DAZZLING

by Paula Wallace

Order this book online at www.trafford.com
or email orders@trafford.com

Most Trafford titles are also available at major online book retailers.

Cover map courtesy of Arkansas State Highway and Transportation Department

Note for Librarians: A cataloguing record for this book is available from Library and Archives Canada at www.collectionscanada.ca/amicus/index-e.html

Printed in Victoria, BC, Canada.

ISBN: 978-1-4269-1781-3 (sc)

Our mission is to efficiently provide the world's finest, most comprehensive book publishing service, enabling every author to experience success. To find out how to publish your book, your way, and have it available worldwide, visit us online at www.trafford.com

Trafford rev. 10/27/2009

North America & international
toll-free: 1 888 232 4444 (USA & Canada)
phone: 250 383 6864 • fax: 812 355 4082

Proverbs 4:18

But the path of the just is as the shining light,
that shineth more and more unto the perfect day.

Preface

THIS BOOK IS fiction. Any similarity to actual people and events is coincidental.

This book is for Americans and all those who uphold her ideals. It is for the military and law enforcement personnel who work and risk their lives to uphold lawfulness and tranquility.

Especially, it is for those ministers of the gospel of Jesus Christ who work to spread the good news that Jesus saves.

> *John 3:16 For God so loved the world, that he gave his only begotten Son, that whosoever believeth in him, should not perish, but have everlasting life.*

May the United States ever stand for righteousness and freedom!

Contents

Chapter 1

DADDY

SEVENTEEN YEAR OLD Mallie dashed across the back porch, and gave the screen door an energetic shove. She barely broke stride as she adroitly kicked back one white tennis shoe to prevent the door's resounding bang.

"Don't let the door slam, Mallie!" came a voice from a back bedroom.

Mallie grinned. No one else these days had back porches with old fashioned screen doors. When she had been small, there had been a hook and eye screw to keep her from "wanderin' off." Then, when she was finally allowed the freedom of the back yard, she had always run in and out, allowing the door to slam fifty times a day.

"Don't slam the door; don't hold the door open! You're letting flies in." came the countless injunctions.

She probably hadn't let it slam in the past ten years, at least not in the last five; but the reminder was as certain, almost, as sunrise and sunset.

Jumping to the back path, she expertly avoided the sagging steps. Quick as a bunny, she jumped some early tomato plants, zigzagged around the crumbling fish pond, and barely skirted a muddy spot beside the flower bed.

"Don't trample my flowers, Mallie!"

She sighed, then gave a delightful little giggle. She loved her mom so much! And sometimes her mom could actually talk without sounding like her needle was stuck in a groove.

Most of the kids didn't relate to Mallie's humorous expression, but Mallie was familiar with old hi-fis, and forty-fives, and seventy-eights, and thirty-three and a third records. She also knew all about eight-tracks and cassettes. She should; the old place housed an eclectic assortment of every piece of junk ever invented by man.

"I was careful of your flowers, Mom!" she returned, turning to run backwards while addressing her mother's open window. "I'll be in my tractor if you need me for anything."

"Did you finish the dishes and make your bed?"

"Yes, ma'am, and I brushed my teeth and washed my face," she replied jauntily.

The morning was achingly beautiful. Severe weather had pounded the rural Arkansas community, and before that, the week had been cold and drizzly. They had feared for their little tomato plants and other little leaves pushing up along the furrows. But now the trees were budding and blossoming; and wildflowers and cultivated blooms seemed to be trying to outdo each other to capture her attention. A cute little bird in the pecan tree winked at her, and whistled sharply.

"Why, thank you, and you look pretty cute this morning, yourself," she responded.

The little bird was right! Mallory Erin O'Shaughnessy was lovely! Tall and slender with beautiful porcelain skin and dancing hazel eyes, she was captivating. These features were made even more appealing by the fact that she was so natural and unaffected. Her hair had deepened from the strawberry blond ringlets of her childhood to luxuriant locks of deep auburn which swung around her shoulders as she hopped and skipped across a small, grassy, stone-strewn field. Lithe and graceful, facing up to the welcoming warmth of the sun, her spirit took wing for the first time in weeks.

Swinging up into the cab of "her tractor", she removed an old towel from her bag to wipe away much of the accumulated grime of the winter.

"Hmmm, maybe the pink outfit wasn't such a good idea."

Rather than trying to clean the ancient seat, she just spread the towel across it and sat down. She bent to wipe a new smudge from her tennis shoe, and frowned when it resisted her attempt. She had spent an hour the night before, trying to make them look newer; now she surveyed them critically. She really needed a new pair!

She hand cranked the dirty window of the ancient rig to let the soft, warm breeze circulate into the musty area and pulled her Bible and journal from her bag. She sat for a moment, drinking in the rural beauty and the tranquil morning, before opening the pages of her most precious treasure.

A wasp interrupted her reverie, and, eyeing him warily, she eased the cab door open to facilitate his escape. After a couple of swoops in the wrong direction, he found the exit and flew away. Her eyes riveted on the departing intruder, and sure enough, he flew to the front of the tractor, and disappeared.

Mallie lurched out of the torn seat, and half jumped and half fell to the ground. Without looking backwards, she ran, sobbing and trembling; not stopping until the screen door banged loudly behind her. She threw herself into the corner of the porch swing, and once again her pain and grief rose to the surface and overflowed.

"Mallie, you let the door bang!"

She caught her breath in a shuddering sigh. "I'm sorry, Mom."

Her mother had come to the back door which joined the kitchen to the porch. The reproach about the door forgotten, she joined her lovely daughter on the swing and pulled her close. The swing creaked ominously, but her motherly instinct outweighed the fear of the structural failure of another feature of the aging home.

"Oh, Mallie, you finally seemed to feel better this morning. What on earth happened to bring you tearing back like this?" It's such a beautiful day, and you were singing again while you were cleaning up the kitchen."

Mallie savored being in her mother's arms. For three months they had mourned the same life-shattering event, but the grief they had in common had driven a wedge between them rather than pulling them closer together. She tried to catch her breath enough to answer her mother's anxious questions.

"A-a -a -a wasp," she stammered.

"A wasp?" her mother questioned uncomprehendingly. "Did you get stung? Where?"

Mallie pulled herself from her mother's arms. "N-no. He didn't sting me, but they have a nest in my tractor again. You know Daddy always kept them from building their nests so they wouldn't swarm me and kill me! Oh, I want daddy; why did he have to die? Doesn't he know how much I need him and miss him? Oh, Mom, I can't stand it! I want Daddy-y-y!" Her voice broke into more heart breaking sobs.

Suddenly cold, Suzanne O'Shaughness, pushed Mallie away and rose to her feet. The swing groaned again, but they didn't notice.

"Really, Mallie! All this over a wasp! You scared the daylights out of me. I miss your father, too, you know. I've never known you to be so caught up with yourself. He left us in a real mess, and I have plenty to worry about without you having a nervous breakdown on me every few minutes. Stop wiping your nose on your hand; get a tissue."

Mallie pushed a strand of hair out of her face, and smiled so suddenly that her mom really questioned her mental stability. But it was too funny! Comfort. Coldness. And then the little "Recorder Box" had come on again- "Stop wiping your nose with your hand; get a tissue!"

"I'm sorry I scared you, Mom, and I'm sorry I let the screen door slam. What's always been the deal about whether it slams or not? It's not like there's a baby sleeping or there are neighbors to disturb? Anyway, I'll get a Kleenex. I know you miss Daddy, too, and you're worried about what happens next. I'm sorry I keep getting crazy when you need me to get stronger. Mom, I do know the Lord is going to help us-"

"Well, He certainly better hurry. I don't know how you keep your faith up, when He has been so awful to us-"

"Mom!" Mallie was horrified. "I keep my faith up by reading my Bible. Faith cometh by hearing, and -" her voice rose in new distress.

"What now?"

"My Bible! I left everything in the tractor when I ran. Can we get one of those cans of wasp spray, please? I'll pay you back when I baby sit again. I can't believe I left my Bible!"

It was a wail, and Suzanne tensed at the possibility of more hysterics.

"I'll see what I can do," she evaded. "Those things are so expensive. Why don't you look on line and see if there are any other ways to get rid of wasps. I have to leave for work. Are you going to be okay? Why don't you have one of your friends come over?"

"Mom, you know I'll be okay. I'll get Daddy's Bible out and have my devotions that way. Maybe he'll feel closer to me, if I use his Bible anyway. I hope my Bible doesn't get rained on, because the window is down in the tractor. Go on to work, Mom. I'm fine."

She gave her mom a squeeze and a peck on the cheek. "You are the greatest! I really love you. Have a great shift and get good tips."

"You had to bring that up! All of these diamond-hunting tourists are just rude and cheap! Their kids are all brats, and they just spill drinks constantly."

"Mom, I'm sorry you have to work such a hard and frustrating job, but I am going to pray for you to have some really nice and generous customers today. The sun is shining; it's springtime, and Suzanne and Mallory Erin O'Shaughnessy are going to make it, or I'm not Irish!"

Suzanne couldn't help laughing at her daughter's sudden humor. It felt good to hear her laugh! It felt good to laugh! It felt so good that she tried to force the moment by laughing too loud and too long. The moment grew awkward once again, and Suzanne turned away toward the kitchen.

Mallie grasped her hand, and reasserted, "Seriously, Mom, we are going to get past this with the Lord's help. Let's have a little prayer meeting right here, and ask for wisdom."

Mallie knelt down near the old threshold, and so did Suzanne, mostly because her daughter was still tugging at her hand. Mallie's earnest prayer poured forth from a heart full of bewilderment mixed with a strange trust. The tears flowed freely, not from some attempt to manipulate God, but from an honest relationship that she had with Him. When she said, amen, she squeezed her mom's hand.

"Your turn." she whispered.

"Um, look, Mallie, I'm about to be late for work. You know how mad Mr. Thompson gets when I'm late. I like to get there a few minutes early so I can collect my thoughts before I have to hit it."

Mallie felt a wave of shock at her mother's response. Quickly, though, she recovered her poise and laughed. She didn't want her mom to see how shaken she really was about the previous comment about God's mistreating them or her refusal to join the impromptu prayer meeting.

Suzanne pulled her hand free and turned back to Mallie from the doorway. She started to say something else, then turned abruptly, gathered her keys and huge handbag from the kitchen table, and left through the front door.

Her car was parked in the grassy, gravel driveway beside the house, and the back door was actually more convenient than the front. Mallie stood amazed for several moments. No peck on the cheek, no long list of the usual orders; then she was out the screen door, standing in the driveway, waving good-bye frantically as her mom's car shot gravel at her as it lurched forward.

No answering wave, no smile, no blown kiss; just spun tires, and gone!

She moved uncomprehendingly back to the porch, then let the screen bang. She sank down onto the swing, and pushed it gently with her tennis shoe. She sat there for fifteen minutes, thinking surely her mom would turn around and come back. Surely she would at least come back and enumerate a chore list, and tell her not to let boys in the house when she was home alone.

Now that she was alone, finishing her devotions using her father's Bible didn't sound like such a good idea. Risking the wasps to retrieve hers didn't sound any better. So she rocked gently on the swing while she contemplated the situation. Suddenly, one end of the swing dropped several inches with a snapping sound, and Mallie launched herself from it before it came down completely. She surveyed it woefully, trying not to dissolve into tears again. She missed Daddy so-o-o much! If he were here, he would promise to get the swing fixed. He wouldn't get around to it, but he would comfort her, anyway.

She wandered into the kitchen and absent-mindedly placed her mom's coffee mug from the sink into the dishwasher. Then she lifted her chin, squared her shoulders, and marched toward the closed door of what had been her father's bedroom. She paused, then turned the doorknob, and pushed gently. Sunlight filtered in around the edges of old dime-store window shades, and the familiar, funny smell nearly shook her resolve. There were a few partially packed boxes and half-filled trash bags strewn around, and Mallie sank down on the bed, remembering. Remembering returning from her father's funeral and the meal provided by the church members, to find well-meaning friends, relatives, and neighbors packing up many of the personal clothing and toiletries of Patrick Shay O'Shaughnessy. Mallie had gone to pieces and, "Made a real scene," as her mother had told her later. Now, as she sat there in her father's personal area, surrounded by his things which she had rescued, the tears broke forth like water over a dam. The tears came, and they came, and they came. She picked up Daddy's top coat where it lay at the foot of the bed and buried her face it. How often she had cried on her dad's strong shoulder when he was wearing this coat! Oh, if only his strong arms were in the sleeves again, his thudding heart beneath the buttons, as he would whisper, "There, there, Mallory Erin, me girl; shh, shh." And whatever her trouble was, it would melt away, from the time she was a little girl.

Gradually, the racking sobs subsided, and she began searching for his Bible. It should have been on the nightstand, and maybe it was. Everything seemed to be on the nightstand. Mallie had often teasingly called him "Packrat Patrick." Now, she was beginning to regret intervening in the well-intended "clearing out". Finally, she found it peeking out from beside the bed. "Right where he left it after reading it that last morning," she thought to herself. Reverently, she bent down, and picked it up; then, as if the room had suddenly filled up with a thousand ghosts, she scurried out into the sunlight and fresh breeze of the front yard.

Trying to settle comfortably into an uncomfortable, peeling, metal lawn chair, she looked toward heaven, and breathed a prayer. Something about letting her feel her dad's presence and the Holy Spirit's power, and wisdom for helping the spiritual crisis her mom seemed to be in, and, oh yes, she needed new tennis shoes.

She unzipped the plastic Bible cover, and allowed the large volume to fall open on her lap. There was a colored marking pencil, which slightly surprised her. Mallie had her Bible highlighted and underlined everywhere in every color, but her dad had not been one to mark much in his. Intrigued, she began leafing through, then became more eager in her search. Maybe he had highlighted some passage in those last few days that would speak to her from across the awful chasm. At last she found it:

Psalm 127:3 Lo, children are an heritage of the LORD: and the fruit of the womb is his reward.

She rubbed her hands over her eyes, and looked again. "Thank You, Lord," she whispered. She rested her eyes, then reread it two more times. "Thank you, Daddy. I always knew you loved me, but thank you for underlining this to tell me again, today. I needed this. Lord, thank You for sending the wasps, and thank You for helping me find Daddy's Bible, and this verse to tell me I am precious! She looked up into the sky, and shouted joyfully, "I'm precious to both of you!" A few wispy clouds continued their journey across the blue, oblivious to the young girl beneath the early green veil of leaves in front of a little tumbledown house in Murfreesboro, Arkansas.

Murfreesboro, Arkansas! The little town sprang into the limelight every now and again. It had begun in 1906 when John Huddleston had been slopping his hogs (livestock-type hogs, and not the popular college mascot), and had -Eureka! discovered diamonds! A diamond rush had ensued, and from that time to the present, the small town had known cycles of booms and busts. Mallie sighed. Mostly, they had been busts. Oh, to be sure there were really diamonds to be found around Pike County. And many of them were breath-taking, gem quality. DeBeers and Tiffany's had immediately showed up on the scene to check out the possibilities. They hadn't stuck around very long; at least, that was the local legend. And there was lots of "local legend".

Mallie's thoughts had drifted without her having realized it, and she returned her attention to the Bible lying open in her lap. After once more reading and savoring the underlined passage, she turned to the New Testament book of Ephesians. It wasn't necessarily where she should be reading. According to the schedule she usually tried to stick to, she should have been somewhere in Deuteronomy or Joshua. But since the sudden loss of her father, she had read and reread the twenty-third Psalm, and other Psalms which brought comfort to her torn and ragged spirit. She also especially loved John 14 about having mansions in heaven, where she knew assuredly her father now resided, and where Jesus promised that He would come again and receive all Christians to Himself in the beautiful Heaven He was presently building and preparing. She squeezed her eyes closed, and tried to imagine the beauties of glory which were surrounding God and her daddy! Her usually vivid imagination failed her, and sighing, she opened her eyes. "Please show, me, Lord," she whispered.

She gazed for long moments at the sad, sagging little house; there wasn't even enough paint now, to be described as "peeling paint," which was how she had described it to herself for years. Some of the windows had ragged-looking screens, others, no screens at all. The old-fashioned window shades that were drawn part-way down seemed crooked and quaint. Maybe the word, 'quaint,' was too flattering.

She suddenly laughed out loud, surprising herself as the sound broke the tranquil morning air. "Well, Lord, at least you showed me what it doesn't look like!" She raised her beautiful, shining eyes toward heaven as she spoke. She so felt His beautiful presence that she could suddenly barely breathe. She sat in rapt silence until she was stirred by a fragrant, cool breeze which whispered caressingly about her and rippled the tender green buds of the canopy above her. Her eyes dropped again to the pages in Ephesians, and for the first time, she noticed how incredibly neat the big study Bible was. She loved her own simple little Bible so much, she was now amazed that there could be a better model. She loved the book of Ephesians about being caught up to sit in heavenly places in Christ. But Daddy's Bible had footnotes and center-column references her Bible did not have. And here was a fascinating piece of information! Revelation stunned her! the footnote to the introduction of the book said, "Ephesus is located in what is now southwestern Turkey."

She read it again, and it said the same thing! "Ephesus is located in what is now southwestern Turkey!" And there were beautiful, full-color pictures of ruins in present-day Turkey of the area that was so central to much of New Testament history.

"I never thought of it as being a real place," she whispered. "The place where you could choose to sit by yourself with Jesus and drink in heaven was a real place in southwestern Turkey!" The pictures drew her; the revelation made her sparkly eyes sparkle more brightly. "I have to go there; I have to!"

Of course, she said that about all of the world's beautiful travel destinations. She wanted to see Ireland, and Boston (where she had actually been born). She wanted to see the monkeys on the Rock of Gibraltar, or even just at the San Diego Zoo. She wasn't particular; just any place to get her "out of Dodge". She laughed at her own use of a trite expression. Her English teacher had hit briefly on creative writing and using fresh and vibrant language, rather than the same hackneyed expressions. The class had fun the rest of the week, seeing how many of the worn-out terms they could wear out further.

Wow, Ephesus was a real place! The pictures were gorgeous! Blue, blue skies, and white, white sculpted marble. Majestic columns lined an ancient acropolis where Paul and John had walked; a huge Roman theater still stood where the Ephesians had rioted about their pagan deity, Diana. The Apostle Paul had said he fought with beasts, here, at Ephesus; and these were real modern-day photographs. There were breath-taking pictures of an ancient library. She tried to imagine what could have possibly been in a library back then. She had heard of the world-famous "Library at Alexandria" of ancient times, one of the wonders of the ancient world. She furrowed her brow at the thought of libraries before printing presses and books. It said something about the ancient city's situation on the Aegean Sea. She had thought she pretty well knew world geography, but she was suddenly unsure of exactly where the Aegean Sea was. It was all so interesting, so fascinating, so mind-boggling.

She laid the Bible aside and stretched her neck; swinging her hair back, she pulled it up into a ponytail, and trapped it in a Scrunchi.

"Wish I had a Coke," she thought longingly.

She stood, or tried to stand, realizing her foot which had been curled beneath her in the hard chair, was really asleep. She stepped forward gingerly, then stamped as the needles jabbed and stabbed at her. She was still limping around the chair, trying to restore circulation when her neighbor pulled into the driveway and lowered her car window.

"Hi, Mallory,"she greeted. The tousled kids in the back bounced forward and joined in, "Mallie, Mallie!

Mallie smiled, and waved, and attempted to approach the car without limping.

"Hello, Mrs. Walters; hi, kids. Whazzup?" She leaned in the back window and tweaked Sammie's knee through the hole is his jeans. He giggled, and pulled his leg back; then deciding he liked the game, he pushed his knee back up against the car door. She tweaked again, and he giggled in delight. Sarah glared from her car seat, not liking her brother to receive attention when she wasn't getting any.

"Mrs. Walters, what are you and these two gorgeous children up to on this fine Arkansas day?" Her smile and beauty dazzled the kind neighbor, who recovered to answer the cheery question.

"Well, Honey, we came to make sure you're doin' okay." Your mom called me and told me you were still really having a tough time when she had to leave for work this morning.

She said she tried to call you several times, and when she couldn't get an answer, she asked if we minded checking.

Mallie appreciated her kind neighbor, but she was horrified to think the phone had been ringing, and in her reverie, she had missed hearing it. It was strange, because they could always hear the phone from the yard when the windows were opened.

"Wow, Mrs. Walters, I apologize! I guess I was on a trip to Turkey," she laughed. "I'm really sorry you had to load the kids up and everything to come be the search party. I'll go in right now and call Mom."

"You really should let her know you're all right. I'll wait out here with the kids while you run in and call."

Mallory thought it kind of unnecessary for the woman to wait, but she didn't argue. It seemed she had already caused too much trouble. She flung herself down in a kitchen chair and dialed her mom's work number. The phone seemed not to be working. Perplexed, Mallory pushed the on and off buttons; there was no dial tone.

"Great!" she thought to herself in exasperation. "Of all the crazy times-!" She felt the tears trying to fight their way out again and bit her lip to keep it from trembling. She wished Mrs. Walters and the kids would just drive off, figuring she was okay and had called her mom. "But, no." She could hear the car's idle and the two toddlers getting restless. In desperation, she tried the phone again, - nothing. She even braved going back into her Father's room to use that extension, but to no avail.

Forlornly, she walked out to the waiting neighbor. "I'm really sorry, but the phones aren't working. Maybe that's what happened; why I never heard it ringing. Maybe there's a line down somewhere or something."

It never occurred to the naïve Mallie that service might be cut because the phone company hadn't received any payment and late notices had been unheeded. She was genuinely perplexed about why the phones were on the fritz, and at such an inopportune time!

Of course, the kind lady had a good idea what the problem was, so she tactfully suggested that the lovely girl hop in the car. "Just get in, Mallie. It won't take ten minutes for me to take you to the lodge. You can show your mom you're okay and tell her about the phone. Then, you can hang around at the lodge until she gets off if you want to. That might be better than spending your Saturday by yourself. Or we can just get a Coke, and I'll bring you back. Whatever you want."

"I'll go in and get my purse-" she started.

"Well, you can if you want, but treat's on me. Maybe you can get these crazy kids to calm down and just sing songs or something."

Mallie grabbed her Dad's Bible from the lawn chair and hopped into the passenger seat.

"Thank you, Mrs. Walters. I feel like I've really disrupted your day already. I really appreciate your kindness. A Coke sounds good. I was just getting up to go in and look for one when you pulled in." She didn't tell her that she had just prayed for a Coke.

And she had breathed that prayer. Strange how the Lord had done it this time. By the phone's not working, And she had been so exasperated! The humiliation of having a neighbor come check on her, of her waiting in the car. "After all, I'm seventeen," she had raged inwardly. "And then, the stupid phones-! Really one thing too much!" And she had really wanted to let go of her Irish Temper, or her Red-headed Temper, or whatever it was, and heave the phone through a window. And God had been working gently through the aggravating circumstances to give her, not just a Coke, but a friendly break in the midst of a long, long, lonely day. She sighed, raggedly, involuntarily.

Janet Walters gave her a quick, sideways glance. "This is a real treat for us. The kids adore you, and I could use some conversation with someone over age five. I'm really glad your mom called. I was going to tackle cleaning out the garage, but the kids just fight and get into everything. I wouldn't have gotten much done anyway. What did you mean that you were on a trip to Turkey? What's Turkey?" She maneuvered the big old car around a huge hole in her lane, then looked at Mallie inquisitively.

Mallie laughed, and began trying to explain about her Bible, and then her Dad's Bible with the notes and beautiful pictures. She unzipped the cover, and opened to the beautiful pictures of Ephesus. Her excitement bubbled as she rattled, almost incoherently, about sitting in heavenly places, and that Ephesus is really, really, really a real place, and it's in southwestern Turkey on the Aegean Sea. "I want to go there!" she finished breathlessly.

Janet was trying to drive, referee her kids, and follow Mallie's excited train of thought.

"It looks kind of pretty, but I bet it would cost a lot. I think you need a passport. Does anybody go there? I'd like to go to Vegas sometime!"

Mallie was frankly taken aback. What did Turkey and Heavenly Places have to do with Las Vegas? Mallie was a real armchair traveler, and she wanted to go almost any place; but not, she decided, to that wicked place! Evidently, they weren't on the same wave-length, and it suddenly occurred to Mallie that the nice lady and her cute kids didn't know the Lord. She needed to witness clearly, and not just rattle like some frenetic teen-ager.

Pulling into a parking space at the little lodge, Janet Walters turned to her passenger, and announced, "Here we are!"

"Yea! Hooray!" shouted the little backseat passengers. They weren't sure where they were, but hopefully they would gain freedom from the restraint of the car seats.

Mallie hopped out and unfastened Sarah. "I'm real mad at you, Mallie!" the small girl did her best to glower, but a smile broke through her stern expression.

"Oh, yeah?" Mallie countered, "why's that ?"

"You know! You were playing with Sammie, and I love you the best!"

"Mallie gave her a hug and lowered her to the ground. "I'm sorry, can you ever forgive me?"

"No!" Sarah retorted unhesitatingly, and marched arrogantly up the sidewalk.

"Sarah!" her mother reproved, but she and Mallory couldn't help laughing.

When they entered the little café in the lodge, Suzanne got up from a seat at the counter and hurried toward them. She gave Mallie and Janet a hug and eyed the twins suspiciously. Children were not really her forte.

"Thanks, Janet," she whispered. When she had been unable to reach her daughter, she had figured the telephone company had cut the service. Though she hadn't opened the late notices, she had known it was only a matter of time before this would happen. Her anger and bitterness toward her late husband and these desperate circumstances were written all over her countenance. And of course, other utilities would also be cut off soon. That was what she had started to confide to Mallie before she had left that morning. But then, the young girl had already been so overwrought, that Suzanne had just walked away. Then, when her conscience wouldn't leave her alone and she had tried to call and apologize, the phone was dead. Suzanne knew she had used her neighbor in a rather deceitful way, but that didn't really bother her too much. "They were having a tough time and everyone owed them help and sympathy." Or, at least, that's what Suzanne Marie Campbell O'Shaughnessy thought!

"Mom, the phone at the house wasn't working," began Mallie, afraid she would be in trouble with her mom for not answering her attempted calls. "I'm really sorry you had to call out a posse. I've been fine, and I can't wait 'til you get off so I can share some of the things the Lord showed me today. It's so exciting, and He's so good!"

Suzanne shook her head. She felt Mallie was on the verge of emotional collapse, and all of her talk about the Lord just some fantasy so she wouldn't have to deal with harsh realities. She was at a loss. She wanted to scream at her to just shut up about that stuff and deal with reality. Usually overly sensitive and easily hurt herself, she seldom considered the feelings of others. Why Mallie so adored her dad and his memory was beyond Suzanne's grasp. He had, after all, been such a total loser, never becoming successful, and then dying so suddenly! No provision! No insurance! No nothing! Now she wondered what had possessed her to stick it out.

Sammie chimed in loudly, announcing his restroom needs with the usual childish bluntness.

"I'll take him," Mallie volunteered. She really did have a helpful and cooperative spirit, but she was suddenly aware that she should check a mirror. "Do you need to come, too, Sarah?" she asked. Sarah shook her head, no. They always seemed to manage not to need to go at the same time. Mallie thought they were absolutely adorable, but she was aware that twins were really a double handful.

She grasped Sammie by the hand and led him to the back of the café. He hurried into the stall, and Mallie focused on her reflection in the mirror. "Good grief," she murmured. She had cried until her mascara was all over her face, she had a few smudges of dirt on her pink outfit, and she was suddenly self-conscious that her outfit had become somewhat snug. Her mind was a jumble; she tried to be so careful with her laundry, and this was her favorite outfit. What had she done to it? She wanted to cry about this new development, but Sammie was calling for help in the stall. Forcing back the tears, she helped Sammie, and they returned to the booth for their Cokes.

"Good grief, Mom," she addressed her mother, "I look like something the dog buried in the yard, and then dug up again!"

Both women laughed, and the twins acted like they got the joke. Mallie's original assessment of herself was that she looked like "something the cat dragged in". But, since she was on a mission to use fresh language, she had invented a new simile. She was pleased with the laughs it brought.

As usual, business was a little slow, so Suzanne brought the soft drinks and joined them in the booth. Mallie had grabbed a napkin to try to dab at the misplaced make-up, then had thanked her mom and Janet Walters for the drink. They were visiting, between interruptions from the twins, when a family entered the café from the lobby of the lodge.

Mallie's jaw dropped wide, she was sure. They were all gorgeous! The ideal American family! "Where were they from? Probably, Dallas," she had made a guess at answering her own question.

Suzanne had risen to show them to a table and give them menus. While they were getting settled in at the table, Mallie tried to take in everything about them without obviously staring.

"Who are those people?" Sarah had questioned in a stage whisper. It was only her awe that had caused her to lower her childish voice at all.

The father was tall, athletic-looking, and really, really handsome. The mom was gorgeous with all the high-maintenance look of a Dallas suburbanite, soccer mom. Flawless nails, freshly pedicured feet in designer-looking sandals, superb tan; and her hair! Oh! My word! Thick, and highlighted in all the most gorgeous blond tones imaginable; it was caught up in a large clip with attractive wisps streaming in just the right places. The perfect build, in an adorable outfit from her color palette! She was amazing-looking! Three perfect stair-step children. Spotless, in brand new looking things from their hair bows to flip-flops, completed the family.

Now, to be sure, people came from all over the U.S. and from around the world to the Crater of Diamonds State Park, so seeing "out-of-towners" wasn't that out of the ordinary. It was jus that the Park kept making so many improvements, that the diamond seekers didn't really need much that the little town had to offer. They were located on the edge of the Ouachita Mountains, but campers and hikers either brought what they needed with them, or they outfitted in Little Rock or Hope.

Suzanne took the orders from each family member, who ordered politely; and, so far, had managed not to spill. She turned in the order and rejoined Mallie's group. She rolled her eyes at the customers in disdain. Mallie was enchanted by them. "What could they be doing here?" she couldn't help wondering. The lady had on a gorgeous wedding set, a sparkling tennis bracelet, and a Rolex. If they were diamond hunters, they must be good at it. Her real guess was that this was their first time, and they wouldn't last long. Or maybe they were on their way to raft or canoe, and their Hummer had blown up. She was sure they had a Hummer; they looked like they should have.

"Excuse me, Suzanne," the man had spoken pleasantly. "Could you bring us some more unsweetened tea?"

Suzanne got the tea, but acted annoyed, and came back and sat down again.

"Mom," Mallory whispered. "I prayed for you to have some really great customers today. Go take care of them; you don't have to sit here with us."

Suzanne gave her daughter a sharp glance as she got up. "Their tea glasses couldn't have been empty for more than ten seconds. People were so rude and impatient!"

The order came up, and Suzanne delivered it to the table: just in time; because Hal Thompson had come in. He surveyed the prosperous-looking diners and rifled through a few sales checks before going to their table to greet them heartily.

"Hello, folks, nice to see you this afternoon. Hal Thompson!" He extended his hand to the dad. The man rose courteously and gave Hal a firm handshake.

"Sit down! Sit down! I don't want to interrupt your family lunch. Do you have everything you need? Suzanne, these drinks are a little low."

"My name's Daniel Faulkner, my wife, Diana. Kid's names are Alexandra, Jeremiah, and Cassandra. Everything looks great, thanks. It's nice to meet you."

Diana and the children had smiled as they were introduced, and they murmured something that sounded polite and appropriate. Mallie couldn't quite make it all out, but she was impressed. They seemed like the answer to her prayer about nice customers, and they looked like they could afford a nice tip. "If only Mom would act pleasant and attentive," Mallie thought wistfully. It seemed like people only reflected her mom's attitude. Her mom had acted annoyed at her employer for trying to make sure his customers needs were being cared for.

Mallie wanted to stick around and watch this enchanting tourist family. "The mom's name is Diana," she thought dazedly. "Like princess Diana." Sadly, though, their Cokes were gone and the twins were getting grumpy. Mr. Thompson looked at their empty glasses pointedly. Not that there were customers waiting for the table, but he really didn't prefer for people to come in just for Cokes or coffee. He was running a lodge and a restaurant; if people needed an office, they could rent one. They didn't have to come camp out in his booths.

Janet was pawing through the bottom of her purse for more change and didn't have enough. She was mumbling that, "Brad must have taken a twenty."

Mallory was thoroughly humiliated that she hadn't grabbed her purse (not that there was any money in it), but Mrs. Walters had said she was treating. Suzanne couldn't bail them out because the morning had been slow, and she hadn't made any tips.

"Hey, Hal," Janet called out. "I'm just going out to the car to round up some more change; I'll be right back."

Before Hal could respond, Daniel Faulkner had risen. He presented his Platinum credit card to Suzanne and said, "Please allow us to treat y'all. Ma'am, if you could just add those drinks to my tab, I'll settle the whole thing."

Hal had the check ready, and Daniel signed with a flourish. Suzanne nearly hit the floor; a ten dollar tip! But she didn't even think about Mallie's prayer or the Lord. She thought it was just because she had kept from saying, "Hold your horses!" when they kept wanting refills so fast.

Mallory and Janet rose to leave, but, of course, now Sarah was whining to "go potty." Mallie rose and led the toddler to the back, acutely aware of her tight-fitting, old outfit and wrecked tennis shoes.

"Come on, Sarah, let's hurry."

Sarah entered the stall and began talking non-stop.

"Hurry up, Sarah, your mom has things to do today!"

The ladies' room door opened, and to Mallory's horror, Mrs. Faulkner and the two girls entered. Mallie quickly helped Sarah, so they could free the only stall, and on the way out she said, "TP's almost out; I'll be right back."

She asked her mom where she could find an extra roll; then took it to the waiting mom.

Diana was impressed with the girl's thoughtfulness. "Thank you so much. What is your name?" Her smile was beautiful and genuine. She had already reapplied her lipstick and gloss.

Mallory was acutely aware of her own appearance. Usually she felt poised and confident in meeting people, more interested in them than thoughtful of herself. "I'm Mallory," she responded, before ducking back out, and running out to Janet Walter's idling car.

The evening was uneventful. After her trip to the lodge, Mallie was restless until her mother arrived from work. They opened a couple of cans of soup, and ate it with crackers. Suzanne was quiet.

"Mom, are you mad at me?" Mallory finally blurted out miserably.

Suzanne was startled. "No, why would I be?" She had thought her daughter might be upset with her about the phone and not confiding in her about it. "No, I'm not mad at you," but she still left the table and acted like she didn't want to talk.

Now Mallory really didn't feel like talking either. The beauty of the morning and her exciting devotions had faded away, and her heartache was back, oh, was it ever back! She placed the pan and bowls and spoons in the dishwasher and wiped off the table. Then she put on her coat against the chilly evening air, exited through the back screen door without letting it slam shut, and walked around in the big old back yard.

The tears came! It felt better. She could tell her heart was beginning to heal; oh, it wasn't there yet. Not by a long shot (a trite expression, but she was too tired to think of something better). But she could actually have moments of time when the grief didn't totally overwhelm her.

When she went inside, her mom's door was shut. It still wasn't late, but Mallie decided to go to bed because there wasn't much else to do.

She said her prayers and climbed into her little bed. Her only prayer was, "Lord, please don't let the dream come!" Her tense muscles began to relax, and she jerked suddenly. Then sleep came. But the Lord didn't answer her prayer this night either. Before midnight, she was in the middle of the nightmare, screaming and sobbing, as she fought to emerge from the horror that had so suddenly befallen her.

The dream was the same. It was Mallie's finding her daddy crumpled over face-first in his room next to his closet door. With a cry of alarm she had been on her knees beside him, shaking him, and crying, "Daddy, Daddy!" When he hadn't responded, she had tried to turn him toward her, sure he would just "come to" from a faint or something, and sit up, and say, "There, there, Mallory me girl. I'm fine! Didn't mean ta scare ya." But when she had turned him over, his gray eyes were staring lifelessly, and the side of his face was dark and terrifying, she had thought from a bruise or something. Later, she had learned it was lividity, where blood had begun settling immediately at his death.

She had immediately felt that his death was all her fault! She should have checked on him earlier, she should have known about his condition, she should have made him go to a doctor. She should have seen it coming - and stopped it!

Now, as she turned on the bedroom light, the horror began to dim, but she sat there hugging her knees to herself with her arms. "I'm sorry, Daddy! I'm so-so sorry. Oh Daddy, you were alone. Were you in pain? Did you have time to be afraid? Oh Daddy, I'm sorry I didn't do anything! Oh Daddy! DADDY!" her voice rose to a shriek and trailed off into sobs, that finally quieted into whimpers. Finally, she was asleep with one last whisper - "Daddy."

Chapter 2

DESPERATION

COLD AND DARKNESS! Mallory sprang up, listening, shivering! Her room had grown bone-chillingly cold since her nightmare had awakened her at midnight. But, what had pierced her sleep? Was it just the cold; had there been a scream? Why was her skin crawling? Trembling, straining, she sank back onto the foot of her bed. Silence! Maybe she was just overly tense. People were thinking she was losing her mind with grief; maybe she was! She exhaled slowly, pulling her little comforter around her closely in an effort to halt the trembling. She closed her eyes, then opened them, trying to wake up, think, be alert, be rational, figure things out.

Cautiously, she reached up and over her head for the light switch. Where was it? This had been her bedroom for fourteen years, but in her terror, her frantic fingers were scraping around the elusive Winnie the Pooh switch plate.

Then there was scraping, crunching in the gravel driveway right outside her window.

Her open window! Why was it open? No wonder the cold night Arkansas air was making her shiver uncontrollably. But why was it open? Had she opened it in her sleep?

Her mind couldn't even consider the possibility that someone else had opened it; someone had tried to "break in" to such an unlikely little house. The ominous crunching sounded again, causing her to respond this time. She leapt to her feet, her face pressed against the cold glass of the windowpane, straining to see who was thumping down the drive toward the road. There was a brief, black silhouette against a slightly brightening morning sky, and the interloper disappeared from view.

Mallie sank weakly to the floor, thanking the Lord for waking her up, for scaring the guy off, for protecting her. Then the questions began to flood her mind like the spring rains flooding the local creeks. "Who was it? What did they want? Was there more than one? Had anyone actually gotten in? Was her mother ok? Had she heard them? Was the local sheriff already on the way? Was anything stolen? What could there be to steal?"

After listening intently as she watched the eastern horizon begin to glow in a gorgeously indescribable pink tone, she decided the house had grown sufficiently silent for her to venture forth. "Lord," she whispered, "Thank you I couldn't find the light switch! Someone was right outside the window, and they would have seen the light come on."

Leaving her bedroom door ajar so that the illumination from the early morning sky revealed the hallway and sparsely furnished living room, Mallie tiptoed forward. After what seemed like ten forevers, she was outside her mom's bedroom. Gently, gently, she twisted the knob, pushed the door a crack; the hinges screeched in the stillness like a stepped-on cat. "Daddy always intended to oil the hinges," Mallie smiled wryly to herself. Suzanne roused slightly, mumbled something, and was back asleep.

Mallie pushed the button for the coffee maker, but nothing happened. Feeling around in the pale light, she could tell the appliance was, indeed, plugged in. Curiously, she flipped the switch for the garbage disposal; nothing happened there, either. Had the intruder cut the electricity? Was it a blown breaker? If it were, Daddy always checked things like that out.

"Oh, Daddy," she moaned for about the thousandth time.

The whole house was freezing cold. Mallie fumbled for a flashlight from the kitchen junk drawer and moved to the thermostat. Still afraid someone might be watching the house, she cautiously shielded the dim beam as she checked the setting. Seventy degrees. She crept back to her room to close her window, but she knew that wasn't the only reason for the cold. She should be hearing the furnace laboring, but it didn't seem to be working either.

Remembering that they had a gas range, Mallie turned one of the knobs, and was satisfied to see the blue flame run around the burner. Placing the tea kettle on the flame, she then turned the oven on, and sat in front of the opening, grateful for some warmth at last.

"Mallie, what in the world----?!"

Her mom's strident and very unexpected utterance nearly scared her to death, which was a trite expression, scared to death, but which nevertheless seemed to sum up her reaction. It also used hyperbole, because she was scared a lot, but probably was really no where near expiring.

"Holy smoke, Mom, I thought you were asleep. You startled me! For some reason, none of the electricity works. I'm making some hot tea to warm up; the furnace isn't running. Do you know how to check the breakers? Wish Daddy were here." She sighed long and sorrowfully, but, to Suzanne's relief, the tears didn't come.

"I was trying to sleep, but you were screaming at midnight and then up and rattling around at the crack of dawn. I would love to sleep! It's Sunday, and I don't have to work until two. I was planning to sleep til noon, which I still plan on doing, if I can get some quiet!"

"Sorry, Mom," Mallie apologized. "Go back to bed. I'll try to be quieter. You must not be planning on Sunday School, but will you meet me in time for church? Daddy liked for us to be in church together. It will get us out of this cold, dark house, and afterward, we can talk about what is going on and what to do before you have to be at work. Then, I can eat at the lodge, do my homework, go back to church tonight, and meet you after work."

Suzanne groaned. "I'm going back to bed. If you want to go to church, call someone for a ride. I'm keeping the car to get to work at two."

"Well, Mom," Mallie began feebly. "We need to talk. How can I call for a ride when the phones aren't working? Why does everything have to break down and stop working when Daddy isn't here to help us? We need to figure out what is happening and what we should do."

"I'm tired, and if you don't mind---" She turned toward the back of the house.

"Mom, did you hear anything, um, strange awhile ago?"

Suzanne pulled an old quilt from the frayed sofa, started to pull it toward her bedroom for added warmth; then she suddenly changed her mind. The warmth from the oven and whistling tea kettle drew her back. She pulled another kitchen chair beside Mallie, brewed two cups of tea, and sat down with a stiff moan.

"Hear something strange like what?" she questioned curiously. "Thought that was just you up banging and rattling around. You're as bad as your dad, -uh- was." she finished awkwardly.

Mallory shook her head bemusedly. Her mother's lack of grief and attempts at sympathy for her daughter's pain were so pitiful they were practically funny.

"I hope I'm like Daddy in all of his good traits," she responded wistfully. "I thought I heard someone crunching on the gravel in the driveway with big boots on," she changed the subject back. "It really scared me. It scared me someone might have hurt you or killed you. I'm glad you're alright." She began to cry. "Mom, I really need you!"

"I know, Mallie, we need each other. I didn't hear anything. Maybe it was just another nightmare. Here, get a tissue. I'm fine! Please don't get started crying. I'll make us some toast under the broiler and another cup of tea. Hurry and get ready for Sunday School. I'll take you; I can wear my sunglasses."

Mallory enjoyed her Sunday School class, visiting with her friends almost like old times. Then she braced herself as she entered the little auditorium, knowing Daddy wasn't going to be standing there greeting people, handing out bulletins, joking, and "stealing the noses" of all the little kids. What a fun person! She dashed a tear away and put on her bravest smile as she waved at Sammie and Sarah. They were in the same tattered outfits they were wearing the previous day, and it seemed pretty questionable if the outfits or the kids had had any soap and water applied. Mallie knelt and spread her arms wide for a hug as they dashed towards her. Their mom was standing out at the curb, and Mallory yelled hello out to her. She knew Janet Walters was dropping the twins at the church because Mallory would keep an eye on them, and Janet could have a respite from the two busy tots. Mallory kept trying to convince her to bring them for Sunday School so they would be in a class geared to their age, get a break during that time, and then attend the morning service. Janet just always used the same excuse that she couldn't get up and get them ready that early. Mallie gave them another squeeze, placed a firm guiding hand on each tousled head, and propelled them skillfully into a pew in the popular back portion of the church.

She was trying to settle them in and answer their noisy whispers when she sensed an excited buzz around her. She felt her jaw drop as the Faulkner family entered the little country church and advanced toward an emptier row down front.

Mallie was dazed! If she had thought they looked enchanted in their Saturday tourist togs, she was really blown away by their Sunday best! Mr. Faulkner was wearing a shiny silk-blend looking brown suit the exact color of his hair. He was wearing a French cuffed shirt in dazzling white with expensive looking cuff links; a brown, white, and pale blue striped tie; and a pale blue pocket handkerchief; brown and blue argyle sox and Crocodile- looking brown loafers. The only thing that didn't look brand new about him was his battered looking Bible.

Then, there was Diana. She had on the cutest dress. It looked like she had cut it from the morning's sunrise sky and whipped in into something by church time with the help of a fairy godmother. It had shoulders that came down on her arms a little ways, then the bodice was fitted, and matching fabric roses accented her small waist, from which the fabric draped gracefully around her to the tops of her knees. Her jewelry was pearls and gold; her sandals and handbag of metallic gold leather. Her finger and toe nails were from the sunrise also. Today, she had opted to wear her hair down, and if possible, it was even cuter than the previous day.

Alexandra, Jeremiah, and Cassandra were all in pastels that reminded Mallory of the saltwater taffy she had gotten at the Galveston boardwalk the previous summer. Alexandra was in a dreamy mint green color lineny fabric in a slim style that made her look grown up. Jeremiah was in a pastel blue cashmere-looking sweater, with little tan slacks, and Cassandra finished out the water color in a pale frilly pink concoction like Mallie used to dream of having when she was little. They all had on new shoes, and the girls had their hair all curled and styled with beautiful and perfect bows. Cassandra had a cute little pair of white lace gloves. Even the kids had on quite a bit of nice-looking jewelry.

While Mallory was taking it all in, her mother had actually slipped into the pew next to her.

"Where's Janet?" she whispered loudly. "Did she just dump her kids on you and leave?"

"Mom, I'm so glad you came. I don't mind helping her with the kids from time to time.

Look, there are the Faulkners," Mallory's voice was hushed.

"Yeah, I saw them and their big fashion parade. Is this Easter? Did I miss something? I think it's just awful to show up at church trying to be better'n everybody. They need to deal with their proud hearts, or something."

Mallory couldn't believe what she was hearing. Her mom had always had cynical and critical moments, but recently--- Mallory guessed her dad had exercised more control over his wife's sharp tongue than she had realized. "Maybe it's just all this uncertainty that's making her crazy," Mallory surmised charitably.

The service was pretty good. Between the two, small, restless children and watching every move the Faulkner family made, Mallie was embarrassed to admit she hadn't been too attentive. They shook hands with Pastor and Mrs. Anderson and exited the small building. Janet was parked across the street, so Mallie helped get Sammie and Sarah loaded, while Suzanne waited in the driver's seat of her own car.

Mallie slid smoothly into the passenger seat. She was hoping she would get to drive, but that didn't look too hopeful. "Well, Mom, where are we going?" Church had run over-time, but there was still time to grab lunch together before her mom had to get to work.

Suzanne had her sunglasses on, as usual, but Mallie realized she was crying. Of course, she began crying, too.

"Mama, what's wrong?" Suddenly she remembered the terrifying events of the morning; maybe someone had done something, maybe her mother was hurt, maybe someone had gotten inside the house. Panic was overwhelming her; she felt like she couldn't breathe, like she couldn't focus, or was afraid to focus on what her mother was saying. "What's wrong?" she asked again, even though Suzanne seemed to be speaking.

"I'm trying to tell you! Stop asking what's wrong, and I'll tell you what's wrong! I gave Him a chance, and He failed me again, just like always! Did I want to go to church? NO! Not really! I wanted to sleep and forget this whole mess, and you, and everybody! I thought if I asked for a miracle, He might squeeze one tiny one out for me. Instead, I get that stupid, free-loading woman's kids for an hour and a half, a boring sermon, and those high and mighty rich people and their airs, and their flaunting their money in my face! That's just a starter for what's wrong! I don't have any money for the phone, the electric, or the butane. I don't have gas money for the car, money for lunch, or food at the house. I told you I have to be at work at two, but I lied; Hal fired me! So, I gave this church thing another shot, and all it got me was another two hours of my life wasted." She paused, and wiped her hand across her nose.

Mallory was so shocked she didn't know where to start to answer the diatribe, so she handed her mom the Kleenex box from the backseat. "Don't wipe your nose with your hand; use a tissue." she intoned with her best serious voice.

"Mallie, you are just like your dad with your jokes and fooling around. He was never serious a day in his life! Everything is so desperate, I've thought of killing myself! I didn't want to tell you how bad it is! I'm leaving for Hope this afternoon. Roger told me I can come back to work for him any time, so I'm driving down there to make him keep his word. We'll go to the house; I'll pack the car; I'll have to live in it for awhile. Who would have guessed we would be this desperate?"

Chapter 3

DANGER

SUZANNE WAS GONE! Without a thought for the daughter she had said she was tired of, she had thrown what little food there was, her cosmetics, and her favorite clothes in the car and headed out while it was light, so she wouldn't get stopped for a burned-out headlight.

Mallory sat on the sagging back steps with her chin in her hands- in shock! If someone had told her on Christmas night what would have happened in the next three months to so totally shatter her world, she would never have believed it! But, Daddy would have gone to a doctor, just to be on the safe side!

Tears did not come, even the ragged sighs had ceased. How long she sat there, she wasn't sure. Clouds had blown up, turning the blue sky into ominous black. Mallie thought idly that her mom didn't like driving in rain. "We don't even have a phone so she can let me know if she made it ok," she thought detachedly. The wind picked up, and Mallie could smell the rain coming. She rose dejectedly, made her way past the broken swing, and into the kitchen. Cupboard doors and drawers were open from her mom's hasty forage for edibles. Mallie didn't mind that she was there without food; her stomach kind of hurt anyway. She raced to the little bathroom, just in time to dry-heave painfully. She had had nothing since the early morning toast and tea. She rested her head on her arm on the toilet seat, and gazed around the plain, little, ugly bathroom. Why had someone tried to break in here?

Slowly, she rose from the bathroom floor. It scared her that the stormy sky was bringing nightfall on early. She never liked being alone at night, and now with no phone or power, and the events of the previous night, she decided to spring into action. She went out to the shed and rolled out a couple of big empty drums. She placed one on either side of the driveway, even with her bedroom windows, and tied a heavy black rope between them across the drive. Somewhat of a heavy trip wire for someone on foot or in a vehicle. It might create noise to warn her, or scare or surprise anyone who shouldn't be in her driveway at night. She rigged up a few other crude booby traps and alarms, both inside and out.

The rain was pouring down, and brilliant lightning forks sliced through the terrifying heavens. Mallory checked all of the windows for the dozenth time. She hadn't checked the two in her father's room, and it bothered her; but she didn't want to go in there right now. She just couldn't! She scrunched her eyes closed, trying to remember if they were down and locked. They should be, she reasoned. She had found his lifeless body on January second. With winter already upon them and his aversion to, "heatin' the whole outdoors," it would only make sense that they were secure. The thought kept nagging in her mind and wouldn't listen to reason, "Maybe you should go in and check," The voice in her brain grew louder, and finally she answered it aloud, jumping at her own voice.

"I will, in the morning," she promised.

"But, it's raining now. What if everything gets ruined?"

Mallory childishly clapped her hands to her ears, even though the voice wasn't external. It seemed she should be able to tune out the pesky recordings from her childhood, and not have to continue to obey every injunction. She searched the darkening room for her handbag and dug out her iPod. Her favorite gospel song was queued, and she tried to concentrate on the beautiful and powerful lyrics, turning up the volume in the thick gloom of the homely little house. Sighing in defeat, she slung the earbud aside and dropped the little device back into her little bag.

The voice sounded just like Daddy's, saying, "Go, do it right now, me girlie. What 'r ye waitin' fer?"

"If everything does get soaked, it's just junk anyway! Who cares?" She tilted her face up and shook her auburn hair in defiance at the memory that was disembodied from its owner. "I wish you were here to make me, to try and make me!" She tried to burst into tears again, but the tears were gone. Stunned, she sat in silence.

A few far-off lightenings shuddered against the drawn shades, and the fearful throaty roars of thunder softened into distant purrs. The tears that she could not hold back were suddenly dried; she could feel the joy mounting within her wounded spirit.

Finally, she picked up the weak flashlight and went out into the sprinkles of the fleeing storm. Not yet ready to reenter her father's sanctuary, she had decided to reassure herself about those two windows by checking from the outside. The sky was clearing, the breeze cool and fragrant. She thought of one of her favorite poems, "Renascence". She wasn't sure why she thought of it, and she was still terrified of whatever might have been out there. Cautiously, she moved around the corner of the house. Little rivulets were running from the downpour, and her best shoes were already wet and muddy. "Great," she mumbled to herself, "what had happened to the recording about getting her good shoes muddy?" Maybe she wasn't big enough to take care of herself without all of the constant reminders, after all.

She heard a rustle that didn't really seem to be from the breeze. She froze! Her heartbeat paused, then surged like a sprinter off the line. She wished the flashlight wasn't exposing her to who or whatever it was. The dim batteries acquiesced to her thoughts, and she was in darkness. Not sure that the inkiness was better, she gripped the useless device helplessly. Fear owned her, and she tried to think of a verse or prayer or something. To no avail. The clouds above had retreated further, bathing the yard and tree stand beyond with pearly light. The girl, frozen like an exquisite marble statue, lost track of time, listening, afraid to move, to breathe!

Finally, she knew two things for dead certain! Someone had been there, and they had slipped away for the moment!

She drew a rasping breath into her starved lungs, and gripping the lifeless flashlight as a club, she approached the first window. It was shut tight and locked. The second one, not even to her surprise, had part of the window frame broken, exposing a fresher wood surface and termite tracks. And evidence that someone had been trying to force the window open against the old locks!

As she watched the trickling waters reside, leaving little eroded "hand-prints," revelation struck her. She was galvanized! There was no JUNK! She had listened to her mother's opinion, which had no basis in fact- for years! "Mom, you were wrong about Daddy, wrong about God, wrong about this place, and wrong about me!" she chortled as she waltzed across the small back porch, giving the broken swing a playful shove. "Oh, Mom, if you only knew! Oh, Mom, come back, I can see it now; I'll show you we have more miracles than Daddy quite knew what to do with! Mom, none of this is junk! It all has value!"

The flashlight was still in her hand, and she held it up to demonstrate her point. "See," she whispered elatedly! "Without good batteries, it is worthless for illumination. But, even without batteries, it's a tool, see, or a weapon!"

Her face flushed with excitement! She was onto something. Her dad had had a very good reason for everything he had done, was doing. He wasn't just a crazy, eccentric collector of eclectic junk! Somehow, some-way, everything here - in defiance of appearance- everything must have value for one reason or another!

"Mom, this is a goldmine," she whispered. "Or maybe, I should say, a Diamond Mine!"

She turned on all the knobs of the gas range, and was relieved when all of the burners and the oven sprang to life. A little heat and light, too. "Thank-you, Lord," she breathed softly. "I'm sorry I missed church tonight; I love being there." She gazed around the dim kitchen; she knew the few sparse items in the freezer and fridge would be ruined. Gingerly, she opened the door. A can of biscuits had popped open so she decided to bake them and give it a whirl. They smelled delicious, and her mouth was really watering by the time they were done. Smearing them with butter and jelly, she gobbled down several.

She wished she had some milk, but started water boiling in the tea kettle and hunted for some tea bags. None. Mom must have loaded them in, too. There was one decaf coffee single, so she brewed it weakly, adding lots of creamer and sweetener. It tasted great.

The night chill was settling around her, in spite of the oven. It was warm enough sitting directly in front of it, but if she moved to the sofa or recliner, it was pretty cold. She looked in the cupboard above the washer, and was surprised to find flashlight batteries. She changed them out, and shielding the light with her hands, she went to her room to get her blankets. They were gone! She was amazed! She couldn't believe her mom actually took off with her Pooh Bear stuff. Mallory had wanted something more mature when they had redone her room five years previously. By now, there was no use even trying to explain the hokie stuff to her friends. She thought about the cold night and her mom spending it alone in the car. "Lord, please watch over my mom, and keep her safe and warm". She pulled the sofa closer to the kitchen warmth, wrapped her coat around her, and was asleep.

The clock chimed one-thirty, and the teen-ager moved uncomfortably on the hard couch. She used the restroom, then tried to see out around the window shades without making it obvious to anyone who might be watching. She was afraid and lonely.

"What time I am afraid, I will trust in him." she quoted in a hushed whisper. She prayed again for her safety, for her mom, for her church, the missionaries, the Faulkners, and America. She picked up her daddy's Bible from the kitchen table, then stopped to wrap the rest of her biscuits for later.

Then, what she had been dreading! She heard an engine, then tires on the gravel outside, and she grabbed a knife from the block as she dropped to the floor. She heard the drums going pell-mell as the vehicle reached her trip wire rope. Tears streamed down her cheeks as she clutched her weapon desperately.

"Maybe Mom came back." ran through her mind. She so much wanted that to be it, that she almost got up to run to her arms. But, no! Mom wouldn't be rolling up stealthily with the lights and radio off. It was something bad! Someone bad! What did they want?

The truck, or whatever it was, was missing, idling rough. She knew whoever was out there had been very surprised by her trick. That meant they hadn't seen her out earlier. Now, they had tried to sneak back again for some mysterious reason. She lay, listening, listening. Finally, she heard the gears grind, and the dark, sinister entity backed away into the night.

Mallory regained the Bible, pulled up closer to the oven, and thumbed through it. For some reason, she was certain her nemesis would return again, but she didn't think he would try again tonight. She spotted a highlighted verse and read it. It was something about slinging stones right or left handed. She shrugged and continued to flip pages. "Why would he underline that?" she asked herself. Too curious to shrug it off any longer, she backtracked to find it again. She grew excited to see her father's handwriting in a penciled note in the margin. Cautiously she shone the flashlight beam on it so she could read it. Her dad had decided American Special Forces should include rock throwing in their training and carry rocks and slings in their gear. She silently hoped he hadn't written the Pentagon. Her face dimpled at the thought of all the Joint-Chiefs of Staff at an important-looking conference table sharing this amazing revelation for this new highly sophisticated weaponry. But, maybe, the thought occurred to her, for a teen-aged girl alone, it wasn't such a bad idea.

Her daddy was a baseball fan, deluxe! Boston Red Sox all the way. He always played catch with her from the time she could grasp a ball. She had grown into quite a pitcher- for a girl! She was definitely a right-hander, though. She was going to teach herself to be the best right and left handed rock slinger in Pike County, Arkansas. She knew where her daddy always kept a slingshot to scare away stray cats and dogs, and she was going to use it, too.

And speaking of cats and dogs, guess I'll find a big dog! Yeah! I always wanted one, and now, neither one of them is here to say, no.

Chapter 4

DIAMONDS

MALLORY HAD NOT permitted herself to fall asleep again! Not that she thought she could. Her racing mind was making the Nascar races her daddy had loved to watch seem like slo-mo! She hugged the Bible hard against her chest; her heart was beating hard and fast. Maybe she was going to die right here, too. She tried to force herself to slow down, be calm. She opened to Psalm 104, and sought for a verse she was certain should be there. The verse she sought was highlighted in all four of her colors in her Bible. Her Bible that was still out in the tractor, she thought forlornly. Finally, her eyes lighted on the verse she was seeking. Verse 24. She would remember the reference from now on. The verse read:

> *O LORD, how manifold are thy works! In wisdom hast thou made them all: the earth is full of thy riches.*

The verse she had loved so much danced and sparkled before her with an astounding new meaning she had never imagined. "Oh my," she whispered. "Oh my word!"

Because, earlier in the evening, when the clouds had scooted off to the east, and the heavens had stretched away, she had seen diamonds! Both in the sky above her head, and in the mud at her feet!

She was trying to absorb the revelation, trying to imagine what to do, who to tell, where to go. How could she pluck a raw diamond from her yard, and sail into the power company with it, and say she wanted her electricity back on? Her laughter rippled with the absurdity of it. Same with the phone. She wondered how long the Butane in the old tank in the yard would hold out. Confusion chased partial thoughts around in her exhausted mind "Lord, thank you for thinking of me when You threw diamonds here. I know the earth is full of lots of other riches, too. The way food grows, and all of Your miraculous design. Best of all, the riches of Your grace and Salvation-- Thank you for the diamonds, but please help me. Daddy always said, 'Never trust anybody!'"

"I wish I could talk to Mom," she thought, then knew in her heart that Mom was one of the ones Daddy didn't trust.

She could see her Daddy's gray eyes twinkle mischievously when he would make Suzanne mad by leaving her out of their secrets.

"Why had they so enjoyed antagonizing one another?"

She returned her attention to the awesome, inspired Word of God which rested in her lap.

O LORD, how manifold are thy works! In wisdom thou has made them all: the earth is full of thy riches.
So is this great and wide sea, wherein are things creeping innumerable, both small and great beasts.
There go the ships: there is that leviathan, whom thou hast made to play therein.
These wait all upon thee; that thou mayest give them their meat in due season.
That thou givest them they gather: thou openest thy hand, they are filled with good.
Thou hidest thy face, they are troubled: thou takest away their breath, they die, and return to their dust.
Thou sendest forth thy spirit, they are created: and thou renewest the face of the earth.
The glory of the LORD shall endure for ever: the LORD shall rejoice in his works.
He looketh on the earth, and it trembleth: he toucheth the hills, and they smoke.

I will sing unto the LORD as long as I live: I will sing praise to my God while I have my being.
My meditation of him shall be sweet: I will be glad in the LORD.
Ps. 104: 24-34

Softly, she began singing, "My Jesus, I Love Thee" as golden fingers of light began clawing at the darkness of the eastern sky.

Still singing, she showered, dressed, threw out what was in the fridge with the rest of the trash, and marched jubilantly out to the road to deposit the bags for the garbage truck.

Gathering her remaining biscuits and her school books, she boarded the school bus just in time.

Usually mom or daddy would take her to school, but in the past three months, her mom had just more and more begged for her to ride the bus so she could sleep. The bus ride was always a zoo, but today, Mallory was grateful for the too -warm ride. The only seat she could see toward the front was next to Martin. He made an effort to make room for her, but with his size, even with her slenderness, there wasn't room. She tried to always be nice to him; she usually tried with most people. But she really didn't like him.

"Hey, Martin," she greeted. "I don't mind standing." Pops had started to roll the bus forward until he heard her say that. He jammed the brakes on to tell her she had to sit down before he could pull away, and the sudden stop threw her right on top of Martin. All the kids hooted! Mortified, Mallie tried to extricate herself. She tried to perch uncomfortably on the little triangle of seat, with her books and biscuits precariously on her knees. Suddenly Martin had his arm around her.

"What do you think you are doing?" She was trying to wiggle away where there was absolutely no wiggle room. "Get your hands off of me!"

"Hey, take it easy, just trying to hang onto you so you don't bounce off on the floor!"

"Hey, I'm hearing your daddy left you filthy rich and sittin' purty," he whispered conspiratorially in her ear. His breath was hot and heavy and disgusting. She hated gossip, and she didn't know where he had gotten his information. She remembered a lifetime of Daddy's serious warnings about trusting no one. She twisted to face him.

"Yep," she confirmed, "Filthy rich and sitting pretty!"

She considered the conversation closed, and focused her attention out the window across the aisle. Thankfully, they were nearing the bus unloading zone.

"Will you marry me?" he blurted out! She had heard him clearly, and she didn't want to hear the question from his lips again, but she was so shocked that she had already whispered, "What?" His mouth was working, and his ugly teeth filled her frame of vision as he was stammering to ask again and explain his proposal. The bus halted, and she was on her feet, desperate for the hissing doors to release her from one more crazy nightmare. Her feet hit the curb, then dizziness hit her, and she fainted.

Martin fell over her in bewilderment, then tried to fumble for her. Before he could touch her, he was tackled and thrown violently to the ground. Someone was on him, and he knew it was Anderson. He let fly with some language, and tried to get his adversary in a wrestling hold. Teachers were rushing up to break up the fight and rescue the stricken girl.

"A great Monday," Tom Haynes, the school principal sighed, as he took in the scenario from his office window. He set his coffee mug on the big, ancient, scarred desk, and hurried to the entrance. Some kids were filing through the metal detectors, but most were trying to stare as the unconscious girl was being loaded on a stretcher, or they were excitedly asking or telling what happened, or they were trying to get in some swings themselves. Most of them didn't like David Anderson too much, but none of them liked Martin.

Years of experience exuded from Tom, and he quickly got the situation under control. "If your name isn't O'Shaughnessy, Anderson, or Thomas, you better get your business taken care of and get to homeroom. Gentlemen, this fight is over!" he asserted authoritatively. He meant David, Martin, and a few others who were still trying to get into the fight. He instructed Coach to take Martin down to his office off the gym, and Bob Grayson, the math teacher, to take David to his own office, and wait there while he checked the infirmary about Mallory.

He heard a siren! "Kids and their cell phones!" he thought to himself. Someone had already called 911. He figured they meant well, but he would address the problem in assembly! All three hundred of them were not in charge! He was!

Mallory was sitting up, trying to stand, and arguing with Marnie that she was fine.

Tom ordered her to sit down and allow the nurse to look her over. He went out to greet the ambulance and paramedics, the fire truck, the sheriff, and the chief of police.

"Morning," he greeted all of them by their first names. The president of the school board pulled up in his Lincoln; then panicky parents began arriving. Collected and organized, he decided the paramedics should check the girl since they had been called. Sadly, since the police had been summoned, the altercation between the boys was now a police matter, rather than one of school discipline. He hoped they threw the book at Martin Thomas, but he felt bad about more trouble for his pastor and his son.

He asked the head of the school board to call the press to explain the incident to the anxious public. Then, he went to his office to call the parents of the three kids.

David Anderson was waiting with Bob Grayson. Tom thanked the teacher and sent him back to his classroom.

"What's your dad's cell number, Anderson?" All businesslike, he had the receiver to his ear.

"Look," David began earnestly. "Can't you just spank me, or something? I really don't want you to get my dad into this. Or my mom," he added. He knew his behavior had repeatedly broken their hearts, and he hated it that it did. He refused to obey their rules, and he was pretty determined to do his own thing. But he hated his mom to cry.

Tom cradled the receiver. "I wish I could spank you! I'd light the seat of your britches real good, but I can't. I can't even warn you and give you detentions or a suspension. Since someone called 911 and the police are here, it's out of my hands. I'm really sorry, but the police will want your dad to come to the station while they talk to you.

David couldn't believe it! The police! Why did everything he did get him into trouble with them? His dad would be furious. "Why do I always get in trouble? Why do I always get caught? My friends do lots worse, and it never catches up with them! And this time, I really did not do one thing wrong!"

Tom didn't know why; he was a stickler for everyone's playing by the rules, but he suddenly felt sorry for the troubled young man.

"What did happen, anyway,?" he asked.

"Like you care!" David had slouched down, and was glaring belligerently.

"Phone number!" the principal demanded authoritatively.

Mallory was allowed to return to class by time for second hour. She tried to put the unpleasant bus-ride out of her mind. She would shudder occasionally at the thought.

She was so romantic! Her proposal would be so wonderful, from someone tremendous with whom she was passionately in love. There would only be one because she would be too honest to lead anyone on. There would be an elegant place, candlelight, soft music, and she would know he had already asked Daddy and Mama's blessing. He would be so tender as he poured out his feelings and begged her to be his wife. She would be loved for herself, for who she was!

What a jolt that that nauseating, overgrown dirt bag decided she was "filthy rich and sitttin' purty," and she would be dying to marry him and buy him large, meat-lovers for the rest of his life!

She didn't know whether to laugh or cry, so she opened her Geometry book and tried to concentrate.

The diamonds, of course, were really on her mind. Everyone in the small town was affected by the carbon chunks, one way or another! Mallie had tried to be different. She wanted to have values that differed from most people who lived here, or who passed through on some quest for magical happiness. It was as though people really believed that finding a valuable stone or two would make them happy, or satisfied. Mallie just basically wanted the diamonds to help through this rough spot and bring Mom back. Or maybe she did really want to be as rich as the Faulkners seemed, but be adjusted, happy, generous, and non-greedy. She knew her mind was exhausted from the past three months, and the past three really crazy, emotional, and terrifying days.

She was hungry, but by the time she had regained consciousness in the infirmary, her books were there, but her biscuits had disappeared. She begged the Lord to help her with the geometry; it had mystified her since the first page, as had Algebra I and II in her freshman and sophomore years. "Wish they had lost the books and kept my lunch," she thought dejectedly. "Lord, I'm starving!" she whispered.

The bell rang, and it was study hall. She planned to work on the geometry assignment as soon as study hall began. Maybe she had paid enough attention that she could work the problems. She slid into her assigned seat in the library/study hall. Right next to her chair in the stacks was a book about diamonds. She had read it before; daddy loved it. It stated that when there was one diamond pipe in an area, there were always more. Sometimes they were very hard to find. The big one at the State Park, discovered by Huddleston, was the only one that was known about for sure. A few stakes were claimed in the area, and each year there were a few more. Claiming a stake was relatively easy and inexpensive.

Getting the claims to yield the stones seemed to be the hard part.

Mallory's dad had often sent his daughter mixed signals about the gems, one day caring about spiritual values, the next rattling on and on that there had to be other diamondiferous pipes, and that there would be alluvial diamonds in the little creeks which fed the Little Missouri river. Then they would be washed, according to Daddy's excited surmising, down into the Ouachita River, into Louisiana, until feeding into the Red River, before joining the Mississippi. Supposedly the Mississippi River Delta and the Gulf of Mexico should be covered in diamonds which could then be sucked up into diamond recovery ships as they were off the southern coasts of the African continent. Her father had often said, "If I could only raise some capital, I'd get me a boat like they use in the rivers in Brazil, and I'd cover ya with diamonds, Mallory Erin, m' girl." His "r's" would roll softly, and she would wonder why he didn't just get a real job and fix the house up a bit better for her and mom. Now the book piqued her interest anew, and she had already browsed through parts she had forgotten. It kind of made her really nostalgic for her dad; but in a sweet way.

She raised her hand, and Miss Richmond nodded at her. She took the book up to check out.

"Oh, I see," the Librarian/ Study Monitor said snippily- and loudly for a library/study hall-it occurred to Mallie. "You have gotten as mesmerized by diamonds as everyone else around here!"

All eyes and ears were front and center, and the hum of the supposedly quiet room broke off, leaving a genuine stillness. Mallory was surprised and embarrassed at the teacher's attitude. She was a teachers' pet with most of the faculty, but this lady always seemed to have a prob with her. And she didn't like having her Christianity or her values judged by someone who had no clue what was in her heart.

She lowered her voice and met the monitor's gaze earnestly. "Actually, I'm mesmerized by Jesus," she affirmed softly. "And He is the One Who has filled the earth with His riches."

"Oh, I see!" She said again. This time her voice was louder and shriller. "So, that gives you the right to claw and scratch like everybody else!"

"What are you talking about?" The student again spoke softly. "I'm sorry, did I scratch you, or something when I handed you the book? Could I just check the book out please? Do I need to go get out my student ID?"

"You know, I can give you a detention for disrespect!"

"Yes, ma'am." Mallory was trying not to get mad, and she certainly didn't want a detention. This was the first time her deportment had ever been called into question. She didn't know what to say, so she stood there.

"Actually, Miss O'Shaughnessy," her voice hissed the "S's" with sarcasm; loud, really loud sarcasm! "You can't check this book out today. There's a waiting list for it." She opened the desk drawer and referred studiously to a non-existent list. Yep, a pretty long waiting list. I don't know how it got checked in and slipped into the stacks without me realizing it." Sorry! Looks like you have to wait until at least next fall!"

Miss Richmond smiled nastily, and snatched the book into her lap as if the girl's next move would be to steal it.

Mallory returned to her seat and buried herself in Daddy's beautiful Bible.

Chapter 5

DESTINATIONS

THE DATE WAS April ninth, and Mallory tried to read the corresponding chapter in the book of Proverbs in addition to her other Bible schedule. Sometimes she didn't get it all done, but she always made a sincere attempt at it. A camp counselor had explained that it wasn't just more assignments or some tedious chore, but a true source of delight. Spending time with Jesus was spending time with a very real Person. "He is very real; but is temporarily out of the room with His physical presence," Marilyn had explained.

Now, Mallory tried to concentrate on her reading.

Chapter nine of Proverbs hadn't been one of her favorites; nothing had ever just stood out to her, that she should underline anything. Mistakenly, she had mentioned that fact to Patrick. You would have thought that she had become a total heretic! He began a strident and ardent discourse that left her stunned.

"It's the best chapter; you aren't reading it right! It's about the two paths that are spread out before every young person who stands where y' are standin'. Ya better take heed, me girl, ye better be takin' heed! There's two paths; the one leadin' to th abundant life, th other t' early death and the fires of hell itself. Go read it again."

"Yes, sir," she had responded. She meant "Yes, sir, next month when it rolls around again." She had laid her Bible aside and had begun cleaning up the kitchen.

"You think I'm talkin' just to hear meself?" he questioned. His voice was level, neither angered or joking. "I think I told you to read it again and get the meanin'."

"You just told me the meaning; about the two paths. I'm saved; that puts me on the path to heaven. I can't lose my salvation. I don't understand the big deal--"

Never the right thing to say to Daddy.

"Lot of saved people wanderin' 'round aimlessly in wrong paths; maybe not the worst paths, but not th' best. You need to be thinkin', decidin' on life now, so you don't waste most of it. Whatever path you choose every day helps decide where you'll be tomorrow. You can't go north on 27 out of here, and get down to Hope, even if you tell yourself you're going to Hope. It's just th' wrong path, headin' th' wrong direction. Time ya turn around, if indeed, there'd be a place t' turn; time and gas is wasted, maybe good opportunities lost ferever."

Only, a sophomore in high school, she had felt he was demanding too much seriousness and perfection. Be sure you're on the best path, not just a good one. Just being a faithful, serious Christian wasn't good enough now? She had to be some super Christian, always, every moment, having to make sure every little decision would be the best because every decision has far-reaching consequences!

She could see his point, sort of, but she was still just a kid! And she was making right choices, getting good grades, checking into good Christian colleges; planning to attend a Christian college and enter full-time Christian work.

Nearly in tears, she had said, "I'm sorry, Daddy, I really can't tell what you're driving at. I'm trying to be what the Lord wants and what you want."

"Yeah, Mallory Erin, ya are; but I see one big danger risin' up, and I'd not be likin' it. I think ya know what I mean better'n ya want ta let on."

His eyes pierced her heart, and she felt flustered. "Oh," she breathed, "you mean David; why didn't you just say so?"

"We're just friends," she had added briskly. "We have been since grade school. He's the reason I got saved, and then you and Mom got saved."

"Yeah," he agreed grudgingly, "he is. But unless ye've gone blind and deaf, ya must be noticin' some change comin' about with him. I'm, askin' ya t' distance yourself from him, Mallory. He already has yer judgment blinded about him, and it'll just be gettin' worse. He'll ruin your life, and if yours is ruined, so will mine be- and your mother's. We couldn't bear to see ya unhappy. I can't, fer the life of me, figure out why bad boys draw good girls!"

"I'm trying to help him," she began eagerly.

He had slapped his thigh impatiently! "His dad's th' pastor, let him help his own kid. It's not your job. You can't do it You'll be burned and scarred fer life. I'm beggin' ya, Darlin' listen to me, please!"

"Well, Yes, Sir," she had murmured, and had started to continue with, "but---"

Daddy's face silenced her. No more said by either one about the subject for the rest of the day.

The next morning at breakfast, he had been in a jovial mood. "Let's drive to Little Rock and find ya some nice new things. Yer dad hasn't spoiled his little lassie in a wee while."

Sometimes his brogue was more pronounced.

Daddy never took her shopping. She wouldn't ask unless she really needed something desperately, because his response would always be the same. He would clasp both hands to his chest and moan, "Oh, ye be breakin' me heart, and me pocketbook! How have I failed to make ye happy that ya can be thinkin' things'll make ya happy? Ya decide it in yer heart, ta be happy Then he would quote her the verse about a man's life not consisting of the abundance of the things that he has.

She would always look around at their meager belongings and think it was a good thing.

But now, he was offering a really fun outing! Little Rock! Mallie thought the mall in Hope was almost heaven. She hoped they could afford something; he always told her they couldn't. Not that she didn't have outings with her dad. She did! And it was always fun. They had good talks and fun jokes between them. Sometimes they would go to the lovely sites which surrounded them. Arkansas tried to vie for tourist dollars, touting itself as "The Natural State." They would make sandwiches and have picnics.

⁂

Patrick Shay O'Shaughnessy had been smitten by Mallory the first time he had laid eyes on her She was the first person to ever make him think of anyone but himself. He loved having something, someone important, to live for. He had sobered up that day, walked away from his friends, and never touched another drop of alcohol. "He'd be needin' his wits about him from now on," he would joke when someone would try to push him to drink.

He had his daughter baptized by his priest and tried to get Suzanne interested in Catholicism. His mother and father had been in the business of importing Irish Linen, and their business had grown and succeeded.

When the wealth had not accumulated fast enough for his older brother, Ryland, he had gotten mixed up in all types of fraudulent and illegal ventures. Not being able to do wrong alone, he had already involved his little brother, Patrick.

That was before Suzanne and Mallory! And although Patrick wasn't "in" as deep with organized crimes as some of the others, you weren't allowed to simply walk away.

He knew there were always "contracts" out on Ryland and himself, and he knew they didn't mind hurting family members. In fact, they seemed to enjoy all the nasty little details that the life demanded.

He tried to find solace and forgiveness in his religion. This delighted his mother, who was an ardent fan of the Pope. and the whole thing. He was always puzzled that the most vicious, cut-throat guys he knew were always at church, too. Always friends with the priest, the archbishop, the cardinals. Always at weddings, christenings, and funerals. How could they be granted forgiveness and absolution from their sins? They weren't sorry. It was how they lived! They weren't trying to stop, or do better "next time"! They were planning to murder, extort, and terrorize whoever was in their way of making a dime. Disillusioned, he would have left the Church before he did; except he was afraid to! Terrified that if the gangsters sensed anything about him, Mallory would be in grave danger, he bode his time Every day she grew; every day she became more adorable, more fun! He had to get out of Boston! Not that the evil empire recognized city limits, but if he could escape their immediate reach, he might be able to think, to plan, to at least save his wife and daughter! He had never figured he would live to be forty-five, before dying of "natural causes".

The life and salvation the Lord had extended to him had given him cause to rejoice, and he had rejoiced.

Every day he had been able to watch his daughter grow and blossom had been a gift.

He had felt like evil still tried to stalk him at times. Sometimes, he was quite certain a new contract on him had been issued. It made him pray more, but now he prayed differently. He had received Jesus as Savior, as Mallory had reminded him, partially because of David Anderson.

The Anderson's had moved to Murfreesboro when Mallory and David were in second grade. The two had bonded to become inseparable friends. David had invited Mallie, and Pastor had invited her family to come to Sunday School and church. So disillusioned with religion, Patrick had refused to go. That was fine by Suzanne; she didn't have any use for it either.

But then when summer vacation had come, David had told Mallory, "We won't get to see each other all summer. You have to come to Vacation Bible School. My mom will pick you up. Ask your dad."

So, she had begged and whined until they relented. Then, her first day there, when she heard the wonderful story of Jesus, she had invited Him into her heart "for forever," she had added for anyone who would listen to her about it.

Little Rock! Mallory raced through her chores and got herself ready, trying to look extra cute for such a special excursion. She applied extra mascara and put hot rollers in her hair. Dressed in her favorite color of soft pink, glowing with excitement, exuding a delightful, feminine fragrance, she rejoined Daddy, who was still at the kitchen table finishing his devotions. And another cup of coffee.

"I'm ready," she announced. "Whenever you are," she had added when he had given her a quizzical look.

"Not readin' the Word today?" he queried.

Embarrassed, she mumbled that she was planning to read it on the way. The only problem with that story was that her Bible was still in her room.

Well, to make a long story short, they never did reach Little Rock that day. That day was an object lesson Mallory would never forget. Her dad had purposely chosen wrong route after wrong route, until they were hopelessly lost, and the entire day was shot. Mallory had been pretty mad at him when he didn't finally end up at some place where they could still shop. He just told her, "These wrong paths have cost you a day, and the disappointment of not havin' time to shop. In real life, you lose more days than you planned on, your youth, your vitality; and you suffer disappointments you can't even fathom now. You marry a bad boy who gets in trouble with the law, gets a record, can't get bonded to handle money, then you get hungry babies, no money, no doctors, no food. A lot of people plan to go to college and be something. They get turned in at the wrong place. That's what Proverbs chapter nine is talking about. Don't miss it, Mallory" He burst into tears. "You're all I got!" He patted her hand and got out of the car. They were home; that was it.

She tried again, to concentrate on the chapter. Her mind had made quite a detour. Concentrating wasn't easy.

She was still trying to forget Martin- and her nocturnal visitor: the two incidents tried to merge together. Could it be Martin who had been terrifying her the past two nights? She tried to think. Martin did have a big, new, black pick-up. All the school kids wondered how he had swung it, and it had quickly sounded like it wasn't running right for such a new vehicle. Mallory didn't know much about cars, but to her, it had sounded sinister; kind of like its owner. The windows had been tinted, but he had customized them even darker. The sound system rumbled the whole town.

"Why was he riding the bus this morning?" she almost asked aloud. Was it so he could scare her some more? Why would he want to scare her? "Cause he's big and creepy and that's what he does!" she answered herself. Trying to corral her thoughts, she pulled out a piece of notebook paper. She stared blankly at the page, then doodled around the punched-out holes. She was pretty certain she hadn't seen him on the bus since he had gotten the truck. Why, then, had he ridden it this morning?

A slight smile crossed her face,"Maybe, just maybe, a couple of old, empty drums had caused some body damage that he didn't want anyone to see!"

The smile faded. Scary to think about Martin's sneaking around her property in the middle of the night. Scary to think about anyone's sneaking around her property in the middle of the night!

She sat, trying not to admit something to herself, trying to ignore a possibility that kept presenting itself. The truck in the driveway seemed like it might have been Martin's, but the dark, booted form on foot the previous morning had made her think it was David Anderson. "Why would it be David?" she finally allowed her heart to question. "Who is sneaking around, and what are they looking for?" Did anyone know about the diamonds? Did everyone know about the diamonds? How could they? How could they not?

The bell rang!

One more class, one more session to try to at least act like she was paying attention, then finally it was lunch hour. Not wanting to enter the cafeteria and try to explain why she didn't have a lunch or money to buy something, she moved slowly along the corridor.

Tammi Anderson caught up to her and grabbed her elbow.

"Hi, Tammi, what's happenin'? Mallory greeted her cheerfully.

"I have office duty this hour, and Mr. Haynes asked me to find you and ask you to come to the office asap! Wait for me a minute after school, will ya?"

"Sure thing," Mallie answered. She didn't want to risk missing the school bus home. She hoped no one knew her mom was gone. If she missed the bus, she would be in for quite a little walk, and "these shoes," she realized, "are not the most comfortable."

She scurried toward the school offices. She hoped Mr. Haynes only wanted to make sure she was feeling ok, and that she wasn't in any kind of trouble. She had never been in trouble at school, and she couldn't think of anything; but being told the principal wants you is still always a scary thing. Then, too, maybe, Mom had called the school to leave a message that she was safe. Mallie hoped she was, was praying she was. She would like the consideration of a phone call. "But, please Lord," she prayed urgently, "don't let anyone find out I'm alone. I'm seventeen. I sure don't want to end up at some children's shelter now!"

The secretary buzzed Mr. Haynes, and he told her to send the girl in.

"Have a seat," he gestured. She sat, and his gaze met hers for several moments. Then he frowned at his cuticles, before beginning.

He seemed embarrassed, then began. "I've been trying to call your mother about your fainting spell-or what ever it was. I keep getting a message that the number is no longer in service. Then I called Hal, at the lodge. He said he hasn't seen your mom since Saturday. Well, I saw you both in church yesterday morning, but- I-really don't know how to ask this. Are you and your mom doing okay? Is there anything Joyce and I can do to help? I mean, we helped with food for after the funeral, but-what can we do now?"

Mallory was touched by his genuine concern. He was a good school administrator; most of the community really liked him. And he was a good Christian. He was chairman of the board of deacons at her church. Her Daddy really liked him. She sat awkwardly, glancing from him to a dead bug, and back to him.

He got up, picked the bug up in a tissue, and dropped it in the trash. "Now, can we talk?" he laughed.

She knew he meant well, but suddenly, she was too humiliated and frightened to talk. She could tell he really wondered where her mom was, and she didn't want to tell him, nor did she want to lie. She had blushed deeply, then blanched white; and the tears were fighting to free themselves once again.

He pulled a few ones from his desk drawer and pushed them into her hand. "Get some lunch," he urged her, "before you hit the deck on me again. Then go home. Come see me in the morning before classes, if you feel better tomorrow and want to try it. Give yourself some healing time. You and your mom better tell Joyce and me if we can do anything-anything at all!"

Without a word of argument, Mallie received the proffered bills, thanked the principal, assured him her mom would contact his wife, and hastily left the office. Walking quickly; no running, she reminded herself; she reached her locker. Most of the high school kids were in the cafeteria; a few had gone out to some tables in the warm sunshine. Mallie shoved everything unceremoniously into the locker, slammed the door, and gave the combination lock a whirl.

Then she moved swiftly along the chain link fence, cut across the highway, and disappeared into a little stand of trees where she was hidden from the high school. She pulled an insect repellent washcloth from its little packet, rubbing it over her the best she could; hair, skin, clothes. Ticks could be a problem, and she didn't want to risk the illnesses they carried. Then, she pulled the slingshot from her backpack and gathered up a few promising-looking rocks. She didn't think anyone would bother her, but she still just felt creeped out about Martin Thomas. She hadn't seen him at school after the morning incident. Of course, she was still "out" when the fight had occurred, so she knew nothing of that, or of the two guilty parties being taken to the police station. She took a practice shot at a tree and enjoyed the gratifying "thonk" it made as it hit forcefully. She took aim at a tree a greater distance away and missed. "That's great," she thought ruefully. "I can't shoot anyone unless I let them get really close." She knew she was going to really work at the sling shot until she could pull it out, aim, shoot fast and accurately, and have disabled any attacker.

While she had been doodling, trying to formulate a plan, some ideas had been coming together in her mind. Nothing she had written down, but a plan, all the same. She had wondered how she would accomplish it between afternoon dismissal and dark! The Lord had surely helped her by causing the kind principal to send her home early.

She was sorry that there hadn't been a message from her mom, but figured she must be ok.

Trying to hurry, in spite of heels, through rough and muddy terrain, she plunged on. This was neither the shortest nor the easiest route, but it was the one that she would be the least likely to be noticed. Finally, she could see her own large, sprawling yard. She gave wide berth to the tractor, skirted around the fish pond, glanced anxiously around the entire area. Rock poised in her slingshot, she eased up the back steps and through the screen door. She closed it as gently as possible and paused. She felt like she was being watched, and she stood frozen, waiting, listening.

She eased out of her shoes, for silence, and because they were muddy. She knew the hinges on the back door would squeak loudly. Already, she had been far from noiseless. The door was unlocked; they always left it unlocked. Finally, grasping the knob, she pushed the door open and squeezed through. Quickly, she turned the key behind her.

She moved like demons were chasing her and charged into her daddy's deserted bedroom. Pushing that lock in behind her, she moved to one of the windows and tried to see if anyone had followed her.

The drawn blinds made the room seem pretty dark for her to execute her plan to look around. Gradually her eyes adjusted.

Now that she was in here, she wasn't' sure what to look for or where to start. People had been going through his things, and evidently they hadn't found anything too interesting. Probably there was nothing in here but his junk. She sank down listlessly on his bed. An intensely private man, his room had been his room, even in the tiny run-down house. Whatever cleaning it received, it received from him. Mallory and Suzanne had just known not to go in Daddy's room. His secrecy had never made Mallory suspicious at all, because that was just daddy. She was never totally sure what he did, or how he earned the little money they had. If there were a sudden need, he could seem to come up with whatever was needed. Before he was saved, he always claimed. "To have the luck of the Irish." Recently, he just always said that," "the Lord helped him." Mallory had never thought to question him. She was pretty sure her mom did. She thought that was probably one of the things they fought about.

She gazed about in the dim light; the room was musty, and she longed to raise the shades and open the windows to the warm spring breeze.

"Lord, what am I looking for? Where do I start? Remember You have promised to help us because Mom is a widow now, and I'm a fatherless child!" Saying it aloud made her want to cry. She was ready to give in to the grief, but an amazing thing happened. The sun had come from behind a cloud, causing a slant of sunlight to shine through the narrow slit along the edge of the window shade. The bright light hit the far wall above a piled up table, which also served as a makeshift desk. The dancing sliver of light, to the girl's amazed gaze, looked like an arrow, pointing directly to a particular stack of papers.

Without hesitating any longer, she crossed the room swiftly, beginning at the stack beneath the arrow. The sun had gone behind another cloud, causing the arrow to disappear. She started to lift the entire stack, so she could sit on the bed to go through it. In doing so, she dislodged the stack in front, sending stuff flying in all directions. Annoyed, she bent to gather everything up. There had been an old cigar box in the stack. It had opened and flung out several stacks of hundred dollar bills. Stunned, she fanned through the packages. They pretty much had non-sequential serial numbers, as far as she could tell. They were not all crisp and new, like they might be counterfeit. She was mystified. There must be more than ten thousand dollars here, she surmised, doing the math. Where had it come from? Why not put it in the bank? Why just leave it lying here with the house always unlocked? Because he always wanted the place to look like a junk-pile; so no one would think to come here for anything valuable.

Swooping up five thousand, she placed the rest back into the cigar box and reburied the box in stacks of paper. She grabbed one of her mom's big purses, filling the bottom of it with the cash, before transferring the contents of her own small bag in on top of the money.

Out in the shed, Mallory dragged her bike into the sunlight by the door, and surveyed the tires forlornly. She pumped them both up, slung the funny, big purse in the basket, and pedaled furiously, making it out to the road, and beyond the mail box before they both went completely flat again.

She was standing in the brilliant afternoon sunshine when David happened to drive by.

His hair had gotten a little long, and his music sounded pretty wild. He turned it down and leaned out his car window. "Having a little tire trouble, are we?" he chortled gleefully. "How is Erin go Bragh?" he always called her that to tease her. "What are you bragging about today? Probably that you are the only seventeen year old in Pike County with such fine transportation." He laughed at his own joke.

She always told him she didn't brag, and he always told her she was bragging by going around with her nose in the air, acting like she was better than everyone else.

She was really annoyed at him now. "Why don't you just go away?" she asked him. She usually tried to be witty, but she couldn't think of anything clever. There was nothing funny about her bike, or the flats.

Trying to remember her Daddy's warnings, she raised her head defiantly, tossing her gorgeous, shining hair carelessly. "Why don't you just go away?"

It hurt to choose the wise path where wisdom beckoned, but she whirled away anyway, trying to drag the annoying bicycle back up the driveway. Tears stung her eyes. She really did want to follow the Lord; why did David have to be so cute?

Chapter 6

DAVID

MALLORY'S WORDS STUNG him in a way he had never expected. He could feel the anger and humiliation of her words making him want to lash out at her in return. He wanted to peel out in a rage, and show miss snooty Irish he didn't care. He resisted the temptation to react hastily, and sat there, watching her jerk angrily at the resisting bike. She had as much of a temper as he did so he felt kind of sorry for the bike.

And she was so mad! Mad that he stayed there, sat there, watching her struggle! She was sure she looked really stupid trying to walk "this stupid bike-" She was sure he was having a really good laugh.

Tears streamed down her cheeks. She flung her head defiantly and slammed the bicycle down. She would not turn to look at him, to see why he didn't just leave like she had told him to. She left the bike where it lay, continuing toward the house as quickly as she could. She could hear his car still idling out at the road.

She hadn't heard him get out of the car; so she screamed, shocked, and frightened, when he caught her by the elbow.

Then, madder than ever because he had scared her, she jerked her arm free and began to run.

"Come on, Mallie, what are you doing?" His voice was earnest, pleading. "I'm sorry for teasing you. Come on, please."

He picked her bicycle up, opened his trunk, and began loading it in. "I'll get a kit tomorrow and fix your tires. Where were you heading? Where's your mom? Will you at least forgive me enough to let me give you a ride somewhere?"

She didn't know what to do. Accepting a ride from someone who had been a close friend for nine years seemed okay. Agonizingly, however, she had to admit to herself that the boot prints he was making along the drive seemed to match the ones that had been made here early the previous morning. She continued to stare at him, big tears welling up and rolling down her face. She wanted to trust him, but her dad had told her not to trust anyone, and had told her specifically to stay as far away from this "no-good" as she could.

"Mallory," he said her name softly again, "get in."

People were driving along, people who knew them both, were waving big friendly hellos, but then they would be on their phones, gossiping. "Hey, I saw Mallory O'Shaughnessy and David Anderson talking out by her driveway. It looked like she was crying. Hey, you think they have something going on?"

The two had a lot in common, but they were really united about hating to be gossiped about.

David opened her car door considerately, removing a pair of binoculars from the passenger seat.

She wondered why he needed binoculars, but she didn't ask. Daddy was right; he had really changed from the cute little p.k. of their growing up years. She was sad, but she didn't really feel frightened of him.

He waited for a break in the traffic and turned toward town. "This is the direction you were going, isn't it? Where were you headed?"

"Into town," she answered without further elaboration.

He turned his music back up to fill up the thick silence. It didn't help, so he turned it off and tried another attempt at conversation.

"You know, Mal," he began, "you really need to be careful of Martin Thomas. You shouldn't encourage his attention. He's weird, no telling what he might do!"

The guy had really scared him when he had made a grab for Mallory. He had kind of had a murderous look on his face. David had been further back on the bus, beside his sister, Tammi. David had scrunched down so Mallory wouldn't see him. He wanted to surprise her and please her when he completed the year. He had dropped out of school at the beginning of their junior year, and immediately been sorry. After Patrick's death in early January, David had gone to Mr. Haynes to see if he could make up the lost semester. Now, he was caught up with the junior class. He was pleased with himself. He was riding the bus because a friend had borrowed his car. Fascinated with his beautiful friend, he had been watching her when Thomas had put his arm around her shoulder. Even from several rows back, he had been able to tell Mallory hadn't liked that. Then he couldn't tell what the guy was saying to her, but she had tried to jump off the bus before it had hardly stopped, to get away from the guy. Then, she had fainted. David had jumped and shoved his way off the bus to tackle the creep. Then at the police station, Martin had been screaming threats at David, swearing, and going into a lot of gory detail about the way he was planning to kill them. One minute he was yelling how Mallory was his woman and was going to marry him, the next minute the horrible, mutilating things he was planning. He was still saying all that garbage when David's mom and dad had come to pick him up. It had scared his mom and dad, too.

Mallory couldn't believe what he had just said. That she shouldn't encourage Martin Thomas's attention!

"You think I would encourage an idiot like that! How insulting! I don't encourage anyone, particularly! I'm only seventeen and a junior in high school. I have college to finish, and I have some dreams and plans! They don't include that big oaf! How did you even hear anything about that, anyway?" she asked suddenly

He pulled over to the curb so he could look at her better.

"Well, I saw you launch off the bus ahead of everyone like the devil was chasing you. Then, you just collapsed, and he was grabbing at you like you, like-like- like I don't know," he finished weakly. "I thought he looked like he might hurt you so I waded in," he finished.

She stared at him, trying to grasp the fact that he was at the school, that he had seen her pass out, that he had "waded in" with a guy like Martin.

"So you were there," she responded blankly.

"I was. That's why I'm saying, don't be nice, don't say 'hi.' Don't smile at him. You can't expect a guy like that to read between the lines and pick up on, "you're not interested". He seems to think you plan to marry him. Why would he even think that?"

Mallory was exasperated. "I don't expect 'a guy like Martin to read between the lines'," she stated emphatically. "I don't expect him to read the lines! I don't think he can read! I don't know who told him my dad left me filthy rich and sitting pretty! Or why he thought that would make me want to marry him. I sat beside him on the bus one morning because Pops told me to!"

She pressed her fingers against her temples and scrunched her eyes closed. She opened them, releasing a new wave of tears. She wished she could go back to Christmas and have her daddy back.

People were still passing them, waving.

She asked him to drop her at the little hardware store. From there, she had some things planned. She needed to ditch him, though. She hopped out of the car.

"Hey, thanks for the ride; I'm sorry I told you to get lost."

"Get back in a minute. What's your hurry? Have you eaten anything today? Level with me; why the hardware store? I mean, you like baseball; you're a great pitcher-for a girl: now if you really like to shop at hardware stores, I know for sure you're the girl of my dreams."

She laughed. "I'm probably not; my daddy really spoiled me; I'm sure I'll ruin some poor guys life. And like I said, I have high school and college to finish. I really do need some things from the hardware store. Thanks for the ride. I don't want to hold you up any more. When I'm done, I'll just go catch my mom--"

"Mallory Erin, do not prevaricate stories. Your nose will grow like Pinocchio's, then you wont' look so cute with it stuck in the air all the time. And, when you lie, you disappoint Jesus." He shook his finger at her sternly. "You are not holding me up. I'm going to help you. Let's do the hardware thing, then get something to eat. What else were you planning to be up to why you played hooky all afternoon?"

"I didn't play hooky; you're a fine one to talk. I'm still really, really, really mad at you for dropping out. Mr. Haynes sent me home because I was still kind of dizzy."

They got the items she needed. Pete raised his eyebrows when she handed him one of the hundreds, but he made change without saying anything.

"Now where?" David questioned. "You might as well tell me what you're scheming and let me in on it. Why don't you trust me?"

"Well, because you haven't been acting very trustworthy lately," she began. "My dad used to really like you, but then you started doing your own thing. He just started telling me to stay away from you. It's weird to me that you are here on the ninth of the month, when I haven't seen you since the funeral." She figured her words were pretty jumbled. She wasn't sure what she was trying to say, herself. He could get her so flustered!

He focused his attention out his window. Her words had stung again, making him pretty mad. He fought to control his words. He had asked her why she didn't trust him; now he wasn't sure he could handle her truthful answer.

"Ah," he began. "So you must have read Proverbs nine today, and now you think I have come to hijack you, get you on the wrong path, and ruin your life. Your dad had the same talk with me. I'm sorry, but I don't think I'm as awful as everyone has decided to make me out to be!"

"He did!" Mallory couldn't believe it. "My dad gave you his chapter nine speech?" she was kind of horrified. "Did he put you in the car and drive you all over western Arkansas?" she asked curiously.

"Uh, no," he admitted cautiously, "just the talk. I think he gave it to all the guys in town. I don't think he took anyone for a ride, though. What's with the ride?"

She described the "object lesson" day, ending up with how mad she had been at him.

Now she was thinking how mad she was at him again for talking to all the guys; like any of them even liked her, anyway.

David was just watching her as she finished the story. Everything about her was so adorable. And, she must like him, if her dad had been so desperate to make his point and keep them apart. Hope began to soar.

"Anyway," he strove for a natural tone. "I'm not as awful as people think. We never did like to be gossiped about, remember?" He was trying to convince her, making it, ' the two of them against the world'.

She met his gaze, then stared out the windshield, sighing involuntarily. She shook her head, but she couldn't speak. Probably best.

Well, that approach hadn't worked very well. He turned the car engine on.

"Okay, hardware store checked off; what's next?"

"Used car lot!" If he insisted on sticking with her, she might as well let him. Her time was wasting, and she still had a lot to do.

"Oooh," he laughed, "the lady has big plans for her big purse full of money. You rob a bank or something?"

"No. My dad did," she responded with a straight face. "Took me 'til this afternoon to figure out what he did for a living."

He looked so horrified! She burst into laughter. "I'm just kidding; it's legal. I'm getting a car; I'm tired of riding a bike!"

"What took you so long?" he laughed with her and shifted into drive. "Let's get something to eat; then we'll still have time to go to Hope. I've seen a car there that will be perfect for you, if it's still there. Anyway, more choices and fewer people who know us and everything we're doing."

He treated her to Sonic; they laughed and talked. The afternoon was gorgeous, and by the time he had driven her to Hope, he knew he couldn't live without her If he had her, he could do what he needed to do, be what he needed to be. She made him a better person.

She was so much fun!

The car was little, cute, seemed to run well, and was well within her price range. David helped bargain with the guy; and he seemed to know about tax, title, license, and insurance. She was grateful that he was along. She knew the used car people would have 'taken her for a ride'. "Ha-ha," she had laughed at her own pun and trite saying.

Finally, the deal was done, and some of her pile of money paid out. The guy had made a big deal out of checking the authenticity of each large- denomination bill. David had seemed nervous, and she kind of had been, too. She took possession of the car keys eagerly; excitement at her new acquisition put a happy skip in her step that had been lost.

Her friend surveyed her as she gleefully checked the headlights, windshield wipers, turn signals. Everything seemed to be great.

She turned it on. He checked the fuel gauge. "Almost out of gas. We'll go right across to that gas station, and I'll pump for you. Pop the trunk so I can check your spare."

Wow! She would never have thought of any of that, she was forced to admit to herself.

The spare was actually pretty good, as were the other tires. He was proud of his deal and the sparkle that was back in her eyes. He started the gas pumping, then hung on her car door, chatting and joking with her while it filled up.

"Hey, buddy, pump turned off!" Some middle-age guy winked and gave him a slap on the shoulder. He hung the nozzle in place, then replaced the gas cap. The attendant hassled him about a hundred dollar bill when the purchase was only twenty-four dollars, but finally gave him change.

The used car dealership and the gas station guys both immediately called the authorities about the two young people with all the hundred dollar bills. It looked "pretty fishy", both guys had said to the agent who had eventually shown up.

"Okay, I don't think you should have a problem, but since she's new and it's getting dark, I better follow you home. I'm gonna put some gas in my car, then we can hit the road. You're a school girl, so you need a good night's sleep."

"Oh-oh," he knew he shouldn't have said that. "Dumb, dumb!" he castigated himself.

She just rolled her eyes at him. It said more than a whole lecture.

He pumped a tiny amount of gas; Sonic had about tapped him out, but he didn't want her to know.

"Ok, let's roll," he hollered.

"Aye, aye, Cap'n Blye," she responded with a wave; and gunned it!

It didn't take her long to lose him. He was cute, but now daylight was waning; she was behind in her plan. Really good thing she had been able to leave school early. She darted around a couple more blocks, then pulled in at the mall. It was eight thirty! Tick-tock.

She flew down the center of the mall. There were always cell phone kiosks everywhere with people yelling at you to get a new phone or change your service or something. Now, when she was in a hurry-

"Scuse, me, ma'am," a voice interrupted her frenzied thoughts.

"Ah, there you are; just who I'm looking for," she responded.

"Really?" he asked, surprised.

It took her awhile, and most of the stores were closing, though the mall doors were still unlocked. The guy had wanted a credit card so he had sent her where she could buy a pre-paid cell for cash. Not the iPhone she wanted, but in an emergency- In an emergency, she interrupted her own thoughts. Now that she had a phone again, who would she call? The sheriff?

Car keys ready, she dashed to her cute new car, hopped in, locked the doors, and turned the key. It hummed to life. She was relieved. Would have served her right for it to be dead after the way she had ditched David.

Her thoughts had returned to the Pike county sheriff. Her dad had spent quite a bit of time with him, drinking coffee, bantering, arguing. Then, one day, when her dad had told her mom for the million and first time that she always talked too much, Suzanne had come back about the way Patrick always "shot the breeze" with the sheriff and some of his friends.

He had calmly informed her and Mallory that he didn't "shoot the breeze"; he just listened. And that the sheriff and the other guys weren't friends. "I need to know some of the stuff they know, but I don't trust them," he had told Mallory in confidence, later. If he had told Suzanne, she would have told them.

Now, the words echoed in the girl's mind, sinister and threatening. Now that she had a phone, she couldn't dial 911. Outside the Murfreesboro town limits, where she lived, the sheriff's department would respond.

Her other errand was going to be the search for a dog; not a puppy, a dog! She had planned to buy a car in Murfreesboro, then go to the animal shelter, be home before dark with some big snarling dog, and then work on her target practice.

Her thoughts returned to David. It seemed like they always did. "Maybe, 'not as bad as people say'," she argued with his words, "but you aren't as good as you used to be." Tears rolled down her cheeks, still April ninth, and daddy and the chapter in Proverbs were absolutely right. Why had he been stealing around her yard? Those were his boot prints. Why did he need binoculars and all those heavy clothes she had seen in his car? Now she wished he hadn't known she had any money.

Why had Martin thought she was rich? How many people had there been, out snooping around, scaring her?

If she had known the answer, she would have been more frightened.

Why hadn't she heard anything at all from her mother? Only a day and a half. Mom was probably already working, maybe settling in somewhere. Probably the time hadn't seemed as long for her as it did for Mallory. She'll call soon," she tried to convince herself.

The night was beautiful. She headed up 278, then dug around in the huge purse until she found her iPod. She felt really grown up with an iPod, her own car, and a cell phone! She started her music, and the presence of the Holy Spirit seemed to fill the interior of the little car to overflowing.

The music built, beautiful, powerful

"...as I glory in His embrace;
as His Presence now fills this place."

The sun had sunk on her left as she headed northwest toward home. On her right she could see the moon putting in its appearance; then the evening star also glowed in the dusky sky. As she drove on, engrossed in her music, the sky continued to darken to the deepest ebony. Millions of stars shone against the canopy. She turned off the car's climate control and rolled her window down. The air was chilly, but clear and lovely.

The night was beautiful. She opened the little moon roof to get a better view of the Milky Way. "Like a diamond in the sky," she hummed, while the gospel played in the earphone.

With the cash she still had with her, she could have spent the night at a motel in Hope. She wasn't sure she wanted to return home to hear the "bumps in the night". But, she fully intended to be at school on time in the morning. She didn't have clothes, make-up or anything for the next day, so she was on her way back. She turned onto 27 and decided to push the speed a little bit.

As she neared her home, she slowed down, turned the music off, and began to pray earnestly. She was afraid and lonely. She slowed slightly as she passed up her driveway. She could see David's car up by the house. He was waiting for her, and she could only assume he would be mad. Like it was such a big deal to get a phone, that she had needed to lose him. She kept going and drove around for about a half hour. When she returned, his car was gone. She eased her car up as close as she could to the back porch, then quickly entered the house. She stood there. All was quiet; it seemed the same, even the familiar smells were the same. No one's cologne, or body odor! She thought of both of her suspects.

David hadn't seemed to think the sheriff intended to keep Martin locked up, even though the guy had acted totally deranged all morning. He was making wild threats, but the sheriff wanted to send him on his way and hold David. Only after Pops had come and made a statement about the bus incident, had David been allowed to leave with his parents. Mallory shivered in the silence. The house was chilly, but she didn't want to try the oven just now, or a flashlight. The little car out there was enough of an announcement that she was in here. Her hardware store items were still in her car. It was only ten-thirty. Cars were still going along pretty briskly on the road.

She stepped out again onto the back porch, then hammer and car keys in hand, she backed her little car to the end of the drive, hopped out with one of her hardware store purchases, and drove the stake of the sign into the ground. "WARNING: NO TRESPASSING! VIOLATORS WILL BE PROSECUTED!" On the other side of the driveway, another sign, BEWARE OF DOG!"

She pulled back up to the house, and David materialized out of nowhere.

She got out of the car. "You mad?" she questioned sheepishly.

"No! Mallory, where is your mom? Why are you staying here now alone? Why don't you go spend the night at my mom and dad's with Tammi? Let me walk in with you while you get your stuff for tomorrow. You're in danger here by yourself; I'll just help you get to my house. Why did you ditch me?" he finished with the question he had wanted to start with.

"I'm not really sure. I just wanted to get a cell phone; that was one of the errands I wanted to do this afternoon. I got one, see?" she showed it to him so proudly that it was hard for him to stay annoyed with her.

He reached for it and put his number in her speed dial. He knew she wasn't planning to go spend the night at the pastor's house like he wanted her to. "Keep the lights off; if you get scared call me. Mallory, listen to me" he pushed her chin up, gazing into her eyes. "Whatever you do, don't call 911. Promise me!" He grabbed her arms and gave her a little shake.

"All right," I promise." Her voice was a soft whisper.

He kissed her hard, then turned and strode away toward the woods which bordered the back yard.

Dazed, she stumbled back into the house; her thoughts were spinning, spinning; she sat down on one of the kitchen chairs and clasped her head in both hands.

She touched her lips; they still tingled from the pressure of his mouth. "He seemed pretty good at it," she thought sadly. "I'm pretty sure my first kiss wasn't his first," and she cried.

Chapter 7

DEFENSE

MALLORY HAD SAT weeping in the kitchen, trying to figure things out. Where was David's car? Why had he left it somewhere and come back on foot? Why did he think she shouldn't call the sheriff? Why hadn't she thought to ask him? In the darkness, she pulled her phone out. He had entered his number. Should she call him and demand an apology for his kissing her? Or just demand an explanation about Sheriff Melville?

Did she just want to hear his voice some more? She slid the phone into her cardigan pocket and pulled the thick sweater around her more tightly. The clear evening was turning into a cold night, and she could hear the wind picking up from the north. Should she turn on the oven? David had told her to keep the house dark. Why?

Finally she grasped the flashlight, and without switching it on, she made her way to her dad's room. She locked the bedroom door behind her. Carefully, she lifted two big piles of papers from his desk, one stack at a time, and set them down in a small, barely accessible area of his walk-in closet. She pulled the closet door closed behind her and dropped to sit cross-legged on the floor. Pulling his bathrobe from its hook, she placed it along the crack beneath the door. At last, certain no one outside could see the beam, she shone the flashlight on the papers. They seemed to be trash. Paper after paper, she scrutinized, before placing them beside her, keeping the same order she had found them in. Some of the dates were pretty far back, and the ink pretty faded. If he had a filing system to his upright stacks, she hadn't figured it out yet. They weren't arranged alphabetically or by date.

Some of it seemed to be invoices for some of his junk, either when he had bought it or sold it. She pulled some of his clothes down to wrap around her for warmth, then remembered his overcoat on the foot of his bed. Burying the flashlight in the clothes, she grabbed the coat and re-secured her closet. She had placed the slingshot and ammunition next to her in her small fortress. She removed her phone from the cardigan pocket and slid on the big wool coat, plunging her hands into the deep pockets for warmth. Puzzled, she drew out a funny-looking little key. She hadn't ever seen it before. She turned it over and studied it curiously in the circle of light before her. She wondered what it was for; she yawned. She was getting warm now, and she was really sleepy.

She wondered if she should risk one stove burner so she could brew some instant coffee. Also, she had left the purse with still quite a bit of cash in it, out on the kitchen table. "No," to the burner and coffee, she had told herself. "Still too much light." But she did need to go get the purse. She dreaded leaving the safety she felt in Daddy's closet.

"Lord, I'm being silly, I know Help me just to grab the purse and get right back in here. Besides, I'm not safe in here without You. I guess I've been trusting 'having a phone', and I haven't even been praying. I'm sorry, Lord, I really need you. Please keep me safe; please bring Mom back; please help David. I wish I could have gotten a dog, but, Lord, You Are my Defense."

She was paralyzed. Why had such terror taken hold of her again? She hadn't heard anything or seen anything, but then, in the closet, she wouldn't. She surveyed her phone and the slingshot; now she wished she had brought in the knives. The purse really didn't matter, or the money in it, or the iPod. She shoved the cigar box with the cash back farther into the closet. She still had that, and probably no one would bother the purse, anyway. No one had actually come in; they had just been outside, rolling up the drive and running on the gravel. Then, she remembered that someone, sometime, had been trying to force one of the windows up in this room.

She looked at her watch; one-thirty. Would morning ever come with its delicate blues and golds? Would she still be alive? Why did she feel so threatened? She tried to remember her drive from Hope in her own, little, new-used car. The music, the afterglow of sunset, the moon, the evening star, the cool breeze, the Milky Way. And David! and the kiss!

Where had he gone on foot? He had had the binoculars hanging around his neck; he was wearing like, that heavy jacket, like hunting clothes or something. What was he doing? Was he a danger to her? Was he defending her, protecting her? He had tackled Martin because he had seemed to think Martin was going to harm her. Why would anyone think she was rich? Oh yeah, because of the diamonds, she had remembered. She was so used to thinking of herself as poor. So, did people know about them, for sure? Daddy sure hadn't confided in anyone. Was that the reason people were trespassing? She thought of her signs. They wouldn't keep people out, but she could now prosecute them more easily, provided they were caught. Caught by whom? The sheriff? She wondered where Martin was and what he had threatened that had scared Pastor and Mrs. Anderson.

Tears welled up again, and she pressed her hand, in the big coat sleeve, against her mouth to muffle her sobs "Daddy, help me; Dear God, please, please, I beg You to help me."

An hour later she was still as gripped by fear as ever. She wanted to press the speed dial, just to hear David say hi, but it was the middle of the night. He hadn't told her to call any time just to chat. It might even scare him that she was in trouble. Besides, it would waste her minutes.

A hideously disfigured man had ordered "to-go" from the Applebee's in Hope, Arkansas. He tried to avoid attention and horrified gasps from people, but he had driven all day, eating only a few snacks, so he had decided on dinner. He pulled up at one of the "to-go" spaces and said he had phoned an order in. His windows were tinted heavily, and his late-model sedan had Oklahoma plates. He wasn't from Oklahoma. He had stopped at a tiny town named Tom, where he had killed an elderly couple for their car. He had transferred his small suitcase and sniper rifle from the car he had been driving into this one. He had chosen this couple and their car because of the dark windows and the helplessness of the old people. Then, removing identification from them, he had placed their bodies into the car he was abandoning, and had left it in a dense area of trees.

A cute waitress came out of the restaurant with his steak dinner in a big bag, and came to the driver's window. He meant to lower the window a crack, hand her the money, tell her to keep the change, and have her open the rear door to place the meal on the seat. However, when he hit the button for the automatic window, it didn't just crack open slightly, as he intended. It went almost completely down before he could stop it. To the horror of both; they were face to face. The girl shrieked with terror; the man, frozen with almost equal indecision, recovered suddenly. Forgetting the fifty dollar bill and the bag of food, he lurched into reverse. Barely missing families in the parking lot, he careened crazily away.

Angry pedestrians were writing down the Oklahoma plate number, others were already dialing 911 on their cells. The terrified server continued to scream and cry. Nobody was sure what had happened. A Hope police officer appeared on the scene; the restaurant manager was trying to find out from his terrified employee what had happened. The police officer was kind and patient; "Some awful-looking guy had rolled the window down!" seemed to be all they could get out of her.

He escorted her to the precinct where a sketch artist and female officer tried to make sense of her story. The young officer shrugged it off. Evidently, the driver had recklessly endangered some of the irate families, but he hadn't hit anyone. The guy couldn't help being scary-looking. He decided to go eat some dinner, himself.

Merrill Adams had been on the wrong path for so long he wasn't sure a right path had ever been presented to him. He had come up "rough", to say the least. He had been in trouble for as long as he could remember. But, he had been a pretty good-looking guy. His reflection in the rearview still repulsed him, even after four years. He had kept going from the Applebee's. Adrenaline flooding his system, his hunger was forgotten. He was on the move, trying to think. The man who hired him was already not going to be pleased when attention came from the "collateral damage" ie, the old couple. Now, this car and plates were probably on the wire, too. He pounded the steering wheel in rage. He should never have agreed to do this gig! The money had enticed him, once again. He now wondered if he would live to complete the job, accept the pay-off, spend any of it? "Spend it on what?" he asked himself bitterly, "a new face?"

Like he could show up at a cosmetic surgery center and tell them an FBI agent had shot his face away; could they please fix it and not tell anyone?

He was speeding along on Interstate 30, and he saw the exit for 278 to Murfreesboro. He decided to run for it. He pulled a couple of big handguns from beneath his seat, and placed them on the seat beside him. Anybody tried to stop him on this run, he planned on shooting them. He pulled the pictures of his two targets from his pocket, unfolding them across the steering wheel before him. The sun set, but there was some afterglow by which to study the names and faces. The sky continued to darken; he didn't even notice the rising moon, the evening star, or the milky way. A little car shot around him.

"Crazy people!" he muttered

His targets were two ladies; he didn't refer to them with such a flattering term. An acquaintance from the old days in Boston had contacted him. He had thought he was off everyone's radar, but when someone needed a hit, they could always manage to find him. So Ryland O'Shaughnessy had managed to find him to help him get rid of some relatives. He laughed to himself. "Thought I was the only one who felt that way about family." Anyway, seems R.O. had some huge gambling debts, owing some of the bigger fish some real cashola. They were leaning on him hard. His baby brother, Pat, had died in this dumb little town in Arkansas nobody ever heard of. His will was going to be read on Friday. Ryland and his two boys were supposedly heirs to some of the "estate", but he figured the widow and daughter to be the main beneficiaries. If they could be "gotten rid of", he figured he would get a lot more. Somehow, the deal had seemed sweeter when it was first presented to him. Now, as he had driven from his oblivion, everything was making less sense. Sounded like Pat's "estate" couldn't be that great, even with the two women taken "outa da picture". He tried to sound like a gangsta for his own amusement. Whatever little money there might be in Arkansas, Adams figured, would go to the gambling debts before his fifty grand came to him. Twenty-five for each target, but nothing if he didn't eliminate both of them. He drove on. Where was this stupid place? He had missed the turn onto 27. It was getting late, and he was in a little place named Dierks. He was tired and hungry and mad. He made a u-turn and froze when a cop turned around behind him. His hand reached for the glock and he pulled it over onto his knee. He slowed to twenty-five, and when he passed the city limit sign, the cop dropped back.

Backtracking, he found where he had missed the turn earlier, the sedan rolled toward Murfreesboro with the sinister killer at the wheel.

He pulled into the O'Shaughnessy drive at one-thirty. He had become sleepy, but the sight of the "Estate" jolted him awake. Had to be a mistake! Had Ryland ever been here? One of his pals had really pulled a fast one to make him think this dump was worth a fortune. He turned his headlights off and the car rolled almost noiselessly to the small frame house.

David was freezing! With the cold front's presenting a strong north wind, the observer's nest in the big, old Pecan tree was the coldest of any night yet. He had worn heavier clothing, but the wind was whipping around him, making him miserable. He was about to abandon his nest to go keep watch from the shed. The only thing he was afraid of was that should he become warmer and more secure in the shed, could he stay awake?

Mallory was suddenly everything to him. Her loss of her father had left her alone and vulnerable. He had to protect her. He was sorry he had kissed her; he knew he had taken advantage of her. He knew her dad would have really been mad. He wondered if Patrick had seen the incident from heaven. He sighed, involuntarily. He knew God had seen it. He had been trying to run from God for nearly a year. "Pretty stupid," he had admitted to himself. With God, you can't run or hide. His rebellion had hurt others; he hadn't thought it would. There was a huge gulf now, between him and his dad. He really loved and respected his dad, but then, when they were together, they always ended up arguing. And making his mom cry. Tears tried to free themselves from his eyes. He stopped them. Too cold; both the wind and his heart!

He regretted the kiss. Whether Patrick saw it was a matter of Biblical conjecture. The fact is, Sheriff Melville saw it, and within an hour, he had posted the photo on-line.

David was just getting ready to descend from the tree when a car moved slowly along the road. It was a late-model sedan with heavy tinting on the windows.

David tensed, watching. The moon was still making the night pretty bright, but there was no other illumination on the property. No street lights, porch lights; the little house was dark. The car stopped on the road, like the driver was searching for a particular address.

Of course, David had been in the tree the previous night to see Mallory's booby trap's damage to Martin's new truck. All day, he had wondered where the truck was; he would have loved to get pictures of the damage. Now, with the tinted windows on this vehicle, his first thought was that Thomas had found another car to use for whatever it was he was trying to do. Now, as the car paused so long on the road, David figured it must not be Martin Thomas. He was dumb, but he knew where the driveway was. Who was this? David had anonymously e-mailed the FBI field office in Little Rock because he had wanted Sheriff Melville investigated. He hadn't mentioned Mallory or this address. The car didn't look like a government agency car anyway. This wasn't going to be good guys to the rescue.

He forgot the cold and wind. The Pecan tree was nestled between some thick evergreens. Even though his tree wasn't leafed-out enough to really hide him, he was pretty-well concealed. Tensely, he watched the car pull forward. The hour was late, almost no traffic along the road. The car turned left across the oncoming lane, shining headlights on the "BEWARE OF DOGS' sign. It continued slowly into the turn, illuminating the other sign.

The headlights switched off, and the car moved toward the inglorious little house.

Merrill Adams pulled the car across the yard, trying to hide it from the house and passers-by, should there be any. The place was so quiet, it made him nervous. He liked the city, neon, and noise. He turned the engine off; he had been swearing and ranting, but as he stepped from the car, he slipped into the stealthy mode of one stalking prey. The car in the drive was different than the one R.O.'s intel had provided. How could he even know if this was the right house? Nothing had been mentioned about dogs either. He had been listening for growling and barking. Even a little dog could alert the women to the fact that he was here. He didn't like it! And it was cold!

He glanced above his head; He had to stretch his damaged neck way around so he could focus his good eye upward. His horrid-looking face twisted into a savage scowl.

David couldn't believe what he was seeing. He must be asleep and dreaming up Hollywood's next horror blockbuster. This couldn't really be happening in rural Arkansas, in this usually too-quiet corner of the world. The night took on a surreal atmosphere as he hung from his branch, watching in horror as the guy pulled a black, hooded sweatshirt from his suitcase and pulled it on.

David should do something, but he didn't know what. He wanted to be brave for Mallory and run and hide under his mom and dad's bed, all at the same time! He wanted to do whatever would be best for both his and Mallie's sake. Why hadn't he told someone else how worried he had been about her? But even with his un-easiness for Mallory's safety, he had never imagined anything this evil stalking around in the dark.

Tears squeezed from his eyes, and he watched.

First, the guy went underneath the windows, listening. Then, he pulled himself up to gaze into one of the windows that had a shade part-way up. He lowered himself again, continuing around the house, out of David's line of vision. He had a handgun in each hand, as he advanced, menacing, threatening, evil personified!

He tried the back door. It was unlocked. He chuckled to himself noiselessly. These two, and he used profane and vulgar terms for his two victims, were going to be so easy to "pop" that it wasn't even going to be any fun.

David was frozen to his spot: with fear; he had forgotten about the cold! He knew he should scramble down while the guy was on the other side of the house. Had he gone in?

"Oh, God, don't let Mallory see him, please. Oh, God, help us!"

He had his cell phone. If the guy scared Mallory and she speed-dialed his phone, it might give his position away. Why had he felt so sure of himself with one hunting knife and a sling shot? If he could surprise the guy, he still wouldn't have enough of an advantage. This guy was a professional killer. His mind grappled with the unreality of it all. Who would want Mallory Erin O' Shaughnessy dead? Why had the sheriff tried to make it look like she had killed her own father? Why had her father had to die? He continued to press himself against the bough of the tree. He was glad he was saved, glad he had invited Mallie to VBS, glad she and her family had been saved. He shuddered as the disfigured stalker reappeared from the far side of the house. Maybe he would leave now. He stepped onto the sagging front porch, trying to be wary of rotting boards, missteps. He silently turned the knob, pushed the door ajar. He stood silently, gazing into the opening for long minutes. He could see into the kitchen where a huge purse rested on the kitchen table. He hadn't been certain anyone was home; he leered. "Guess they're all tucked in tight."

He pulled the door back closed; hinges whined just a little, and he winced. He stood on the dilapidated porch surveying his surroundings in total disgust. He shivered; from the cold and a sudden dread. He could see his terrified victims from earlier in the day, could hear them pleading with him, could feel their weight as he transferred their bodies to the other car. He shivered again; nothing like this had ever bothered him before. Nothing personal; he just wanted the money. He tried to shrug it off.

Re-crossing, the yard, Adams looked everything over, from the shed on the far side, to the garden, to the fish pond, to the tractor. The tractor caught his eye. Looking around, as though he felt he were being watched, he circled around the tractor a couple of times. Finally, he pulled himself up onto the cab, and then onto the roof of the cab. Although, it had rusted badly in the weather, it was still strong enough to easily support his weight. David was having a harder time seeing him now; the angle wasn't as good. He adjusted his binoculars, crawling out more on the branch at the same time.

The guy was standing on Mallie's tractor going through the motions of sighting someone in with a rifle. Aiming at the driveway, swinging the imaginary barrel back and forth slowly, pulling an imaginary trigger.

David's heart filled with dread and hope. Maybe he was just casing the joint tonight. Maybe he was planning to leave and come back later. Maybe he was planning to shoot Mallory as she was getting off the bus, checking the mail; or Mallie's mom as she drove in from wherever she had gone.

The guy finally seemed to be coming back to the car. David figured he had as good of a shot with his sling shot as he was ever going to get, but he hesitated. If the rock didn't hit hard enough, with enough accuracy, all it would do was let the guy know he was there. He would use one of the two guns on him; then the shots would waken Mallory, and he would shoot her, too. He wished he had faith like the real David had when it was time to face Goliath. Instead, he clung there, waiting, and praying.

At long last, Adams got in the car. Everything in it made him think about the old couple. He needed to lose this car anyway. He started it, turned around in the yard across Suzanne's garden, back onto the drive way, and out onto the main road. He planned to find some food and lay low, maybe nap. Then, when the school bus brought Sissy home, BAM. That one down! One to go! Tuesday morning! Time the will's read Friday morning, these gals are dead, and I'm long-gone!"

Psalm 7:10
My defense is of God, which saveth the upright in heart.

Mallory had quoted the verse over and over as she had spent the long night, terrified, in her daddy's clothes closet.

Finally, she had emerged. The morning was bright and cold, with the wind continuing to bluster. She had looked around carefully; no one seemed to be around. The house looked the same. The big purse, her keys, and her iPod were still there. All the money was still in the purse. She finally turned on a burner; ah good, still gas. Then she tried the faucet, still water. And it isn't going to matter after today, she told herself grimly. She wasn't spending another night in Spooky Hollow. She found an oatmeal pouch and was overjoyed. She found some sugar in the canister, and the breakfast tasted pretty delicious. She knew she should shower, but she was still scared. She placed the slingshot, the phone, and a big butcher knife beside her and cleaned up as well as she could at the kitchen sink. She dressed quickly; she didn't have many choices to begin with; now many of her things had gotten tight. Maybe she would go back to Hope after school and look for a few new things. She would have to do her homework in study hall.

Even now she was worried, because her Geometry homework wasn't finished and the class was second hour. "Lord, please help me," she whispered once more. She applied some shiny stuff to her cheeks and lips and a coat of mascara to her eyelashes. Then whistling, she stepped into the back porch. Her breath caught in terror, the whistling dying suddenly, leaving her standing there with her lips still puckered, her eyes widening as she gazed at the muddy footprints everywhere. These were not from David's boots. She was glad of that. Had Martin been here? Had he gotten this close, and then had he just decided to leave?

She hurriedly got into her car, locking the doors, and getting the key in the ignition in quick succession. She backed up the driveway toward the road, and gazed with consternation at the tire tracks around the yard and across her mom's garden. She waved at Pops and the school bus, then pulled out toward the high school. She needed to get there as soon as possible, get her books, and try to do some of her math assignment.

Chapter 8

DISAPPOINTMENT

SUZANNE HAD GROWN continually more desperate with each day that had passed since her husband's death. Because she really did seem totally unable to keep anything confidential, he had given up on letting her into the loop of anything that was going on.

They had gotten married one night when they were both drunk. Trying to be a good Catholic and please his mother, Patrick had stuck with the marriage. Before long then, Mallory had been on the way. Some of their friends hadn't been the best. When Patrick had received a small inheritance from his paternal grandmother's estate, he had loaded Suzanne, little Mallie, and their stuff in a rent car, and left Boston. They had kind of gone all over for awhile, then finally settled in Murfreesboro, buying the house with the sprawling yard when Mallory had been about three. Patrick had always wanted Suzanne to go to Confession and Mass is Boston. He had finally kind of gotten disappointed in all of that, and Suzanne had been glad. She had grown up, never going to church, and she had liked it just fine that way.

They had both adored their temperamental little daughter, but they had a hard time finding common ground otherwise. Suzanne always had friends that she told all about it. She always said her life was an open book and she didn't have anything to hide.

"That woman would tell anything," he had found out to his dismay. "Nothing about their marriage, their life, or anybody else's was sacred to her. If she knew something, so did everybody."

That's why she didn't know anything about their business. If he acted as middleman for an astrolabe and earned twenty-five thousand in commission, it went into an account she didn't know about. If she knew about it, so did everyone! All of Murfreesboro, and eventually his brother and some of the other characters from his past would have their hands out. They could suck the life out.

Sometimes, he would try again to try to get her to be more discreet. It always just made her mad. What was so mysterious and secret, anyway? What's the big deal--? He had hated it when Mallory had started asking that, sounding just like her mother.

By the time Mallory had turned seven, she and the new pastor's kids had already become good friends. Patrick had liked the nice kids, including little David, with his kind ways and his big brown eyes. Mallory had her daddy around her little finger to such an extent that Suzanne had already become jealous of the father-daughter bond. As he shared his secrets more with their daughter and closed her out more and more, she was left more and more with the feeling that life was disappointing. She had expected to find joy, or contentment, or excitement, or something, in being married, or at least in becoming a mother. If any of that had come to her, it hadn't lasted long.

She had taken to nagging her husband. "Why didn't they have this, or why couldn't they get that?" Then, if he tried to please her by coming up with whatever the demand was, she would be on the phone, bragging to everyone. Then, since they asked her where the money had come from, for whatever it was, she would badger him to tell her. She always made him think of Samson and Delilah. "Oh, if you loved me, you'd tell me! Wah! Wah!" She'd bawl and carry on; then he would say, "Ok, if you promise not to tell." She would promise not to tell, but she always did.

Patrick had gotten into enough legal trouble in his youth that filling out employment aps and being bonded would be a problem for him. When he had received his grandmother's money, he had realized it gave him a chance. He had always been a saver. His mom used to say he seemed more Scot than Irish; he could be so tight-fisted. His goal had been a nebulous one about a future for Mallory. He had begun investing in whatever way he could safely gain on his money. It was slow, at first. They really were about as poor as they seemed. Gradually things had picked up, but by now his best defense for the growing value of his property and antique items was the rumor that they didn't have anything. He let Suzanne help spread the rumor that he was just kind of a crazy junk-collector. Yacking was what she did best.

He had figured if anything ever happened to him, she wouldn't have a clue what to do. As Mallory had matured and proved she could keep confidences, he had confided a little bit to her. What bits and pieces he had left her with hadn't helped her much. But Patrick had figured his daughter would check out some of the contents of his room sooner after his death than she had. He had never intended for her to have the three months' of agony she had; or Suzanne, either. He had really loved them both. He had certainly never thought Sheriff Melville would do what he was doing.

Suzanne had given Mallory a ride to Sunday School, then had taken Mallory's little baby-sitting stash, put some gas in the car, loaded the trunk, and met her daughter in time for church. She really had prayed for a miracle, and the Lord had been faithful! He always is. But as usual, the woman had done what she had always done: judged appearances. "Appearances" were often misleading, Patrick and Mallory had both often tried to explain to her. Once her mind was made up, though, there was no changing it. In her mind, what appeared to be- was!

She had brought Mallory home, loaded the rest of the things she had prepared, and had taken off.

And, her plan had really been to find Roger Sanders and ask for her old job back. When she had quit her job, he had told her she had been a good employee, and he would gladly rehire her should she ever consider coming back. He had meant it. He had been a pretty good boss back then. Then, due to the influence of Patrick and Mallory after they had gotten saved, he and his family had gotten saved. His marriage and his relationship with his kids had been rescued, as they had all been baptized and had begun serving the Lord together.

Actually, Suzanne, had cost him some important deals and revenues. Even though he had explained "confidentiality" to her during week one, she never had totally seemed to get it. A couple of times her indiscretion with clients had done some real damage. Then, she had seemed to kind of develop a crush on him. Before his salvation, he had flirted and carried on with women. He had never figured it would be good for his business to be involved with one of his employees. He liked Suzanne, ok, but she wouldn't have been his choice. When she finally resigned, he had been relieved.

⁂

She had gotten to Hope late Sunday afternoon, just before dark. She had gone into McDonald's to eat some supper. She didn't even consider that she was using Mallory's baby-sitting money, while she had left her alone without utilities and food. She bought an ice cream cone, and sat back down. She smiled at a guy sitting there; he folded his Sunday paper up to leave.

"Excuse me, Sir," she had smiled sweetly. "Are you finished with your newspaper? I'm new here in Hope, and I'm starting to look for a job-"

The guy obligingly dropped the paper on her table and strode away, not listening for her to finish her story.

"Well, about rude," she had mumbled after the retreating man. "People aren't very helpful or friendly!" She huffed her way out of the restaurant.

When she reached her car, she burst into tears. She was old and fat. She scowled at her reflection angrily in the rear view mirror. Here's why her life was dead-ended and she was facing living in her car, for at least one night. Her cute looks and her small figure had vanished. She could have, should have used what she had when she had it. Then she could look like that Diana Faulkner; she could have had a happy, smiling, handsome husband; she could have had three perfect kids- She stopped herself. (Mallory was pretty perfect, and Patrick had wanted more children, but Suzanne had not.) She let her angry thoughts continue to spill out. She should have clothes and jewelry like that, pedicures and fancy fingernails. She gazed through the tears at her fingertips, disfigured from years of nail-biting. She yanked at a little wisp of over processed do-it-yourself bleach and perm job hair. Her dark roots looked really tacky, she observed. Then she noticed tiny flecks of gray in the roots and began to sob harder. It was all Patrick's fault. He shouldn't have been such an unmotivated, lazy bum, loser. All those nosy-neighbor church people always telling her to stay. She hated them; she hated everybody. A few customers noticed the lady sitting in the car, crying. No one stopped to ask her if she were all right.

The sky had turned black, and lightning flashed angrily; it had struck really close-by. Maybe she shouldn't have told God she hated Him and all the Christians. Another bolt!

She screamed involuntarily and turned the car engine on so she could get a weather report. Tornadoes terrified her.

When the storm had finally eased up, she had reapplied some make-up and driven to the mall. She sat in a book store until nearly closing time, before using the restroom and going to her car for the night.

She would try to get some sleep. She didn't have enough gas to keep the car running for warmth, so she would wrap in the blankets she had brought. Then, in the morning, she would go to her former boss, and see what might happen. She would go in someplace and really fix herself up first.

There were a few sprinkles still coming down. She had found a quiet, residential neighborhood where she thought she could park without drawing attention. She opened the trunk to get out some of the snacks and blankets and make sure her clothes were still lying smoothly so as not to wrinkle. To her sad surprise, everything was soaked. The downpour had inundated the trunk of the old car. Too tired to cry anymore, she pulled out the top outfit to hang in the back seat. She planned to wear it to see Roger. Maybe it would dry out ok.

Then she drove around, looking for a laundromat so she could dry the blankets. It took quite a few quarters; then she drove back to the street and tried to sleep.

Morning finally came. Monday morning! She was stiff, and her head ached. Tiredly, she peeled a shriveled orange and ate it. Her face was puffy, and her outfit was still wet. She drove to the warehouse area where Roger's company had started up, then found a gas station where she used the unsavory facility to try to wash up and become ravishingly beautiful for her former employer. It seemed like the more cosmetics she applied, the older and worse she looked. Then, tears had begun streaming from her red, tired eyes, further destroying her efforts. Mascara was all over her face, and someone was banging on the door. She pulled her sunglasses down and ducked past a line of women who were waiting.

She saw a drive-in and ordered a cup of coffee. Then, making one final attempt to "fix her face", she drove slowly to try to find her former boss. His company had grown and moved, so she had to find a phone book to learn where his company was now located. She had to stop and put more gas in the old car; her small amount of money was nearly gone. If Mallory hadn't gone so nuts about Patrick, she would have had more baby-sitting jobs this spring. Of course, now it was Mallory's fault Suzanne was in a jam. There was always someone to blame.

Suzanne couldn't believe what she was seeing. Never had she imagined that Roger Sanders could grow a business like this! "And to think, I knew him when...." She was still shaking her head in amazement.

The spread was impressive, to say the least. The whole place seemed to be part of the same operation. Finally, she found a building which said Executive Offices. She parked the old land yacht in one of the "visitor" parking spaces next to some really sleek, sporty, and expensive cars. She should have parked a few blocks away and walked. It would have given her clothes more opportunity to dry. A really handsome gray-haired man looked at her quizzically. She looked like she was living in the derelict-looking vehicle.

Suzanne tried to smile her best seductive smile.

He just shook his head and disappeared into the best of the best of the best of the cars which were parked there.

A really young and cute secretary smiled cheerily as Suzanne entered the office area.

"Good morning" she had greeted. "How may I assist you this morning?"

Her voice was modulated, professional, assured.

Suzanne was crushed. She didn't know what she had expected. She guessed she had expected her same old desk and her same old job with her name Suzanne O'Shaughnessy, on the battered desk

The secretary was still smiling, waiting expectantly for Suzanne to speak "May I help you, Ma'am," she questioned again

At last, Suzanne, had spoken. Not lifting her sunglasses, she had mumbled something stupid and literally run from the Executive Office area. Falling into the battered old car, she had thrown it into gear and roared away.

She was devastated! She had planned to run into Roger, where he would be so happy and relieved to see her. He hadn't been able to find good help. Welcome back! Can you start right now? She would be back at her desk where she would call Mallory with the good news that they were saved! She would get a check and be home Friday night. Little by little, they would make it.

It didn't look like Roger Sanders needed her at all! And bitter disappointment raged in her heart.

It shouldn't have! As usual, she was jumping to conclusions; judging appearances. As usual, everything wasn't what it had seemed to be!

Chapter 9

DEVELOPMENTS

DAVID HAD CONTINUED his observation of the O'Shaughnessy property, even after the stranger had departed and Mallory had left in her new little car. She looked cute in it, and he was glad he had taken her to the larger town where she would get a better deal. A bird scolded him brightly, and he laughed.

"You throwing me out of this tree? You can have it!" He climbed down nimbly, then kind of collapsed. Pulling himself back together, he began to cautiously ease through the woods behind Mallory's yard. He had been leaving his car hidden here each night that he had kept his vigil over her. He had thought it was hidden; in this town, nothing was. There were eyes everywhere. In comparative cover, he had become less careful. He had formulated a plan and he had to find his dad as quickly as possible. A woodpecker startled him, and he paused. It was a good thing!

The boy's heart lurched wildly! He had almost stridden boldly into the little clearing. He had stopped just in time! There was the car that had stolen into Mallory's yard earlier; and the terrible monster was going through things in David's car. David pulled back into the cover of the trees. He knew his registration was in the guys hand; it was in his dad's name with their address on it. The guy continued to look through the contents of the vehicle. He pulled out the case for the binoculars, turning to look around the clearing. He couldn't figure it out. Maybe just a hunter. Nothing to do with him or his quarry. He pulled out an awful-looking knife and started to slash the tires. He decided not to. That would probably just make unnecessary suspicions in this neighborhood. He knew who the Andersons were. The pastor was invited to the will-readin' too. He took another long look around, craning Sitting there, he turned the engine on. Things didn't feel right. He scratched at his ankles and continued to sit there. At long last, he backed out of the clearing and bumped through a field, to a dirt road, and away from town. Time to steal another car!

David sprinted for his car. Now he really had to find his dad. He pulled his cell phone out and speed-dialed the number. His mom answered his dad's phone.

"Hi, Mom, is Dad there?" He tried to sound calm and casual.

"Son, I think you better come home," his mom began.

Terror gripped him anew! He hadn't been aware that it had ever really released its grip.

"Why, what's wrong?" his words would hardly come. Dread flooded over him in wave after chilling wave. Had the guy already hurt his dad? Who was he? What did he want? Was the sheriff behind all of it?

"Just get here as fast as you can!" The voice boomed. It was his dad, and he sounded mad.

The boy silently thanked the Lord. His dad sounded ok.

FBI special agent in charge Erik Bransom had knocked on the parsonage door at seven-thirty A.M. on Tuesday, April the tenth. Lana Anderson was used to early morning callers. Between church members and her kids' friends, the place usually hummed with plenty of activity. Still, after Martin Thomas's wild threats of the previous day, she had been extra careful today. Looking out the window, she had seen the big, black car. Puzzled, she had opened the door slightly. She still hadn't been prepared for the FBI.

When he had showed her his ID, she had felt like she was going to be sick.

"Please, come in." She had tried to sound pleasant, but her heart was sinking within her; she felt like she couldn't breathe.

"Sit down, please," she had showed him graciously to the sofa. "May I get you some coffee?" He waved his cup to indicate he was good, but she had disappeared into the kitchen.

"What now, Lord?" she had whispered as she was running water into the carafe. She and her husband had had a terrible night. Since David had decided to move out, their lives had been shaken to the roots. They had seen all five of their children accept Jesus as Savior at young ages, and they had all seemed happy enough here in Diamondville serving the Lord. Then, suddenly, (tears spilled down her face again), David had grown angry and hostile-about everything, finally moving into a tiny apartment up at Kirby.

After his fight at the school on Monday and hearing the Thomas boy's threats at the police station, they had driven to Kirby together to try to make sure their son was alright. They were even ready to make some concessions about the rules if he would agree to move back home. They couldn't find him. When his friends knew where he was, they wouldn't tell. Lana and John had taken turns all night, driving all over the county, searching for him or the car. He wouldn't answer his phone, even after John had left some angry messages. Then, about six in the morning, Sheriff Melville had e-mailed them a picture of their son kissing Mallory and saying David's car had been hidden by her house all night.

They had both been in shock since then. Finally, John had stormed, "I'm gonna kill me a son!" Lana knew he wouldn't really. She just kept numbly repeating, "I thought we had taught him better."

Lifting her head bravely, she re-entered the living room. "Coffee's started. I'll tell my husband you're here, Agent-" she faltered.

"Special agent-in-charge Erik Bransom." He was reaching for his badge again, but she had scurried away.

John was in his cramped study looking at his computer.

"Any more e-mails?" she queried. Her face looked so miserable, and her husband reached for her and pulled her to him.

"Everything's gonna be ok, Sugar," he whispered.

"There's an FBI special agent -in-charge guy downstairs," she whispered.

He released her, his face as anguished as hers had been. He headed down the stairs to greet the agent. He had left his cell phone next to the computer, and it rang. Lana grabbed it as she started downstairs behind him. David's number. She answered.

David was asking for John, trying to sound as casual as could be. Her faith tried to soar upward. Surely, he wouldn't be calling his dad if he had spent the night with Mallory, would he? Surely, Mallory would never-

The FBI agent, special agent-in-charge, she reminded herself, had risen to greet her husband; he had his badge in hand -again, or still. Seemed real proud of it.

David's voice had sounded frightened when she had told him to just come straight home. She had told her husband it was David, but he was trying to listen to the FBI guy, so he had grabbed the phone and just yelled like he always did.

She went to the kitchen to pour them all some coffee. She figured David wouldn't come now, since John had yelled at him to get home.

The door flung open, and David dashed in. He was dressed in heavy camouflage and muddy boots. A pair of expensive binoculars hung from his neck. His face was ghastly; he was so pale. His brown eyes, large, and terrified, had dark circles under them. He sneezed and wiped his nose on his sleeve. To his mother, he seemed to have grown up overnight. His chin was covered with a heavy stubble. He coughed a croupy cough, and she instinctively felt his forehead.

He kissed her on the cheek and headed toward the living room. "There's an FBI special agent in charge," she had tried to warn him. She guessed she was trying to help her son evade arrest.

"About time!" He winked at her and strode toward the two men. Pour me a cup, too, will ya, Mom?"

Erik Bransom had stood to shake hands with David as he entered the room.

"I'm here in response to your anonymous tip that you have a problem with the local sheriff," he began. "You should have known we can track down the senders of most of our e-mails.

"Figured," David answered easily "I mostly didn't want the sheriff to know it was me. I'm glad somebody finally responded."

"Well, we get a little busy," the agent defended, watching the teenager shrewdly. "Good thing everybody that gets in trouble with the law doesn't have us investigate their LEO's"

David wasn't surprised that the Federal officer had taken that slant. He was neither offended nor angry. He needed to make his case with this guy, and convince him fast.

"Son, what have you done?" his dad interrupted.

"In a minute, Dad."

David took a sip of his coffee. It tasted good; he was still frozen. He pulled out his cell phone and brought up a photo.

"This isn't real good," he apologized as he handed it to the agent. "I was going to print it out up in my dad's study. I know your lab can enhance it. You can hardly see how scary this guy looks on this little image, but believe me-" Bransom could hardly believe what he was seeing. "Where did you take this?" he demanded.

"From the pecan tree at the O'Shaughnessy place," he answered. "I've been trying to protect my friend. The sheriff is behind this for some reason. He tried to blame my friend when her dad died, frame her for murder. The coroner ruled his heart gave out, but he has just hassled her. He's been trying to ruin her reputation. I think he hired one guy to scare her, but this guy's a killer! Sir, I have been in trouble with the sheriff's department, but you have to believe me. She is really in danger!"

His words broke off. He reached for his phone back, but the agent was already forwarding the photo to other agents.

Slow down. Start over from the beginning. Mrs. Anderson, maybe we all need some more coffee."

Mallory's new little car stirred quite a bit of interest with her friends when she drove up. She was really proud of it. She parked it in a visitor space and ran up to the office to ask for an SPP (student parking permit). She was glowing, despite her sleepless night of terror.

"Morning." she greeted. She smiled happily at Mrs. Oliver. She presented her Arkansas Driver's License and her new tag number.

"Mallory, I -uh-uh, think Mr. Haynes wants a word with you." She ignored Mallory's paper work. Mallory glanced into his office; his door was opened, and he was talking to someone.

"He looks busy," she told the woman. "Maybe I should make an appointment to come back later. Do you mind doing my parking permit?" She didn't want to seem impatient, but she was in a panic by now about her Geometry.

Mrs. Oliver handed her paperwork back to her. "I'm pretty sure he wants to see you right away. Have a seat, Mallory."

Sounded like she was in trouble, but that was what she had thought the day before; and she wasn't.

She started to take the indicated seat, then decided to go to her locker. She would need her books before first hour, and she could try to work on her assignment while she waited for the principal

She rushed from the office complex, walking as fast as she could. The corridor was becoming crowded. She saw Tammi and waved. It was the first time she had thought about meeting her after school; she had totally forgotten. Tammi failed to acknowledge the greeting, and Mallie sighed. She grabbed her thick notebook and her books for her morning classes. "Tammi, I'll talk to you at lunch; save me a place," she told her friend.

Silence!

Loaded with books, she headed back to the offices. Mr. Haynes's visitor was gone, his office was empty, and he was standing in his door frame, looking at her.

"Good morning, Sir," she said politely. "Mrs. Oliver said you would like to see me?"

She was trying to be normal, but he was acting strange She ducked past him, into his office and folded into one of his chairs, dropping her armload of books into the other.

He sat across from her with his elbows resting on his desk, his fingers steepled upward. It was a guy power play, David had explained to her. She met his steely blue eyes. They burned into her! She continued to look him in the eye. She was growing annoyed. Had he found out her mom was gone? Was CPS on the way to pick her up? She had been as respectful to everyone as she knew how to be. If the guy had something to say, why didn't he just say it?

"Mrs. Oliver felt like you wished to speak to me," she finally said, a slight edge to her voice.

He cleared his throat importantly. "I hardly know where to begin." He sounded pompous; like she had committed so many offenses he didn't know where to start with the indictments against her.

"Then I'll start." the assurance of her own voice startled her. "I got busy yesterday afternoon and never did eat lunch. Here's your money back. Thank you for lending it to me. Thank you for saying you and your wife would be glad to help us, if we need you. Everything's great, but you don't know what the offer meant. The people from both the town and the church have been wonderful. You told me to check in with you this morning. I feel great!"

She rose to her feet; "was there anything else you needed?"

Wow, he thought, talk about power play! Was she dismissing him? This was his office!

He couldn't believe she had developed such poise, but he had been at this business of dealing with students longer than she had been alive.

"Sit down, Mallory! There is something else!" He whirled his monitor around so she could see the picture of David kissing her. "What do you have to say about this?"

"Awesome," she chortled. "Do you mind printing me off a couple of copies?"

The FBI special agent took notes, going over and over David's story, asking more questions.

Finally, in exasperation, David had blurted out, "Look, if you don't believe me, why don't you talk to Mallory O'Shaughnessy? I need to get back to where I can keep an eye on her if you guys aren't going to do it. I'm telling you the truth. The guy had a big town car with black windows and Oklahoma plates. He pulled into the yard about one or two. I don't have a clock in my tree-house. He went all around the house; he left muddy foot prints and tire tracks everywhere. Why don't you go check it out?"

"You said he was going through things in your car, then. Why would he do that?"

"I don't know! Why don't you pick him up and ask him? Maybe he figured I'd seen him; I don't know. He was reading the car registration. I'm worried about my mom and dad and brothers and sisters Is this guy your department or not? Maybe I should have just phoned Sheriff Melville."

The special agent-in-charge closed his notebook. His phone rang, and he answered it. Other agents in black FBI windbreakers had arrived. They were going over David's car inch by inch.

Mrs. Anderson didn't understand it all, she thought they were still after her son, for some reason.

"No ma'am," Erick Bransom had explained. "We know who this guy is, and we have BOLO's out for him all over Arkansas. He killed a couple in Oklahoma yesterday to get the car he's been driving. Now, we're sure he'll be targeting another car. David said he doesn't know why the sheriff would hire this guy to kill the girl. What can you tell me about her?"

The entire time he had been listening to David Anderson and going over the facts, pulling more facts from the boy's memory by his skilled expertise, agents had already been covering the area. They had been to the Applebee's in Hope, the used car lot where Mallory had bought her car, the gas station, and the little hardware store in Murfreesboro.

They had been pretty interested in the teens with a big purse full of hundred dollar bills. Four agents had been dispatched to the high school to find Mallory, to protect her, and to ask her some questions. They were photographing all of the evidence at the O'Shaughnessy residence. There was so much evidence, that one agent had finally said, "Look, this guy is a total clown about evidence. I think he has us looking for him, and maybe someone else is set up to really make the hit." They had finally put together a fuzzy picture of the Boston connection. One of the agents had worked the east coast. "If Ryland O'Shaughnessy is her uncle, and he wants her dead, God in Heaven can't help her!" He had dropped his voice to a whisper, but David and John Anderson both heard him.

John had pulled his son to him, clasping him tightly. The exhausted young man was overwhelmed with grief and worry. Sobbing loudly, he allowed his dad to hold him. He finally pulled away and wiped his nose on his hand. "God can too help her," he said fiercely. "Daddy, would you pray?" The family joined hands, and the pastor sent a short fervent prayer zinging to heaven, while the agents stood there awkwardly.

Speaking of agents; they were everywhere. There were numerous divisions of the FBI, ATF, DEA, IRS, and Departments of the Interior, both federal and state. The ABI had agents on the scene, as well as other officials from Little Rock, the state's capital. They had assembled a real "alphabet soup", as John Anderson had whispered to Tom Haynes. Quite an entourage had convened at the high school just as a second hour assembly was dismissing.

When Mallory had been trying to figure out who was on her property, she would have been truly amazed. Between the bad guys, the good guys chasing the bad guys, and the good guys investigating the other good guys, the short list would have been of who had not been sneaking around the little fifteen acre spread.

Haynes had gotten word earlier in the morning that the FBI was offering a reward for the capture of Martin Thomas. He had been shocked. He hadn't liked the kid who was so far behind in school, so unwilling to try at even Physical Education. Coach had wanted to turn the big kid into a football player, but he was too lazy and too much of a loner to do that for more than one day. Curious, he had tried to find out why the feds wanted the student (maybe a loose interpretation of the word) he had thought bemusedly. They weren't in a position to say.

Anyway, the reward idea had played nicely into the principal's hand. He was still annoyed that so many kids had used their cell phones at school. They were supposed to leave them at home, or in their cars or backpacks, turned off. Now, under the guise that they might be eligible for a crime buster reward, he had called an assembly during second hour. He always rotated the hours for assemblies so the students didn't always miss the same class. (This had saved Mallory, getting her out of Geometry and the consequences of her incomplete homework assignment) The principal had told the student body that their calls had summoned the police and sheriff so that Martin had been apprehended. That caused a buzz that took awhile to settle down. Finally, he had explained to the students that whoever had made calls should come to the office after the assembly to see about sharing whatever reward might be forthcoming. He had mumbled the end of it about after a trial and conviction. Some of the students basically thought they would have hundreds of dollars by lunchtime if they just saw Mr. Haynes

Mallory was still mad at him about the morning encounter. She could see through his ploy. She thought it was pretty obvious. It occurred to her that if there really were a reward about Martin, that David should get it; he had tackled the big oaf. She was mad about the picture of the kiss. How had Mr. Haynes gotten it? Was he watching every move she made, too?

Her dad had often told her that if the townspeople would take as much care of their own business as they did of everybody else's, everyone would be better off. She sighed, then realized she had dozed off. Assembly was over, she had escaped Geometry, and the entire student body was heading to the office to line up, except for her.

Mallory entered study hall, and Miss Richmond glared her disapproval at her.

"Good morning, Miss Richmond," Mallory said politely.

"Surprised you aren't down shoving and pushing for reward money with everyone else," she whined maliciously.

Mallory shrugged her shoulders. "I was out cold when it happened, so they'd know it wasn't me. Besides, I haven't even had a phone until last night." She held it up innocently, but proudly. "It's turned off," she added quickly as she settled into her place. She hadn't read her Bible, but she needed to do her assignment, too. She hadn't had time to accomplish much of her plan. She thanked the Lord about the assembly's keeping her out of trouble.

"There's always time," her dad had always said, when pressure would start to get to her. "When there isn't enough, it means yer priorities 'r out a whack!"

Tears had welled up, and she thought of her mom as she pulled out a tissue. Daddy was so wise; she just missed him so much. She was grateful for his words. She pulled out her Bible.

Miss Richmond was glaring viciously, but that was her prob.

Actually, the teacher was aggravated to have a student in here this hour. She needed to get to the office herself, to claim to have made the call.

Mallory had turned to Psalm 104 again. As the morning before, her troubled thoughts were of Martin Thomas. It didn't make sense! Why was he in trouble with the FBI? She wasn't sure what the boundary was of stuff they handled. Why had he and David mixed it up? She was trying not to think about David; he made her head ache (maybe lack of sleep had something to do with it, too). They weren't allowed to sleep in study hall. She tried to marshal her thoughts away from the kiss and the picture. Back to Martin. David had said he was making horrible threats that were scaring everyone who was having to listen to him. The Murfreesboro police wanted to hold him, but Sheriff Melville had been about as crazy, trying to make a case to let him go. David was pretty sure he was free now. But if Mr. Haynes was saying there was a reward for his apprehension, maybe the FBI did have him. She would like to know; she would feel much safer.

Mallory whispered to the Lord that she was sorry about the kiss and asked him to tell her daddy she was sorry. She turned to Proverbs 10, but her eyes were drawn back to chapter nine. She desperately wanted to be on the wise path that would take her to the destination she really wanted. She wanted a happy life, filled with service to the Lord and other people. She wanted to finish college and be filled with knowledge for the path or career that stretched ahead. She wanted a great husband and happy marriage with kids and a nice house with a big yard. Always, though, in her dreams, the good husband looked like a cross between David and his dad. Her kids looked like David's little brothers and sisters.

"Is he my destiny? she whispered hopefully. "I'm willing for him not to be."

Suddenly ten people with dark windbreakers and drawn weapons were in the room. Glancing out windows and across the school yard before closing the blinds, they motioned to the terrified teacher to get on the floor.

"Where was Mallory O'Shaughnessy?" they were demanding.

Finally, Penny Richmond was able to get out a stuttering answer. "She said she had a headache and wanted to go to the office for some aspirin. I knew she was a criminal. Is there a reward for her?"

Special agent, Jon Reisman was annoyed by the sniveling woman. "There was one, for ten million dollars, but you let her get away." He was already out of the room. The teen was in mortal danger; he had to find her.

Miss Richmond wailed in earnest at that. One of the female agents cut crisply into her theatrics. "Miss O'Shaughnessy is not a criminal; she is in danger from people who are. There's no reward for her. SHUT UP!"

⁂

Mallory couldn't figure out what was wrong with her. She fled the high school building and hopped into her little car. Everything around her seemed a little crazy, but in her dash, it hadn't registered.

Noisy, excited kids had flooded the office. Even kids with no phones were trying to claim money. All of the agents looking for Mallory had assumed she was somewhere in the throng. It was kind of pandemonium for awhile. When some of the kids finally realized there were so many law enforcement agencies on campus, there were stampedes in all directions as many members of the student body fled to get rid of all of the various and sundry items of contraband they had stashed. Tom Haynes was stunned! He had so prided himself on his squeaky-clean campus. There was a lot of toilet-flushing going on.

Mallory raced away from the school. She had never done anything like this. She was really going to ask for Tylenol or something, but then, the craziness around the offices made it look like getting an aspirin could take all day. She was probably still in trouble with Mr. Haynes, anyway.

The north wind was still pretty chilly, but the sky was brilliant and beautiful. The April green had deepened, and the countryside seemed to sing along with her little, rumbling tires. A beautiful day to play hooky, she thought joyously. It scared her. She had a car, a phone, and a little bit of money; it was already ruining her. She knew she had to finish high school, even if her mom didn't come back.

"Lord, please bring her back," she pled earnestly. "I don't think I'm to be trusted."

Her plan was to go back into Hope and shop for some new clothes, shoes, everything she needed for spending the night at a motel. Maybe she could find her mom while she was in town. Maybe she could be in touch with her mom's former boss, Roger.

She had switched her phone on as she left the high school. It rang, and a number came up for the lodge. She answered. "What's up, Hal?"

"Hi, Mallory, hope you don't mind me calling your cell. I have a check for your mom for this past week end. It's not for much, but if you want to come pick it up, I have a cola waiting for you."

"Passing that way in five," she answered affirmatively. Soon, she was skipping up the steps to the restaurant side of the lodge. It seemed to be hopping; she was slightly amazed. Hal met her with the paycheck and the promised drink.

She gained the privacy of her little car and sped away again. "Thanks for the set-up, Hal!" she mumbled to herself as she gulped the drink gratefully. She dug a couple of aspirin from her little bag; they were contraband at school, too. She swallowed them with a big swig of the soft drink.

The parking lot of the lodge had been full of government-issued cars. Seemed to be a law-enforcement conference or something. She had no idea they were looking for her and for a dreadful individual named Merrill Adams. She shrugged. She doubted Martin Thomas was that important to any of them.

She had shopping on her mind.

Chapter 10

DISCIPLE

MALLORY HAD JUST left from the lodge, headed south on 27, when a huge, black pick-up, coming from a gravel side-road at a fast speed, nearly broadsided her. By the time, the driver of the truck had seen the stop sign, it was practically too late. He had tromped down on the brakes, but on the loose gravel, the heavy truck had barely lost its forward momentum. He managed to stop inches from the little car. He was nearly fifty years old, but this was his first experience with driving on gravel. He was an urban man, and proud of it.

"Dumb roads!" he had growled.

The near miss had terrified the girl. The truck with the black windows was definitely Martin Thomas's. Shaken, she continued to sit there. The drums had definitely dented both sides of the vehicle, and there was quite a bit of blue paint transfer.

Merrill Adams was in the truck. He had disappeared deeper into the countryside with two immediate needs! Food, and a different mode of transportation. He had scored with both objectives. He had broken into a pretty good-looking house and snagged lots of groceries. No one had been home, fortunately for them. No beer! he had been disappointed. But, with the job before him, that was probably best. With only one eye, he had found that his shots lacked the accuracy they had once had.

He had traveled farther up the road, where it forked into two smaller trails. He had followed the less worn one, finally coming to a tumble-down barn. The place looked totally deserted. He had pulled the Lincoln up to the back side of the building. To his total amazement, a nearly new black pick-up truck was parked underneath the shelter. He had planned to eat some of his stolen food here; now he wasn't sure the place was as abandoned as it seemed. One of his hand-guns at the ready, he had approached the truck. It was locked.

He gazed at it longingly. He knew some of R.O.'s guys from another branch of "the business" would have been able to jack it already, without a sound, with no damage whatsoever to the dark glass. He knew how to hot-wire it once he was in. But getting in! He was sure it had an alarm that was set. He sat down next to it and opened a bottle of water. Then he savagely attacked a package of lunch meat, then chips, finishing with some little packaged cakes. He belched.

The wind was brisk, so he put his sweatshirt back on, pulling up the hood. Then he fell asleep. He started awake, grabbing for his guns. Some horse had wandered toward the property where he was and had whinnied.

"Geeze, give me horns honkin', or sirens or somethin! This country stuff is gettin' on my nerves." He gouged at his legs again; now his hands were starting to itch. He looked at them more closely, to see little, watery blisters.

"Guess my trigger-finger's gettin' kinda itchy," he smirked to himself. He squinted his eye toward his big wrist-watch. "If I'm gonna pop sister this afternoon, guess I need to get a move-on."

He had been torn with indecision about whether to appropriate the pick-up or continue in the same car. He knew the Town Car would be futile.

"Unless you plan to ride Horsey over there," he mocked himself, "take the truck.." He broke out the rear window of the cab on the passenger side, and the alarm began beeping. He tightened his grip on one of his guns; he had no idea how to silence the alarm. He left it honking, transferring his rifle and other things from the sedan. He pulled the car farther behind the shed, deep into a heavily forested area, and left it. He should have wiped it down, but he didn't. And for the first time, he noticed how much trouble the Arkansas mud could potentially be for him. There were deep tracks to where he thought he had so cleverly hidden the stolen car. When he hot-wired the truck, the alarm stopped. Knowing the afternoon was waning, he had gunned the truck toward the O'Shaughnessy property. He could barely believe how bad the engine sounded. "These country jerks never heard of oil," he muttered contemptuously. It was rough, but he was clipping about fifty when the accident had barely been avoided.

He had recognized the car, but he had erroneously surmised that it was Suzanne driving toward whatever job she had found in Hope. He was pretty sure the girl rode the school bus every day, and his plan was to have somewhat of a sniper's nest atop the old hunk-of-junk tractor by the time the bus usually dropped her off. Bam! Nail her and beat it back to the truck parked in the woods! Out of here for the night. Find Mom at the job! Whacko! R.O. inherits the trash farm. Everybody's happy!

"Long as I get my fifty G's," he ammended.

It was about one-thirty in the afternoon when Mallory reached the mall. The previous night when she had rushed in to find a phone, she had seen some signs up, advertising good sales. Some things were as much as seventy-five per cent off. She knew that with Easter's arriving soon, merchants would be getting rid of stock to make room for new spring and summer merchandise. She tried to resist the temptation to even look at the new, full-priced goods.

"Was that just last night?" she thought incredulously. The past four days seemed like eternity. She could hardly get her head around it; the aspirin didn't seem to have helped her headache, either. Her phone had been ringing during the entire drive. Exasperated, she switched it off. She grabbed lunch at the food court, then purchased a cute little suitcase. She shopped quickly for items she would need for overnight and school the next day. It was like the Lord had prepared really cute things for her at really good prices. She had found a really cute ribbed knit turtle-neck sweater that was a chocolaty-cinnamon color. It was stunning with her hair. She knew it was. She was thinking now of the Faulkner family. They had somewhat taken up residence in the back of her mind, since her thoughts had been on weightier matters. She found a really cute, long blue-jeans skirt, only one size left; it fit perfectly. Then, there was a darling pair of shoes the same color as the sweater. Then, a handbag, larger than her little-girl one; but considerably smaller that the ones her mother always chose. As she passed by one of the major department stores, she noticed a beautiful glossy poster for one of the cosmetics companies. They were offering a free gift, with so much of a dollar amount purchase. Drawn, she paused by the tantalizing display. She chose a lovely fragrance, then tried a lipstick, hesitantly; a deep, rich shade like she had never imagined. The same tone as the sweater. She had always stuck to pale pinks and a natural, minimum look.

She laughed to herself. "Daddy barely tolerated that." She sighed. Oh, if only. She pouted her sad lips in the mirror. The color did look good. The pout gave way to a sunny smile. "Sold," she announced, handing the sales lady another hundred dollar bill. Then she bought some big, chunky sterling silver; a pendant on a heavy chain to compliment the lines of the turtleneck, a heavy bracelet, a "statement" ring, and large hoop earrings. She purchased a large hairclip, a cute flannel sleep shirt with funny monkeys cavorting all over it, and a few other personal items she had been needing desperately.

She stopped at a drug store for toiletry articles, then checked in at Holiday Inn Express. She was having so much fun. She checked out her room; it was cute. She was surprised it had cost way more than a hundred dollars for just one night, but she took all of her new things out of her suitcase so they wouldn't wrinkle, and arranged everything.

It was four o'clock.

Adams drove through the middle of town in Murfreesboro on his way to the O'Shaughnessy place. He felt concealed, safe, behind the dark tinting. He rumbled past the Sonic. An Arkansas Bureau of Investigation agent was finishing some kind of shake-concoction. He frowned at the truck. He knew whose it was, but they hadn't been able to locate it. Martin Thomas and sheriff Oscar Melville had neither one admitted to knowing where it was. It would reveal some major evidence, but an area-wide search had failed to produce the vehicle. He thought of a couple of suspects who had been held in Hope until they could be transferred to Little Rock today. Concerned that one or the other had somehow escaped from custody, he made a phone call. He had wanted jurisdiction over the two, but as usual, the feds had trumped him. Seems like he never got credit for his hard work. If either one of the goons had escaped federal custody, he was ticked. He pulled out behind the pick-up and requested back up. His call confirmed that Thomas and Melville were still locked up. He explained the appearance of the truck. Thomas's father had been uncooperative with all of the law enforcement agencies' questions. He had seemed relieved to have his son behind bars. Something about always sleeping with one eye opened. He had claimed not to know how his son had gotten money to acquire the new truck and said he didn't know the location of the vehicle at the present.

"Must be the dad," the agent surmised. "Who else would have it?" The mom had left years before. Agent Summers shuddered. He wasn't for parents abandoning their families, but seeing the pitiful place, and the entire situation, he felt kind of sympathetic to a woman who would have wanted out. "Totally creepy!" He wondered if anybody alive had witnessed things as awful as he faced day after day. He was sure they did, and figured the federal guys stories could surpass his by miles. He shook his head sadly.

The maroon Crown Vic was anything but subtle. The agency guys and the bad guys always laughed about the "Unmarked Car" moniker. "They might as well have targets slapped all over them," they would complain whenever new vehicles were issued "Are you trying to get us all killed?"

Actually, it was a couple of miles before Adams noticed him trailing. Color drained from his hideous face. The truck was hot, both overheated and stolen; he had been pushing it harder than it would go. The buses would be rolling soon. Adams rubbed his fiery hands; they were covered with some kind of angry rash. His face was swelling, too, affecting his eye. He had barely heard of poison oak or poison ivy in Boston. He swore! What had convinced him to leave? An eerie feeling had come over him, but he shook it off. He would never leave a city again for some job in the sticks. He pulled his foot from the gas so he could scratch at his ankles. They were an agony of itching and burning. The maroon car dropped back as the pick-up slowed. Suddenly, the pursued slid into a u-turn, racing back toward the state vehicle. Adams pushed the hood of his sweatshirt back, and rolled down the window. He shot out two tires and put four in the grill as he came back past Summers.

Not even drawing his gun, the agent stopped his disabled car. He sat there, stunned. At the briefing of the joint agencies at the lodge earlier in the day, he had seen this guy's picture, heard his history, been issued the BOLO on him. And he was connected to Thomas and Melville? How else could the contract killer be driving this particular pick-up truck? That must tie the locals to the crime-boss from Boston. Shaken, he called the FBI office in Little Rock.

Mallory pulled out the phone book and Yellow Pages that were in her hotel room. She had intended to try to contact Roger or his company to ask about her mom. Then, she decided not to. Her mom hadn't tried to contact her for two days to be sure she was ok. She was suddenly angry at her mother. Then, finally, she had admitted ashamedly to herself that she didn't want her mom to know she was skipping school and spending all of this money.

She got her Bible out and actually read from the book of Deuteronomy; she loved the entire Bible, both Old and New Testaments. Then she read Proverbs chapter ten and began a new prayer journal. (Her old one was still in the tractor from the Saturday morning incident with the wasp.)

She prayed, confessing how angry she had been at Mr. Haynes about the picture of David's kiss, her bad attitude toward Miss Thompson, the study hall teacher; her hatred of Geometry class.

She had been angrily considering moving down here to Hope and transferring schools. Then - she had known that she could never do that. She had to be right with the Lord, and her pastor, and the people of her little town. She had to face them in spite of the fact that her "good name" was being smeared. She knew she hadn't helped things by skipping out of school today.

She knew God's will for her life was to be a good high school student, graduating with honors like her mom and dad wanted. Peace flooded her. More than anything, she wanted to love the Lord supremely, with all of her might and mind. Beyond David or anything else. Once again she chose to put the Lord first in her life. She wanted to be a disciple!

It was four-fifteen.

Chapter 11

DEATH

Merrill Adams had raced back toward the road that approached the forested area on the back side of Patrick's property. In the rear view mirror, he could see the red swelling, forcing his eye nearly closed. No cars were behind him. He pulled off the road, crashing the overheated truck through dense stuff as if it were a bulldozer. The path it had left was far from subtle. He thought about John Anderson's car that had been parked here early this morning. He knew R.O. was gonna be hot about some of this stuff. So were some other people in Boston who were tired of Mr. O.'s suddenly becoming such a loose cannon. Tired of him using their assets for his own personal stuff. You didn't do that; they didn't like it. If they didn't like stuff; there was trouble." He shrugged. "Shouldn't be his problem. Long as he got paid before bad stuff happened."

The truck engine seized up, making a puddle of oil. The hit man shrugged again. He would have sworn there wasn't a drop in it.

Grabbing his rifle and tripod, he lifted himself to the top of the funny old tractor's cab. He assembled the tripod and the weapon, sprawling behind it. He sited it and waited. The postman stopped, shoving a few pieces of mail into the rusting mailbox. Adams sited him in; just for fun, just for practice. He squeezed the trigger slightly; adrenaline was pumping. The mailman drove on, totally unaware he had been in the crosshairs.

From where Adams perched, he knew he would be able to see the bus as it topped a hill, before descending into the lower area of the O'Shaughnessy yard. He stiffened as it appeared. His eye was watery and swollen; he rubbed it with his fiery left hand. He could hear the motor and tell when the bus slowed for the driveway. It ground to a stop! Bingo! Sister was appearing on cue! The doors didn't open. Anxiety seized him; maybe the driver thought she was on, so he stopped; but now no one was getting off. The seconds dragged interminably; the bus rolled, then stopped.

The killer's thoughts were in confusion as he gazed, first through his scope, then around it, trying to figure out what was happening. He needed a spotter and a headset, the thought had occurred to him. But he had always worked alone before.

Finally, someone had exited the school bus. It was Tammi Anderson. In light of what had actually happened, she knew she owed Mallie an apology for not speaking to her. Pops had stopped here, out of habit, so Tammi had decided to jump off to see if her friend was home.

Robert Adams knew immediately that this girl was not his quarry. He relaxed slightly on the trigger. Long as the little girlie didn't see him, she was nothing to him.

Meanwhile, the feds and the Arkansas bureau had responded to Summers. They were already spreading out, looking for the suspect and the truck. A helicopter whirred into sight. Tammi looked up curiously, helicopters hovering around here were a pretty rare sight. She had yelled Mallory's name a couple of times. She knew Mallory loved to retreat to the old tractor. They had all played around in it when they were smaller. Now she knew it was her friend's quiet spot. She circled around the yard, between the fish pond and the pecan tree. She froze in horror as the old tractor came into view. Too terrified to scream, she stood there.

Law enforcement was closing in. The murderer, for some inexplicable reason, was still planning on getting away - in the black pick-up. Summers had viewed it amusedly as he advanced past it with his drawn weapon. It had made its last run!

Frozen eyeball to eyeball with the little girl, the criminal had made one last decision. He shifted his weight slightly to squeeze off the shot.

No twenty-five G's for this one, but she was in his way to an imaginary freedom, a supposed walking away, to return another day. His shattered face should have been a warning to heed, but he, once more, and finally-chose one last, wrong path.

A combined and coordinated contingency of law enforcement officers moved forward cautiously, slowly. Knowing their target was within their pincers, they advanced. Knowing for certain that the man's two targets were both fifty miles away, their only assumption was that the desperate man was simply hunkered in someplace to stage a final shoot-out with them. Their most recent intel of the property was that the mail truck and the school bus had come and gone; no one out here but Adams.

Radioing their positions to one another softly, Summers, with his agents emerged from the backside of the property in coordination as Bransom and the other feds edged forward around the cover of the shed. They figured the guy would make his stand from the cover of the house or the shed.

The sudden rat-a-tat of a woodpecker froze Summers and his group just as they were preparing to cross the open area of the yard. The recent rains had made the grass deep, hiding muddy places. There wasn't much cover. The window shades covering the back windows of the house hadn't moved. Things looked quiet. He swept his field glasses around again. His hands froze with horror.

Instantly, he recognized the girl. He had noticed her at the high school. She had stood out to him. With her slight build and her dark hair and eyes, she had reminded him of his own teen-aged daughter. She was going to die before his eyes, and none of them were in any position to help her. His guys were watching him in puzzlement; then they, too, saw the sniper's nest on the old tractor's roof and the young girl frozen in terror in the sights of the high caliber weapon. One of them had issued a terse "hold it" into his mouthpiece.

Adams hadn't spotted them as they hovered just behind the tree line. His attention was totally on the teen.

The tractor was too high, shielding the man too much, for any of them to get a shot. Summers had never felt so helpless. Bransom and his team had halted their advance when he had heard the breathless, "hold it". From their position, they couldn't see Adams or the other team. They didn't know Tammi was there. They waited!

Adams shifted slightly to his left, cold, calculating. His swollen eye narrowed slightly more. He licked his lips, grinning maliciously.

Something drove painfully into his right hand, just as he had begun to pull back on the trigger. He jerked in pain, sending the barrel of the gun upward. The shot split the air, but the shell missed its intended victim.

Confused and swearing viciously, the man tried to re-establish his hold on his weapon. As he grasped at it, it clattered to the ground. By now, another wasp had stung him on the ankle. Now more of the enraged insects were buzzing at him menacingly. He stood to swat at them futilely. They were attacking; stinging mercilessly, on his bare skin, through his clothing. Losing his balance, he fell heavily toward the ground. Summer's gun barked and flashed. The dealer in death had been dealt with!

> *Romans 6:23 For the wages of sin is death; but the gift of God is eternal life through Jesus Christ our Lord.*

> *Revelation 21:8 But the fearful, and unbelieving, and the abominable, and murderers, and whoremongers, and sorcerers, and idolaters, and all liars, shall have their part in the lake which burneth with fire and brimstone: which is the second death.*

The wages for his sin were twofold. He had never received the gift of God which had been offered to him by the sacrificial death of Jesus. He immediately stepped from the torments of the miserable rash, the stinging insects, the gunshot-into the incomparable horrors of the second death!

Chapter 12

DELIGHTS

BY FIVE O'CLOCK, Mallory had grown restless. She had absolutely no idea of what had been taking place at her little house, by her little tractor. She knew David had kissed her goodnight the previous night. She knew he had left his car someplace; she didn't know where he had materialized from. He had told her to keep the house dark and not to call Sheriff Melville. She didn't know it was the sheriff who had taken the picture of them. She didn't know David's car was in the woods behind her house, or that the sheriff had blazed that implication all over cyber-world (or their little corner of it, anyway). She couldn't explain why she had felt so terrified the entire night as she had sat in her daddy's closet with her phone and slingshot beside her.

She shivered at the memory. She hoped to sleep tonight. She pulled her school books from her school bag and opened her notebook, and the Geometry text. She doodled on the paper.

She pulled her billfold from her purse to look at a picture of her mom and dad and herself. Sighing raggedly, she pulled the photo from its plastic sleeve and set it up on the desk in front of her. She thought her mom and dad looking at her might give her the motivation she needed for her work. The assembly had saved her this morning. She fully intended to be at school early tomorrow. She would have to apologize to Mr. Haynes for all of her behavior, admit to just skipping out; no use trying to lie. Maybe she could just tell him, too, that the math had her so discouraged. Maybe he could help her find a tutor. Her mom and dad had been able to help her with it a little bit. She was sure the whole town must know her mom was gone. Would anyone just leave her alone? Let her take care of herself? Live by herself and finish school?

It brought her thoughts full-circle. She would have to stop imagining such crazy things, go visit the sheriff, get her power restored, act like a grown-up. Her mom probably was working this week for Roger Sander's company. She would probably come home, at least for weekends. There would be a new normal. Everything would be fine. Mallory would gradually get all of her daddy's stuff sorted out, selling some of the valuable antiques, putting out feelers about the diamonds. She would stay active in church and ignore David. She would live down the picture of the kiss, the insinuations the sheriff had continued to make. She would finish Geometry, Calculus, and high school. She would finish college, choosing paths that would make Daddy proud.

Her gaze wandered to the landscape beckoning beyond the large plate glass window. Her new little car was calling her name. She hated to admit it, but the money was "burning a hole in her pocket." She tried to think of a less trite expression for the truism. Laughing, she had to admit that that really pretty well described it. "Why fight it?" she laughed helplessly to herself as she grabbed her car key and bag from the bed and skipped out the door.

The evening was still a little chilly, although the brisk north wind had finally tapered off to a few whispers. The air was crisp and fragrant. Mallory inhaled the fragrance of the landscaping, noticing the neat shrubs and flower beds appreciatively.

It was so beautiful she wished she could stay outside, enjoying the evening air, the sunset, the spring dusk. "Sadly, I must go back to the mall; so much for the great outdoors!"

Agents from various agencies had taken notice of the girl. A couple of cars surreptitiously pulled behind her little car as she headed back the short distance to the shopping center.

They all knew that the danger surrounding her had lessened considerably with Adams lying in the morgue and Melville and Thomas locked up under heavy guard in Little Rock. Still, the fear that the one agent had voiced, remained with them. Maybe Adams had been a ridiculous, hideous, decoy, drawing their attention away from another plot. They all knew that their Massachusetts counterparts had been seeking the girl's uncle, but had been unable to find and arrest him. Word was, he was planning to be here, in Arkansas this coming Friday when the will was to be read. If he hadn't been arrested or taken out before then, these guys and ladies were planning to make sure he never knew freedom again.

Mallory never noticed her convoy. Parking her little car, she walked jauntily into the mall. Her plan was, to shop, shop, and then shop some more; until the mall closed and someone told her she had to leave now. Then, she might look for an all-night discount store.

She found so many cute things! There was a beautiful wool suit in a deep olive color. Next to the bright pastels of the spring merchandise, it looked drab. It was very nice, though. The style was very cute, the fit flattering, the color enchanting with her eyes. She found a beautiful dressy, white blouse to go with it. Then she found some metallic copper high-heeled pumps with a matching handbag. She spotted some clunky, coppery, costume jewelry to complete the look. She was sure the Arkansas weather would still present a cold snap or two, before yielding to the summer's heat. Excitedly, she completed the purchase. She took the unwieldy bag out to the car, depositing it in the trunk, out of sight. Then, she drove around to one of the other department stores.

Suddenly, she had felt that she was being watched. She observed the dark car curiously; then deciding nothing seemed too dangerous, she turned her phone back on as she hurried toward all of the welcoming entrances of the big store.

She stood, just inside the entrance. Departments stores had always enchanted her, much to her father's chagrin. She just stood there, drinking the ambiance in greedily. She loved the place. She wandered around for a few minutes, enjoying the soft bustle, the dings of the manager-paging system, the fragrances wafting from the cosmetic counters. The store wasn't hectic like Christmas, but there were quite a few shoppers. People seemed to be looking for Easter outfits, or at least for new, bright things for spring. She broke down, grabbing some full-priced items to scurry into the fitting rooms with. Everything was so cute!

"Lord, I'm going crazy" she whispered guiltily. But she was having fun. The burden of grief had eased, leaving her infused with life, and energy, and excitement. She was excited about her life that lay ahead.

She had entrusted some of her selections to a saleslady while she looked around some more. Now, she was in the fitting room again. Her reflection smiled back at her. She leaned into her reflection, whispering confidentially, "The earth is full of thy riches."

She found a really cute deep aqua casual outfit, noticing with great satisfaction that it brought out the blue flecks in her hazel eyes, making them appear bluer. She bought several pieces of the coordinates from that grouping. She found neutral colored espadrilles and a canvas tote. Noticing a sunglass display, she tried on several pair until she found the ones she thought looked just right. She stacked it on top of her other selections. The pile was growing. She found a basic, new black skirt; her faithful old standby was faded, had lost shape, and she had outgrown it. This one was cute and new. She picked out some new black shoes; they were kind of high-heeled, but she liked them-a lot! Then, she went to the ladies' dress department. Quickly, she chose two dresses to try on. One was a very stylish basic-black dress, that looked fairly dressy. The girl from the small country town admitted there was really no place to wear it; she shouldn't. It was cute, though. It had capped sleeves, a scooped-out sweetheart neckline, but wasn't low-cut like most of the dresses in stock. It fitted in at the waist, then had two self-fabric bows at the waist, from which the skirt folded into soft pleats. It came to her knees. She looked self-possessed and sophisticated. She liked the fabric; it was stiff and rustly. The black heels looked great with it.

Then, her eyes rested on her new Easter dress. A new rack of merchandise had just been rolled out from a stockroom. The color was a glorious, golden, peachy, sunrise! Her hands trembled as she held it up. The radiant hue made her skin shimmer. Some people shopping around paused to stare at the beautiful girl and her reflection. One of the shoppers was a female agent who was continuing the surveillance. The girl was absolutely stunning. The price tag on the dress was as breathtaking as the garment. How could she? She came back to reality, suddenly wondering what her total was going to be.

She went to the fine jewelry counter and picked out a double strand necklace of fresh-water cultured pearls and a pair of pearl earrings.

She was finally ready. It took the lady a while to ring it all up. The girl paid in hundred dollar bills. It was a lot. The sales lady never batted an eye. Mallory didn't look like a teen-ager who shouldn't be in possession of large bills. She looked like a very well-off and elegant young lady who was accustomed to money.

These bags were really heavy, so she made another trip out to her car, placing her most recent acquisitions in the trunk with her earlier purchases.

She shivered in the night air, and drove around to one more anchor store. There, she found a cute navy pleated skirt with a matching blazer. There was a soft, yellow sweater. Then she found some cute navy loafers and a metallic, slouchy, silver hobo bag.

She left the mall just before they had to ask her to.

She went to the same McDonalds her mom had visited a couple of days earlier. Starved from all of her hard work of shopping, she ordered a super- sized burger meal, to go.

Back in her room, she quickly showered. It felt good to have electricity again and not shower in the dark, or bathe in the kitchen sink by the "dawn's early light". She spread her purchases around on the king-sized bed, rearranging some of the items in different combinations.

At ten o'clock, she turned the news on. Like most kids, she had always resented how she couldn't talk during the news, or the weather, or the sports! For the past three months, hearing any snatches of news, weather, or sports had brought her tears of grief springing to the surface again, reminding her again of her loss.

Now, since she had some new clothes, she was suddenly interested in the weather. Would it be warm enough for this spring outfit? or cold enough for the heavier items. Either way, she thought jubilantly, she was covered!

A really, sadly deformed man's picture was on the screen. Mallory instantly felt sorry for him. She turned the volume up to find out what had disfigured him so. His picture left the screen, to be replaced by hers, then by Sheriff Melville's and Martin Thomas's. Then there was a story that moved so fast and seemed so convoluted that she could hardly follow it. Then, there was a picture of Tammi Anderson and her mom and dad. The story was that the teen-aged girl narrowly escaped a bullet from a contract killer.

Mallory shuddered with disbelief. She couldn't imagine what her friend could have done to merit a contract killer. Nothing like that ever happened in the whole state, let alone the little town of Murfreesboro.

She continued to watch the kaleidoscope of images, there was her house; there was her tractor; there was a dead man in the tall grass beside her tractor! Yellow crime-scene tape seemed to be stretched everywhere over the entire acreage. They were showing Martin's truck and talking about murders in adjacent states.

Mallory turned to CNN. The little diamond town was making national headlines, again!

Chapter 13

DINKY

MALLORY HADN'T SLEPT really well, even with more sense of safety. The hard king-sized bed with the equally hard pillows had only been a minor part of the problem. Of course, all of the television stories and images had hardly been conducive to her being able to fall asleep quickly and sleep soundly. Then, she had been afraid she would oversleep. With all of her surfing channels to ferret out the whole story, she had missed the announcement that the Murfreesboro High School was going to be closed, at least for Wednesday; and possibly for the entire remainder of the week.

By five a.m., she had been awake. The alarm went off, and the wake up call came, but by then she was nearly ready to grab some of the complimentary breakfast and check out. The breakfast wasn't totally ready, so she sat down in the pleasantly decorated breakfast nook to wait. She had gotten herself a cup of coffee; well, more like a cup of cream and sugar. Sitting down at one of the small tables, she spread out her free newspaper. Like her dad, she pulled out the sports page first. Eagerly scanning the baseball stats, she was bummed to see that the "Sox" had lost; that was bad enough, in itself, but the "Rangers" had also won. Her eyes flashed! That made two reasons why she hoped she wouldn't see David Anderson today!

In spite of her indignation over the kiss, she couldn't help secretly hoping she would see him. She was wearing the new outfit with the chocolate-cinnamon sweater and lipstick. She was young and radiant enough that the sleepless nights were not in evidence at all.

More of the food was out, so Mallory fixed a plate-full. All of the TV stories had taken her appetite away, so she had only nibbled at her hamburger the previous night. Suddenly, the front page of the newspaper caught her eye! There it all was, again. Over night, the agents had been trying to piece more of the story together. Somehow, everything was linked to some murders of young women in a multi-state area. One from Oklahoma, one from Texas, one from Louisiana, and the other from here in Arkansas. The similarity of the crimes had been missed at first because each crime had been treated like a local crime by small local agencies. The larger picture of a serial killer on the loose, had only been pieced together in the past couple of days.

There were pictures of her, of her home, of her mom, the Sheriff, the Andersons, the disfigured man, and Martin Thomas. The entire issue seemed to revolve around her little town and her friends and acquaintances. The picture of David's kissing her had been removed since the broadcasts of the previous night.

Too dazed to be hungry, she took her heaped-up plate of food with her. She didn't want to throw it away in front of the lady who was keeping the buffet supplied. She was now much more aware of the agents who were shadowing her. According to the paper, it seemed as though everyone she knew was under investigation. Well, the sheriff, she could certainly see that! But what had Mr. Haynes done wrong? or her pastor, or any of the nice Arkansas Park Rangers? There were both state and federal investigators everywhere. She wondered if they were following her to see if she might be guilty of wrong-doing. "I don't think the g-men follow teen-agers around to see if they're skipping school," she had laughed to herself.

But then, remembering her promise to the Lord to be in school and humble herself to whatever discipline would come, she hurried to her car and headed up 278 toward Pike County. She had been hoping the animal shelter would be open by about seven. She hoped to find some kind of dog that could at least bark. She was sure no prize-winning breed watch-dogs would just be waiting for her.

She turned in on the poorly marked road where the shelter was. It was kind of sad-looking. She couldn't hear much barking, or anything to indicate there might be any dogs here at all. The hours said eight to five; closed for lunch. They were really even far more relaxed than that.

Mallory was so disappointed she felt like crying. "Lord, I told You I need a dog." she had prayed petulantly. Immediately, she was sorry. "I'm sorry, Lord! You have protected me without a dog for more than seventeen years. Especially, You have cared for me since You called my daddy home.!" Tears flooded down her face again. "Lord, thank You for everything. Thank You for that arrow that showed me where Daddy had that money; no one would ever believe that, but I know You were helping me. Thank You for my iPod, and my phone, and my car, and all the new clothes."

She was heading back toward the main road; but just before she reached it, she nearly hit a huge dog. She jumped from her car. She was pretty sure she had missed him by a good margin. He had been tied to a fence post, she guessed. But, with his jumping and straining at the rope, he seemed to have worked the loop loose. Mallory didn't make any sudden moves, but bent down, making soft little kisses, her empty hand outstretched. The dog just looked at her. For some reason she had brought the petrified burger and fries from the previous night, and the bagels and danishes. She had offered it gingerly. Evidently, like a man, the way to his heart was through his stomach. Every morsel disappeared in a couple of huge bites, and the dog seemed to have made up his mind about his new owner.

Mallory had grabbed his collar; she just knew he had a home and some little kid was already calling to him. To her amazement, there was a note attached. Evidently, someone had been trying to leave this dog at the shelter, but after a few attempts, and not finding anyone there, had just looped him to the fence. It said, "My name is Dinky. I have a huge appetite! I'm good with women and children. I have a problem with men."

Mallory laughed joyously, extending her hand. "Put 'er there!" Dinky graciously "shook" her outstretched hand. "Looks like we have a lot in common, already!"

The Lord never ceased to amaze her. He was so faithful and kind.

She still had both an ABI and an FBI car following behind her. She started her iPod playing. She pushed down on the gas a bit. Now, she would have to go all the way home to leave her new dog, then backtrack to school. It was going to be close; she was afraid now she would be late. Woefully, she turned off her music. Digging out her phone, she punched in the number for the high school. Maybe if she called, there would be less of a problem if she arrived a few minutes late. To her amazement, there was a recording saying to check back later for another recording as to when school might resume sessions.

Her heart soared, but then, she still figured it was too good to be true. She cut across a gravel road from 27 that was a short cut to the school. When she arrived, she was amazed to find no cars in the faculty lot or the student parking lot. No buses! She looked around nervously, no Martin! Mr. Haynes' car was in its usual space; he spent a lot of time at work. He was in Whose Who in American Educators. There were some official cars from various agencies and people with different letters on their windbreakers. Mallory wondered what was going on. Then, she thought of her dad, always telling her just to mind her own business.

Yes, Business! First thing, get more food for Dinky. He was still whining at the empty styrofoam plate and burger sack. She would need a couple of big bowls for him, a new collar, and a better leash. She gave his head a scratch, and he tried to lick her hand affectionately in return. "Ew! No licky," she commanded, tapping him on the nose with her index finger.

Then, she needed to go to the power company and pay whatever was necessary to get the power back on. She planned to pay the phone company what was owed, but discontinue it in favor of a cellular. She still wanted an iPhone.

When she pulled into her driveway, she was still amazed by the sight before her. She had seen this scene on TV and in the newspaper, but she was in shock that it all seemed suddenly true.

She tried to pull her car in amongst all of the agency vehicles, some huge, non-descript truck, various news crews with their vehicles, and a big crowd of curious gawkers. Her docile doggy was going ballistic! He was tense, growling threateningly, baring his teeth.

"Good boy!" she whispered in his ear.

Bransom had started to approach her car; the agent following her had called him to tell him the teen finally seemed to be returning to her home. The dog caused him to back away. Mallory opened her window a crack. "I'm sorry, sir," she was trying to apologize.

The dog's growl intensified.

"Dinky, be quiet!" she ordered. "He had a note on him that said he doesn't like men," she was explaining helplessly. One of Bransom's guys was giving instructions to different drivers to get their cars moved so she could get closer to her house. Then, he was motioning her to pull up. She could see where this was going and she shook her head, no.

One of the female agents had approached Mallory, telling her she could pull up.

"You know, I'm not sure what everyone is doing here. I have up a 'No Trespassing' and a 'Beware of Dog' sign. Would you please send everyone away that doesn't absolutely need to be here?" She had unfolded from her little car, holding her dog at bay by wagging her index finger in his face. "Please tell that guy I'm not pulling up until I know for sure my car isn't going to get hemmed in. I have quite a few errands to run!"

Agents had begun sending the spectators on their way.

"Why didn't I think of that?" Bransom berated himself.

Some of the agents who hadn't seen the girl before couldn't help exchanging glances

Chapter 14

DEFENDANTS

BRANSOM HAD BEEN busy out in the shed, so he hadn't been aware of the big truck that had pulled into the yard. The driver had waved some paperwork at one of the agents, saying he had an order from Sheriff Melville to start clearing some of the junk away from the property. The sheriff had told him the owner was dead, and the place was an eyesore. The agent had helped him courteously.

Now, as Mallory pulled her car up farther into the yard, she was totally dismayed by the scene. The garden had been obliterated by all of the traffic, and now somebody was over messing around with her tractor. She had left her car door open as she strode angrily across the expanse of yard.

"Hey, what are you doing?" she had demanded angrily before she was even close.

The guy sneered at her. "Orders from the sheriff! He told me to start haulin' trash, said the county would pay me. Just doing my civic duty to tidy up this nasty corner of the county."

Mallory had already reeled back from him with disgust; she could swear to the fact that tidiness usually wasn't one of his priorities. "Don't lay so much as a finger on my tractor," she hissed at him defiantly.

Dinky was at her side, eyeing the hauler suspiciously, growling, snarling ferociously.

"You think you and that junk-yard dog scare me, lady, you couldn't be more wrong!" he had replied viciously.

Mallory wheeled back around toward her house, whistling for her dog to follow. He gave another warning growl and a bark, before reluctantly obeying his new mistress.

Grinning at his victory, the man lowered himself to the ground beside the antique. He groaned, as he stretched underneath, trying to find a secure place to fasten his tow chain.

The wasps stung him twenty times before he could get up and get started running for his truck. He didn't die, but he went to the hospital.

"Score two for the wasps," one of the agents had whispered with awe to another.

Erik Bransom greeted Mallory again as she re-approached her back steps. This time he had pulled out his badge, and was introducing himself officially. He and Dinky were still eyeing one another with maximum distrust.

"Ma'am, I'd like to ask you just a few questions, if I may?"

The girl's head raised defiantly, and her eyes blazed before filling with tears.

"I didn't murder my daddy, if that's what this is all about again!" The dog had moved closer, nudging her empathetically. He continued to watch Brasom.

The agent couldn't have been more shocked.

The girl was trying to stop crying and regain her composure.

"You can see the autopsy report; I mean, I guess you can order another autopsy if you want," she had faltered. "What did you want to ask?"

"You know what?" he had said, "Why don't you follow me to the lodge? We have a joint-task force operating from there. I'm hungry, so I'm ready to go eat some lunch there before I have a briefing later on this afternoon. What did you mean about your father? Is someone thinking it's a murder case now?"

He couldn't believe how the scope of the crimes seemed to be escalating beyond his ability to keep up. Never underestimate the secrets of a small town, he had surmised to himself.

He headed toward his car. If Patrick O'Shaughnessy had been murdered, his brother or people from his former life in Boston, would seem far more likely for it, was the FBI man's take.

He pulled out his notes from his interview at the Anderson's. Now he wished he had paid more attention to some of the boy's complaints about Sheriff Melville. He had been so convinced before he got here that it was just a vengeful ploy by the teen to get a law officer investigated. Anderson's words were that the Sheriff had actually harangued the distraught girl for five or six hours, accusing her, trying to get a confession. There were no arrest records. If the Sheriff had indeed, behaved this way, he had been out of line- way, way, way out of line. If he thought there was a murder, well-first of all-evidence would support the theory. He would like to see the Sheriff's evidence. And then, based on "probable cause", he would have arrested her, Mirandized her, questioned her with her mother present, or, at the least with an audio or video tape. She should have been appointed council. Surely, Sheriff Melville would not have strayed that far from the legal high road. Why would he want to deal so much grief to a seventeen year old girl, that he would jeopardize what little he had? The agent was deep in thought. Maybe he had tried something with her; she was a minor; he was afraid she would tell? That didn't make sense, either. Anderson said the Sheriff was trying to smear the girl's reputation; he had showed the agent the picture and the innuendo that the Sheriff had e-mailed. To the agent, it smacked of voyeurism; he had issued a memo to remove it from the media coverage. He gulped down four big headache pills without any water. He had reached the lodge. Mallory had followed him; he had been so engrossed he had never checked the rear view mirror.

The sky had become overcast, the north wind had grown strong again. Bransom was thinking maybe he shouldn't have left his trench-coat at the house.

He walked briskly to the restaurant side of the lodge. Mallory was still giving orders to Dinky. Waving her finger with her "statement" ring on it, she had ordered, "Be a good dog. I don't want bad stuff to happen in my new car, if you know what I mean." He started to lick her hand ."Ump, no!" she reminded him.

Reluctantly, she headed toward the door where the agent stood waiting.

She had been surprised to see so many cars. Law enforcement people by droves, along with media personnel and tourists jostled for tables inside. Someone whose face she recognized as being from one of the TV stations had jabbed a microphone into her nose with such force it hurt.

Bransom muscled in, and placing his hand on her elbow, he propelled her toward the conference room. By now she was really hungry; the food she had bypassed smelled delicious. To her relief, there was already a buffet set up in the room. Some of the agents had already served themselves. Bransom courteously allowed her to precede him in the line. She got a plate and loaded it with Chicken 'n Dumplin's. It was always the daily special on Wednesday, and it was Mallory's favorite. She got some iced tea, and took a seat where the agent had indicated. She bowed her head and closed her eyes. It wasn't just going through the motions; she was really grateful.

She dug into the delicious luncheon, as did the agent. Others had brought their plates over to join their table. They were all kind of quiet. Mallory tried to sneak a couple of aspirin out of her purse; four hands shot out. Laughing, she shared.

"Bunch of babies!" Bransom chided his men. They didn't know about the four pills he had just swallowed. One of the agents stacked their plates on a side table. Other people were filtering in for the upcoming briefing. Drizzly rain had begun to fall, making the chicken dish more appealing than ever. Agents were loading up with the great food. Mallory was glad the agent had brought her here. She was still apprehensive about the questions he wanted her to answer. One of the guys had loaded up five or six plates with blackberry cobbler and vanilla ice cream. He was met with applause and whoops of delight. One of the others was bringing cups of coffee. Mallory accepted one, and instinctively, every one pushed the cream and sugar her direction.

"I guess my reputation precedes me," she laughed, noticing that every one of them was drinking the awful tasting brew black.

Finally, Bransom rose. He had a lady agent escort her to the powder room. "Am I in trouble?" she asked the woman anxiously.

"No, I don't think so," the agent responded. "He just doesn't want everyone in your face"

Mallory was glad for that.

Bransom had frankly been shocked about the girl's frightened reaction to him. Suddenly, he felt like she didn't owe any more answers to anybody. He wanted to fly to Little Rock right now and punch the sheriff in the nose. Too bad no one had asked for the Pike County Sheriff's office to be investigated sooner. He had felt like Mallory would be able to fill in some of the gaps he was missing and corroborate some of the rest of the statements he had been given. Now, he decided to ease back from her.

When she returned to the room, she asked him what he wanted to know.

He had sipped his coffee, gazing at her quietly. "Not really that much. Just tell me what you know about Melville and Thomas."

Mallory was shocked, "like, what do you mean?" she asked, puzzled. "I don't know whether to say I don't know anything about either one of them or 'don't get me started'."

Bransom held up his mug for more of the strong, hot coffee; the girl was still drinking on her "milk".

"Let's do the 'don't get me started' one." He laughed and got his notebook out. He listened intently, skillfully getting her to spend about a half hour on both of his suspects. Then, he had asked her about her family in Boston, her paternal grandmother, her Uncle Ryland, her cousins, ending by asking if she had any idea why they might send a contract killer to Murfreesboro. Was there a chance that they had murdered her father.

When he had come back around full-circle to saying her father had been murdered, she had begun to cry again. "Why do you think someone murdered him?" her voice was anguished, and annoyed "They told me that he used to drink a lot when he was young. It messed his liver up, but he had quit drinking by then, so he didn't know his liver was weak. Then, when he started having heart problems, the drugs for that had quickly aggravated his liver. He had needed both a heart and liver transplant; he knew it, but he hadn't told Mallory and her mom. "I guess I did kill him," she confessed tearfully. "Tell the sheriff I did; he'll be pleased. I didn't know he was so sick, and I just kept making him worry." She dropped her head onto her arms and sobbed. "I should have known he was sick; I should have made him go to a doctor. If I didn't actually murder him, it's my fault he's gone!"

One of the ladies had moved in sympathetically. He waved her away.

"Mallory," he spoke her name firmly. "You have been a really big help. I will need the coroner's report; one of the agents is getting it for me now.

It was probably natural. Did you ever know that your father once had ties to some organized crime members in Boston?"

Mallory shook her head negatively and emphatically. "No," she was wiping her nose on a paper napkin. "I don't know anything, except we moved here when I was three. My grandma really loved me. Then, when I was in second grade, the Anderson's moved here. I got saved, then my daddy and mom. After that, Grandma was always mad at me because Daddy wasn't a Catholic any more. I'm not sure how he got money, if that's what you're trying to ask. In my heart, I'm pretty sure my dad was way above-board honest. He always demanded it of me. I don't know my uncle or my cousins; I wish I did. I know my mom's side of the family a little bit better. Do you know where my mom is?" she finished tearfully.

When Agent Bransom finished his visit with Mallory, he rose. "I have three defendants to prosecute. You aren't one. Agent Haskle will see you to your car. If anyone tries to bother you for a news story or anything, turn your dog loose on 'em."

Bransom had watched Haskle get the girl out to her car. She was letting the huge animal walk a little bit. It kept barking and growling nastily. He was impressed; he couldn't figure out how the girl, with hardly any time to look around for a dog, had found such a perfect one. It was a strange-looking mutt. It looked like Great Dane and an Irish-Setter mix. It was kind of a dusty red color, with hair between the lengths of the short-haired Dane, and the longer haired Setter. The shape of the head and ears was mostly Great Dane. He was a fearsome size, and his posturing was definitely terrifying. And she could just wag her finger at him, and he responded.

He thought about the guy with the tractor before lunch. He hadn't been scared of the dog. "Must have had a piece on him," the agent had muttered angrily. He intended to find out who had permitted him on the property. The agent knew the tractor was really, really valuable; he was pretty sure the hauler knew it to. If he was really acting on the orders of Melville, and he intended to find out, then Melville was falling into an ever deepening hole. People entering his crime scene, trying to rob huge and valuable things in broad daylight from underneath his nose- He didn't think so!

The girl had retreated to save her dog's life. Still, he and his agents had done nothing! He was enraged with himself, and with them. "Good thing there's a wasp nest out here," he raged to himself. Otherwise Tammi Anderson would be in the morgue now, rather than Adams.

An agent interrupted his reverie. He had the autopsy report on Patrick O'Shaughnessy and preliminary findings on Adams. Adams had died of the shock of the stings before the bullet hit him Good! That would save an investigation on Summers for the shooting.

He couldn't help smiling as he read further into the report; then he was chuckling. Adams had Poison Ivy, Poison Oak, and nine embedded ticks, and counting. There were fifty-seven welts from the wasps. "This guy should have stayed in Boston!"

He shook his head in wonder. He didn't know why, but a Sunday School story from his childhood had come to mind. It was about Absalom's revolt against his father, king David. He found a Gideon Bible in the nightstand in his room at the lodge. It took him a while, but he found the verse.

> *II Samuel 18:8 For the battle was there scattered over the face of all the country: and the wood devoured more people that day than the sword devoured.*

The special agent in charge was charged up for the briefing he was about to hold!

Chapter 15

DISCARDS

BRANSOM ENTERED THE conference room at one forty-five. Hardly anyone there! He was planning on jumping everyone about everything. Some of these guys better have found a few things that they had been assigned earlier in the week. Bransom couldn't stand for things to bog down; especially if it were because of lazy, half-hearted work. Hal Thompson seemed to have found some extra help; sandwiches, desserts, and coffee seemed to be arriving more smoothly. Erik had signed off for the guy to receive his funds for the food and lodging from the Feds. He had told the guy to keep the Arkansas State account separate from his tab. He knew that would be a confusing thing for the lodge owner, but he wasn't going to allow that to become his or his agency's problem.

A few more people had assembled; now there were some new faces, from an auditing group of the Treasury Department. He had sighed in annoyance, but he was hardly surprised. When the guy with the truck had nearly left with such an invaluable item, he had known it would be investigated-sooner or later. They would find out which of his agents had been so accommodating; and why! There was so much stuff on the O'Shaughnessy property that Bransom had actually been relieved to have an extra accounting and oversight of it. And that was before Mallory had confided to him that the place was sprinkled over with millions and millions of dollars worth of diamonds!

He thought of his three defendants; two in Little Rock, under heavy guard: and one in Hope, in what he hoped was somewhat of a cushy confinement. He knew the other guys were making jokes behind his back. He was sure his judgment was clouded. Two of the criminals, he wanted the book thrown at! He wanted them buried. He was coming up with a lot more questions to ask the two in Little Rock. The one in Hope, he had to admit, was just someone who had struck him as being really cute. But, she was in a lot of trouble!

A couple of guys handed him some things. Thomas's truck had made it to the FBI crime lab in Little Rock, where forensics was beginning to coax some of its secrets into the open. Impatient, he wanted all of the answers now! But, he knew that couldn't be. Haste really did make waste, he had admitted to himself; and he didn't want one hair, or one shred of evidence missed. He didn't want Melville or Thomas to have a loophole: he wanted the death penalty. That would require patience. He was really glad Adams was deader than a doornail. Maybe Ryland O'Shaughnessy was dead, too. Boston couldn't find the guy. Word on the street was that Delia O'Shaughnessy and her grandson, Shay Patrick had first-class airline tickets to fly into Little Rock today at- he looked at his watch-about now! Of course, they were coming because of the will. He studied the grandson's name; looked like he was named after his uncle.

The other item was about two murder victims whose bodies had been discovered a couple of hours away in a small Oklahoma town. They were an old man and his wife. Their light blue Lincoln was missing; they were found in a different vehicle. The local sheriff's department said they had been careful not to disturb evidence. Bransom sighed wearily. He was sure that wasn't true. If Adams had been in that vehicle, had killed the elderly couple, had stolen their car, crossed into another state to commit crimes, it was another big chain, tying all of his culprits together. Those were Ryland O'Shaughnessy, Oscar Melville, Martin Thomas, and Merrill Adams.

Time to get started! He began his briefing with a tirade.

⁂

The drizzle seemed colder, the wind more cutting. Mallory had returned to her home from the lodge. The electricity was back on; she had forgotten to go to the little, local window, where Murfreesboro residents could pay their utilities. She thought it was a miracle that the house was bright and warm when she returned. It made her almost expect her mom or dad to be there. They weren't; the place was still just buzzing with people everywhere doing whatever it was that they were supposed to be doing. She was still tired from not sleeping. She picked up the telephone receiver; it buzzed with the dial tone. Maybe she was waking up from a bad dream, and none of the crazy things had happened at all. She shivered: they were real, alright.

Dinky was beside her, continuing the menacing growls, being far more menacing with the male agents than with the women. "Dinky, give it a rest!" she ordered. He dropped tiredly beside her. She yawned; they both took a nap.

The phone rang; one of the agents grabbed it before she could fight away the sleepy stupor and answer it. She had slept for an hour. She wasn't sure she liked these people here, grabbing her phone.

She waited in line for her bathroom. "Sorry," one of the agents apologized when he squeezed out past her.

She went to the kitchen to get a glass of water; all of the glasses were in the sink, dirty. She was annoyed. She noisily placed all of the dirty dishes in the dishwasher and started it running.

One of the ladies whose jacket said "Treasury Department" on it, handed her a bottle of water. "Sorry everyone is making such a mess." She was very aware of all the muddy footprints everywhere. Could you come out to the shed with us for a few minutes? We need some answers, if you can help us."

The girl felt a sudden sense of panic. She was only seventeen; she sure couldn't figure out exactly what Treasury Department meant. Her sudden perception was that there was all of this stuff here, that was kind of valuable, so she was going to owe some huge tax amount they would never be able to pay. Her cute, new clothes; the money in the cigar-box; her new car; the antiques; the little house; probably there were not really any diamonds here: it all seemed to melt away. The path ahead of her suddenly appeared dark and hopeless. In terror, she followed the lady out to her dad's shed.

It was a nice shed, both larger and newer than the little homestead house. Mallory had played around in it occasionally, but Patrick had eventually convinced her that some of the varied antiques had blades or things where she could hurt herself. And, that had been true. She followed numbly behind the "Treasury Department" letters that had ordered her to follow. There was a narrow path amongst all of the strange items. The lady pushed a button and held it in. A ladder descended automatically, and they climbed to the loft. There were more pieces of junk scattered around up here, but suddenly they were in an enclosed space that was hidden cleverly behind the array of antiques. Mallory could feel the nice warmth, and realized there was an air conditioning unit, too, so the area would be equally comfortable in the summer. There was a phone line with a phone, a television set, a computer with high-speed internet, and a printer/fax machine. She had had no idea this was all up here. "What a sneaky little man," she had admitted to herself. Suddenly, she was fearful that they, not only, owed a lot of taxes, but it was all illegal stuff, too. She stood there dumbly, gazing around, wide-eyed.

TD was speaking again, and Mallory was watching blankly as the woman's lips moved. He head was spinning, and she could only hear whooshing noises in her ears.

The guy at the desk had been rising to his feet to acknowledge the introduction. He caught Mallory just before she hit the floor. Dinky had decided to come looking for her, and he was barking frenziedly down below the loft.

The frightened T-people weren't sure what to do, so they interrupted Bransom's briefing.

Mallory sat up with a moan, looking around. The guy who had been at her father's desk was surveying her frantically through thick glasses.

"I'm fine," she had mumbled, somewhat thickly.

"Oh good," he was relieved. "Ma'am, do you have any idea where the key might be to this filing cabinet, what the safe combination is, or his computer password?" I mean I can get it all eventually. What's his password first, did he ever tell you?"

"No," she admitted honestly. "I never knew he even knew how to turn a computer on."

The lady TD who had showed her up had opened Mallory's water bottle. She handed it to the girl. "We have some sandwiches," she offered.

"They're chicken salad, from that cute little lodge." She hollered down to someone and a plate of sandwiches and potato chips was urged into the girl's hands.

"Thick- glasses" repeated the password question. The TD lady also said, "Honey, if you know, you can really save us some time."

The whole scenario seemed so unreal: this little office tucked up here; these people!

Mallory set the plate of sandwiches aside, dropping her head into her hands. She felt woozy and nauseated. She wanted to cry - no- more like scream. She wanted all of these crazy people to go away, who seemed to have so many more questions than they had answers. She rubbed her face with both hands. She undid the clip that had been holding up her heavy hair all day. It seemed like a week ago, at least, since she had checked out of her hotel room, found Dinky at the shelter, found out school was canceled. She gazed around the neat office once more. She raked her fingers through her luxuriant hair, massaging the places where the clip had been pulling. She wished school hadn't been cancelled. She would prefer to be in an all day Geometry class than here.

With a bewildered sigh, she had extended her hands forward, palms up. She didn't usually think she talked with her hands, but her body language was open and trusting. She was trying to think. She had fallen so sound asleep-

"I found a funny little key in my dad's coat pocket; I think his coat is on the floor in his closet. I couldn't figure out what it might be for. I didn't know if it was for a locker or a safety deposit box, or a PO Box. Maybe it's for the filing cabinet. I can't think of what he might use for a computer password. When we played with walkie-talkies, his handle was always "Irish Spud". "Thick-glasses" laughed, and she was mad she hadn't told him to figure things out for himself. Dismally, she was thinking, "Why should I help them hang us?" Suddenly, she wondered if they could compel her to say anything that might be self-incriminating.

Sam was the guy's name; the lady had said it again. His fingers had flown like lightning, but "Irish Spud" hadn't gotten him in. He drummed the desk idly, then suddenly tipped the chair forward onto all four legs.

"What was your walkie-talkie handle?" he questioned curiously.

"Tater Tot," she answered him softly.

"Ha! That's cute!" he smiled at her. "Irish Spud to Tater Tot, come in Tot!" He was playing like he had the radio, then he was making static sounds.

Bransom had a dry board, and one of the agents had written on it, what they had. Then, there was an area of questions that needed answers. The light blue Town Car had been found out in the country. (Bransom pretty well thought it was all country). Anyway, farther out in the country. Strangely, some of the tire tracks out at that scene were from the Thomas pick-up. So, Adams had switched vehicles out there. Martin or Thomas must have told him about the pick-up, but in Bransom's mind, this new development wasn't fitting. Some of the guys were trying to make it all fit. He had started out on a rampage; now this set him off again. "Don't make a theory, then try to force everything to fit around it. Whatever doesn't fit gets filed! That's not what we're doing here, gentlemen! That isn't the way I operate!

The sheriff wouldn't furnish the hit man with a vehicle that is already connected to other crimes. For some reason, Martin and Thomas had tried to conceal the pick-up. We are not totally certain about those reasons. Forensics will have a lot of answers about that within the next week to ten days. There was broken window glass at the scene where the truck had been stored that matches where the back passenger window was broken out of the truck. Maybe Adams wanted to ditch the town car, and he found the truck by accident. He didn't know or care that it had a history. In that case, maybe he doesn't have a real connection with anyone from Pike County. He was simply hired from Boston.

Get out there and canvas anyone who might have been around that area in the past few days!" He nodded to a couple of his guys on the front row.

"Excuse me, Special-agent-" It was one of the Pike County deputies. Bransom didn't trust any of them because he wasn't sure how loyal they still were to Sheriff Melville, or if they were possibly involved with him.

He didn't appreciate the interruption at all.

"What?!" he whirled to the guy in total exasperation.

"Well, we do have a crime report from out in that area; we didn't think it was very important," he explained hesitantly.

"Well, what is it, ?" he roared.

"Well, a housewife, Mrs. Joyce Haynes, was away from her house; she had to take Tommy, Jr. to the doctor. When she got back yesterday, the kitchen door was busted. Nothing much taken but some groceries. We went out and looked; must have "just been a hungry transient."

Bransom couldn't believe anyone could be so dumb. He held up an evidence photo from the crime scene. Their criminal obviously hadn't minded leaving a trail of litter. The photos were of water bottles, a lunch meat package, a Cheetos bag, and some cake wrappers. Just a hungry transient! How about a hungry murderer? Mass murderer? Did you take any prints at the Haynes house. That's another major crime scene. You just walked away, and now the evidence is really tainted. He had the deputy arrested. There was stupidity; and their was duplicity! He couldn't believe anyone could really just be that stupid!

Then, he addressed the combined group once again. "Don't overlook anything; don't dismiss anything; don't make your own decisions about what may or may not be important! Don't concede defeat to the bad guys. Don't increase the stature of any of these thugs by speaking of them in awe. We are the awesome ones. We are on the offensive. We're the good guys. We are winning; we are going to keep winning. Don't stand around with your weapons holstered waiting for a bunch of bees to do your jobs for you. Don't let anyone, I mean anyone, on the O'Shaughnessy property, without turning them inside out! When you use the radios, try to make sense. Shoot until you run out of bullets, then throw rocks if you have to! Are there any questions?" He strode from the room without waiting for any.

He went to his guestroom, and phoned the treasury agent. She thought Mallory was feeling better; they were not sure why she passed out. She had helped them get into her father's computer and his filing cabinet. Seemed the guy was a true genius. His taxes had all been properly filed, his income declared. Somewhere, he should even have quite a treasury check refund for the previous year. Looked like he had a PO Box in Hope. His wealth seemed to be tucked away in different places, as he had sought more and more to increase it without calling attention to it. Bransom spoke to her for a few more moments before ending the conversation.

He had a call from his office in Hope. Someone had come in and posted bail for his detainee who was being held at the police station there. He wasn't sure if he should be glad, or not.

Mallory had watched with relief as the agents at her home were sending most of the people packing. She could see that many of them were trying to argue. They needed a story, or they were Mallory's friends, and she had asked them to come. The agents were searching them, although their search wouldn't have revealed concealed diamonds. That story wasn't out yet. Bransom wanted to make sure it didn't get out before the will was read on Friday morning. By then, a civilian security firm was supposed to be in place, as all the federal and state agents would be withdrawn at that time. Their job was to protect America and her citizens. If the citizens had diamonds, they had to protect them themselves. Bransom was willing to give his life for America and the people he was sworn to protect. He wasn't eager to give it, but willing; if it came to that. He wasn't interested in dying for rocks.

Now, more people retreated from the dismal property where the bone-chilling drizzle had left the yard a series of deep, muddy ruts. Mallory had coaxed the stubborn shade over her bedroom window to go up so she could watch the retreat. She still had most of her bottle of water, so she dug out a couple of aspirin. Wearily, she swallowed them. She was nervous. She wasn't sure what the fine-toothed comb search was digging up. She wasn't really sure if she were some criminal suspect. She was pretty sure the cash she had secreted in her daddy's closet had been found and confiscated. She watched a couple of the agents who were engrossed in a conversation on the back porch. She crossed the little kitchen as innocently as she could and entered her father's room. A man and a lady were working in there. The chaos was ordered, boxed, labeled. She gazed around in confusion.

One of the lady agents asked her, with genuine concern, if she could help her.

Mallory wasn't sure how to phrase her question tactfully, so she just said, "My Daddy had a cigar-box full of hundreds in here. Have you seen it?"

Nearly everything in the room was cataloged and boxed. The agent hadn't seen it, and she had the oversight of this side of the house. Her mind was suddenly filled with dread that someone had taken advantage of the confusion to remove what she was responsible for.

She could hardly force the words out. "Well, where was it, Honey?"

"I spent the night in the closet, and it was beside me, and I pushed it way back in." She shuddered again, thinking of how terrified she had been.

Relief swept over the agent. "We haven't gotten into the closet yet. Go ahead and take a look."

Mallory rummaged around for a few seconds; she came out with the cash in the cigar box and a baggie that had been in her daddy's robe pocket. It contained two, sizeable, uncut diamonds.

"Thanks," she nodded to them, before retreating to her room.

The woman immediately phoned her superior; she wasn't sure the girl should have taken the cash without her permission. Bransom called the head of the team from treasury to tell them to watch his agents more carefully. It was for all of their protection. He had dealt with things like this before, removing valuable items, cash, drugs, establishing a chain of evidence. This wasn't a crime scene; the valuables weren't evidence. The best he could sort it out was that it they rightfully belonged to the girl and her mother. "Well," he had corrected himself, "the inside of the house was not a crime scene. That was because Adams had never actually entered the house. He had stopped after leaving muddy prints on both porches. Bransom could still hardly believe he hadn't completed the hit on Mallory at that time.

Mallie freshened up for church, grabbed her daddy's big Bible, and with Dinky at her side, she drove away toward town in her new, little car. She had been relieved when the agent hadn't insisted on hanging onto the cash. Now, she wasn't certain what to do with it. Curiously, she wondered if "thick-glasses Sam" had been able to open the safe that was up in that office. She wondered what might be in it, if her daddy had left large amounts of cash around in cigar boxes.

As she made the drive into town, she couldn't help thinking about her daddy's constant lessons to her. Things aren't always what they seem; things aren't usually what they seem. One man's trash is another man's treasure. Already, today, Mallory had become aware of a gentleman who had been trying to buy her tractor for the past eight years, offering more and more for it each time. Daddy wouldn't sell it because Mallory had bonded to it. She laughed to herself, "Wish he had told me someone was offering twenty-five thousand for it and let me decide if I loved it that much or not."

She pulled into the Sonic and ordered. Dinky whined, reminding her that he was hungry, too. She ordered an extra burger for him, explaining to him that he better not get spoiled; she was on her way to buy him dog food.

She knew a few of the pieces of stuff were valuable, if you could locate who might be in the market. A lot of it was part of the subterfuge, a very clever subterfuge. Mom had never guessed at any of it. Smiling, she remembered one of the most vivid stories

One day, when Mallory had probably been about seven, she had been playing in the big back yard after a rain storm. Playing in the mud, which she shouldn't have necessarily been doing, she had discovered a very "intriguing" rock. She had been certain she had found a diamond, running to her dad to show him. Excitedly, she had asked him if he thought it might be anything good. He had examined it carefully, then had laughed and told her the only diamonds were in her eyes when she got so excited.

He had kept it, though. A few days later, he had decided to put in the "fish pond" right about where she had been playing. It had never held water, never housed any fish. It was just there. Over the next few years, Mallory would occasionally come running to him with "pretty" rocks. He would tease her and keep them. He always told her all of the diamonds were much smaller than what she was looking at. The older she got, and the longer she lived in diamond country, the more she would come to him.

"Daddy, are you sure? If they aren't diamonds why do you always keep them, instead of giving them back so I can play with them?"

All the while, Patrick was working to build his daughter a future. He had to keep the secret as long as he could, cringing when Suzanne had decided to take up gardening, then beginning to refuse people access to the acreage, even to repair things.

Suzanne had never suspected one thing; except perhaps that Patrick was completely nuts!

Working behind the scenes, he had eventually allowed Mallory to go to camp for a week, and Suzanne to visit her sister. They thought Patrick had stayed home. Immediately after seeing them both off, he had flown to New York City in a chartered jet out of Mena. Having the largest and loveliest uncut diamond with him, he had kept an appointment with a diamond expert he had been exchanging e-mails with.

Mallory didn't know any of the story at that time. Even now, she was unsure of the details. The diamond had cut into two very beautiful stones, faceted into the newest, most dazzling cuts, and set into Platinum and eighteen karat Gold. Suzanne's was eleven carats of stunning perfection. Mallory's had come in at slightly over nine. The custom jeweler had nestled them into white velvet in discreet white leather ring boxes.

Pleased, Patrick had flown back to Arkansas to meet Mallory and Suzanne. Neither knew he had been gone. He had been excited. They had packed a picnic supper and headed up to the Narrows Dam to enjoy it at the picnic grounds up there. It was a beautiful place, and the meal had been fun. Patrick had cleaned up their site. Then, beaming proudly, he had pulled out the white leather box for his wife. He opened it proudly. The ring sparkled brilliantly in the late afternoon sunlight. Mallory had drawn closer, and gasped with amazement.

Suzanne, for some reason, reacted as she usually did. Something about the plain white leather box, without a jewelry store logo on it, led her to believe the ring wasn't real. Despite the beauty of the piece, she had made up her mind. There was no way she could even grasp how her husband might possibly, actually come up with anything valuable for her. Enraged, she had flung the box, with its priceless contents into the river.

Mallory had been so stunned that she had dashed toward the falls. Terrified, her father had actually been afraid she was going to try to retrieve it.

"Mallory! No! Leave it be, girl"

At first, Patrick had been stunned by his wife's reaction. That had been replaced by the real fear that Mallory had nearly fallen into the river. When Mallory had stopped short of the river bank, she had turned back, shaken, tears rolling down her face. Her mother had still been storming and raging around about how she was no fool, and she could tell the difference. And real diamond ring boxes were always from real stores!

They had driven home in silence. The finished work of art had appraised for a figure which had astounded Patrick. Even so, he was already figuring maybe it was for the best that it had gone in the river. He wondered what had been wrong with him in the first place, to have gotten one of them cut. But, he had been wounded-again.

The next day, he had taken Mallory to Sonic. While she was devouring her hamburger, he had handed another little white box to her. She had opened it and gasped with wonder. She didn't know if it was real. She didn't know if the rocks she had found were diamonds. She had thought they might be; she didn't ask. It didn't matter. It was a present from Daddy. When she had given him a hug and kiss and slipped the ring onto her slender finger, Patrick knew he had made a mistake.

Suzanne had thrown away the ring; deciding for herself it wasn't worthwhile. She made that erroneous assumption because she had already decided her husband wasn't ever going to be successful. All his Christianity was making him too nice, too honest, too whatever. She was envious of Ryland and his wife and their two sons for what she perceived was surely a better life. As was so often the case, she couldn't have been more wrong.

Mallory had been lost in her reverie of the past incident. The Sonic was busy, for as miserable as the weather was, so it had taken them a while to get the food out. She took the food, making sure she gave a good tip as she paid. She always tried to, but this was one of her school friends. She opened Dinky's burger, starting to order him not to make a mess with it. He swallowed it in a bite, not leaving a crumb. He watched eagerly as she bit into hers.

A long, sleek, silver car pulled into the space beside her.

Chapter 16

DELIA

DELIA O'SHAUGHNESSY, AND her grandson, Shay, had traveled first class on Wednesday morning from Boston to Little Rock, where one of her cars had already been shipped ahead to meet them. Her driver had pulled up at the arrival gate just as all of their luggage had arrived at baggage claim. Some of her other employees had already gone ahead to a lodge where her secretary had finally managed to reserve some cabins. The word, "cabin" had thrown Delia into somewhat of a dither. Shay had tried to calm her down by telling her Arkansas might even be fun. Now, as they had left Little Rock behind, heading west on Interstate 30, she was only hoping that it would at least be tolerable. She gazed out the window at the miserable drizzle.

"Grandmother, you haven't eaten any of your lunch," Shay had startled her.

She looked at the foil wrapped sandwich on her tray; she would hardly define it as "lunch" she had thought to herself.

Delia O'Shaughnessy always told people who regarded her beautiful cars and elegant lifestyle, that she wasn't rich. Shay always laughed. "I'm not rich," she would always affirm. "Just comfortable."

Delia O'Shaughnessy had taken "being comfortable" to a whole new level. She had made it into both an art and a science. Every morning her staff would make her bed up with freshly laundered and ironed fine

Irish linen sheets. Her Boston mansion was sumptuous and refined. Her breakfast was always served exactly on time on impeccable china and attention paid to every detail. She would then bathe and dress elegantly, working from her boudoir office, checking into every detail of the company business. In the early afternoon, she would sometimes shop or get her hair or nails fixed at a luxury salon. Tea was served promptly at three thirty. Sometimes her grandson would join her. Lately, though, she would sometimes break the tea tradition and join him at a coffee shop, having a latte. When she did that, she would invariably stop by the church to pray for her deceased son.

Patrick's death had hit his mother hard. In trying to inflict punishment upon him, she had come to realize she had hurt herself far more. His early death had been such a total shock. She had refused to attend his funeral. He had wanted it held in that horrid little church that that horrid little girl had talked him into embracing. An elegant linen handkerchief caught more tears. She straightened her back resolutely, forcing herself to stop sniffling.

Her attorneys had been at work, and her plan was to return from this wretched place after the will was read, with her son's body in her possession. She hoped there wouldn't be too much of a scene; she hated scenes! But she had to give her son a proper burial, with a priest and a mass. She remembered Suzanne, and wearily concluded that a row was going to be inevitable. She was still hoping the attorneys could reach an agreeable settlement.

She turned her attention to her grandson. He had grown tall and handsome. He was within a month of being seventeen. Her heart swelled with pride in him. He seemed older than his years; that was because he had endured a great deal. Ryland and Miranda had finally split up. Shannon, the oldest of Delia's three grandchildren had already hardened into a vicious copy of his father. At the split, though, Shay had asked to go with his mother. That had enraged Ryland, of course, and his ex-wife had perished in an automobile "accident" within six months. Of course, that had even been too much for Shannon, too, until Ryland finally convinced his son he had had nothing to do with it.

Shay had begged his grandmother to allow him to live with her so he could help her with the growing business responsibility. He had been a quick study. Even now, he was completing his high school, while working on several college courses. She had feared her son's wrath would be visited upon them. So far, it hadn't. Maybe he still had some regard for his mother; but she wasn't counting on it.

"Here, Shay, eat my sandwich." She was offering it to him.

He unwrapped it part-way, then acted like it was an airplane as he zoomed it at his grandmother's mouth. "Open the hangar," he coaxed.

It worked. laughing at his funny antics, she had tried a bite. Allowing it to grow cold hadn't helped it any. She cut it in two, agreeing to eat half. He finished it hungrily.

She turned his laptop to see what he was working on. He had been really busy, working to acquire an operation in Ireland that produced quality wool. She had been amazed; if it went according to the projections, they might actually get rich. It was such a natural acquisition, she didn't know why she had never thought of it. She had been obsessed with linen, which had offered some handsome reward. But the wool was brilliant, she had to admit.

At Malvern, the car exited onto 84, which would take them to Kirby, near their lodge. The advanced staff had already arrived, getting the clean, neat beds changed with Delia's personal linen. They told Shay it wasn't too bad. The cabins were actually doublewides with log exteriors. They had full kitchens and baths, central air and heat, washers and dryers. They even had hot tubs. That was at least some relief. That was the closest accommodation they could find. Seemed like there was an FBI convention, or something. They would have to drive several miles south on 27 to reach Murfreesboro.

Delia leaned back on a small neck pillow which was encased in monogrammed linen. Patrick checked the headline news on his laptop. He had been following the stories surrounding his cute country cousin. He had seen some of it during the previous couple of days. He had hardly been able to believe it. The reason his father was leaving him alone right now was because he was obviously involved in his sinister business elsewhere. Shay was pretty sure his grandmother wasn't aware of these newest developments. She tried to glance at the newspaper each morning, but she didn't allow herself time to just watch TV or follow much on-line "drivel".

Shay Patrick had spent the rest of the road trip working on some course material, then had answered a couple of e-mails about the upcoming acquisition. He was excited; he was glad his grandmother was pleased. He hoped her "corpse" fight wouldn't cause her too much distress. They pulled up in front of the "cabins'.

She had surveyed the cabins quietly, glancing about her without too much disgust. She had instructed how and where she wished her bags unpacked. The scenery was really very nice; the lodge was on a lake.

Paying scarcely any attention to the surroundings, she was eager to move on. She wanted to go straight to Murfreesboro; Shay wasn't sure about it. "I don't think there's much to do there," he had tried to explain to her.

"Doesn't look like there's anything to do here!" she had retorted. So off they had gone. Delia had longed to come to this little tiny place in nowhere since the moment Patrick had chosen it for his home. She had missed her son, and his livewire little daughter! She couldn't say she had missed Suzanne. Looking back, though, she had to admit to herself that maybe she had cut out the wrong side of her family. She had been furious, well more just terrified about their souls, when they had left the Church. At least, they had ended up being better people. She knew more about the headlines than she had cared to discuss, and she felt sick about her older son and his actions.

As they neared the town, Delia had gazed eagerly through the wet car windows to try to take in all of the places where her son might have been. There wasn't too much to see; just a typical small town, USA. Delia instructed her driver to turn southeast onto 301. Just a couple of miles out of town, they drove past the entrance to the diamond mine. It was an Arkansas State Park, and it was fixed up attractively. Delia liked diamonds; her hands always sparkled with them. She thought they always spoke volumes when she talked with her small, expressive hands.

The cold rain, and the lateness of the afternoon were neither one conducive to diamond hunting, so there were few cars there.

"Ready to get a shovel, and go after it?" her grandson teased. He was still never sure exactly how much to tease. She was every inch a proper Boston lady, and he always tried to show her more respect than familiarity. He adored her and felt very protective of her.

He hadn't been able to help his mother. He should have, would have gone with his dad, if he had had any idea. The horror still haunted him; his mother's funeral. That was why he already felt a kinship with Mallory. They didn't remember one another from the early Boston days, but he was sorry for her losing her dad. He felt like he would have enjoyed knowing his uncle.

Now his grandmother had been answering him about the shovel. She had no intentions of lifting a shovel; that was one of the things he was along for.

They drove back into town, where they pulled in at the Sonic.

Chapter 17

DETAINEE

SUZANNE HAD RACED away angrily from the Sander's Corporation headquarters on Monday morning. She was so dazed, she could hardly think. For several years, Roger had continued to send a Christmas card to the O'Shaughnessy's. But, then, his empire had expanded so, that their name had been dropped from the list, as many other names were added. Word had reached Roger, about Patrick's death, and he had been saddened. He had intended to attend the funeral. He felt he owed a great debt to the man for his present happy and prosperous life. An ice storm had made that plan seem unwise. Since he had been so short-handed in the secretarial area, he wasn't really sure that flowers had ever been sent. Every day, he had felt like he should check on Suzanne and Mallory, but there was always so much going on

He had tried to fill quite a few positions in the Executive Offices. For one reason, or another, if they were any good, they didn't stay. If they were bad, he still had them, or had been forced to fire them.

He had been in Hawaii when Suzanne had showed up to ask for a job. He had left the main reception desk in the capable hands of his daughter while he and Beth had taken a one week Island vacation. His daughter, Constance, was expecting a baby; it would be the first grandchild. She had agreed to keep everything together in the offices so her parents could go. She had recognized Suzanne, or thought she had; but the woman hadn't seemed to recognize her at all. Rather than running after the strange-acting lady, she had called her dad as he was taking a golf swing. He gave his daughter instructions to call Suzanne and ask her to come back in; then, since they had reached the turn, he dialed the number himself. He was concerned to hear the recording about the phone's being out of service. If he could get Suzanne back, he wanted her. The problems she had caused were extremely minor compared with what he had dealt with since. At least, he knew Suzanne, knew what he would be getting. He knew her weaknesses; but she had a lot of strengths! Sander's Corporation needed what she could bring to the table!

He had instructed his daughter not to let her get away again.

"Gladly," she had responded. "I don't want this job anyway."

Suzanne had gone to the mall. Everything made her more miserable. There was a pay phone, and she wanted to call Mallory to make sure she was ok. But she couldn't stop crying. She cried harder thinking about the phone's being disconnected anyway. The food in the food court smelled good, but she had almost no money left. All of the things for sale in the mall seemed to taunt her, that they were out of her grasp. She didn't have enough gas to get back home. So, she had walked until mall security had begun to eye her suspiciously. Then she had gone to the park, trying to enjoy the nice weather and the flowers.

But she was angry. She was angry at Patrick, angry at Roger Sanders, angry at Mallory, the Andersons, the rest of the church people- oh- and Daniel and Diana Faulkner, too. She was mostly mad at God. She hadn't said that again since the previous night's lightning strikes, but with the seeming safety of the light breeze and the sunny, blue sky, she was saying it again.

When darkness brought a chill to the air, she found a grocery store, used the restroom, bought snacks that she hoped would be the most satisfying with the rest of the money, and found another residential street where she would try to sleep in the cramped quarters of the car.

Someone crazy nearly hit her parked car as it careened wildly down the narrow street. It was a light metallic blue Lincoln Town Car with tinted windows. It had Oklahoma plates. It really had been a close call; she just had no idea how close!

Wrapped in blankets, including Mallie's Pooh Bear stuff, she had actually slept fairly well. She still awakened with a headache. There was no change at all left for a cup of coffee. She munched hungrily on some store-brand cookies. She had no idea that Mallory, in her brand new little car, had come within a block of her.

Tuesday morning was bright and beautiful, but the wind was cold. Rather than calling attention to herself at the mall, she had gone to the public library. Some homeless people seemed to have thought of the same thing, but Suzanne was too tired to cry any more. Eventually, she had followed some of them for a block or two. She had actually hoped they were heading for a soup line. She went back to the library where her car was, and napped in it for about an hour.

Finally, she had made a decision.

When she had planned to leave Murfreesboro on Sunday morning, she had dropped Mallory off for Sunday School. Then, she had returned to the house. That was when she had grabbed Mallory's blankets, her baby-sitting money, a cute sweater set she had gotten for Christmas, and Mallory's little jewelry box. She had prayed for a miracle, truly she had. She didn't know exactly what she had expected. Maybe for someone to invite them over for Sunday dinner; maybe something placed in the offering plate for them, maybe a voice from God. The thing that had made her the maddest was that Faulkner family! How could they have so much, and not care anything at all about people going without? Everything about them had been an affront to Suzanne and what she imagined being a Christian should be about.

Now, by late Tuesday afternoon, her desperation had only grown deeper.

Mallory had just left her hotel room to return to the mall for more shopping. She didn't see her mom pull in to the Western Arkansas Pawn Shop.

Suzanne was aware that she didn't look good. She had brought her cosmetics and changes of clothes with her, but she felt hopelessly old, and fat, and bedraggled, as she entered the store.

The proprietor, Herb Carlton, advanced toward her. "How may I help you, ma'am?" he had asked. Courteous but professional had been her assessment of him.

He was studying her with equal curiosity. Kind of cute, but red eyes from crying a lot. She looked tired, and he felt sorry for her.

She had placed the box on the counter, pulling out a few little pieces that were cute, but not worth a lot as far as borrowing went.

"Can you give me anything at all for any of this?" she had questioned, eagerly, but with no real hope.

The last item out of the box had rolled across the counter and dropped at his feet. Speechless, he had bent to pick it up. Trying to don his best poker face, he was studying the ring intently. He couldn't keep his hands from trembling. It was the most gorgeous thing he had ever seen in his life. He was trying to remain calm outwardly, but his mind was racing. Did this woman not know what she had? Evidently, she didn't, or she wouldn't be here with it, saying "Can you please possibly give me anything for this?"

Still trying to appear calm, he had just casually asked her for her name.

Suddenly embarrassed, she had asked him why he needed it.

He didn't know what to do. He didn't have cash to begin to touch the ring; he wished he did. It was dazzling beyond his imagination. He had wondered idly if it were a "Conflict Diamond" from the forbidden diamond-producing areas of Africa. It wouldn't matter to most buyers; he was certain of that. It was odd that the lady didn't want to give her name. She didn't seem like the criminal type, or a druggie. He dealt with all types, but this lady with her six figure ring was just totally out of context.

His gaze returned to the mesmerizing jewel in his hand, even to have touched it- Its beauty took his breath away! He rotated it to catch and fracture the light rays.

Suzanne had been searching his carefully neutral expression anxiously. She was hoping for at least ten or twenty dollars. She knew Mallory wouldn't mind. She was sentimental about the stuff, of course; she was sentimental about everything about her dad. But she could get over it.

Her eyes had dropped from his face to the ring he continued to study.

"I'm pretty sure that's a fake," she confided. "What about some of the other stuff? Some of it's fourteen carat gold, and-"

"So, are you in a divorce, or something?" he had asked? Why do you think this is fake?"

At some point, she had told him the jewelry wasn't really hers; it was her daughters. That had set the alarms off in his mind.

Herb had been in the jewelry/pawn business for forty years. He knew gemstones and artificial. Without his diamond tester, he would have staked a lot on the fact that the diamond was real. His hands were still shaking when he placed the tester against it, and then his loupe confirmed the fact that the setting was Platinum and eighteen carat Gold.

"Ma'am, I might be interested in some of it." He handed her a tablet of forms, and asked her to fill one out.

She didn't want to, but he told her she would have to, that the law required it. Another customer had entered the store. Before Herb had placed the beautiful ring back into the box, the customer had caught a glimpse of it.

Suzanne had grasped her box back and exited the store. In her car, she had begun fuming angrily to herself about the "jerk" and his paperwork, and the law.

Herb Carlton called the police. He hated to have them show up; they didn't help him much with some of his clientele. But he thought they should know about the fabulous diamond, and the fact that someone was trying to fence it who wasn't the rightful owner.

The customer who had entered the store, had left almost immediately on Suzanne's heels. He startled her when he tapped on her car window. She locked the car door, but lowered her window a crack.

""Scuse me, miss" he had started. "I saw you havin' some trouble in there wit yer stuff. You needin' t' raise a little cash, I know a guy. Follow me. Believe me' there's people out here that are a lot more understandin when yer havin it tough."

"Where do I have to follow you to?" she cut into his speech. "I don't have much gas."

Not believing his luck, he had pulled away in his car, with the desperate woman following close behind.

Since the fiasco of the previous evening with the Hope police department's not following up about the incident with Adams, the FBI had begun routing all calls through their office. Bransom had returned to, Hope, and was sitting in the FBI office when the call came in from the pawn shop. The concerned owner said he was afraid the woman was handling stolen jewelry, but then that she didn't seem criminal as much as naïve. He was worried that a man had followed her from his store. He knew he was speaking to the Hope police dispatcher; he didn't know the feds were listening. He had restated, in a near panic.

"That diamond was worth killing for."

Bransom was already giving orders for all law enforcement officers anywhere in the area to be on the lookout for Suzanne's car, and that of the character she was following. He was racing to his own agency vehicle.

"No diamond is worth killing for!" he had raged to himself!

The pawn shop owner's supposition had been that they would head onto the freeway immediately. That probably would have been the plan, but Suzanne's car had run out of gas almost immediately. By the time the guy realized she wasn't behind him, he had to circle back a couple of blocks. He came back and told her to just get in his car. She was telling him that she wouldn't; that he needed to go get her some gas, or go get his nice friend who was so understanding and bring him back.

Bransom and four black and whites descended upon the two while they argued. The man had snarled in rage, but he knew he was caught.

He was taken into custody without further incident.

Bransom cuffed Suzanne, himself. "You're under arrest for attempting to fence stolen goods!" he had charged her. "You get a 'D' for 'Dumb'," he had whispered in her ear.

"Read her her rights," he had ordered one of the police officers.

She was booked in, after which, she received a pleasant meal. She was alone in the cell. If she was still mad at God, she didn't say so.

She had spent the night in shock. She had never expected to find herself in jail. She hadn't used her phone call. She figured Mallory would not have been able to get the phones back up. She didn't know who else to call.

A state appointed defense attorney had showed up at eight: thirty on Wednesday morning; her arraignment was scheduled for ten. His advice was for her to plead guilty to the charge, and he would request leniency in sentencing.

"But I didn't do what they said," she had tried to argue. "I came on a trip looking for work. I brought my own stuff from my own house. My husband is deceased, and I pretty well think what little he left me is mine," she had stormed.

The defense attorney was aggravated. If people knew so much, how did they end up in jail without means of even hiring an attorney? Everybody he advised always thought they knew so much more than he did. He tried to make his response sound more patient than he felt.

"Well, your late husband's will actually may sort all that out on Friday. You told a Herb Carlton, the owner of the Western Arkansas Pawn Shop, that the jewelry in question, actually belongs to your seventeen year old daughter, Mallory Erin O'Shaughnessy. Your daughter is also heiress to part of Patrick Shay O'Shaughnessy estate. If these items were presented to her as gifts throughout her lifetime, they are hers, according to the law, even if they were purchased by you. Did she give you permission to remove them from the home?"

"Well, not exactly, but she wouldn't have minded. I really just brought it along so I could wear it to a job interview."

That was the truth, but the situation had grown beyond her control.

The attorney was about to reaffirm his position for her to plead guilty, when three new visitors had been buzzed in. He knew the men, and he greeted them with handshakes and back-slapping before he made his exit.

Roger and Beth Sanders had returned from Hawaii, tanned, but not relaxed. Roger had gone to work to try to get hold of Suzanne. He had gone on line, just in time to see her mug shot get posted. He had immediately been in touch with his corporate attorneys, and of course, they knew the best defense attorney in Western Arkansas. Trey Johansen was his name, and Roger had liked him immediately. He paid the hefty retainer without flinching, and the guy was in Suzanne's court-literally.

"The whole thing may get thrown out, anyway," he confided to them. "If it does, I may give you back some of your money. Seems like the evidence managed to disappear."

"What, you mean that big O'Shaughnessy diamond?" Roger had let out a long whistle of disbelief.

Suzanne didn't think she could ever remember being so humiliated as she had been to have Roger come bail her out with his high-priced attorney friends and his checkbook.

But she was glad; it was the miracle she had prayed all night for. She had made some promises to the Lord, and now, she intended to keep them.

She was still feeling dazed when Beth and Constance had met her outside the courtroom. The arraignment hadn't taken long, now she was free to go as far as Pike county. Roger had scolded her for assuming he might not need her. He told her he wanted her to come in on Monday, and they would get "the ball rolling" to get her rehired.

"Of course," he teased her, "after Patrick's will is read on Friday, you may not need a job! Maybe I should get you to sign a twenty year contract today!"

He had just purchased a shiny new SUV to make room for car seats and the grandbaby. He sent the three women off to the mall in it. Roger and his attorney returned to work.

Beth and Constance said they had been dispatched to take Suzanne shopping, and they were relishing the project. Then, they told her, the plan was to meet at the country club for lunch. After lunch, they were planning to all take Suzanne home to Murfreesboro.

Between the three of them, they managed some serious shopping in just an hour and a half. Most of it was what Suzanne had gazed at so longingly just two days before. Everything had seemed so hopeless. She still kept pinching herself; nothing could really turn around like this, could it?

The country club lunch was a dream come true for Suzanne. It featured a very attractive buffet, and some menu items were also available.

She had hated to seem ignorant, but no one had notified her about the will. Perplexed, Roger had told her what he knew. Actually, Sheriff Melville was to have notified her and Mallory. With his having been arrested, he hadn't accomplished the task.

Suzanne didn't know he had been arrested. She didn't know anything. Roger and Beth, in Hawaii, hadn't paid as much attention to the news as they normally would have. Constance had breathlessly filled them in on the excitement that had been in the news during the past few days. It spilled out in something of a jumble.

"A hired killer had tried to shoot the pastor's daughter in the O'Shaughnessy's yard. Sheriff Melville had hired the killer and a high school kid. The high school kid had the Murfreesboro high school blueprints, and had been planning to plant some bombs, so the high school principal was being fired. And there were all kinds of agents from everywhere all over the place."

Roger and Brent, Constance's husband, had listened to the rambling story with some degree of skepticism.

"You sure you got all that straight, Baby?" Brent had teased his wife. He hadn't paid too much attention to the continuing coverage, but he was pretty sure his wife's condensed version had probably gotten the facts pretty mixed up.

Suzanne was wearing one of her new outfits; it had seemed so far out of her reach. Now, she was sitting with the Sanders, eating lunch at a country club. She had tried to be low key, watching what they were doing so she would be correct. She was trying to forget that they had just bailed her out of jail.

The chattering group left the country club, loading into the SUV. Brent Watson was driving, with Connie riding in the front seat beside him. Beth and Suzanne had climbed into the back.

"You two want to watch a movie?" Brent had teased them

Beth laughed. "No, we have some catching up to do; guess we'll just visit."

Roger was following them in the sporty ivory Jaguar he had been driving for the past two years. He didn't own it; his corporation did His corporation owned everything! That saved him a lot on his income tax! He was planning to leave the Jaguar with Suzanne in Murfreesboro. One of her job perks was going to be the sporty, company car.

Roger laughed. He and Beth had both doted over their daughter's 3D sonogram. He had his grandpa car now; he couldn't believe the joy the Lord had given them about this next phase of life.

The convoy pulled into the Christian school where the two youngest Sanders children were enrolled. Emma aged fifteen, and Evan, aged eleven bounded out of the building ahead of their mother who had gone in to get them released about an hour early. They loaded nimbly into the third row of the massive SUV, and immediately started trying to con their big sister into starting a movie. Beth got back in, and the movie idea vanished before the better idea of doing homework.

"Moms are so mean," she had laughed to Suzanne. Suzanne laughed, too. She greeted Emma and Evan, and they had responded as politely as they could manage, considering they were bummed out about no movie.

"Watch out, or there won't be a movie on the way home, either," Beth had warned them. She didn't like getting "attitude" from them.

"Where's Catrina, now?" Suzanne had asked. She had hated to say she didn't even remember that Constance had gotten married.

"College," Beth had answered proudly. She filled Suzanne in briefly about the four children, ending by apologizing for not having invited them to Connie's wedding.

She had explained that they got so many shower and wedding and graduation announcements from people they had hardly ever known, from years before. "We didn't want to be that way," she had finished with a laugh.

Suzanne had suddenly remembered about her car. She didn't have any idea where it might be. The last she had seen it was where it had run out of gas right near the pawn shop. Maybe she could get Janet Walters to take her back to Hope in time for her upcoming appointment with Roger on Monday. She tried to put the problem out of her mind. Suzanne's thoughts had returned to the guys who had arrested her. She was real mad at the one that told her she "got a 'D' for Dumb"! She thought it was bad enough they arrested you without getting insulting, too.

Beth had gotten busy, trying to look over her shoulder to help with homework. Evan had gotten kind of upset about missing his friends and his Awana at his church. He hadn't known the plan was for attending a different church. Emma was a really cute fifteen year old, and she wanted to check out some of the boys in a different town.

The weather was miserable, and they had all been hoping the mess wouldn't freeze into a sheet of ice before they could complete their trip Amazingly, the temperature had continued to hover above freezing. The wind chill and damp made it feel much colder.

They arrived in Murfreesboro too early for church. They had planned to have dinner after church at Hal's restaurant at the lodge. But since a snack sounded good, and there was time to kill, they had all pulled in at the Sonic.

Chapter 18

DECISIONS

JOHN ANDERSON GAZED out the window from his cramped office in the church building. He had an office in the parsonage, and one here. Combined, they weren't twenty square feet. He had been working on his Wednesday night Bible study message. He enjoyed studying; he loved reading his Bible and serving the Lord. The weather had turned back to definitely miserable. He thought about his hard work getting ready for the service. He was pretty sure the threat of ice would keep everyone away. He leaned back in his desk chair and closed his eyes. The lump was still in his throat when he thought about Merrill Adams, now lying in the county morgue, who had nearly ended Tammi's life. He felt like he should hold a funeral for the guy, but he didn't want to. He felt like he should go to Little Rock and visit Martin Thomas and Oscar Melville in jail.

David had dropped by his office; the father had wanted to grab onto his son and never turn him loose. David had been in danger from all of the recent events, too. Had deliberately placed himself into harm's way. He had been pretty scared early the previous morning when he had seen Adams show up at the O'Shaughnessy home to case the joint.

David had just come to visit with his father about wanting to clear Mallory's name from all Melville's implications. This had been the first time his son had ever actually confided to him about being so in love with Mallory. David's eyes had shone the way they had when he had been a little boy. It didn't seem that long ago! How could his son be so grown? But then not really? He had been excitedly going on and on about how he could be what he needed to be, if he had Mallory by his side. He had it all worked out, how he was going to live his life for her. He had thought he was doing a good sales job on his dad.

Sadly, John had finally broken into the fevered stream of words. "Maybe Mallory could do all of that; but why should she have to?"

"What?" David had been surprised.

Leaning toward his son, while silently praying for wisdom, John Anderson spoke from his heart.

"If you love her as much as you are telling me you do, and I believe you really believe you do, why do you think that it would be her responsibility to be the strong one? Why should she have to help you be good, do right? Isn't that why you just told me you need her? She's strong! She has a strong personality, and she has strong faith. Maybe she could help you, but she deserves better than some spiritual cripple who needs her. What about what she needs? When you can come in here and tell me you need the Lord, that He can help you, and prop you up, and make you what you need to be; when you love Him and can't live without Him, then maybe I could recommend you to Mallory O'Shaughnessy! Right now, I can't! You're both way too young for this anyway!"

David had sat there stunned. John had started to go on, but his son had held up his hand.

"That's enough, Dad!" He had risen to his feet and stridden out. His father's words had stung him. He thought parents were supposed to think their kids were too good for anybody; not the other way around. He jogged from the little church building, past his car, and out to the road. The drizzling rain mixed with his tears, rolling down onto his t-shirt that peeked from under his battered leather jacket. He ran harder, his feet were pounding along the pavement. His every foot fall pounded out, "He's right; he's right; he's right; he's right; he's right!"

Disregarding the mud, he ducked beneath a fence, and sloshed through a pasture. The cows all ignored the sobbing boy. He dashed through a little wooded area, coming out by a shack that was so nasty, it made Mallory's little tumble-down house look like luxury living. Pigs were rooting around in the yard; there were a couple of spindly, underfed dogs that whined weakly as he jogged past them. He was starting to barge in through the battered door. He suddenly paused! He had heard that Martin Thomas had made kind of a stalker-type shrine of Mallory. That he had pictures of her plastered all over his wall! His intention had been to rip it all down. Now, he just backed away. He had been trying so hard to help Mallory, and he had been going about it entirely wrong.

Leaving the property, he cut back around another way. He had come out at Mallory's. There were a lot of people milling around; a bunch of the big cars in various dark colors. Mallory's car was there. As he stood there watching, she had come out with her Bible, and driven away. She had an immense dog with her. She had been wearing a new outfit, and she really looked extra cute. "Had on a lot of lipstick, though," he had thought disapprovingly. He was thinking he would have to tease her about it.

He ran up the opposite direction from the one Mallory had taken and cut back through town to the church. There were a couple of other cars there. It was too early for church. One of them looked like one of the FBI cars, and the other one belonged to Tom Haynes. The young man drove quietly away. He was hungry, out of gas, and he had caught a cold. He coughed and spit the junk out the window. He was wondering what those two cars were doing at the church. The news had said his dad and the church were under investigation. He had laughed when he heard it; gossip was always so crazy. But Mr. Haynes was the chairman of the board of deacons; maybe some disgruntled member had tried to cause trouble. If anyone was stealing money, it wouldn't be his dad; he knew that. Well, for one thing, there really wasn't any to steal! But if there was, his dad would never-, and neither would Mr. Haynes. They certainly didn't get along well enough to be partners in crime, or in anything else-! He shrugged. He was planning to be in church tonight. If there were a problem, his dad would address it to the congregation. He planned to be in church from now on. "And not just because of Mallory," he had told the Lord. He was truly sorry for his behavior of the past year. He had come to another pathway, and he was determined never to take the wrong way again. He had made a decision. He asked the Lord for His help in sticking with it.

⁂

When his son had left, John Anderson had watched his heart walk away. Lana always said he should listen more and lecture less. She would be upset with him again. They had disagreed about David and how to handle his rebellion during the last year, more than they had disagreed about anything in the twenty-two years they had known each other. They had met in Bible College, had known they were perfect for one another, had waited three years to get married. Nothing had tested their love and commitment to one another like this had. He wanted to beg the Lord to let the trial end; but as he did so, he knew he sounded like King David had, when he hadn't wanted any harm to come to his son and heir, Absalom.

There was an awkward knock at the door frame of his office. It was the FBI guy. John was trying to remember his name. "How's it goin', Branson?" he had made a guess.

"Bransom, 'm' on the end, the man had corrected. Call me Erik. You got a few minutes?"

"I guess so," the pastor had agreed. "I kind of thought I had explained everything to all the other guys. Is this about money again?"

"Not at all." the agent had paused awkwardly. Now that he was sitting here, he didn't even know why he had come.

Anderson suddenly suspected it had something to do with a spiritual need. "Would you drink a cup of coffee if I brew a pot? It's so cold out I feel chilled to the bone. A little jolt of caffeine will perk me up before the service." He was already on his feet, getting the brew started.

Bransom watched him. He was relieved for the break in the conversation. He almost wished he hadn't stopped. And he had too much going on with the ongoing investigations to sit around sipping coffee and yacking about his emotional stuff. The nagging in his heart wouldn't go away. He had tried alcohol and a lot of stuff. Now, the problems were compounded by that; he felt like he couldn't go on. He worked so hard to try to clean up the world, but no matter how desperately he mopped at the mess, it just continued to grow. Kind of deal with one mess, and there was something even uglier, more disgusting coming at him. He felt like he was alone, fighting a losing battle against evil, unspeakable evil. He knew other agents regarded "Born-again Christians" as another problem, another group of crazies to be surveiled and guarded against. Bransom's short time in the little town, and his brief exposure to this pastor had made him feel like he did have an ally in the fight. Pastors like this guy were doing more good in America than all the other agencies and police departments put together. If people didn't have something inside of them, helping them do right, there couldn't be enough law enforcement to prevent total anarchy. Anarchy! He had been afraid to say it. Now he felt like America was tottering on the edge, and she was going to sweep him and his futile efforts into the abyss, as she sank in deeper Herself.

Instead of returning to his desk and pushing the agent, John had watched the pot brew. His heart had left with his son, and he felt too drained to help anyone else. "Please, help me, Lord," he had breathed. And He always did.

"Black?" he guessed. Bransom had nodded; feeling like he was going to start to cry. Anderson set a steaming mug in front of him, then sank back into his chair, taking a sip of the hot beverage. It tasted good.

The agent across the desk had done the same. Anderson watched sympathetically while the other man struggled to get himself under control. He guessed the feds must still have him intimidated. Usually he began every session he held with a word of prayer.

"I'll start with a word of prayer" he informed the guy.

"Dear Lord, we need your help today. I don't know what Erik has on his mind; I don't know what's happening in his life. But You do, Lord. You know everything about him. He needs a touch from You, today. He has a hard job. I don't know how he sees what he sees and keeps going, Lord. We need him, Lord, in our battle; and other good men like him. I'm asking You to help us both, give us the strength we need for the fight. Give us the victory, please, In Jesus Name, and we'll give Him all the glory. Amen."

With the prayer ended, Erik Bransom only continued to weep harder, sobbing and shaking with anguish. Anderson watched him quietly. He had never seen any man cry so hard. He envied the man. Maybe if he had had tears like that for David, maybe he could have moved God's heart more. He was sure the entire rebellion had been his fault. He hadn't been there for his son; while he worked to patch up other families, his own had been falling apart. His own tears had begun to flow; tears that had refused to come until now. His own voice rose in a moan. The sobs racked his body. He felt like he was more out of control than the other man.

Tom Haynes was beating on the door frame.

"Am I interrupting something?" he demanded. "I could hear you guys clear out at the road; with my car windows rolled up, and the music blasting. If you guys are starting a new choir, you sound just awful! I thought I had stumbled into a cat-drowning, or something." He jabbed his outstretched hand to the agent, "Tom Haynes," he introduced himself. He had met Bransom at the high school the previous morning, but he re-introduced himself.

Haynes had come by for a little counsel from his Pastor, too. The Arkansas State School Board, and the Murfreesboro Police, the DEA, and the ABI had all taken turns grilling him about how he had been handling his position as principal of the high school. He was pretty sure he was going to lose his job. One woman had even gone so far as to say she was planning to do everything in her power to make sure he never got a job in Public Education again. He had always thought he was doing a pretty good job.

Both men had stopped crying, even laughing at Haynes's funny entrance.

"Can I cry with you guys"" he asked. Before they could say yes, he already was.

For nearly an hour, the three men wept; each one broken with his own load. Part of the time, one would try to console one of the others. Then each would be immersed in his own personal grief, once more.

John Anderson finally rose to his feet. He unrolled some toilet paper that was in his desk drawer, drying his eyes. He blew his nose loudly. That struck Haynes funny, so then, he was laughing and crying at the same time. He was really on the verge of hysterics, and John was immediately concerned.

"Breathe, Tom!" he ordered.

"Lord, help us get control of ourselves," he had breathed softly.

Tom Haynes had reached for the TP and was drying his eyes. He turned to the agent; he couldn't see him very well, and he figured all of his crying must have washed his contact lenses out.

"Are you a Christian?" he asked Erik.

On the spot, Bransom had started to stammer.

"It's real easy," Haynes had offered. "Pastor will lead you in a prayer, and you just repeat it after him. Pastor-"

Not knowing exactly how to better handle the situation, the pastor had led out in the sinner's prayer.

Bransom, at an equal loss, repeated the words obediently. When he had repeated the 'amen', his spirit had taken wing. He rose to his feet, knowing in his heart that the salvation transaction had been complete. He felt energized to retackle the world of crime.

Shay and Delia had ordered food at the Sonic. Shay had recommended the foot-long chili cheese coney with tater tots and a shake. His grandmother and her driver had both ordered the same. Shay had been amazed at that; then they had both eaten the greasy, unhealthy stuff with quite a bit of gusto. They hadn't even complained about anything's not being Bostonish, for at least the past hour. He was pretty sure that wouldn't last.

Delia had been watching her surroundings with both interest and amusement. She noticed every car that drove around, teen-agers, honking at each other, families grabbing food on the run for someplace. A big new SUV had pulled in across from them; the driver was trying to get a whole load of people to decide, so he could try to get the big order straight. An ivory Jaguar had pulled in next to the SUV; the people seemed to know one another. Under the canopy, they could have their windows down without the rain spitting in at them. It was pretty cold, though. A cute-looking girl with a big dog beside her was in a car next to them. Usually people noticed the big silver classic Rolls-Royce, but she seemed to be miles away.

Delia was watching the little bustle of a little world, the world where her son had chosen to settle, where he had died. In her heart, she had felt like a Boston doctor, a Boston hospital, something from her world could have saved his life. She couldn't help smiling now, even in her grief. He had been really happy here. She thought of her other son. Patrick had lived longer here than he ever would have in Boston. Even as she took in the bustling, small-town drive-in, the parade of cars, she was on the alert- for anything that even hinted that Ryland was here, or Shannon.

⋄

Mallory had redialed the high school number. The recording was still saying to call back later for another recording-. She had punched the button to disconnect, frustrated. That meant she still better get the Geometry assignment finished. She offered the uneaten portion of her meal to Dinky.

She checked her watch; just time to go to the store for dog food and the bowls before the store closed and church started. She backed out.

"Follow that car," Delia spoke softly and the elegant car responded.

"Grandmother, is that Mallory?" Shay had questioned. "Maybe we should go back to the lodge for the night and let the attorneys handle everything

She smiled at him mischievously, "What makes you think that's your cousin? I thought you said you didn't remember her." Her phone vibrated. Frowning, she checked the caller ID. It was one of the private investigators she always kept busy. She answered. Her little hand grasped at Shay's coat sleeve; her fingers dug in.

"What happened?" she listened. Shay could hear the voice, but couldn't make out any words. "When?" The voice talked on. "You're sure? You're not mistaken? All right; call me back if there's anything more." The call disconnected; Delia O'Shaughnessy continued to sit quietly, gazing at the hypnotic windshield wipers, her grip on Shay's arm finally releasing slightly. The windshield wipers held her attention, or the little car they were following. The car pulled in at the little grocery.

"Not too close." Her driver applied the brakes.

While the girl entered the little grocery, Delia O'Shaughnessy had turned toward her grandson. "Shay," she spoke softly, "your father is dead." She heaved a big sigh for such a petite lady. They both sat silently, not knowing what to say. Shay felt like he should comfort his grandmother, she feeling that she should comfort him in the loss of his father. Both were aware that their own safety was now more certain than it had been. What could they say? A heavy silence filled the air. Finally, Mallory had reappeared from the store. She loaded the unwieldy bag of dog food into the trunk and sped away.

When the big car had once again pulled out behind her, she decided it wasn't a coincidence. She sped up and went straight to the church. She wasn't comforted that the car seemed to have out of state plates. In the rain and approaching darkness, she couldn't tell which state. She didn't want it to get close enough so she could tell. She was afraid that with the rain, not many people would be at church to help her. Not that she wanted anybody at church to be in any danger. She pulled into a parking space near the grass and let Dinky get out.

A handsome stranger had emerged from a brand new Porsche. She had noticed the car on the church parking lot. "Wow! I'm envious," she had laughed to herself. Now, she tried to watch without being too obvious. The man was walking toward Mallory rather than the building. Dinky growled threateningly and barked sharply.

"Be quiet." she told him.

"Excuse me, ma'am." Mallory looked around; she wasn't sure who he was talking to. She didn't know him. He was dressed very nicely, and he was carrying a Bible.

He drew a little closer, despite Dinky's now somewhat muted protests.

"Are you Miss Mallory O'Shaughnessy?" The dog was a concern to him but he needed a few words with the girl before the church service. The weather had slowed him down as he had made the drive from Dallas after an afternoon deposition.

The girl hadn't answered him, but he knew it was Mallory. She looked like her father, and Patrick had shown him her picture at least a hundred times.

"Mallory, my name's Kerry Larson. I am- was- your father's legal counselor. He retained me to represent his interests in various legal areas. I helped him draw up his will. He requested me to continue to represent his estate, you, and your mother, until such time as you require my service no further."

He paused. Mallory hadn't moved. Her gaze traveled to the car that had pulled to the side of the road, then back to the man standing in the parking lot. She ordered Dinky back into the car and got her Bible out.

"I'm on my way to church; can this wait?" she didn't want to be rude, but she felt like she couldn't handle what he had already said. He had drawn up a will. Had the whole world known her dad was dying but her? Just when she felt like her wounds were healing, there was more.

He had fallen into step next to her. She had looked around, the big silver car had pulled farther forward. A crowd was finally arriving for church; but still she wasn't recognizing the cars that should be arriving.

"Like I was informing you, I believe I am your legal counsel. Your father had wanted me to represent you in all of your legal affairs for at least five years after his demise. After the will is read on Friday and you hear his wishes expressed, I can go into more detail with you, about some of the plans that have been formulated. Your father tried really hard to make sure you would be protected. He passed away before everything was in place. He never guessed you would be in so much jeopardy. I mean, I guess he knew; none of us could fathom it!"

They had entered the church, and there was a crowd gathering, in spite of the weather threat. Some people passed Mallory and spoke. She responded. They looked familiar, but she couldn't really place them. The small membership that was gathering had noticed their local girl talking with the Porsche guy with the Texas plates. One who saw it, was the pastor's wife, Lana Anderson. She was immediately jealous for her son's sake. Determined to break up Mallory's earnest conversation, she had swooped over. Without acknowledging Kerry Larson, or apologizing for interrupting, she had grabbed Mallory by the arm and was pulling her away.

"Hey, Mallory," she had begun. "Do you mind playing for me? My head is killing me; I may have to slip out and go home. It's time to get the prelude going, please, help me out," she had wheedled. She scurried away before the girl could protest.

Mallory hadn't touched the piano since January, but she had made her way up to the instrument which was over to the side on the little platform. She had sat down; and her hands had automatically begun to float across the keyboard. It was out of tune; her ear picked that up every service. The church needed a new piano; it needed everything. She played beautifully, she was a natural, with a real feel- for both the instrument and the Christian music. She had begun the prelude with one of her favorite Fanny Crosby hymns, "Tell Me the Story of Jesus". The music was so powerful that the crowd had actually silenced ahead of time. People were finding their pews and getting settled.

Mallory was trying not to cry. The hymn was one of her daddy's favorites; and the attorney, and a will; she hadn't been expecting any of this. And Pastor had told her he would like for her to play an offertory again, whenever she was ready. Lana Anderson never turned the piano-playing over to anyone for anything. Now, suddenly, she couldn't make it, could Mallory, please...

She moved smoothly into another song, "I Am Resolved". She sat up straighter. It was seven o'clock. Preacher and the song leader of the night, Jack Fielder had come onto the platform. The prelude stopped, then pastor was opening the service. Tom Haynes had come up to the platform for opening prayer. During the prayer, Mallory had peeked around at the crowd. The little auditorium was packed. There was the regular Wednesday night crowd, then there were still a lot of government agents. She wondered if they were all Christians, or if they were protecting her, or if she was still some kind of a suspect they were watching. The Faulkner family was there, looking greater than ever. Then Mallory spotted her mother; and that was Roger Sanders and his family who had spoken earlier. Her mom was sitting with them; she must have gotten her job back. Kerry Larson, the attorney, was sitting across the aisle from the Faulkners.

Tom Haynes had said "amen" Usually he prayed longer.

Jack was trying to get everybody to sing; he always tried; they never did. Mallory didn't know whether to play louder or softer. Suddenly, she decided to modulate into a lower key. It helped; people seemed more comfortable not having to screech out so many high notes.

Out in the Rolls, Delia and Shay were involved in a little family spat. Delia wanted to follow the crowd into the little church building; her grandson thought they should go back to the lodge and go to bed.

Delia informed him she had never gone to bed that early, even when she was a child; and she was not a child now, to be told when it's bedtime. Everyone in this little town seemed to be here. She knew it was the Baptist church, but she had never heard of church on Wednesday nights. She thought it was just a town meeting; whatever was going on in this little town where her son had lived and her granddaughter had grown up, she suddenly wanted to be part of. Usually she and Shay hadn't argued. She had seen Kerry Larson introduce himself to her granddaughter; her snooping hadn't been limited strictly to her son in Boston. She knew her attorney would be dealing with him now, about Patrick's body. She thought about the news she had just received. If she could win the battle for Patrick's body, it looked like both of her sons would be getting a Catholic funeral

Someone else had driven up to the church, parking on the shoulder of the road directly in front of the Rolls. The little parking lot had overflowed.

It was David. He knew he was late, but there had been a wreck on the narrow road from Kirby. His dad didn't appreciate lateness, but David had promised God. He hopped from his car, noticing that people were getting out of the sleek Rolls Royce at the same time.

All three of them entered the little church together.

Pastor John Anderson was amazed at the sudden leap in attendance. All the newcomers looked really prosperous, too. Suzanne O'Shaughnessy and her employer and his family were all dressed up. The Faulkners; wow, they had been intimidating. Then the guy who had driven up in the Porsche, and finally the Rolls Royce people. The young guy was wearing a charcoal gray suit, with a deep forest green and white striped tie. His pocket handkerchief was monogrammed linen. He had on a gray herringbone topcoat. The lady with him was wearing gray, also. Her beautiful gray hair was styled attractively, despite, the precipitation. Her trim suit seemed stylishly custom-tailored. She had slid out of a silvery-gray fur coat, before gliding into a pew. They didn't carry Bibles.

Mallory, sitting at the piano, knew her jaw had dropped. David hadn't come on a Wednesday night in over a year. That had to be her Grandmother O'Shaughnessy and one or the other of her two cousins. She couldn't imagine why they would be in Murfreesboro, and she really couldn't believe they were here in church. She decided she must not have much faith; they had certainly prayed for other members of the family to get saved. There was the rest of the song service, announcements, another prayer, and she played an offertory. She played "Face to Face," her slender fingers moving confidently and caressingly across the keys. Tears streamed down her cheeks as she finished and moved to the front row where she had placed her purse and Bible.

Pastor had opened his Bible to *Matthew 14:3* and read in his authoritative voice:

"But he answered and said unto them, Why do ye also transgress the commandment of God by your tradition?"

He read through the passage to verse 9.

"BUT IN VAIN THEY DO WORSHIP ME, TEACHING FOR DOCTRINE THE COMMANDMENTS OF MEN."

Mallory had cringed. This really was where they were in the Bible study the pastor had begun in January. She had a feeling he was about to start blasting Catholics. She prayed. "Lord, please prepare the hearts of Grandmother and Shay or Shannon, or whoever; please save them."

Pastor Anderson had explained the words of Jesus. He was rebuking the Jewish hierarchy of His day for making up their own religion. To this day, he explained, men continued to try to make up their own rules for coming to God. Many of the religions had strayed far from Biblical truth. Many of them were deceived, themselves; others were purposely involved in deception, making money, making merchandise of people whose souls were at stake. He didn't single out Catholicism, or Islam, or any particular group. He explained the gospel simply and sincerely and began the invitation.

Startled by the brevity of the message, and not being accustomed to playing for the invitation, she had jumped up pretty suddenly to get to the piano. It made her head spin again. She had begun to play "Amazing Grace" softly. She put her soul into it. Pastor had given her a quizzical look; usually he wanted, "Just As I Am" for the invitation. He repeated the sinner's prayer, inviting people to repeat each phrase after him, in their hearts. When he asked if anyone had prayed that prayer, several hand had gone up. Mallory kept playing "Amazing Grace". She hadn't heard it since the bagpipe had played it at her father's funeral. People were getting saved; she had been afraid to look toward her relatives. Members had come to the altar to pray. David had come down; then he had been hugging his dad and mom. They were all crying.

She was crying, too. Lana and Tammi were taking down the names of people who had come forward for salvation, if they wanted to give their names. Delia and Shay had slipped out.

Chapter 19

DINNER

AN EMOTIONAL CROWD was heading out of the little church building. Mallory was excited about all of the decisions. But she was mentally and physically exhausted. She was trying to get past people and get to her mom. She was hoping just to tell the Sanders "hello and good-bye", grab her mom, and head for the house. She hoped all the agents would be gone.

All of the out-of town people seemed to be meeting one another, and they were all excitedly planning to go to the lodge for a late dinner. Suzanne had already seemed to have disappeared by the time the girl reached the back doors.

She was disappointed; she thought her mom could have at least asked her if she was ok. She wondered if her mom knew or cared people had been trying to kill her. She glanced hopefully around the parking lot; no sign of their car. Other cars were filing out, and she waved at them as she headed for her own car. Kerry Larson pulled up beside her just as she reached her car to make sure she was going to the lodge.

She told him she wasn't planning on it; that she was pretty sure her mom had gone home, and that she would be expecting her.

Of course, he knew better. He was pretty sure Suzanne and all of the Sanders were going out to eat, and so was almost everyone. It would be a lot of fun. He told her Pastor and his family were all going. Mallory found that hard to believe. They never went out after church. Usually she loved to eat at the lodge and be around a big group of church people like that. But, she had eaten at the lodge once today already. (It did seem more like a year ago.) She told him she had some homework to do; then decided that made her sound like a little school girl.

"There isn't school tomorrow. I really need an opportunity to visit with you before Friday. The lodge will be a good place for us to do that. Hop in!"

"I'll come in my car; do you know the way? Follow me," she had acquiesced. She certainly hadn't wanted to "hop in" with someone she didn't even know. She pulled around past him so he could get behind her. The Rolls was still over on the shoulder of the road, and David's car was parked in front of it. Kerry pulled out smoothly behind Mallory, the Rolls behind him, and David trailing behind the Rolls.

Mallory's head still hurt; she wanted sleep. Suddenly, in occurred to her that Kerry Larson could answer some of her questions. She had been too numb to think of that. She thought she should call the school to make sure it was canceled for the next day, but she decided to just take his word for it. If there really were school, and she missed it, she would just say that in all the confusion, she had been misinformed.

In the darkness, she powdered her nose and reapplied her pretty new lipstick. She was suddenly excited about a get-together on what would ordinarily be a school night. She was excited about her pretty outfit, although the chunky turtleneck had begun to chafe her skin under her chin. Her cute new shoes had gotten kind of wet in the drizzly weather. Now, the precipitation had finally stopped. At the lodge, she had to park on the shoulder; the parking lot was crowded. The three cars behind her parked on the shoulder, too.

When Pastor Anderson had begun the invitation, and Mallory had begun playing "Amazing Grace", Delia had tapped Shay on the knee. He had been engrossed in everything. He had followed his grandmother wordlessly to the car. She hadn't said anything; he couldn't believe how angry she must be at what she had heard. He had tried to keep her from going in; he hoped she wouldn't be mad at him. The silence between them continued. Finally, she had begun to search for something in her handbag; her handkerchief. Tears were rolling down her face; he didn't know if the truth had just sunk in to her about his father's demise. He hadn't even asked her what had happened to him. Still without speaking, he had placed his arm around her. She actually had allowed herself to be comforted longer than he had figured she would. Then her back had straightened, and she was telling the driver, "follow Mallory."

As the car moved smoothly forward into the little convoy, Delia finally spoke to Shay.

"Everything Mr. Anderson said tonight was the truth, you know. That's why it made sense to Patrick. I prayed that little prayer in my heart; did you? I'm sorry I never listened to Patrick or Mallory when they tried to explain. If I had, maybe things would be different. Maybe both of my boys would still be alive. Shannon wouldn't be as hard as he already is-you prayed it, didn't you, Shay?"

"I did!" he gave her a happy hug. "We'll both pray for Shannon."

Mallory ordered Dinky to keep being good, and headed into the lodge. It was crowded. There were still all types of law enforcement people, some who had been in the service, some who hadn't. Tom and Joyce Haynes were there, and they were at a big table with Pastor and Lana Anderson, and Daniel and Diana Faulkner.

Mallory's mom was sitting with Roger and Beth Sanders, and another man and his wife; who looked pretty expectant. Then Mallory realized it was Connie. The kids and teen-agers were all at a different table. Kerry Larson had spotted a table for two, and had pulled the chair out for her courteously. She had been heading for Tammi Anderson and the kid's table, but took the chair across from the attorney. She felt like there must be a thousand eyeballs drilling into her back. David had come in by himself, and his dad had grabbed a chair so he could join their group. Finally, Delia and Shay had entered. The Andersons were trying to fit two more chairs into the already crowded table.

Delia was introducing herself and Shay, then had suggested that her grandson go join all the cute teen age girls at their table. He didn't need a second chance. He shook hands with the pastor and David and Daniel Faulkner as he passed them.

Lana Anderson had been trying to think of another way to get Mallory away from the handsome attorney, but John had shaken his head at her.

She turned her attention to Delia, expressing her sympathy for Patrick's death, telling her what a beloved church member they had lost. John knew more of the story, so he had entered the conversation smoothly.

"It was so nice to have you in our services tonight. Your grandson really looks like Patrick did, and like Mallory. You have another son, don't you? And another grandson? We are really glad to meet you.

Erick Bransom had come in, and he joined Roger's table. Roger didn't have a clue who he was, but of course, Suzanne did. She was mortified.

"Who let you out?" he chortled at her. The buzz at their table had died away.

"She's free on bond," Roger had whispered to him. "You have some kind of problem?"

He had no idea the guy was a federal agent.

The server had come to take his drink order, and he didn't seem to be moving along.

Roger's family just stared at him. "Oh hi," he greeted them all jauntily, "Erik Bransom, can I join your cozy little group here?"

David had noticed the Porsche with the Dallas plates on his way in to church. Even though he was already late, he had jogged nearer for a better look. He couldn't imagine who might be driving a car like that. He had already been jealous before the guy seemed to have taken up with Mallory. When he had met Delia and Shay O'Shaughnessy, his hopes had soared that maybe the driver of the Porsche was another relative.

She had looked really beautiful up playing the piano, but he had noticed she still couldn't stop crying. He was glad to see her mother back from where ever in the world she had taken off to; he had heard lots of different gossip about that. He hadn't believed any of it until the agent had just sat down next to her; maybe she had been in jail. He wondered if Mallory had heard it. He was splitting his attention among the adults at his table, the kids and teenagers behind him, and the couple in the corner.

Finally, he had risen from his seat and headed towards the men's room.

"Rangers' won!" he announced triumphantly, dipping in toward Mallory as he spoke.

"So did the Red Sox; double-header," Larson had come back quickly. He rose to his feet and extended his hand. "I'm Kerry Larson. Patrick retained me to provide counsel for Mallory. I'm bringing her up to speed on a few things, the best I can, before the will is actually made public, and Mr. O'Shaughnessy's wishes read."

David had shaken hands, giving his name in return. He went on into the restroom; he kind of wished there were a trap door somewhere to fall through. What, was the guy a "Sox" fan, just because Mallory was? How did he know their little private rivalries? The guy wasn't wearing a wedding band or anything. He wondered if Patrick had given Larson the Proverbs nine talking to. How could he have set up a guy like that to walk into Mallory's life?

He splashed water on his face and rejoined the adults at the table.

Delia and Diana were visiting as if they had known one another forever. They were both involved in the fashion industry, and they both looked it. Delia, of course, couldn't rave enough about her Irish Linen. Diana was a silk fanatic; her main emphasis was screen-printing on fine silk. She adored the feel of silk and its affinity for color. She was all about color. Delia had to admit, the design the woman was wearing was positively stunning. She was wearing a silk knit pullover sweater with the heavens literally spangled across it. The moon was rising toward the Milky Way, drawing the Evening Star behind it. Along the hem, *Psalm 147:4* was lettered in a silver script that was both beautiful and easy to read:

> *"He telleth the number of the stars; he calleth them all by their names.*

The Evening Star actually sparkled with a diamond, and diamond dust illuminated the sweep of the Milky Way. She was wearing it with a black suede suit and black suede knee boots.

Diana really admired Delia's deep gray suit. Delia wore gray a good deal; it flattered her lovely hair and coloring. She, of course, had a delicate, ruffly, linen blouse.

The sweater Diana was wearing was from a photo she had taken the previous Monday evening. She pulled out a different one she had designed from a photograph of the thunder storm Sunday afternoon. It was amazing. The angry gray storm clouds were split with a streak of silver-white lightning. It was beautiful with the suit the linen icon was wearing. Diana was giving it to her. Delia was genuinely moved with emotion, but she had still laughed and said she wanted diamonds on hers.

The pastor's wife, who seldom had anything new, and the principal's wife, that was facing unemployment had been trying to make their own conversation.

David was trying to listen to the men. They had been trying to figure out what exactly, the Faulkners were doing here; besides taking pictures of the sky. He was pretty ambiguous, saying he would be able to say more after "Friday". It suddenly occurred to David that they were making inferences about Mallory; that her father may have made plans for her beyond the realm of tiny Murfreesboro. Surely, he wouldn't have planned to uproot her before she could graduate from high school with her class, would he?

He was already praying,"Please, Lord, no!" under his breath.

Shay seemed to be enjoying himself. He had never really been around girls his own age. Tammi Anderson and Emma Sanders were both really cute, and they all kept the conversation lively. Tommy Haynes was saying even less than usual. He had been having a bad week, and he was hoping his dad <u>would</u> get fired!

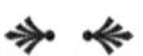

Mallory had listened to Mr. Larson for nearly an hour, as he explained the way he had set up all of her father's corporations, and established this trust, and that fund. She thought he must surely be talking to the wrong person. She was wanting to know all the stuff about her world. Was she in trouble with the FBI, with the IRS, did people really think her responsible for her father's death? Was Martin Thomas in jail? What for? What about the sheriff? All of that was the reason she had joined him, rather than sitting with her mom and the Sanders.

Finally, she had cut in, "Let's go join the party." She had risen with her tea glass and introduced herself to her cousin. He had risen courteously, then given her a hug. He started to cry when he told her he was sorry she had lost her father. He was crying for himself, too; he had recently lost both.

Mallory pulled up a chair next to the FBI agent. Not having learned anything interesting from her attorney, she had decided to try a different angle.

David had moved to the chair Mallie had just vacated. "Could I ask you a couple of things?" he had begun the conversation with an edge to his voice.

"I'm not at liberty to divulge anything about Miss O'Shaughnessy's legal matters with you," the attorney had responded with an equal warning tone.

"Can you tell me anything at all about Sheriff Melville?" David asked. Like Mallory, he hadn't been able to find out anything he wanted to know, either.

"Sheriff Melville," Larson had repeated uncertainly. "Fill me in"

"Gladly!" David had leaned forward earnestly and begun at the beginning- when Mallory had found her dad, dead. Her loss, her self-blame, and the sheriff's having jumped on that to harangue her with murder accusations and attacks on her character. It had gone on for three months, finally the feds had come; and the guy was in jail in Little Rock. David hadn't heard anything more than that. He wanted the sheriff to put out an apology to Mallory and the community. He told about the sheriff taking a picture of David's kissing her and sending the e-mail with the bad insinuations they had spent a night together. He had finished by telling Kerry that he was planning to send an e-mail, or a blog or something about the sheriff's actions.

The entire story had left the attorney stunned. Some of it, he had heard; and the attempted hits, and the murders, and who had done what. He thought they were still trying to get it all sorted out. He didn't know about accusations Mallory had murdered her father. "If she had,"he told David, "she wouldn't receive the life insurance or an inheritance!"

David didn't know there was an inheritance or a life insurance policy! He guessed the guy had divulged more than he was supposed to!

"She didn't murder her father!! It was something crazy about the sheriff; he violated her rights! Is anyone doing anything about it? Should I send an e-mail, myself?"

Bransom had passed by, "No, don't send any e-mails! I know you want to do something because this is slow. If you send accusations against Melville into cyber-space, a judge could rule that, 'he couldn't get a fair trial any place, even with a change of venue'. The entire case we've been working to assemble against him might get thrown out, in that case."

David and the attorney were both glad for the answer.

The table service for so many people late in the evening had been slow, but everyone was enjoying the conversation, moving from one table to another to speak to different people. Mallory had tried to move toward the Faulkners, but she seemed to keep being herded away from them. She didn't realize that it was deliberate, and that it was another piece of the puzzle that would make more sense after Friday!

Erik Bransom had finally edged Suzanne away from the rest of the group. "How were your accommodations in Hope?" he had teased her.

"What is your problem?" she had whispered back savagely. "I didn't appreciate that "D" for "dumb" comment you made. You didn't have to throw me in jail, anyway. Mallory doesn't even care that much about her jewelry."

Well, it's still nice if you check with people before you just take stuff. Your daughter might care about things more than you know. Besides, I changed my mind about the "D", you get an "F" now."

Suzanne turned to end the conversation, but he had grabbed her elbow, pulling her out onto a porch. She had her back to the wall, literally. He had her cornered "Have you thought about starting to date anybody yet?" he had asked her.

"Not anybody that gives me bad grades and calls me dumb," she had pouted at him-real cute, really, really cute!

"Ok, then, how about a 'B-' for less than brilliant? Don't ever agree to go with someone like that that you don't know again, when you have a big diamond with you! Or even if you don't have a diamond. You have really given me a couple of scares. You were in jail for your own protection. Will you please go out with me sometime?"

"Like when?" she asked.

He looked at his watch. "How about breakfast?"

The Andersons seldom went out for dinners. They were always on a tight budget. The Faulkners had invited them to join them at lunch on Sunday; then again after church on Sunday night. They had turned down both invitations. Then today, Faulkner had called John and begged them to let him buy their dinner. John had agreed . He had known Lana would enjoy a great meal at the lodge, but he knew she would feel intimidated by the other family's material wealth. John had tried to cheer her up by telling her about all the rewards they were going to have in Heaven. She knew all that, of course, but it hadn't made her feel any more comfortable around Diana. He had been trying not to like the family; to be judgmental of their seeming to have so much. They really seemed to be an awesome family, though, showing more pure, radiating joy in the Lord than anyone else the pastor had ever known. He was suddenly feeling like they should be teaching him.

Finally, he had asked, "so what is your persuasion? Are you 'name it and claim it?' 'health and wealth?'"

Daniel had laughed,"Well, we would love to have it that way? Who wouldn't? We have learned that God answers prayers and invites us always to pray for more. He is Gracious beyond-" his voice trailed off. "We believe like you do, Pastor. God has a sovereign will; sometimes, oftentimes, he tells us, 'No'."

Lana didn't think they looked like God had told them, 'No'very often. She had felt like the heavens above her were brass; both about ever having a pay raise approved, and about David and his rebellion. She was trying not to feel resentful about them.

Daniel had suddenly shared something at the table that they had shared with few people. Diana wished he hadn't become so candid with these people quite so soon; the subject was extremely sensitive for her. He was telling about the miscarriages they had endured, even though they prayed for successful pregnancies and healthy babies. With them, it had been lose one, have one, lose one, have one, lose one, have one. From six pregnancies, they had three children.

"I guess it makes us extra thankful for the three we have," Diana had broken in tearfully.

Then Daniel had made the announcement that Diana had now carried another baby, their seventh, into the second trimester. Everything seemed good. "If we could 'name it and claim it,' we would have seven children by now."

Lana and Delia exchanged glances like they might claim something different than seven children. Joyce Haynes knew the heartache the Faulkners had shared. It hadn't been their plan for Tommy, Jr. to be an only child.

At last, everyone had been served, with desserts for those who had ordered them; and plenty of soft drinks and de-caf coffee. Everyone had paid out. Shay was still talking to the girls, so the pastor had helped Delia into her coat.

"May I speak with you a moment?" she had asked him.

"Certainly," he had drawn her off to one side. He thought she was probably going to tell him off for the sermon, for making her son leave the Catholic church.

"Thank you for coming here when you did, and for what you have done for Patrick and Mallory." She interrupted herself, "Do you feel like you ever did Suzanne any good? That girl hasn't spoken one word yet, to Shay or to me. Anyway, now I know for sure that Patrick is in heaven, and I know I'm going there, too. You can not imagine what that means to me. Shay prayed that prayer, too. Thank you for staying here all through the years. You may not know how much good you're doing."

Bransom had come back in to shake Anderson's hand and tell him the same thing.

"Bransom, just don't get me started crying again," John Anderson was backing away defensively. But the tears had already come to his eyes at Mrs. O'Shaughnessy's words.

David was crying, too. For years, Mallory had prayed for her family in Boston to find the Lord. He wondered if she knew, but the attorney dude had closed in on her again.

⁂

David was amazed his car had made it so far on empty. He had left from the lodge, driving back toward town. The church parking lot was empty. He pulled in; he had a lot on his mind. He was thankful about the people who had gotten saved. He didn't know what to make of any of it. He had a feeling that his world was about to turn upside down for him on Friday. Surely, Mallory and her mom wouldn't move away. She had always been here; since his first day of school here. She had walked up to him and told him she could beat him at anything. She was a pretty tough adversary. They had always had fun together. He couldn't remember exactly when he had started calling her Erin go Bragh, but it fit. He had walked into the dark church; it was always unlocked. He had knelt at the altar and sobbed.

At last, he had risen resolutely. He needed the Lord, whatever the next few days might bring forth.

Chapter 20

DESERTED

PROVERBS 29:15 THE rod and reproof give wisdom: but a child left to himself bringeth his mother shame.

Martin Thomas had gone crazy on Monday morning. It was the first Murfreesboro knew about his viciousness. The entire town had felt that he was a little slow, lazy, and slovenly. He didn't seem to have friends. It had just been Martin and his dad, for years, barely making it. They were both known for their tempers; sometimes getting into fights with one another.

Mardy, his mother had left years before. Not knowing how to handle either her child or her husband, she had left when she had gotten the chance. No one in town had heard from her since. The story was, that she had scraped together enough money to go to the State Park and hunt for diamonds. The entrance fee had always been small, but they didn't have much. After paying the fee, she had dug and sifted for hours; then had left suddenly. She disappeared and never came back. The supposition was that she must have found a diamond good enough to at least pay her way to another state.

Since 1906, when the first diamond was discovered, there had been at least seventy-five thousand of the gems found. The 40.23 carat Uncle Sam was the largest diamond ever found in the U.S. Diamonds found at the mine could be quite significant, or quite insignificant. The deal was, that many people who found diamonds would take them in to the visitor's center for verification and weighing. These were the ones that were in the count. No one could guess how many diamonds had been found by people who just left quietly with them.

The Crater of Diamonds State Park was interesting, fun, and family oriented. Its popularity and attendance had continuously increased, drawing people from all over the world. Tourism dollars, of course, were an important part of the state's revenue. For that reason, the Arkansas State Parks Director had sent his investigators to Murfreesboro.

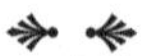

Martin Thomas! David Anderson had grabbed him on Monday morning as the school bus had been unloading. When the fight had been broken up, Haynes had ordered coach to escort Martin down to the athletics department to hold until the police came for him. The kid had been wild; coach was a big, strong guy; but it had taken half of the football team to subdue the student. Coach didn't believe in "demon-possession" he was saying later, but Thomas Martin had looked and acted really weird and scary. He had still been acting like a wild-man, resisting arrest when the police were trying to get him moved. Kicking and screeching, he had been making violent and gruesome threats. He wouldn't shut up, even when they told him to. He was pretty much freaking out every one who had to listen to him. He had refused to answer any questions. He had hardly slept or calmed down, in his high security confinement in Little Rock.

What they had surmised so far, was that Thomas, deserted by his mother, had "snapped".

They believed he had entered the Diamond Mine on three or four different occasions. Rather than digging for diamonds, or "surface searching" as other people were doing, Martin was looking for victims. No crimes had actually been committed in the State Park, itself. But several hideous murders might have had their beginnings in the broad, open, plowed field of the Kimberlite pipe. Obviously, that wasn't what the Arkansas State Parks Director wanted to have happen. The diamond mining was supposed to be fun and safe; finders, keepers. Nothing horrible like this was supposed to happen. That was why, by the time the killings were linked together with a possible connection to the mine, the powers that be in Little Rock were relieved to have the perpetrator already in custody. There had been a big meeting with all Park Rangers to be more alert about people who might seem strange, who might be watching other people find diamonds, rather than finding their own.

That was what Thomas had done. Filled with such rage that his own mother had gone there to find a diamond so she could leave him, he hated and resented all women. They shouldn't be looking for diamonds. That was bad. The first girl had been a twenty year old from Oklahoma. Small and cute, she had looked like a little western cowgirl doll- before Martin had finished his work. Not even attempting to cover his tracks, he had sold the diamond and bought the truck.

The second victim had been a college student from Weatherford, Texas. They hadn't been able to figure out if she had ever really found a diamond, or if the killer just thought she had. The body was left the same way.

With somewhat of a method to his madness, he had driven to Missouri, in pursuit of his third choice. He had gotten money from her account before ending her life. Much of the bloody money had been found in a box in his room, crudely printed with "snack money" in black magic marker. So far, his truck was yielding evidence for all of the murders.

The fourth victim had been a mother of a two-year old; her body had been found in the Ouachita National Forest. The National Forest crime scene had brought investigators from the US Department of Agriculture. All of them who had tried to question the suspect had come away shaken.

The one who had finally linked the four cases together was Ivan Summers, from the ABI. He was the one who had been so sickened by the body in the National Forest that he had done a search and had come up with the other cases in three adjoining states. He had just made the connection and notified Bransom. Bransom had just arrived at the Murfreesboro Police Department as part of his investigation into Melville. He had been in the police station and had heard some of the crazy ranting and screaming Thomas was doing. Both of the boys were being held for fighting at school; hardly a police matter, Bransom had thought; sure not anything to him as a Federal agent. But the way he was threatening to kill the other boy and the girl (he guessed the fight was over a girl) was detail for detail like the four dead young women. He couldn't believe that the killer was already in custody, before they even had completed the profile.

Sheriff Melville had come to the police station, which was odd; the two departments were separate entities. He had been trying to get the quiet kid held, and had been throwing a fit to try to get the Martin kid released. Bransom had stepped in.

He had immediately taken the profane, screaming Martin Thomas into federal custody. The sheriff hadn't liked that at all; he was still working on freeing the big, overgrown Thomas kid. Even after Bransom had brought up the four murders cases for his consideration, the sheriff had still claimed not to believe it, swearing he had known Martin for the boy's entire life. Bransom had been forced to believe that some of the allegations against Melville must be true.

Now, he just couldn't determine what the relationship between the two men might be.

David Anderson's complaint about Melville had mentioned an incident of the sheriff's paying some money to Martin. Bransom tried to dismiss the incident. "Maybe Thomas had done some odd jobs for the sheriff, or something."

David had shrugged; he wasn't convinced. Martin Thomas was hardly known as being a worker, and the sheriff was pretty broke for hiring anything done. His statement was that they had been "acting sneakier" than that. Part of the investigation of Oscar Melville would be his financial situation, anyway.

Martin Thomas was now being held by Federal agents, as was his friend, former sheriff Oscar Melville.

Chapter 21

DREAD

Isaiah 41:10 Fear thou not; for I am with thee: be not dismayed; for I am thy God: I will strengthen thee; yea, I will help thee; yea, I will uphold thee with the right hand of my righteousness.

SUZANNE HAD BEEN up bright and early, trying on some of the various new outfits Connie and Beth had helped her pick out. They all looked pretty cute; she couldn't decide. She decided to ask her daughter's opinion. Mallory had curled up groggily on her mom's bed.

"Wow, I don't know, Mom," she had finally concluded, "It's all so cute. Are you meeting Agent Bransom this morning?" she had asked curiously.

Guiltily, Suzanne had begun stammering. "Um-uh, well- I was going to talk to you about-"

Mallory had stretched, still sleepy. "Mom, you don't need to talk to me. I don't mind if you two like each other. He seems pretty nice; I'm just kind of scared of all of them, still." She gave a willies, spooky shudder, making a face at the same time.

Suzanne laughed at her. "How did you manage to get the lights and phone back on and get a car, and a dog and a cell phone, and the new clothes- all in two days?"

Mallory had yawned. "It hasn't been two days, Mom; it's been two years, I think. Did Roger really give you the Jaguar as part of your job?"

She and her mother had still not really talked, but at least her mom hadn't seemed too mad about Dinky. She refilled her mom's coffee mug and poured herself one. She tried it without so much creamer and sugar; then hating it, she had doctored it up some more. Better. She placed her mom's mug on the dresser.

"Go with the blue." she had advised.

Her mother had looked gorgeous as she slid behind the wheel of the sporty car. "You go, Mom," Mallory had laughed and blown a kiss.

She shrugged into an old outfit, just so she could wash her "Monkey" nightie with the rest of her laundry. She was glad to have electricity. She didn't know Bransom had ordered the power company to restore it so they could carry forward their investigation.

She sat down at the kitchen table with her daddy's Bible. No more "quiet time" in her old tractor, ever again. The agents had processed it because of the hired killer, but since he was dead, they hadn't felt much was really necessary. They had already released it for the sale; the check had been issued, and Mallory had endorsed it and turned it over to Kerry Larson so he could stash it into some tax-sheltered account. Everything she had left in the tractor the previous Saturday had been ruined. She had thrown it all away. The crew who had been sent to load the old, rusting antique had come prepared to deal with the wasps. The wasps had gathered national attention, and almost, but not quite, given God the credit for saving Mallory and Tammi's lives.

Mallory opened the Bible. She felt a strange listlessness and dread of the future. That was not like her. But then, she hadn't really been herself since she had lost her dad. She kept trying to fight her way out of the grief, but she felt like every time she fought her way to the surface, a new, crushing wave would sweep her back under. Now, sitting alone in the tiny, humble kitchen, she was afraid. Some of the things Kerry Larson had been saying were sinking in more now. He had said something about getting her relocated away from everything and a guardian, and some other things that had been really troubling to her. She was struggling with life in general and possible changes looming large, when Dinky had begun to growl; then she had heard slamming car doors. In consternation, she realized the property was about to be overrun with agents again.

Hurrying to her room, she grabbed the new yellow sweater and the navy skirt, gathering what she would need in preparation for the shower. She made the safety of the little bathroom and locked the door. She showered and dressed, then was working on blow-drying and styling her hair. Someone banged on the bathroom door. She opened it indignantly. "Do you mind?" she hissed savagely, "someone still lives here!" She grabbed her cosmetic bag and hand mirror and swept past him. Every place was crowded; now it was mostly Treasury department people trying to establish that the empire Patrick had established didn't have ties to Ryland and the old Boston days, or anything else illegal. Mallory didn't know what they were looking for; she had no idea of anything but the diamonds. No one seemed to be looking for them at all. That was a relief to her. She had thought the attorney might say something about them, but since he hadn't, Mallory hadn't mentioned them either.

She got in her car, and finished her makeup. The yellow sweater was like the soft sunshine. She was glad she had chosen it. The color was so flattering that makeup was hardly necessary. She applied some shine, mascara, and the new lipstick. Today, she softened the rich, deep tone with lip gloss; then surveyed herself with some satisfaction in the rear view mirror. She went back into the house to release Dinky from the confines of her bedroom. As soon as she did, agents had rushed in there. Shaking her head in disbelief, she had grabbed her handbag, leaving them to search for whatever it was they thought they were going to find. "At least I have an attorney, now." she told her reflection. But that was one of the things that had her worried.

She drove aimlessly for a few minutes, the big dog by her side. She had her phone in a compartment of her console, and was listening to her iPod. She had no idea when her mom would be home. She remembered, suddenly, that she should have written a note. In less than a week, she seemed to have forgotten a lifetime of instruction.

She drove by the church. There were no cars there, so she stopped and went in. She sat down at the piano and began to play softly. She poured her heart into the music for about half an hour, then sat there in the semi-darkness thinking about the service the night before. Several people from the different government agencies had gotten saved. David had been in church, hugging his mom and dad. Agent Bransom had gotten saved, and he seemed to like Mallory's mom. The Faulkners had been back, and Kerry Larson. Mallory still could barely believe that her cousin and grandmother had attended a baptist service. She played "Amazing Grace" once more, modulating from key to key, making up her own arrangement as she played. Then she played "I Don't Know About Tomorrow", because she didn't. She was dreading the whole "will" ordeal. Her heart felt like a stone; she wished she could cry some more; but the tears hadn't come.

She got the Bible out of the car, and sitting down on the church steps, she decided to make another attempt at her devotions.

❧ ❧

David had returned to the parsonage late Wednesday night. The house was pretty dark; he figured his family members were all asleep. He had crept in as quietly as he could. He knew he didn't have gas or gas money, so returning to his apartment was out of the question. His cold was making him feel pretty miserable, so his plan was to flop on the sagging sofa in the den. As he crept into the kitchen, he had heard his mom and dad talking softly. They were trying to decide who should take the first turn to drive around looking for him. Then they had decided that since he had been in church, maybe it would be ok for them both just to go to bed. David was ashamed, now, of what he had been putting them through. His mom was speaking again.

"I just don't understand why he kissed Mallory, do you?"

His dad's laughter had roared, and she hushed him so he wouldn't "wake the children!"

John had pulled her toward himself, and kissed her passionately. "Yes, I understand why he did; I wish he hadn't. I love you, Lana. All those people got saved today, partly because you have been so wonderful. His eyes met hers. Let's get some rest, Sugar". They ascended the stairs, arm in arm.

David was standing alone in the dark silence of the kitchen. Without even removing his boots or the leather jacket, he was sound asleep on the sofa. When he awakened, it was because his little brother, Jeff, had sat down on him in the semi-darkness as he had grabbed the remote to surf for cartoons. David had moaned; he felt worse than ever.

He sat up and gave his little brother an affectionate punch. They watched cartoons together for a few minutes.

Suddenly, John Anderson had let out some war-whoop sounding shouts from upstairs. He scared the entire household. Lana and the three kids still trying to sleep were jolted wide awake, not having any clue what might be going on. David heard the racket above the noisy television and sprinted up the stairs two at a time. Dread was suffocating him that his father was falling victim to another hired assassin, or he was having a heart attack like Patrick had. His dad had emerged from his small home study into the upstairs hallway, holding a letter limply at his right side. David couldn't imagine what could be such dreadful news.

"What is it, Dad?" He could scarcely speak as he tried to reach for the paper. His dad was standing, rooted to the spot, staring at him.

"What is it, Dad?" David had asked again.

Lana had found her robe, and the bedroom door flew open. "Mercy, what's going on?" she was staring at her husband, too.

Finally, his eyes had filled with tears. He was nearly as overcome with emotion as he had been the day before. Lana had pulled him back into their bedroom, where he had sunk numbly onto the bed.

"I can't believe it," he had spoken at last.

By now, all five kids had assembled, "Can't believe what? What can't he believe?" Tammi was asking as she had heard her father's hushed voice. "Is it something bad?"

Like a man emerging from a trance, the pastor had blinked, shaking his head.

"No, not bad!" A huge grin had finally broken across his face. "It's too wonderful to be true. We need to thank the Lord right now!"

"Oh no," Lana shook her finger at her husband. "I'm not thanking Him for anything until I know what it is. You scared us all to death with your war whoops. Now you have some 'splainin to do"

"Yeah," they all chimed in in agreement.

Mallory was still sitting on the church steps when David had driven up. She really was still trying to finish her devotion time. Her mind was still so clouded with fear and uncertainty. It seemed like she couldn't find any time or place for quiet when she had so much to sort out. He had parked his car and was walking toward her. Dinky started to go even crazier than usual. Mallory watched David's approach, saying nothing to Dinky. The dog had taken an even more menacing step forward.

"You gonna call off your dog?" he demanded of her.

"I haven't decided," she had closed the big Bible and risen to her feet. Dinky growled again, barking sharply, baring his teeth and snarling. David was watching the dog in total disbelief. He was pretty sure Christians and baptists didn't believe in reincarnation and coming back as higher or lower life forms, but he could swear this dog had to be some form of Mallory's father. He could remember Patrick's last conversation: "If you mess with my daughter, I'll come out of my grave and pull you back in with me!"

David didn't bluff easily, but he had been pretty sure the man wasn't bluffing. Now with the snarling and bared teeth, the dog looked pretty much like the little Irishman had the last time he had seen him.

"Uh, where did he come from?" he asked, almost afraid to find out.

Mallory had finally moved forward, coming between David and the animal. She waggled her index finger at him and he had flopped down like a rag doll. David moved toward her, and a growl erupted, though the dog hadn't moved.

"I came into a fortune of twenty bucks, so I wondered if I could buy you a burger for lunch."

Dinky stood up eagerly, and whimpered.

"He wasn't inviting you," she laughed. The dog sank back down dejectedly.

"Thanks, David, I really can't," she had begun.

He held his hand up. "No problem. I wanted to apologize for kissing you and everything else that happened because of it. It was your fault, though."

"Ok, whatever," she was heading toward her car.

"Yeah," he was going on; she didn't know she had encouraged him. "You just looked so cute, I couldn't help it. You just looked like a cute little raccoon. Yeah, like a cute little raccoon with a really big purse!"

She slung a rock at him, and missed. He chuckled and started his car.

"Later," he said, and he drove away.

⇝ ⇜

Mallory, for some reason, had decided to drive up to Daisy State Park on Lake Greeson.

She pumped some gas into her car, and bought a hot dog and coke at the station. The sunshine wasn't brilliant, but after the cold rain of the previous day, it seemed like a pretty nice day for an outing. She started her music and headed toward the lake. She still wanted some peace and quiet; she was terrified of what the following day might hold in store for her. She felt as threatened as she had felt as a little girl, knowing her closet was full of ghost and monsters. She wanted to spend another day in the beautiful, familiar surroundings she had grown up with.

"Who might her father have chosen for a guardian for her? Why would he have? Maybe that was for when she was little, if something had happened to both her dad and mom. That would make sense. But if that were the case, why had Kerry Larson shown up?

She suddenly wondered if she had to go to the ordeal tomorrow; if there were any way they could compel her. Maybe she could sleep through it, and her mom could fill her in later. She could just tell she wasn't going to be able to keep from crying hysterically at whatever they told her. Would they force her to go someplace strange with people she didn't know? If she fought them would they put her in a straight jacket? She knew her imagination was running away with her.

She tried to focus on today, on the rich pines and their fragrance. She opened her windows and the sunroof. The hardwood trees were bursting with delicate green, and wildflowers spread in a vivid carpet to the small whitecaps that lapped against the lakeshore. She inhaled deeply and tried to sing to her music.

When she reached the campground, she left Dinky in the car and skipped across some logs and stones to the picnic table they had usually tried to lay a claim to. Too late to retreat, she had looked up from her little obstacle course. "Their" table was covered with a linen tablecloth, and a beautiful picnic hamper lay open, exposing china and all kinds of elegant looking foodstuffs. Delia and Shay were both staring at her strangely.

"Hello, Dear," Delia had greeted her graciously. "How did you find us? Would you like to join us?"

"What are you guys doing here?" She was startled; she hadn't meant the question to sound so blunt. "Not just here, at this picnic spot, but why are you in Arkansas?"

"Well, we came because we had been informed that my son had included us in his will."

Mallory sank onto the picnic bench. It had little white cushions on it. The table had a fresh flower arrangement. She kind of wondered what the point of a picnic was, but they were on the edge of the shimmering lake, beneath a beautiful canopy of trees. Birds were singing. She guessed it was a melding of outdoor beauty with indoor elegance. All in all, not bad! Just not the way it was usually done in Arkansas!

Shay was grabbing at the stuff that was in her hands. "What are you holding out on us?" he was teasing.

"Shay," Delia had made eye contact with her grandson. She couldn't tell now whether Mallory had been looking for them, or not. Now, the girl had perched for a moment, looking as if she were prepared to flee if frightened.

"Please stay, Mallory," she urged. "I apologize for treating you so badly all of these years. I'm sure you can never forgive me- You weren't really looking for us, were you? Are you meeting your boyfriend out here? This place is actually rather nice."

Mallory had handed her stuff over to her cousin. "There you go, a hot dog, a coke, and my Bible. Well, actually, the Bible was Daddy's. Mine got left in the rain and got ruined. I've been using this one for a few days.

Delia's hands were trembling as she had reached for the Bible. "Patrick's Bible," she spoke it like poetry. "May I?"

They asked Mallory to bless the food, and they all dug in. They were sometimes all talking at once; then there would be some awkward silence. Over all, Mallory was enjoying them both very much. Delia had asked her again if she had a boyfriend, and acted surprised at the girl's answer.

Finally, Mallory had said with amazement, "Grandmother, you don't sound Irish."

She had laughed. "Probably because I'm not. My father-in-law was, your grandfather wasn't into it much. Mostly the O'Shaughnessy name now, and the company dealing in Irish linen."

"But, Daddy was so Irish," she had begun in confusion.

"What?" she had asked incredulously, "he was still doing that? We always just said, 'Cut it out, Pat'." She gave a little nonchalant flip of her wrist.

The girl was stunned, but tried not to let it show. "Who was he, really? she couldn't help wondering.

Some uniformed people came and stiffly cleared the picnic table. Mallory went with the two to look at the cabins they were staying in. She thanked them for lunch and hurried back to her car.

As soon as she was gone Shay and Delia both sat down in the living room in front of a fire, and read the Bible together.

Suzanne had a great breakfast with Erik Bransom. Various agents had interrupted a few times to ask him questions, and he had taken a few phone calls. He hadn't ever fallen so hard for anyone before. He didn't want the breakfast to end, but he had so much to do! Reluctantly, he had walked her to her car, asking if he could call her again, apologizing for the interruptions. He opened the car door for her. He couldn't help being amazed at the difference between the Jaguar and the beater she had been in when he had arrested her. He was dreading the will, too. Would she be so rich she wouldn't want him? Maybe she already didn't. Would she have to move away? He would transfer, if she offered him any hope at all.

Suzanne had driven home in a happy daze. Tears were trying to escape; now, she could finally understand some of the things Mallory had tried to share with her about the Lord. Patrick had too, she guessed. She tried not to think about him; she had tried to act as grief-stricken as Mallory had been, but she wasn't really. It was all her fault, she was sure. She thanked the Lord again for lifting her up, when she had been so low, and for putting a song in her heart.

When she returned to her home, there were still agents everywhere. As she entered the house in bewilderment, the phone had rung. It was Erik. He had heard about some guy running Mallory out of her own house. He told Suzanne to gather up her stuff, and he would approve the expense for a hotel room for them in Hope. He told her that his sources had informed him that Mallory was nearly home.

"Ok," Suzanne had agreed. Like a typical mother she asked, "Did your sources tell you where she's been?"

"My sources have informed me that she has been up at Daisy with her grandmother and cousin. They had a "comfortable, Boston-style picnic".

❧ ❧

Ivan Summers was back at Sonic, ordering whatever the thing was that he had had Monday before Adams had rumbled by on the way to O'Shaughnessy's Even now, he was still eyeing traffic warily. The word was that Ryland and Shannon O'Shaughnessy were planning to be in town by ten in the morning. They must be as bad as, or worse, than their reputation. The hardened agent shuddered involuntarily. He wondered how many more guys like Adams they could bring into play. Law enforcement hadn't received the word about Ryland; Delia hadn't told; neither had her source.

Diana Faulkner had appeared in the yellow Hummer. Summers knew they were staying in their extremely luxurious motor home at the Crater Of Diamonds State Park campground. The weather was pretty nice, so she and her three children had exited the vehicle in favor of a picnic table. She had immediately begun scrubbing the table down with a wet wipe. That struck the agent funny; he wasn't sure why. He watched as they ordered their food. They were all real, real cute. The kids were well-behaved. All of the agents had noticed that, so they weren't really surprised when they had observed the Faulkners were church folk. He thought vaguely that he might "give it a shot" sometime. A couple of honey bees had buzzed by; Diana and the children had instinctively ducked. Summers looked around, once again eyeing traffic on the street, cars pulling in at the drive-in. He returned his attention to Diana; the kids were still there, but he had lost track of her. She had emerged from the Hummer with a can of wasp spray. She was chasing the unwelcome insects with it. Summers couldn't help thinking about a guy who had recently killed a fly in front of TV cameras. Mass murderers didn't get the cries of outrage that the fly-murderer had received. He laughed to himself as the mom continued to battle the threat to her little cubs. He thought about filming it with his phone, then decided, better not. One of the offending pollen-gatherers had flown close to his agency car; she sprayed the car, and him, and his drink. Finally, one of the bees had dropped, next to his car door. He clasped his hands over his heart, "Oh, man, Lady, I think you just killed my uncle!" he had moaned.

He had startled her, and she retreated from him, real fast. He hadn't meant to scare her.

"Oh great!"her husband was just pulling in next to the Hummer. She was at his window, telling him the agent had said something to her. Then she was pointing toward Summers. The guy was striding purposefully toward him.

"Hi," Daniel greeted him cordially enough.

"Afternoon," Summers replied. "Look, I didn't mean to scare your wife. But she was on a real killing spree; you could see the murder in her eyes. I told her she killed my uncle.

Now I think you may have stepped on his body!"

Faulkner roared with laughter. "Get over it!" He slapped him on the shoulder and joined his family at the table.

"What was so funny?" Diana had demanded.

He explained it to her the best he could. It had to do with zealous animal-rights' groups. They included everyone from little old ladies who loved cats to Hindus who were entering the country every day, believing in reincarnation. He told her about the outcry over a guy swatting a fly. She knew most of it; she owned several fur coats, and she knew people were violently against that. It amazed her that there was so much national concern over animals, and now, evidently over honey bees, when so few cared about millions of aborted babies.

"Am I in trouble over it?" she questioned seriously.

"Honey, no," he laughed. "Guy didn't mean to scare you. I think he might have been flirting a little bit."

All three kids giggled, all turning to stare at the maroon car as if on cue.

Summers, sitting there trying to decide how poisoned his drink now was, saw that they were still talking about him.

He got out of his car and joined them. "Hey, kids," he greeted. He gave them all a little Junior ABI badge; they thought it was great. He was still tense, alert, even as he had been engaged in conversation.

Daniel was aware of it immediately, although Diana hadn't seemed to pick up on it.

"You think there may still be more trouble?" he had asked. He and Diana had prayed a great deal about this whole situation before they had agreed to become involved. They hadn't known it would involve personal danger to themselves and the children. Maybe, Patrick had tried to give a veiled warning, but if he had, they had missed it. Anyway, they had both still felt peace, even this morning, that they were doing the right thing; and that it was the Lord's will.

Summers had laughed. "Just have your wife keep that can handy, and everything should be ok. Do you have a license to carry that?" he was teasing her again.

Daniel had laughed testily,"You married, Summers ?" he had questioned pointedly.

"No," he responded.

"Well, my wife is!" He had placed his arms possessively around her waist. "Tell you what, why don't you come visit my single's Sunday School class in Tulsa some week-end? There are about a hundred fifty or so, on average; way more than half of them are women. They might even be desperate enough to give an ugly guy like you a chance. You see, the trouble with meeting women in bars, is that you find the ones that have all kinds of problems."

"We are known as the church match-makers," Diana had laughed.

Summers was stunned; jolted! It made sense that if you wanted a marriage made in Heaven, you were more likely to find it by going to church. "Are you there every Sunday?" he asked. He was serious.

"This Sunday, we'll still be around here, but after that, we should have quite a stretch. Let us know if you're coming; we have lots of room at the house. You can be our houseguest." Daniel bit into a corn dog.

The agent threw the drink away and pulled out to patrol around town. He still had flashbacks of Tammi Anderson frozen in the sights of Adam's high-powered weapon. He was watching for rental vehicles, Massachusetts plates, any out of state plates. He was tuning in carefully to any suspicious activity reported by any force. A stolen car, a scared waitress, anything they had missed before. He circled around the O'Shaughnessy property, then to the Diamond Park campground, then up to the Daisy Campground. Everything seemed quiet, but he couldn't shake the sensation of dread. He was closer to the site in the Ouachita National Forest where the one girl's body had been found. He still felt profoundly affected by that. There were a lot of parts about his job that he really liked, but even now, he was wondering how long he could do it before he finally buckled under the load. If he could just get the images out, just erase it like a hard drive- He sighed wearily. He had swung back around by the cabin where the O'Shaughnessy woman and boy were staying; he froze!

The agent had made Daniel concerned about his family's safety. He hurried them back into the Hummer; they were hastily gathering up their unfinished food, protesting. He had rushed Diana into the passenger side and sprung into the driver's seat himself.

"Dad, you're forgetting your car," Jeremiah was trying to help.

"Yeah, I know, Jer," he responded. "For right now, I want us all to be together."

He wished he had gotten the gun out of the other car, but there were other guns at the Motor Home. He pressed down hard on the accelerator, and the Hummer roared out of town.

Kerry Larson was now more concerned about the revelation that was to take place in the morning, than he had been. He was pretty self-confident, and usually he could negotiate the necessary deals. After finally meeting Mallory O'Shaughnessy, now he wasn't so sure. Patrick had warned him that she could be a real handful; that hadn't been his impression so much. It was just that she had lived nearly her entire life here; all of it that she could remember. She was so entrenched! He had grown up among the apple orchards of the Northwest. He knew how easy it could be to kill a tree by yanking it up and replanting it somewhere else. Even if the soil, and rain, and the environment were basically better, it was hard to convince a dying tree of that. It was his responsibility to carry out Patrick O'Shaughnessy's wishes. He hoped the guy had known his daughter as well as he had thought he did. She was entrenched, playing the piano at her church, helping in Awana and vacation Bible school. The same high school, same friends all her life, even the same house, even though it wasn't much. He was already feeling like a villain, even before her fear of what he was telling her had been so evident.

The Faulkners were being too eager beaverish about it, too. They were already about to scuttle the deal about no "conflict of interest". Which there really wasn't. Just the entire deal would look better if they hadn't already approached the girl. He had tried to convince them to come later in the week. He had known they would hardly be able to keep from running into one another in such a small town. Then Daniel had already bought Cokes, before he knew it was Mallory: yeah, like the girl had a look alike.

He sighed. The biggest problem he could still see was the one Patrick had feared, her affinity for the pastor's son.

He had risen and was pacing. Of course, none of the gangster stuff was really settling to him, either. The last he had spoken with Special Agent Bransom, no one had heard or seen anything of Ryland in a couple of days. The attorney swirled his glass of iced tea before setting it back down. Bransom might be a wrinkle, too. Didn't seem like Patrick O'Shaughnessy had foreseen the possibility that his widow would have another interest so soon. Bransom might have some ideas about offering legal advice contrary to what Kerry was hoping for. Lawmen usually seemed to think they could double as attorneys. He was praying he wouldn't have any opposition.

As an officer of the court, he had been forced to investigate the possibility that the Anderson kid had brought to his attention. So, he had to ask the FBI if there could be any truth to the rumor that the girl had been involved in the death of her father. He had thought Bransom was going to take a swing at him.

"I have to ask, you know that!" he had told the guy.

Bransom filled him in that he had investigated the same thing, told him all about the sheriff and some of the things they were still trying to find out about his questionable activities. Now, Larson was verifying the story, himself. Seemed as though Oscar Melville was going to be involved in a civil suit with Miss O'Shaughnessy, in addition to his other mounting legal woes.

Finally, he had been forced to admit to himself that his client wasn't the plain little school girl she looked in the photo Patrick carried. He drained the rest of the tea. He hoped she wouldn't end up hating him.

Chapter 22

DISCUSSIONS

BRANSOM FINALLY FELT as though some of the different organizations underneath his control were beginning to dovetail and bring loose ends together. He was going to be relieved about the resolution of the various investigations. John Anderson had come to the attention of law enforcement because some large amounts of money had been deposited into the church accounts and his personal accounts through mysterious, shadowy, paper organizations. The immediate reaction of the FBI and IRS had naturally been of money laundering, tax fraud, or any number of illegal activities.

When John Anderson had been aware of the first large deposit, the anonymous benefactor had instructed him not to let anyone know about the deposits, and not to put the funds to use, until a later time. With both the church needs and the needs of his family being so great, it hadn't been easy for him to do. It had been difficult for him not to confide in either his wife or his elder son. Then, government agents had been grilling him. He hadn't been able to tell any of them what he didn't know, himself. He didn't know who was depositing the money, or if they had paid their taxes, or if the money was earned by legal means. He wasn't familiar with the DiaMo corporation. Then, there had even been the concern for the Pastor, that he might owe a great deal of money to the IRS. Large donations had been placed into his personal account; the government considered it income from the date of its appearance. John's contention was, that surely, it wasn't income for him, before the benefactor gave the approval for him to begin using the money.

He had been mystified as to who might have so much wealth, who was aware of the crushing needs there were for him, and for the church.

The Andersons always brought their petitions to the Lord, and they knew there was no limit to His understanding. They knew He was able to help from sources they could never imagine. Still, it sometimes seemed as though it were too little, too late.

When he got his first personal checking account statement reflecting the initial deposit, he had made a dash to the bank to show them what a mistake they had made. They showed him the transfer from the corporation. It had the pastor's information and his account number. When he couldn't understand it, the bank's fraud division had investigated it. If someone fraudulent had this information, maybe they were planning a scam, first depositing money, then removing the amount of the deposit, as well as the Anderson's deposits and balance. Concerned about that possibility, they had avoided using their account for several months. They certainly couldn't afford to lose what little money they received.

A letter had arrived at the parsonage a few days after the original deposit, stating that more deposits would be made, both for the church, and the Anderson family. Then, they had been instructed to wait for further instruction. By the time of the investigation, when Anderson had shown the letter to all of the agents, he had read and reread it, until, if it might have ever yielded anything useful, it certainly didn't by then.

Wednesday night, Kerry Larson had handed the pastor an envelope; people were always handing him things when he was on his way to the platform. He had gazed at it curiously for a moment; it had no letterhead, and he didn't know the guy. He had automatically shoved it into his Bible cover, where he had forgotten about it.

When he had risen early on Thursday morning to slip into his study for his daily Bible reading, the envelope had slid onto his desk. He vaguely recalled the guy placing it in his hand. Intrigued, he had slit the envelope with his letter opener, pulling out a sheet of stationery. It had an impressive letterhead. It was from the DiaMo Corporation. John had read it with trembling hands. Finally, the instructions had come about the disposition of the funds. His hands shook; every instruction eclipsed his hopes and dreams by light years.

The letter was signed, Patrick Shay O'Shaughnessy, CEO, DiaMo Corporation!

Although his mind could still hardly fathom what was happening, that was when he had begun shouting. Then, even better than that, David had been the first one to reach him. Maybe his son was home, too! When he had finally been able to explain the wonderful news to his family, he had gotten them to agree that they needed to thank the Lord. They had all dutifully formed a circle and thanked the Lord, but John could tell, none of the wonder had yet begun to dawn on them. He was pretty sure it would take awhile. The only reason he had a better grasp at all was because he had been watching account balances soaring for more than a year! Finally! The moment had arrived! Right on time.

He had called Bransom about the letter; the agent was busy with safety and security about Mallory and Suzanne and the settlement on O'Shaughnessy's estate the following morning. He said he would get with Treasury, and they would be in touch with the pastor.

Everyone was still looking for Delia O'Shaughnessy's other son and grandson. They had been tracking Shannon's cell. It hadn't been hard. So far, Bransom couldn't figure out why any of these thugs had struck any fear into the heart of any FBI agents. He didn't think any of them had made any smart moves yet. But, then, he thought about Tammi Anderson and her rescue by a nest of wasps, and his smug grin had disappeared.

"Lord, we need your help. This guy may be smarter than we think. Then, there are so many more besides him. Lord, we need You to help us vanquish evil."

Back to Shannon's cell. The only calls he had made since Monday night had been to his father's cell; calls which were not being answered. He had wondered curiously, if Mrs. O'Shaughnessy had any information, and, if she would share it. He knew she and Shay were at the Self Creek Lodge up at Daisy. He was trying to figure out if he should take the time to drive up there himself, or send someone else. He wanted to see Suzanne again and make sure she and Mallory were getting safely relocated. He also wanted to finesse information out of Delia O'Shaughnessy; she had an army of attorneys. He was sure she must have some sympathies toward Ryland and Shannon.

While he was deciding, his cell rang. It was Summers. He answered. "Hey, where ya at, Summers?"

"I'm up here at Lake Greeson. Swung up here a while ago. I was just circling around a second time, caught a sniper's nest!"

Bransom had to bite his tongue to stop what had been his habitual swearing. Since his salvation, he had suddenly found himself at a loss for words. Most of his vocabulary was gone!

"Sniper! What? Where? Up at Greeson? You check on gramma and the boy? They OK?"

"Oh, yeah, they're fine! It's her hired muscle. Seems she got word that Ryland is at the bottom of the Charles River, but Shannon is still on his way here. She evidently isn't totally trusting us. Guess she doesn't trust her grandson, either."

Bransom still felt like swearing. "Yeah, but she can't do that. I mean, private security and body guards are one thing, but a sniper? I'd say that's pushing it. You get any threatening posturing from the guy?"

"Nah, but I'm in this big maroon Crown. If he's her security, which I'm guessing, he knows I'm on his same side. Just if someone shows up in a car that even resembles the kids, they might get one by accident."

"How'd you hear about the Charles River?"

"I went into the lodge for a cup of coffee; Shay was in there. He told me. Course, it's his dad and her son. They can hardly even grieve because they're so relieved. How does life get so mixed up?"

Bransom could feel the emotion in the other man's voice. "I don't know. John Anderson thinks a lot of it stems from that atheist woman, O'Hare, in the sixties, getting the Bible thrown out of schools in America. A week ago, if someone had said that to me, I would have laughed. You know, we worry more about the Bible-thumpers in America than we do about the real threats. I would have said that's totally irrelevant, or too simplistic, at best. But think about it, when did America's break-down really begin? When did crime and drugs really jump into high gear? Now we don't have Bibles in schools; we have kids with guns and bombs, no consciences, and hearts full of hate."

"What should I do about the tree-house shooter?" Summers was surprised by Bransom's impassioned speech.

"I honestly don't know." Bransom's voice. "Leave him alone; he may come in handy."

"You sure?" Summers was surprised.

"You there by yourself? You want to tell him to get down? I don't have any manpower to make him come down. O'Shaughnessy, the dad, was after Mallory and Suzanne; they are the main beneficiaries, you can count on that. If Shannon's on his way here, I'm pretty sure he won't head to Daisy first. You see anything else strange up that way? Good eye, by the way."

"Thanks, you want me to stay up this direction?"

"Guess so, unless they leave. Keep an eye on em. They seem to check out pretty clean. What's your take? How accurate you think her intel is about Ryland?

"Seem nice enough; she's pretty shrewd, about business and life! I bet she's a pistol-packin' mama, though. She probably doesn't pay the money she pays to get served wrong information."

Bransom had to admit the guy was sharp. He either needed to cut across and join the feds or move way up the ladder in Arkansas.

He disconnected. Course gramma was packin', so was Shay, so was the driver. You didn't just cruise the country in a car like that, for one thing, without someone's deciding to try to take it away from you. He thought sadly of the elderly Oklahoma couple killed by Adams for their car. They should have had a gun; no they should have the liberty to own something nice without fear of people like Adams. He was pretty convinced that America had once been a nicer place, filled with nicer people. He knew John Anderson and men like him, were the key, even before the line of law enforcement he represented. Even more law enforcement people, like Melville, couldn't be trusted to serve the interests of the citizenry. The police were more and more needing to be policed. He had argued vehemently with anyone who said the US was on her way to becoming as corrupt as Mexico. Public servants on the take, bribery, and perversion of justice. A bitter chuckle had escaped. One of the things his agents struggled with the most, was that the criminals they rounded up, had so many ways of getting off. Bribery, plea-bargains, clever attorneys getting relevant, and hard-searched for and processed evidence thrown out for one reason or the other. Gruesome crime-scene photos, like those of Thomas's victims, being dismissed because they might inflame the jury against the perpetrator. "Maybe it's time for people to be enraged and inflamed," he had raged inwardly. Then, he had quickly disagreed with himself about that. As one, whose main objective was to keep America's streets peaceful, he realized inflamed passions weren't the ticket, either. Thinking of the ramifications of that, he had sighed wearily. The wisest course seemed to be just staying at it.

He called the office in Hope. "Need a metal detector up here yesterday!" he disconnected before the secretary could argue. He was annoyed with himself. He suddenly realized everybody had a gun. What was wrong with him? Well, Mallory and David only had sling shots; he couldn't help smiling. Both were getting better. And Mallory had her dog; he planned to petition the judge to allow the dog in during the proceedings. But now, the agent was pretty sure that Delia, Shay, the limo driver, Daniel Faulkner, and Roger Sanders, all carried guns. All good people, surely legal and licensed, but aware of the fact that, if they had anything at all, someone would be after it. He sent an officer to research handgun licenses, and Brent Watson, too, Roger Sander's son-in-law.

⁂

When Mallory had returned to the house, her mother had been waiting for her. "How was your breakfast?" she had greeted.

"It was fun. Then there were people here going through everything, so Erik called me and told me we need to go to a hotel for the night. He has a room reserved. Get your stuff together for tomorrow; when you get ready, I'll call him back. He wants to help us get settled. You didn't write me a note," she had ended. "Where have you been all day? Get your stuff together first, though."

Mallory had thrown her load of laundry into the dryer, then pulled down her new little suitcase. She had thrown a few items into it, she really needed the clothes to dry quickly. She was planning to wear the new wool olive-colored suit for the next day, the white blouse, and the copper heels, jewelry, and bag. She was wearing the navy skirt and yellow sweater with the navy flats. She changed into the copper heels, throwing the flats into the bag, and putting on the blazer that matched her skirt. She planned to leave her clothes hanging so they wouldn't wrinkle. She was trying not to resent her mom's dig about a note; she should have left her one. She threw her toiletry items in and her hair dryer and curling irons. She remembered the big clip; that looked good, even if it did hurt after several hours. That made her remember the office in the shed and the safe. She hoped everything really was going to make more sense by tomorrow afternoon. She was trying not to think about what might have transpired by then, The terrifying uncertainty had gotten on her nerves. She got some aspirin out of the medicine cabinet, and threw the rest of the bottle in her bag for later. She decided to add the new basic black dress and the black heels.

"Mallory, where did you get all that stuff?" her mom had asked suspiciously from the doorway.

"Mom, there you are. Have you seen my jewelry box?" she had been pretty sure her mom had taken it with her, but it hadn't found its way back into her room, yet.

"If you're about ready, I'll call Erik," Suzanne was moving toward the phone in the living room.

Mallory knew her little pre-paid phone was about done for; she really had wanted an iPhone. Now, she realized she had left the study Bible with Shay and her grandmother. That gave her a real sense of panic; she was planning on reading it all night in preparation of what tomorrow was threatening. Tears of anguish had welled up. She kind of had a brief sense of what Christians suffered who lived under persecution, having only small portions of scripture or what they had been able to memorize. She had suddenly nearly laughed at herself. "And I think I have problems," she had scolded herself.

"Mom, my stuff isn't dry yet. Did you hear me about my jewelry? Have you seen it?"

Kerry Larson had called John Anderson around noon. "Did you ever read that letter that I handed you last night?" he had questioned immediately. He had thought that the guy would have surely pulled it out, at least by the time everyone had gathered for dinner at the lodge after the service. Finally, he had wondered if it had gotten lost.

Anderson had still been slightly dazed. "You pray and pray;" he had mused inwardly, "then you're still so totally amazed." He had thought about the story in the book of Acts about the church's praying for Peter's release from prison. An angel had set him free, but the Christians praying didn't believe God had answered them. He still felt that same wondering disbelief.

"I guess I should have called you," John had begun to apologize.

"No, no, I wanted to give you some time," the attorney had responded graciously. "I would like to get with you, right away, if possible, and discuss some of the things Patrick really had on his heart. I'm sure you stay busy, but this is important. Patrick loved America, but he didn't want the Treasury Department to have any more than necessary. He tried to set everything up so you don't have to pay a lot, either. I guess they have already been raking you over the coals. Don't talk to them any more without representation. I can't represent you and the O'Shaughnessy's, but I have a colleague I recommend highly to you."

"I have pretty good tax breaks, being in the ministry," Anderson had interrupted. "I have a CPA; I don't have anything to hide. I told them I'd talk to them as soon as I found out anything. Now that I know more, I have to fill them in.

"I'm telling you, we know more about this than you do. For one thing, by this time tomorrow, there's going to be more, and you are going to want everything as sheltered as your benefactor wanted it to be. The feds are getting ready to secure and take over your church for the next twenty-four hours. Come to my hotel room in Hope. Bring your family and let them shop at the mall; we can talk."

Larson hung up, and swirled his ice around. He began to pace. He hoped it wouldn't take all day for them to load up, and for them to get here. He wanted his colleague to turn the pastor into a corporation. It was so easy and logical, but Pastors usually preferred to take heavy tax hits, rather than engage in anything that seemed dubious. It wasn't.

Larson was convinced that in the conception of the American Nation, the Founding Fathers had intended for religious institutions and their leaders to be free from taxation. All of that had been heavily encroached upon, as the treasury had turned into more and more crushing national debt. Larson frowned into the empty tea glass. Like taxing all of the underpaid preachers in the country would refill the coffers! What the law makers seemed to miss, was the fact that preachers and churches were the best ally they could have in maintaining law and order.

"If people don't learn to fear God, we're all doomed."

Kerry Larson was a Christian; he had asked Jesus to save him when he was in junior high school. He didn't agree with many of the religions and cults; he thought they misled people into hoping they would get to heaven. But, even if their doctrine were wrong, even if the religion taught a concept that there was a God of some kind Who would judge wrongdoing; that helped maintain order, as opposed to chaos of people who feared nothing.

The young attorney was an extremely active member in his church in Dallas. He had helped his own church and some of the staff. It hadn't been easy. Of course, he received an exemption on all of his giving to his church, as well as every other break he could find.

He thought of some of the extremely large ministries across the nation, with wealthy preachers, skiing trips in private jets, and some of the things the press wanted to bring up as often as possible. The attorney sighed. As an attorney, he could be hard working and innovative, teaching courses, writing books, doing everything he could, and people wouldn't have that hard of a time with it. Well, there were always a few jealous people. But, people would never make the outcry about an attorney's having access to a private plane for a ski vacation, like they did for a "minister". Kerry thought any American who worked hard deserved to enjoy the fruits of their labors, including, and especially people in the ministry. He laughed about Congressmen trying to decide if a trip was ministry related, or for pleasure. Christians were supposed to be Christians where ever they went and whatever they did. If they were skiing, they should be good testimonies in the lift lines. In other words, every trip is a business trip for a Christian.

If pastors did immoral acts, that was something else.

Kerry had heard one well-intentioned old saint say that preachers shouldn't be flying around in corporate jets while people were dying and going to hell.

Kerry had said maybe more people could be reached faster and better if more preachers had jets. Even as he thought that, he was deciding

John Anderson should have one. He was excited now, about his upcoming meeting.

He refilled his tea from the carafe room service had delivered. His face clouded somewhat as he pondered what would be the best way to deal with Mallory; and in a manner that wouldn't make the judge mad.

Diana Faulkner's eyes were sparkling. She was wrapping some lavish and expensive gifts. She loved to give people presents, and she had been planning this party for a while now. She carefully tied an elegant bow in place; she was humming.

Daniel was watching her with a mixture of pride and trepidation.

"You seem pretty sure this will go off without a hitch," he had interrupted her happy thoughts.

She seemed surprised. "Well, sure! I mean, we've prayed about it for months!"

He didn't know what to say in the face of her optimistic faith. He worked at a lot of things, and he thought he pretty much tried to pray about everything. The facts were, sometimes deals came together; sometimes they didn't.

"You're letting Kerry make you nervous," she accused.

"Well, Honey, he's an attorney; making us nervous was what he needed to do. We should have listened to him and not even have gotten to town at all until about now. He's right; we've made this messier than it needed to be."

Her eyes were angry now, and starting to brim with tears.

"Well, it just has to come together. We promised Patrick!"

Mallory and Suzanne had arrived at their junior suite, escorted personally by Special Agent Erik Bransom. He had a security detail, and his orders were that they could either go to the mall with the agents trailing them, securing fitting rooms and ladies' rooms for them, or they needed to stay in their hotel room. He told them everyone was tentatively planning to get together for a dinner later. He had winked at Suzanne, before leaving them in the care of half a dozen agents.

Suzanne wanted to go to the mall. Mallory was already numb, and she just wanted to go someplace and hide. She thought about the words of the Psalmist, "Oh, that I had wings like a dove, for then I would fly away and be at rest." She had felt that way, often in her short seventeen years, but never as much as now. Well, maybe in the first week after her dad's death and surviving through the funeral, she had amended her thoughts.

"Oh, Daddy!" the sobs had begun to break loose again.

Delia was growing restless. In a way Shay was glad; he was bored, too. But he felt a certain sense of security within the perimeter he had set. Contrary to the ABI agent's surmising, it was Shay who had placed extra security around their cabins. He felt like he knew more what his brother might be capable of. Grandmother still viewed Shannon as somewhat of the adored first grandchild. Shay had smiled at her; she was busy studying samples and arguing with suppliers. She never stopped. Not that she had played favorites between him and Shannon, spoiling them both as much as she could. She had certainly turned off the adoration she had for her only granddaughter when Mallory had left the church, dragging her father with her. Delia had vilified her to a terrible little heathen enemy. He was pretty sure Grandmother was as delighted by her now as Shay was. She seemed like a long-lost treasure. Even now, he wished he had her phone number.

Tea was being served, and he slipped into his place. His grandmother usually "poured", but sometimes she would have him do it so she could be sure he knew how to do it right.

"This place is getting on my nerves, Shay, let's go someplace.

"There isn't any place to go." He should know by now that arguing with her was futile.

"I'm going to change for dinner. What you have on is fine," she had told him pointedly.

That meant dress up.

Leaving the tea untouched, she had gone to her room. It wouldn't take her long, so Shay rushed to his room. He quickly chose a pair of shiny gray slacks with a white dress shirt and a black wool crew-neck sweater. He changed to black dress sox and Italian leather loafers. He slid on an onyx signet ring and a Tag watch with a black leather strap. He gave his hair a tousle and sprayed cologne. His five o'clock shadow was there; he figured he didn't have time to shave again.

"Are you going to be all night?" she was demanding!

Chapter 23

DUSK

THE WORLD LOOKED magical when Suzanne and Mallie had left the hotel for the short drive to the mall. The sky had been a pale wash of a blue throughout the day. Now, a few clouds had banked to the west, where a brilliant pink sun had begun its slide toward the horizon. Silvery rays shot upward, as the pale sky had kaleidoscoped into mauves and lavenders. It was a rapturous sunset, and even as Mallory had savored the loveliness, breathlessly, she had been praying, "Even so, come, Lord Jesus."

They left the light to fade, as the agents rushed them from the curb to the protection of the mall.

Shay was busy with his laptop as he and his grandmother had been riding toward the larger town of Hope. She thought he was working on the acquisition; he hadn't tried to give her that impression. But, when she had assumed that, he hadn't clarified anything for her benefit. He was e-mailing Jerry, his guy in charge of security back at the lodge. He wanted to know of any changes in anything. Jerry had e-mailed earlier that the maroon crown vic that had circled around and around the lodge throughout the afternoon, was tailing them now. Delia's driver had noted that immediately.

"We just get the state guy, and not the Fed?" was all his grandmother had said.

Shay had laughed at that. He was glad for anyone, and he knew she was too. He pulled up headline news. There were still some stories about the Arkansas heiress and her daddy's will. Then there was another story about that big Thomas freak, and his arraignment in Federal Court, and that he was being held over for trial without bail. There was more about a reward for his capture if he got convicted.

Delia was watching the enchanting sunset beyond the deep green of the pines. She was sure it was even more beautiful back at the lodge, with the beautiful tints reflected from the lake. She thought about her new-found designer friend. Pulling her phone from her bag, she punched the speed dial and had Diana on speakerphone. "You getting pictures of this one?" she questioned.

"Oh, yes!" came back the enthusiastic response. "I probably have captured fifty images in the past fifteen minutes.

"Make that fifty-million images," Daniel's teasing voice had inserted itself.

They could both hear her hitting him, and then he had yelped in pain.

Delia laughed, as she broke the connection. "I always like to know I'm causing trouble."

Delia cut the connection and punched another button. Two or three rings, but then Beth Sanders had answered. She had known it was Delia by her caller ID.

"Good afternoon, Mrs. O'Shaughnessy," she had answered. "What can I do for you?"

"Shay and I got a little lonely so far away from everyone up at that lodge, so we've driven down. We were wondering if you could tell us what the best restaurant in town is."

"Well, this isn't exactly the epicurean center of the world," she had laughed. "Roger and I really enjoy McKenna's steak house. The food is actually delicious, and on a week-night, you might about have the place to yourselves."

"We had the lodge to ourselves and didn't like it; that's why we're driving down. We want to get a party started. Shay said he wants to buy for everyone. I know it isn't much notice, but could you join us, please?" she had wheedled sweetly on the end. "We aren't eating until late."

Shay laughed. She always got what she wanted; she was amazing.

Beth was saying something like, it was a school night; she would have to see if Connie could stay with Emma and Evan. Delia could hear both of them saying they were big enough to be left, without their big sister.

"Hold on a minute," Delia had interrupted. "Shay and I don't like to be around old people; it was all the kids we were inviting, actually." She had winked real big at her handsome grandson. "It's Constance and Brent, and Emma and Evan we liked. You and your husband, what's his name, are welcome to come along, if you must."

The other woman was saying she was sure it would be too late on a school night.

Roger had been listening in, "Hey, if you cool people will allow us old worry-warts to join you, count us in." He was laughing at over- riding Beth's objections. H e was grateful she was such a great mom; but sometimes, you could throw caution to the wind and have fun with your kids. "See you around nine-thirty, but Shay isn't treating when y'all are in my town. Bye." He hung up before she could argue.

The kids were excited. Emma was already on the way to her rooms to change clothes and re-do her hair.

John Anderson had pulled the battered mini-van up in front of the mall in Hope at about two-thirty. He had handed each of his five children a hundred dollar bill and told them to have fun.

He had given his wife five hundred. He had kissed her, and told her he might be a while. "Where are you going?" she had questioned in alarm. "Where did all this money come from?"

"It came from Patrick; I have a meeting with an attorney about it. I'll be as quick as I can. If I get tied up, I'll call you on David's phone. Why don't you look into a phone deal while you're in the mall? You can get a plan, and you can get a cell for yourself and Tammi."

"Here's my phone, Mom." David had thrust it at her. "I'm going with Dad."

"No, you're not. You're going with your mother and your brother and sisters, please, David." he could see the obstinacy all over his son's countenance.

"Dad, what if it's a trap?"

John laughed his deep, easy laugh. "I'm pretty sure it isn't a trap. But if it were, then I would really need you with Mom and the other kids. Find yourself something nice with the money; some high dollar label stuff you're always wanting. Be back as soon as I can. He shoved a fifty dollar bill into Lana's hand with the five hundred. If you get hungry, get some snacks. We can all go have a nice dinner together later when I get back for you. School's canceled tomorrow; I just need to be at our church/court before ten in the morning for the proceedings."

Kerry Larson had been on his balcony watching for the pastor to arrive. He had handed him his colleague's business card, and that of a highly respected accounting firm first thing. They were both in Dallas. John's immediate impression had been that he had, indeed, been set up.

"I thought that was who I was meeting with here, now. Thanks for the referrals; I may give these guys a call. Seems to be no reason for me to stay; guess I'll go join my family.

"Please have a seat," Kerry had interrupted him. "These guys are really great guys; when you hear some of the things Patrick has been planning, it will make more sense. Right now, I really just need a word with you about your son."

He had plunged in headlong when he had intended to use a more subtle approach.

John Anderson felt himself bristling inside. He didn't want anyone bringing his son up to him in this guy's tone. It was a sensitive thing with him, anyway. Only the fact that he had been Patrick's attorney, and now seemed to have plans for Mallory, caused him to be willing to sit down. He didn't want to act in haste, losing the much needed money for the church. He had to admit, they desperately needed the cash personally, too.

"What about David?" he had questioned, his voice laden with misgivings.

The young attorney had poured yet another tea refill, offering a glass of the beverage to his guest, as well.

"I'm going to order up a sandwich," he had decided, proffering the room-service menu to his guest.

The pastor had surveyed it quickly before deciding on the Club. Larson phoned the order in for two Club sandwiches and another tea carafe; then he decided to order coffee, too.

"Remember the word "tip" is an acrostic for "to insure promptness"," he instructed who ever had been taking the order.

John had been following the other man's actions detachedly. The guy had barged in, now he was backing off, giving him some space. He appreciated it. He sat quietly, refusing to reopen the conversation about David. If this man had something to say about David, he could re-gather his courage to start again. John Anderson made it a practice not to open doors he didn't want to walk through.

"What were we talking about?" Kerry had finally begun again.

"You gave me these guys' business cards and recommended them to me. You were saying I should incorporate for more tax shelter. The church is already incorporated as a non-profit organization."

The attorney had tilted the chair back; something that always got on Anderson's nerves. He was gazing at the ceiling, steepling his fingers. He smacked his chair down suddenly onto all four legs. His gaze was back on the pastor sitting in front of him.

"I know you're a really good guy; I'm not questioning your integrity or your willingness to serve the Lord. You've shown that. That's why Patrick O'Shaughnessy thought so highly of you. He sat through the meetings when they ripped you and your family apart in front of you, to try to justify not giving you raises. He was becoming wealthy, even then. He wanted to tithe on every penny he was making; but if he did that, people would discover how wealthy he had become, before he had everything in place the way he wanted it. He's been building a house for you; he wanted you to own a home. Hardly any baptist ministers live in parsonages any more. He knew that if something happened to you, your family would get pushed out of the parsonage, almost immediately. He wanted to be certain you get a life insurance policy, again for the sake of your wife and family. He wanted your family to get to take fun and educational trips together, before your children are grown and gone. He wanted the church buildings to be repaired, rebuilt, expanded; preferably by an architect. He said he would have liked there to be something, somewhere between a totally derelict-looking baptist church and a Catholic Cathedral. He had purchased some beautiful mountain property not too far from here to build a Bible Camp. He always felt like your wife and children tried hard to enhance you as a man and a pastor, but some people just pick-picked all the time."

John Anderson had begun to cry softly. He was starting to like the attorney; or at least appreciate Patrick's kind heart, even more.

A knock at the door of the suite meant the sandwiches and beverages had arrived. Larson rose and answered the door, allowing the bellman with the tray to enter and arrange the food. He signed, including a generous tip.

"See, these expenses, including tips can all be deducted from my income, because I'm incorporated. All my expenses on the road, hair cuts, dry cleaning, vitamins, prescriptions, gym membership all come out before I'm taxed. That means I'm not taxed on much. It isn't illegal, immoral, or even really questionable. This will actually free you from so much oversight by church people. Look at the way you are living right now. The parsonage belongs to "the people" so they feel free to come at any hour of the day or night to see if your wife and kids are keeping it up in a way that meets with every-one's approval. They'll talk to her about it, or just get on the phone and yak about it to one another. She must really love the Lord to stay so gracious"

Anderson leaned forward and bit into his sandwich. His mouth was full when the attorney had continued on.

"That brings us back to your son. Mr. O'Shaughnessy has always loved your family; he really sympathized with the kids for the pressure that they always felt. He really was always glad he moved here, and that Mallory had your children for friends. He credited your ministry for his salvation and he was always glad for your wisdom and friendship. He really loved you and your entire family."

"But?" John had been able to tell there was some sandwich psychology going on here. He was ready to hear the guys point and go rejoin his family.

"Mr. O'Shaughnessy had become increasingly alarmed about his daughter's feelings for your son. He liked David, but he was worried they were far too young to be such close friends. He tried to limit their ability to be together. He wanted Mallory to get beyond this little town. In such a small school, there aren't that many boys and girls to choose from. Then, since we only want our children to like other children who are saved, that narrowed the possibilities down even more. He thought they liked each other so much because they didn't have more choices."

John wasn't in total agreement, but he sat silently. No use trying to argue with what Patrick thought. He was in heaven.

The attorney had paused to take another bite. He chewed, giving Anderson a chance to respond. The pastor took another bite of his own sandwich. He felt like he was about to be informed about the detail of whatever their dastardly plan was. He was dreading it, for his son's sake. What if whatever they decided about Mallory knocked David out of the saddle again?

Then he remembered his own words to his son; that he had to decide for the Lord. "Whatever happens, please keep his eyes on You," he had petitioned the Lord in his heart.

Kerry still hadn't continued on. Finally realizing John Anderson wasn't any novice at taking control of a situation, he had gone on.

"Patrick had a lot of money. He has some really great things for Suzanne and some of the others, including you and your family. Mallory is his primary beneficiary. One of the things he was trying to get finalized before his death was finding her a home where she would be safe. I think maybe he knew his brother would be capable of trying to have her killed. We were shocked at the danger, though. He found her a beautiful home on the north side of Dallas that has the security features in place for her. After the will is read, tomorrow, we would like to get her situated there as soon as possible."

John Anderson had risen to his feet; he hadn't been hungry for a sandwich. Now he felt as though he might be sick.

"So, who do you mean by "we"?" he had questioned. Who is in on this deal with you? That Faulkner family? What if she doesn't want to go?"

"That's why I'm sharing this with you. If she doesn't want to go, will you help us persuade her?"

"I'll pray about it," he meant it; he always meant it when he said that!

He had driven slowly the four blocks back to the mall. He wished Patrick had talked to him about this before he had involved these other rich and heartless people. They probably just wanted to isolate her from people who genuinely cared about her so they could get her money. He gave himself a shake. It scared him when he found himself thinking like his son.

He had a huge lump in his throat, and his stomach was still misbehaving. The sky was beautiful. He pulled over for a few minutes, just to watch the changing light, the gilded cotton balls, the last brilliant coral remnant of the sun. He had told David that Mallory was too good for him. He didn't like hearing the same thing from Patrick O'Shaughnessy, or his attorney. Still, everything he had said financially made sense. He was finally convinced to be in touch with the other men.

He had stayed too long, listening to Kerry Larson. Then, he had watched the sun set. When did he ever do that? But the tranquil beauty had helped him feel more of a sense of the beauty and wonder of the Lord.

When he arrived at the mall, he actually found Lana first. She was loaded down with huge bags of sheets, and towels, and bathroom rugs.

"Honey, you were supposed to be getting something for yourself and the kids for Easter," he had fussed at her as he relieved her of the heavy packages.

"Oh, you didn't tell me that. But, honey, we hardly have any decent towels at all; and the sheets don't stay on the beds any more."

"How did you lug all this stuff this far?" he had asked her in amazement. Here's the Food Court. Let's sit down and have a drink; you hungry?"

She told him they had all eaten a snack soon after arriving. She had met up with them again a couple of times, on the hour. Everyone was due to check in with her again in about fifteen minutes.

He ordered a large diet drink and rejoined her with it.

"Honey, you are not going to believe this, but Patrick is building us our own house; no more parsonage!"

"Patrick is?" she teased. "Is he working on our mansion in heaven, or does he have passes to come down here someplace and build on something?"

"Ha ha," he laughed at her. She really was still pretty cute and funny. He clasped her hand, then kissed it. Sorry! Guess I should have slowed the guy down to find out more about that. He said Patrick had purchased acreage in the mountains to build a camp, and he wanted the church plant to be all spiffed up better than new. It isn't just the money in the accounts. Larson thinks there will be more, tomorrow; or more details. Patrick wanted me to have life insurance and a retirement, and vacations. The attorney wants me to see another attorney and CPA for sheltering some of it."

Lana could still hardly grasp the meaning of everything, but she loved seeing him so happy and light-hearted once again. The past year of the problems with David added to the tremendous financial burden, had really taken its toll on him. She smiled at him through tears.

"It's good to see you so happy again, and David seems pretty happy, too. Those are some wonderful answers to prayer. What else did that lawyer say? you were gone a long time. I didn't like him much last night before church when I first saw him speaking with Mallory."

"M-m-m, so, is that why Mallory ended up playing the piano?" he had asked her curiously.

"John, what else did he say?"

"Honey, I can't tell you all of it right now," he had started.

"Is it something that is going to hurt David?" she had asked.

"Spoken like a true Mom. What do you mean by 'hurting' David. It might be like a shot, that hurts right away, but helps a lot over the long run."

"She isn't leaving here, is she?" she was already starting to cry.

"Look, Sugar, I don't have my crystal ball with me. Why don't you go start looking for Easter outfits? Start with something beautiful for yourself; then work down the line. I'm going to take these home goods back for now. We can pick out stuff together when we know what the new house is going to need."

"Hope it looks better than his house does," she had whispered gloomily. "I'm on my way to look for an outfit; you want to sit here and wait for the kids to check in? They should be coming any minute."

⁂

Mallory had sped toward the bookstore as soon as they entered the mall. She had to find a Bible. "Mom, you want a coffee drink?" she had offered. Get me something, too; I shouldn't need too long to pick a Bible out." She handed her mother a twenty.

Suzanne ordered the drinks, and Mallory was back in under ten minutes with a Bible similar to the one her grandmother had kept. They sipped their drinks together, pretty much in silence. Mallory was busy checking out some of the features of her new Bible. Finally, she had slid it back into the bag.

"So, Mom," she had drained her drink. Let's go do some serious shopping. She handed her mom a couple of hundred dollar bills and told her she would meet her at the entrance at eight thirty. The agents didn't like it really well that their charges were going separate directions, but the two women could be pretty headstrong.

Mallory had begun at the cosmetic counter. It was the same lady who had helped her earlier in the week. Mallory asked for water-proof mascara, which was produced immediately. Maybe no one would tell her she looked like a raccoon, now The woman suggested she purchase another tube of the attractive lipstick. One for her "vanity" and one to carry in her handbag. Mallory made the purchases. She really liked the shade; she was uneasy about whether she would have any liberty to shop or do anything she enjoyed. She smilingly paid for her purchases, trying to force the unpleasant thoughts to do an about face and march right back out of her mind.

She looked at some more clothes. She still had quite a bit of cash with her. She couldn't really focus on shopping. She had no idea where she might be going, if anywhere, or what she might need. She had started through the men's department to get out to the mall. She saw David Anderson, but he hadn't seen her. He had gotten a hair cut; he looked really handsome.

She had turned and hurried away. Walking quickly back to the bookstore, she had loaded her arms with books; all the classics she had always intended to read sometime. She purchased about ten heavy volumes. If she were a prisoner somewhere, she had a Bible and some books. That actually had helped her feel a little better.

⁂

Erik Bransom had tied up some loose ends; his cases were by no means, closed; but his plan was to meet Suzanne and Mallory at a steakhouse as soon as the mall closed. After dinner, he was planning to pull an all-nighter. He finished a briefing. They were planning roadblocks along every traffic artery into Murfreesboro. It was a relief to him that the proceedings were actually taking place in such a small town. The State Parks Director had requested that they not hinder access to the Diamond Mine. They should be able to cooperate with that; no problem. The word was that Shannon O'Shaughnessy was still heading in their direction. Bransom couldn't find any real grounds for just picking the guy up; which would seem the easiest. If he just arrived at one of their roadblocks, where they were looking every car over, it would be easier to look the car over for weapons or drugs.

He hurried up the steps to the most highly recommended steak house; Suzanne and her daughter were already seated.

Mallory had tried to beg off; she really felt like an intruder having a steak dinner with her mom and the agent. Their security detail had refused to allow the girl to return to the room before Suzanne was ready to go.

"Evening, ladies!" he greeted them; "Hope you have an appetizer coming, I'm hungry."

He had slid into a banquette next to Suzanne and ordered coffee. Both of the girls already had iced tea. The server had returned quickly with the steaming cup of coffee and a basket of fragrant yeast rolls. Bransom had taken Suzanne's hand and extended his other hand to Mallory across the table. Startled, she had joined hands with him, and he had said a blessing over the meal. He gave Suzanne a kiss on the cheek, then offered the dinner rolls to them, before helping himself.

"Did you two have good shopping?" he had begun.

"Not bad," Suzanne had responded. "I found some great things; Mallory bought out the bookstore."

Two of the agents in the security detail had been seated at a table for two by the window. The other four were outside, two circling the area in a vehicle, and the other two disguised as grounds keepers.

Suzanne had asked Erik if he knew where Ryland and Shannon were.

He just told her everyone had eyes and ears on the situation. They still had no official confirmation on Ryland; he wanted to alleviate some of their worry about everything, but he couldn't give details.

He had started to talk to Mallory about Oscar Melville and Martin Thomas. She had hardly had any appetite. Hearing those two names didn't help any. "I still don't know anything at all about what's going on," she had confided wearily.

"Well, as soon as I get you two girls off my hands tomorrow, I'm going to Little Rock to find out more from those two. Martin has been indicted in one of the murders, and he's bound over for trial without bail. I think Melville is implicated in the murders, but I can't prove whether he was at the scenes, or if evidence just transferred onto him and his clothes due to contact with the truck after the crimes. If we can't prove he was guilty in the capital murders, he may receive bail. We want to stall that until you are both clear out of the area. Of course, Mallory, Kerry Larson is working on bringing a civil suit against Melville for the way he has violated your rights since your father's death. I'm pretty sure he'll do some time for the criminal aspect of his misuse of authority. But, if we can't prove he helped Thomas murder those women, he may not do much time."

"Why are you only trying Martin for one of the murders?" Mallie had asked fearfully.

"If we try all four at once, and we can't get a conviction, he walks. If we try him for one, and for some reason, he wriggles out, we can still try another one, and another one, and another one. I want the death penalty"

Tears had welled up again in Mallory's eyes. "You know, David and I always used to try to get him to come to Sunday School, or Vacation Bible School, or Summer Camp. I wish we had tried harder. We always sort of didn't really want him to come, you know?"

The Anderson family had shopped until closing time, finding new things for the special upcoming holiday. David had agreed to haul back all of the heavy home goods and get the money back. He seemed to be the same kid he had been before he had decided to train-wreck.

The family couldn't believe they were going to Mc Kenna's for steaks. John and Lana had been able to go one time for their wedding anniversary. Meals at any restaurant were a rare treat. Now, they had been to the lodge for dinner the previous evening, and a steak dinner now.

Daniel and Diana Faulkner had stayed in their luxury motor home for more than twenty-four hours. As a wealthy executive, Daniel was always aware of safety and security matters for his family. They were the most treasured of all his possessions. The Coach was armored, the glass bullet-proof. The Park Ranger at the "Crater" campground had noticed that the pad was suffering beneath the weight of the vehicle. His supervisor didn't know what to do; this was a first.

Diana had convinced them, finally, to venture forth, so she could photograph the beautiful sky. They had been relieved to get out. Daniel had called Agent Bransom to get an assessment of the danger level

"I can't make you any guarantees," he had told the guy honestly. "Obviously, I think there's a real threat; I'm not sure where, or when, or from whom. I can't tell you what to do about your family; that's on you."

Diana wanted to go out for dinner; so surrounded by private security, they had decided on steaks at the nicest restaurant in Hope.

They were chagrined to see the two Federal Government vehicles. Since they hadn't seen the Jaguar or Mallory's new little car, however, they had assumed that Suzanne and Mallie were not at the restaurant. Larson was trying to keep them apart for another sixteen hours.

As soon as the hostess had opened the door, the Faulkners had seen Mallory, and she had seen them. The Faulkners had all acted wrapped up in one another and passed the threesome without speaking. Mallory had begun to sense that they were pretty friendly to everyone, but they didn't like her-for some reason. She wondered if they had heard some of the things about her that were not true. Did they think she had somehow caused her dad's death? Did they think she had allowed David to spend a night with her? Maybe they just didn't like her; that was certainly their right. She had heard that they were in town for the legal proceedings. Would they get a lot? Would Grandmother and Shay? What had Mr. Larson been saying, exactly?

Her eyes had followed the fascinating family, longingly. When she had picked out her cute, new clothes, she had somehow done it with Diana Faulkner in mind. Would she like this? Would she compliment that? She had seemed so nice on Saturday. Now, every time she appeared someplace where Mallory was, she looked the other way. And she always looked so exquisite that Mallory felt like a frumpy, little, country girl; even with all of her new clothes. Once again, what Diana was wearing surpassed anything Mallory had ever imagined. Tonight, she had on an oceanic-aqua silk, shantung suit. The coordinating silk sweater looked like an underwater dive scene, with brilliant-colored fish and deep green seaweed backed with the beautiful color of the water. Her heels and bag matched the golden orange of one of the fish. The aqua matched her beautiful eyes. She was laughing at something one of her children had said. Her jewelry sparkled. Mallory wished she had on the ring from her dad.

"They sure aren't friendly," Suzanne had observed-vocally. "Wasn't that guy just talking to you on the phone? You give him his information, and then he doesn't know you?"

Bransom shrugged. "Guess I'm not really in their league. Doesn't bother me either way. I want to talk to you two, anyway. About a certain box of jewelry!" He was watching Suzanne's reaction, shrewdly, yet teasingly.

"Roger said it disappeared before it got to evidence." Suzanne was trying to get Erik not to mention any more about it in front of Mallory.

It hurt Mallie's feelings; the Faulkners didn't want to talk to her; she was on a stupid date with her mother and her mother's stupid boyfriend. They didn't want to talk in front of her. She had pushed her chair back; she could wait in the car!

"Whoa, sit down!" the guy had barked at her.

She realized she was too dizzy to stand, anyway, so she had complied.

"You aren't in our way, Mallie," he had said kindly.

He looked back at Suzanne. "I lied about the jewelry getting lost! I had to transport it by myself, and I didn't want to die over it. The charges have actually been dropped, and the jewelry will be delivered by armored car to Mallory on Monday."

The Sanders arrived and were led to the table Roger had reserved in advance. They were quickly joined by Shay and Delia.

Then the Anderson family had showed up. It was the same group as the previous evening, with the exception of Kerry Larson and the Haynes family.

Chapter 24

DIVISION

MALLORY HAD SLEPT poorly, once again. She was awake before dawn. She was thankful for the junior suite. She was trying hard not to disturb her mom. She had grabbed her new Bible, and with new marker in hand, had turned first to Proverbs 13. The first verse jumped out at her, and she underlined it: "A wise son heareth his father's instruction: but a scorner heareth not rebuke." The third verse grabbed her attention, and it, too, was highlighted: "He that keepeth his mouth keepeth his life: but he that openeth wide his lips shall have destruction."

She copied both verses into her journal; the entry date was, "Friday, April thirteenth."

She read some more, but she knew the Lord had already answered her desperate prayers for wisdom. No verses could have been more perfect. "A wise son (or daughter, in her case) was to hear her father's instructions, and obey. That's what Kerry Larson had said; that Mallory's daddy had written a letter about what he wanted to have happen in her life. The uncertainty was in not knowing exactly what that was going to be. She was pretty sure it meant, "no David Anderson." Well, in a few hours now, she would know something more definite. She paced, then reread the verses. Whatever happened, she had to do what her dad wanted. She wasn't wise enough or mature enough to make her own decisions. She was to listen, and agree. Sounded easy! She was pretty sure it was going to be harder than it seemed.

"Lord, please help me to be quiet about what I want, and do the will of my father, like You submitted to the will of Your Father"

She showered and dressed in the olive wool suit. She didn't know if the weather was supposed to be springy or wintry, but the suit was the best she had. She was thinking, aggravatedly, that Diana Faulkner would be there looking like Spring, personified, while Mallory was clad in olive drab. Why were the Faulkners even here, circling around the carnage left by her dad? How did he know them? Where did they meet him? Were they really rich? Or had they bought a lot of stuff, hoping to leave here rich?"

She was trying to look extra-nice, but this morning, she didn't like the way the color made her green eyes stand out in the stark pallor of her face. She tried the nice lipstick; then, she really thought she looked like the "Joker". Finally, with a defeated sigh, she had given up. Her hair had looked cute in the clip a couple of days before; now, it looked all lop-sided. It felt like it was all going to come down, anyway. She gave up on the clip, allowing the shiny strands to swing freely around her shoulders. She stepped into the hallway. There were different agents than the ones from the previous night. Three of them spread out to cover her, and three stayed to watch over Suzanne.

Shannon O'Shaughnessy had continued to panic more, the longer he went without hearing from his father. Shay was much more a natural leader, between the two brothers. Shannon didn't have a clue what to do without orders from his father. He had continued on toward Murfreesboro, Arkansas because that was the last order his father had given him. He had stopped for a couple of nights on the long road trip, but it was still farther than he had thought, so Thursday night, he had had to keep pushing, in order to reach his destination by Friday morning before ten o'clock. He kept using a credit card; and he repeatedly used a fake ID to buy liquor. Neither of the two things were particularly smart.

Both overly-tired, and inebriated, he had finally hit an icy spot on 84 just to the east of Kirby. He had spun his yellow, pride and joy Corvette into a tree. Summers, who had followed Shay and Delia back up to Daisy after their dinner in Hope, had been in charge of setting roadblocks up there. It didn't take him long to get to the scene of the one-car collision and get the dazed young man into custody. An ABI chopper set down, and Shannon was on the way to hospitalization under guard in Little Rock.

Bransom was continuing with the security, anyway. No one had ever said that Shannon and Ryland O'Shaughnessy were the only threats. Just because those two seemed to be out of the picture, didn't mean Mallory and Suzanne would be safe.

A news crew had tried to get through Bransom's roadblock, and he had refused to grant access. He thought there was already too much media. The reporter had been carrying on about his right to free speech and freedom of the press. Finally Bransom leered in his face. "Guess I haven't seen that memo! I said, turn around, and go back!"

Then the guy was going to write him up, so he asked Bransom for his name.

"My name is, 'the guy with a lot of fire power'! I said, 'Go back!'"

"Freedom of the press," he had muttered, finally, at the retreating vehicle. "More like power of the press." They seemed to think they should get the final say in every situation. He thought they always made his hard job harder whenever they were around.

He had been amazed that Shannon, had indeed been heading to Kirby, where his Grandmother and brother were staying. He didn't know if Shannon knew they were staying there, or if the maze of roads and alternate routes into Murfreesboro were just as confusing to him as they were to most people. He was glad Shannon had wrecked his car before he had gotten to the lodge. If the sniper had taken him out, it could have caused charges to be brought against Delia O'Shaughnessy. Shannon hadn't had any weapons with him!

Daniel Faulkner had agreed with the FBI agent that other dangers could still be lurking; but he was extremely relieved that Shannon had been apprehended. He could hardly believe the guy had been driving across the country without a weapon. He expressed that to Bransom.

"Where all did Ivan look?" he had asked.

"Who?" Bransom didn't even know Summer's first name. "Oh, you mean Summers. I guess he searched all through the car and luggage." As he said it, he knew what Faulkner was thinking. Whatever weapons Shannon O'Shaughnessy might have had with him, wouldn't have been licensed. The kid was barely twenty years old. He probably had an automatic weapon, which was illegal. He ditched the weapon, as he wrecked, or afterwards, before Summers had reached the scene. He had started to call Summers, but his phone was already ringing. Just as Faulkner had surmised, there were some weapons; and ammunition; an excessive supply of ammo! Bransom was relieved. He knew they couldn't have held him long, just for the under-aged drinking, and driving under the influence. Pity! 'Cuz those things were pretty bad.

Shay and Delia were shaken that Shannon had come so close to them. Delia still hadn't known about Shay's extra security measures.

By nine o'clock, the church had been converted into a temporary court of law. Since it was an Auxiliary of the Arkansas State Court System, the ABI was in charge of security. Summer's superior, Janice Collins, was issuing orders. She had agents stationed at all of the entrances. No one was to go in or out anywhere but the double doors at the back of the auditorium. That was where the metal detectors had been set up and tested. There were state agents who were to tag and store any weapons that people had in their possession. Due to the small size of the building, the judge had ruled "no photography" during the court session. The reporters were not particularly pleased. Bransom had asked for permission to allow Mallory to keep Dinky by her side. He explained the dog's nature, but told him Mallory had excellent control over him. A temporary bench for the judge had been set in place; he had already been escorted in, where his "chambers" were a small Sunday School classroom that opened onto the front of the auditorium.

The press members were already in place, with sketch artists, rather than intrusive cameras.

John and Lana Anderson were the first to arrive of those whose names were included in the will. David had insisted on accompanying them. John had argued with him all morning. He wasn't invited; he wouldn't be able to keep his mouth shut; he would end up getting them all cited for contempt of court.

"Why? What are they going to say that would make me mouth off? What do you know that you haven't told me? What are they gonna do to her, Dad?"

It was the panic in his voice that had let John know this wasn't a good idea. But, with one more warning, and one more promise from David, they had acquiesced.

David had stopped at a large decorative mirror at the back of the auditorium to survey himself anxiously. His new haircut looked strange, and he could feel a zit popping up by his eyebrow. He knew this was going to be an extremely well-dressed crowd. He was afraid he might cry when he saw Mallory. He thought she had looked miserable the night before at the steak place. He tugged at a spike of hair that wanted to fall over.

"Hello, Narcissus!" Mallory was greeting him. He hadn't seen her coming. "You say I brag. I'm not about to get sucked through the looking-glass," she was teasing.

She was so white he about wanted to call an ambulance. She was all eyes: Huge, green, limpid, mystifying. She was beautiful; a classic tragic heroine! He wished he were an attorney, with expensive clothes and a new Porsche. He would sweep her away from whatever was coming down here. The color would flow back into her cheeks, and she would smile.

"Did you call me Narcissus?" he demanded. "Isn't that the little dude that loved to see his reflection in the pond each morning? And then, didn't he fall into his own reflection and drown?"

"That's who I mean," she affirmed sweetly.

He leaned back into the mirror, even though people were trying to get past them, and they had drawn a crowd. He gave himself an approving nod and flexed his muscles slightly. "Ah, what a way to go!"

His response sent her into giggles; he had intended for it to!

The bailiff had come to escort her to a table in the front. It had two chairs at it, and Mallory seated herself in one, her back ramrod straight.

David joined his parents a few rows back.

A distinguished looking silver-haired man had approached Mallory. He was dressed in an expensive navy suit. His tie was navy and gold striped. His attache case was alligator.

He had pulled a set of papers out, and was showing them to her. David seemed to be the only one noticing. He couldn't hear.

"Miss O'Shaughnessy!"the man had startled her.

"Oh yes, I'm Mallory," she had responded. He stood there, then recovered slightly.

"Yes, good morning. My name is Lawrence Freeman. I represent Ms. Delia O'Shaughnessy. I have filed a motion on her behalf to petition the courts for her to claim the remains of her son, Patrick Shay O'Shaughnessy."

Mallory had looked shocked. Her eyes were sweeping the crowd for her grandmother and cousin. They hadn't mentioned anything to her about it before this. Her mom was sitting toward the back with Mr. Bransom. Mallory had thought her mother was probably going to be sitting beside her. Her gaze swept back up to the attorney, standing beside her. She rose to meet his gaze.

I'm not sure I understand what you said, Mr. uh Freeman, was it? My father's body doesn't need to be claimed. We held a funeral for him in January. Mrs. O'Shaughnessy chose not to attend."

"Yes, ma'am, I understand that. She is willing to settle this out of court. She's prepared to offer you ten thousand dollars if you don't try to fight her about this. You should take the offer. I don't think you can win, anyway."

Mallory had spent the night determining that she wouldn't cry, no matter what happened.

"Mr. Freeman," her voice was icy, "you may tell my grandmother my father is not for sale! My dad is in heaven; he doesn't need 'his remains' any longer, and I don't either!"

She sank gracefully back into her chair, turning away from him; but then he wanted her to sign the papers. She scrawled her name with a decisive flourish. She would not cry!

She was desperately clutching a box of tissues, even though she was determined not to shed a tear. Shay came up, trying to trade a beautiful stack of the monogrammed linen handkerchiefs for the box. Mallory relinquished it without looking up.

"Is your mother going to sit beside you?" he had asked.

"I'm not sure," she had replied stiffly. She could sense that the church had filled up behind her. She refused to look. Kerry Larson had finally come forward and taken a seat beside her. Reluctantly, Shay had retreated to sit next to Delia. She had rewritten her verses from Proverbs thirteen onto a scrap of paper. She untwisted it and reread them.

The bailiff had stood at the front and told everyone to rise. When Mallory had sprung to her feet, dizziness had hit her again. She remained on her feet, but she was steadying herself against the table. She had begun to tremble.

The judge had taken the bench and pounded the gavel to begin. Dinky had growled, then settled down like he understood the seriousness of the situation. Her attorney had risen and was addressing her. He was saying something about he didn't know whether he should read the will first, or the letter from his client Patrick Shay O'Shaughnessy to Miss Mallory Erin O'Shaughnessy. Mallory thought he was trying to be theatrical; the judge looked bored. After some more tedious legal-speak, he was announcing that he had deemed it best to begin with the letter. She tried to get a glance at her verses again, and he had told her she had to look at him while he read the letter.

She tilted her face toward him defiantly.

He had begun:

"*My Darling Mallory*,

I wish I could have made it to see you graduate from high school, and then college. I wish I could walk you down the aisle at your wedding. I wish I could live long enough to be a grandfather to your children.

Thank you for being such a joy to me. I love you.

Because you are still so young, and you will be in control of such a large estate, I have asked a very good friend to be your guardian for five more years from the time of my death. That will bring you to twenty-two or twenty-three. I want you to finish college and keep serving the Lord in that time. I know you think you are more ready for the challenges of life than I think you are. Guess Daddy's always think their little girls are little girls. That is my wish for you. Five years probably seems long to you. The man I have asked to watch over you is someone you don't even know. I'm asking you to transplant before the completion of your junior year, to a house I have chosen for you in Dallas, Texas . All of the details of the guardianship are not expressed here; but with a very good couple. I hope you always remember what I've tried to teach you. Please, Mallory, Darlin' consent to this. Trust me; I know what's best.

Love,
Daddy"

When the letter had been read, the room remained hushed.

"Miss O'Shaughnessy, do you understand what you have heard?" the judge asked her.

"Yes, sir," she had responded.

She didn't really. It was still as much of a riddle as it had been all week. She couldn't begin to imagine who she was agreeing to live with. He hadn't named names. She had a feeling this was why the Faulkners had come, but they already wouldn't even talk to her.

"Do you agree to your father's stipulations?" Kerry Larson was asking.

"Counselor, approach the bench," the judge was frowning. Larson was surprised.

"Yes, your honor?" he replied.

"It seems to the court that you are, indeed, representing the deceased. Are you saying you are representing the best interests of Miss O'Shaughnessy, also?"

"Miss O'Shaughnessy, would you like to reconsider your counsel and reconvene this court at a later date?" the judge was asking her.

"No sir," she had responded. "I can decide right now. I'm not opposed whatsoever to my father's request. I agree to it."

She could feel the entire crowd sigh together in relief; she felt some relief, herself.

"Very well! So note!" the court reporter had it all down.

They began with the will. There were several corporations that covered quite an array of enterprises. Many of the antiques had been disposed of according to directives Patrick had signed earlier. There were specific instructions about the creation of the diamond mine. Even before the diamonds had been mentioned in the will, a firm had been moving onto the acreage, moving the house. They were erecting fences and security measures to protect a diamond-mining operation. There were claims along the rivers that washed many of the diamonds along toward the gulf. The size and quality of the O'Shaughnessy diamonds were remarkable. The safe had contained numerous, beautiful rough stones, more cash, stocks, and bonds.

The reading seemed to go on endlessly. There was supposed to be a board meeting during the remainder of the afternoon.

Beneficiaries of Patrick O'Shaughnessy's estate were: Mallory, the church, Suzanne, John and Lana Anderson, Delia O'Shaughnessy, Ryland O'Shaughnessy, Shannon O'Shaughnessy, Shay O'Shaughnessy, and Robert and Lynn Campbell. Suzanne couldn't believe he had bequeathed so much to her mother and father.

The division of the man's goods had been carefully thought out, and there was quite a bit of detail.

Mallory had continued to sit stiffly.

Suddenly, David had whispered hoarsely to his dad, "Dad, they railroaded her. That wasn't fair!"

John had been afraid of this. The judge had banged the gavel, ordering the court to come to order. His son had caused quite a flutter. He gave his son a desperate, sideways glare, not wanting him to say anything further.

"Dad," he was still trying to plead.

"Young man, approach!" the judge had ordered.

David had obeyed.

"Do you have something to say about these proceedings?"

"No sir, It's just the way the attorney chose to read the letter first; he made it sound like she would be disinherited or something, if she didn't agree to the guardianship and moving away."

"Be seated; no more outbursts or you will be held in contempt."

The judge addressed Mallory once more. "Your attorney's maneuverings struck me the same way. You are the main beneficiary whether you fulfill all of your father's wishes as expressed in the letter, or not. Does your previous response still stand?"

"It does, your Honor," she had replied softly.

Then this court places you under the guardianship of Daniel Faulkner for the next five years, dating from January second, when Mr. O'Shaughnessy passed away. You will receive further orders from this court as the guardianship continues, to ascertain that you do finish the education, as expressed in your father's written wishes."

"This court is adjourned!" the gavel banged.

Chapter 25

DANIEL AND DIANA

DANIEL AND DIANA had made a beeline for Mallory as soon as the gavel struck. They were thrilled with her decision! Patrick had been right!

Daniel had watched David Anderson's angry retreat past the metal detector. He had been right, too. Mallory had been set up. Faulkner was determined not to make her sorry she had chosen to obey her father's wishes.

Diana had grabbed Mallory to give her a big hug and Daniel was shaking her hand. She looked terrified, but everything would get settled down. They were pulling her toward the motor home which had been moved from the campground. She dreaded to step into their world; she didn't know why. They were insisting, so she had allowed herself to be pulled along.

"Please, sit down," Diana had urged. She sank into the seat in the kitchen nook that Mrs. Faulkner was indicating. "Would you like something to drink?" she was asking. "I thought they had it way too warm in there." She opened a diet coke and took a sip. "What sounds good?" she had asked again. She placed a coke and a diet coke in front of Mallie.

Daniel had plunked down in the driver's seat and was maneuvering the coach onto the road. "I'll take a diet drink, please, Honey," he told her. She handed him a can of pop before sitting down at the little table, too.

"We're on the way to the lodge. Hal is fixing lots of the Friday special of the day, Catfish. I think everyone is coming. It's going to be a lot of fun."

"Oh yes, Hal's catfish is pretty good," Mallory had echoed. Her voice sounded a little flat, in spite of her effort to match Diana's excitement. "Where are your children?" she had tried to sound interested.

They're already at the lodge. We thought this might run longer than it did; we knew the children would be bored and hungry.

By the time they arrived at the lodge, the place was packed. A group of attractive people in matching uniforms had met the coach.

"You girls ready to dash for it?" Daniel had asked. Diana had answered affirmatively, and evidently Mr. Faulkner had thought she was speaking for herself and Mallory. They stepped from the bottom step, and they were encircled with the security. And they were making a mad dash. Somehow, Mallory had managed to stay on her feet, in spite of her high heels. She was propelled past a long line of hungry people, TV cameras, demonstrators with signs, and she wasn't sure what all else.

She was suddenly from the chaos to the calm! The banquet room at the lodge had been vacated by Erik Bransom, his dry board, and all of the various agents. The room was now crowded with tables spread in snowy Irish linen. Beautiful china and silverware graced each place setting. There were live flowers on each table; the neon beer sign had disappeared.

"Wow, I like what you've done to the place," Mallory had laughed.

The buffet tables set up along the sides of the room were being loaded with silver chafing dishes full of appetizing dishes. Sterno cans were being lighted by someone new Hal had hired. He was busy supervising everything.

Diana and Mallory had made their way to the restrooms, once again, encased behind a security team. A lady team member had checked the ladies' room for Mallory. One of the men had secured the men's side for Diana. They returned to the banquet room where people had begun to assemble. Diana seemed to be shielding Mallory, even from the crowd they all knew. She had guided the girl to the head table and indicated her seat.

"Sit down," she had encouraged.

Diana really didn't prefer a buffet line; she liked the food plated and served. Still, this was pretty nice. Catfish wasn't necessarily a banquet dinner, but Diana had admitted it looked pretty delicious. She was standing behind Mallory's chair with her hands resting lightly on the girl's shoulders. She was greeting everyone and pointing them toward where they should sit. Her children and the Anderson's two youngest had entered and she moved swiftly to corral her three. There was a table for the children, and Daniel had already been saying for the moms to go ahead and fix plates and drinks for the little ones. Alexandra and Jeremiah could pretty well get their own, but she was by Lana Anderson as she had prepared a plate for Cassandra.

Daniel Faulkner asked John Anderson to bless the meal, and then he instructed the ladies to go through the line first. Diana had come back to the head table, picking up her own and Mallory's plates.

"I'll get your food; you just want some of everything?" she had smiled at Mallory as she headed toward the line. Of course she got all the usual teasing about getting so many plates of food. "Yeah, yeah," she had agreed as good-naturedly as possible. Daniel had brought them all glasses of iced tea by the time Diana returned with the plates of food.

Mallory had been watching Diana as she had moved gracefully to assist her children, as she had greeted everyone by name, and with a smile. She had a real ease around people; she had already eased some of Mallory's worries away, just by the light touch on her shoulders. She had placed Mallory's plate before her, just so. The catfish toward her arranged correctly on the beautiful dish. It made Mallory relieved that she hadn't jumped up to serve her; she would have done it all wrong.

She was more gorgeous than ever, Mallory had decided. Today she was wearing a wool suit. The skirt was slightly flared, and the jacket was a little bit boxy. The color was a delicate Hydrangea blue, and the fine gauge silk sweater was printed with the lovely flowers. Her jewelry was Diamond, Tanzanite, yellow Gold, and Pearls. Her heels were ivory kidskin, and she had a California manicure. Her fragrance wafted about her, not overpowering, but definitely there.

Daniel had filled his plate in total disregard for the China pattern, and had set it down with the catfish on the opposite side from him. At least he had grabbed the correct fork. Hal had brought baskets of corn bread and hush puppies to each table. Daniel had asked his wife if he had to use a bread plate for cornbread and hushpuppies. She said, "Yes, unequivocally." So, he did.

Mallory was watching everyone and everything. All of the Sanders were back, including Constance and her husband. The Haynes were sitting back a ways. Her mom and Agent Bransom were by themselves. Shay and Grandmother were talking to Kerry Larson. Even Brad and Janet Walters were eating with the crowd, although Sammy and Sarah weren't anywhere to be seen. All of the Anderson family, John and Lana in the middle, Tammi by her mom, and David next to his dad; they hadn't joined the other teens.

"Mallory, you have hardly touched your food," Diana had spoken at last.

Mallory took a mouthful of coleslaw, and crumbled the hushpuppy that she had placed on her bread plate. She dabbed at her mouth with her napkin, before sipping her tea. She just didn't feel hungry. She suddenly realized she had lost track of Dinky.

Servers were clearing the table. Daniel intervened before they could take Mallory's plate.

"She isn't finished. You have to eat more than that," he had told her.

She ate a few fries and one of the catfish fillets, and he allowed her plate to be removed. She was terrified of him! It was going to be a long five years!

The meal ended without dessert. There were going to be some corporate meetings, and dessert was going to be served later during some breaks in that. The group was released to move out into the yard for a fifteen minute break. There was a security perimeter. The Faulkner's motor coach had been pulled up to secure one side, and it was opened up to make the restrooms available to the group. The facilities in the lodge were "woefully inadequate," as Diana had described them. The coach was beautiful.

Mallory had sauntered out into the brilliant sunlight. She had dug a couple of aspirin out of her bag, and had rinsed them down with her iced tea. The various members of the group were strolling the enclosure, surveying the luxury of the coach, and chatting. Kerry Larson had approached her and asked her if she was okay. She had assured him she was so he would go away. Usually, Mallory was friendly and outgoing, now she wished she could just go hide in the solitude of her little room.

She thought about what they had said. Her house was already being taken somewhere, so a diamond mine could be where it had been. She thought about how she had always pretty much hated the crumbling eye-sore of a house. She had been so embarrassed by the ridiculous Winnie the Pooh stuff, even when she was twelve; that hadn't gotten better by the time she turned seventeen. She was thinking sadly, that you didn't appreciate what you had until you lost it. Right now, she would give almost anything to be able to hit the wobbly, little-girl bed, and pull all the Pooh pillows and blankets over her head.

People were filing back into the banquet room. The buffet tables along the side were set up with coffee, iced tea, soft drinks, and bottled water. There were some mints, and nuts, and a big bowl of beautiful apples.

Mallory had chosen a bottle of water and one of the apples. Daniel had grabbed her elbow and was guiding her back toward where she had been seated earlier. She had surreptitiously reapplied her lipstick. She had managed not to cry, and the waterproof mascara still appeared to be in place. She powdered lightly.

"Where did you find that apple?" Diana had questioned.

"I'll get you one, Honey." Daniel had retrieved one of the apples for his wife and returned to his seat. There was a harmonious hum about the room. He had left once again. He got coffee for himself and his wife. Then he went back again for soft drinks.

Roger Sanders was passing out notebooks and pens. The notebooks were heavy leather and the pens were Mont Blanc. That had created a stir! Everyone was settled back in their places exactly within the fifteen minute time parameter.

Daniel had winked at Mallory. "You ready?" he had asked. She had brought her hands up and shrugged.

He had risen to his feet and moved behind a podium. "Ladies and gentlemen, our new CEO will open our meeting. "Miss O'Shaughnessy," he had nodded at her deferentially. Everyone clapped.

Mallory rose to her feet and moved swiftly to the podium.

"If you're trying to help me look stupid, I don't need any help," she had smiled.

Everyone laughed.

"Pastor Anderson, will you please begin our meeting with prayer?" she had stepped aside, and her pastor had taken the podium.

He prayed for every decision to be filled with wisdom and for the Lord to be magnified and glorified. He closed with "in Jesus Name, amen." then added, "this board meeting is now in session!"

Daniel Faulkner had thanked Anderson. Mallory had made a good move.

Mallory had picked up the Mont Blanc and was making a pretense of writing down the opening phrase on the linen napkin. "This board meeting is now-" Diana was in stitches. Delia had thought Mallory was really writing on the napkin; served her right about the fight over Patrick's remains

Faulkner was chairing the meeting when he suddenly realized no one was recording the minutes. "Does anyone have a Dictaphone, or a secretary in their pocket?" he had asked hopefully. Everyone was looking at each other, but nothing was happening.

Mallory had risen and taken the microphone. "Mom?"

"Ah, yes, Mrs. O'Shaughnessy, please," Daniel was laughing. "Can you help us out here?"

Suzanne was moving forward. She had on a new green outfit today; Mallory was proud of her.

"I can take the minutes in shorthand and transcribe them later," she had volunteered. "I need to sit closer so I can hear everything." she was pulling a steno notebook from her cavernous handbag.

Faulkner was impressed.

"Don't be getting any ideas, Faulkner," Roger was warning good-naturedly.

"Shorthand! Whatever he's paying you, I'm willing to double-"

Roger had risen to his feet. "Faulkner, you want to go outside for a meeting?"

"No, not really! I don't like outside meetings. I'm much too pretty; don't you think so, David?"

The entire room erupted with laughter. Most of the group had either heard, or had heard about, David and Mallory's exchange about Narcissus.

"I've seen prettier," David had responded. He had acted like he was checking his reflection in the screen of his phone.

Faulkner told Roger Sanders he looked as ugly as he did because he had been punched in the face one time too many.

The entire thing was so funny, because, truthfully, everyone in the room was knock-em-dead good looking!

Suzanne had it all recorded.

The group was voting to make Mallory CEO in place of her father. The new people were being voted in as members of the board. There were discussions about new corporations and new divisions within existing corporations. A report was presented about feasibility studies for mining the rivers. There was a vote about the acquisition of a corporate jet, two new helicopters, and construction of helipads at both Mallory's home in Dallas, and the Faulkner's home in Tulsa. It was lively and fun. Mallory had almost forgotten to be terrified.

The group needed a break, so Faulkner had released them. The camaraderie was even warmer. They had accomplished a good deal, so Faulkner had suggested thirty minutes. Desserts were appearing, chocolate cake, coconut cream pie, banana pudding, blackberry cobbler, and apple crisp. Shay was trying to decide, and Mallory had appeared at his side. "Take one of each; it's all good, I can assure you," she had instructed him brightly.

"Doesn't the Bible say not to be a glutton?" he had responded.

"It does," she had concurred. "But we try to ignore that part!"

"You look gorgeous, by the way," he told her, growing serious. "You look really nice in that color. I'm turning into Diana, but I took a picture of you. I'm ordering a suit for fall in the same color."

"How's your brother?" she had changed the subject.

"I think they're saying he's going to make it. But that's only till I can get my hands on him. Then he's gonna die for totaling that yellow 'vette."

Mallory's face registered total disgust. "He totaled a yellow 'vette? Oh, death's wa-a-a-y too good for him!"

"I'll be sure he dies painfully. I knew I liked you!" Shay had laughed.

They high-fived, and Mallory had wandered along the table, trying to decide on a dessert.

"Good afternoon, Mallory," It was her grandmother.

"Good afternoon, Grandmother," she had replied. Her grandmother looked beautiful. Mallory kissed her on the cheek. "I think people are heading back to their places; I want to talk to you more later." She opted for the blackberry cobbler and her milky, sugary coffee and returned to her seat.

The second part of the meeting was about charitable causes. Everyone was in agreement, that they should all have to do with the propagation of the gospel.

There was also a reaffirmation about responsibility to act like Christians and not corporate hot shots, wherever they all went, but especially when they were abroad. We need to do all we can to not be the typical "ugly American".

The conversation turned to John Anderson. Patrick had wanted his pastor with such a humble, servant's heart to have his ministry expanded. He hadn't been short on tall ideas. He knew John had computers full of sermons, books, pamphlets, and Gospel songs that he had written and never considered publishing. The pastor and his family were ordered to come up with an appropriate name for the corporation. Then, the home that had already been partially constructed was shown on a screen. Lana had screeched with joy. It had been involuntary, and then she was embarrassed. "We don't like this house, do we?" Faulkner was leading the assemblage to shake their heads, "No," in unison with him. He superimposed another house over the existing photo. It had added bedrooms, bathrooms, living areas, patios, a pool with a cabana and spa, a game room, and a home gym. It had a four car garage, and the artist's rendering illustrated beautiful vehicles parked around. They voted on the proposal, then decided to add a helipad here, too.

On the same acreage, there was a drawing for a ministry headquarters building. It included administrative office space and a sound studio for the pastor to prepare broadcasts. It would also be a way to assist Christian musicians to make high-quality recordings. They had plans for promoting the gospel around the world; radio, television, cyber-space. They had already made arrangements with a secular business rag to run a weekly column by Anderson. They were calling him the 'Chaplain of Wall Street'.

Everyone in the meeting believed in capitalism and free-enterprise. They felt it was Biblical and American, but the unbridled greed and economic plundering that had been happening, was something that needed to be addressed.

Diana had taken the floor next. The talk turned to the diamonds; then to her design label; then to Delia and Patrick with their Irish Linen and Woolen Imports. She read a study about other luxury fibers: Cashmere, Silk, Vicuna, and Alpaca. They all voted to restructure to increase profitability and trim expenses, including taxes. They still had some other issues to resolve, so they voted to hold another stockholders' meeting in three weeks. It would be in Tulsa. The main agenda at that meeting would be security issues.

A few members of the DiaMo Corporation security had entered, and they were handing out gifts in addition to the heavy leather notebooks and Mont Blanc pens. Everyone in the meeting received an Arkansas diamond ring. They weren't shabby. Each was in white velvet in a plain white leather box.

"The diamonds are real," Daniel had laughed. "Don't anybody throw them in the river! This meeting is adjourned!"

Chapter 26

DESIGNER

AS SOON AS the meeting was adjourned, Diana had immediately invited Mallory to join their family in going for steaks at McKenna's.

John Anderson was trying to work his way against the tide of people to reach her.

"Excuse me, Mrs. Faulkner, could I borrow Mallory for a little while?" he was asking as he was pulling Mallory away.

Diana had thought he must be coming up to say how overwhelmed with gratitude he was.

She was still standing there staring at him with a mixture of annoyance and puzzlement on her face.

"Relax, Honey," Daniel had whispered. "He isn't trying to sneak our new little girl away for his son."

"How can you be so sure?" she had demanded.

He had placed his hands on her waist, leading her gently from the place at the head table.

"You feel okay?" he had questioned tenderly. "The day was pretty long and busy. I don't want you to overdo it. Pastor grabbed Mallory because Erik and Suzanne are getting married in his study in a few minutes.

"They are?" Diana was enchanted. Daniel had already expressed his opinion that she could have waited until Patrick had turned cold. Diana had responded that Patrick was likely to turn colder, faster, once Delia could get him reinterred in Boston.

"What?" he had asked her incredulously? "What are you talking about?"

She told him what she knew about it, and he was furious. "I can't believe Kerry let that happen!" he had stormed.

"Well, Honey, the guy was smarter than to do it in front of him. I don't think he knows about it yet."

"You said this happened this morning before the judge came out? I thought ABI was doing security. How come they let some strange guy get that close to her? He could have been an assassin; they don't all look like Adams did."

Pastor Anderson had Lana act as one witness and Mallory as the other as Erik and Suzanne exchanged their vows. They both seemed totally smitten with one another. They had driven off in the big FBI car without saying where they were going. Mallory had kissed her mom good-bye. She was really happy for her. She liked the big, husky agent. He had given her a hug, too.

He was totally aggravated that Anderson had pulled her out, and she didn't have one security person with her. He felt like calling Faulkner to tell him what he thought of his first day of guardianship of the girl. He decided against it. He wanted Suzanne to have his undivided attention; that should be easy.

John and Lana drove Mallory to Hope to her hotel. That was when they had confided to Mallory all of their misgivings about Patrick's vision for their ministry.

"Well, he really loved you all; he meant well. Only you guys can know for sure what the Lord's will is for your lives. I thought it all sounded really exciting."

Her pastor could tell he had hurt her feelings. "We love his vision, Mallory! We just think everyone seems to have more confidence in us than we have in ourselves!"

"Yeah, it's an amazing group," Mallory had agreed softly. "Isn't that called 'Synergy'?"

Everyone plans to help every one else make it. Wherever I go, I recommend Irish Linen sheets, wherever Delia goes, she leaves one of your pamphlets. Different people ask you to come preach, and we let people know about the recording studio. We have conflict diamonds all right. Maybe they can help us win the fight with the devil."

She was asleep in the back seat of the battered van.

John's cell phone rang; it was Faulkner. "Hey, Daniel," he answered. "You hunting your new charge? We are nearly to the hotel. Is that where you want us to bring her?"

"Meet you there." He was waiting on the hotel lot when they pulled in. He had security with him.

"You and Lana haven't had a chance to have dinner, have you?" he had asked them. "My family is already at McKenna's. Come join us. Where is Mallory?"

"She fell asleep. We'll follow you, although we have already had way too much to eat today. Thank you for everything; we don't know what to say."

McKenna's had opened up an extra area to accommodate the DiaMo Corporation crowd. Mallory, still trying to awaken, had been guided toward a table piled high with beautifully wrapped gifts. She opened the first one; it was large and a little bit heavy; it was a Louis Vuitton suitcase. It had travel books in it; the one on top was "Turkey". She had stared at it in amazement.

The next gift was an IOU. The board of the corporation all wanted to travel together to view the places Mallory had been so thrilled about. The seven cities of the seven churches of the book of Revelation: Ephesus, Smyrna, Pergamum, Thyatira, Philadelphia, Sardis, and Laodicea. The travel arrangements were being worked out. Everyone who didn't hold a current passport needed to get one asap!

The next gift was a stunning Lynx jacket. Mallory was overwhelmed.

Diana was apologizing that she probably wouldn't be able to wear it until fall.

There was a lot of conversation and excitement, but then, exhaustion had hit everyone at just about the same time. Suddenly, everyone seemed to want to finish their steaks; no dessert. A couple of the teens wanted dessert, but tired parents had overridden them. There had been plenty of desserts all day.

Tom Haynes had announced that they were going canoeing at the falls in the morning. "That sounds like fun," Tammi had chimed in; "Yeah, Daddy," Emma had begun.

"Okay! Anyone interested meet at the lodge at nine for breakfast, we'll check out the canoeing from there," Daniel had taken charge.

Diana was on her cell, giving Hal a heads-up about their crowd being back for breakfast.

She handed Mallory a new iPhone. "Here's one I forgot to wrap."

Alexandra, Jeremiah, and Cassandra were asleep the moment their heads were pillowed. Daniel had bent down and kissed each tousled head again. "G'night, girls, I'm heading for the sack," he had announced wearily to Diana and Mallie.

Diana had cleared some of her designs from one side of the room. The RV had extensions for making the space larger; it was a good thing. She was preparing the daybed for Mallory. Mallie was in awe of the way Diana could take a photograph one day, and be clothed in the images within a day or two. Diana was tired, and she knew Mallory had already fallen asleep on the way from Murfreesboro. Still, having Mallory's enthusiasm for her passion had reenergized her. She showed her a picture of the pink Hydrangeas. She had taken the picture at the same time, she had taken the blue. Both of them were so beautiful, she could hardly decide. She showed Mallory the pink outfit. It was designed as a sleeveless, fitted pink silk shantung dress. The coordinating shantung coat was screen printed with the repeating pattern of the beautiful pink blossoms. There was a matching silk flower pin. Her jewelry was pink tourmalines and pearls. Of course, she had shoes in the same lovely pink. It was her Easter outfit

Mallory was more dazed by her now, than she had been the Saturday before, when she had first seen her.

"It's all so beautiful," she had gasped. "That blue you had on of the ocean. Is everything you do inspired by nature?"

Diana had laughed, a lilting laugh that sounded musical. "Nature?" she had laughed again.

"Everything is inspired by God! He Is such Beauty; he surrounds us with such beauty! The realm of nature is His design. People have nearly made a goddess of 'Mother Nature'. Anything nice, she gets credit for; any thing tragic, blame God."

Mallory caught a glimpse of a glorious red. It was an outfit similar to the Easter outfit, but the dress was solid red with more flare to the skirt. The peplum jacket was printed with large elegant red roses.

"Let me show you something about the "Ocean" one; then we better sleep before it's time to eat again."

She pulled out the lovely blue sweater. "Study the ocean floor, and tell me what you see," she had instructed, her blue eyes alight.

Mallory shook her head; she wasn't sure what she was supposed to say.

"See what looks like a little, round rock, or something?"

The teen continued to focus on the spot. "It's an eye!" she announced at last. "Is that a shark?"

Diana was folding the garment carefully. "Is that scary, or what? When I came out to fix the kids' breakfast this morning, Jeremiah said, 'Why don't you wear the outfit with the shark on it, again?'"

"I told him I don't have anything with sharks on it, and he told me he saw a shark on my sweater when we were at the steak place. I pulled this out, and he showed me. It scares me to death to think about it. We were all down there that day. Here's this huge shark. The dive master never saw it, I'm positive. Daniel works so hard to always try to keep us all safe." She gazed at the camouflaged shark, barely discernible in the picture. "This is as scary as a 'roaring lion seeking whom he may devour'. the Lord must have sealed his mouth like he did with the lions in Daniel's lions' den."

⇝ ⇜

The cute little room had an adjoining three-quarter bath. Some of the security people had brought Mallory's things from the hotel, and Diana had told her good night. They had brought Dinky; he had been looked after by one of the ladies on the security staff. Mallory had tried to warn her hostess that the dog shed a lot of hair. She didn't care; she was never the one to vacuum. She praised the Lord that everything had gone off-pretty much as planned. Diana was asleep almost instantly.

Mallory had lain quietly for quite a while, thinking. She was still trying to make sense of the jumble the day had been. Her mom was married, to a guy named Erik. He lived in an apartment in Hope. Her mom was going to start working for Roger Sanders again. Erik and Suzanne were planning to build a home with Erik's GI bill he had never used. Her mom had inherited a very nice settlement from Daddy, and he had left money for Mallory's other grandparents.

The Faulkners lived in Tulsa; Mallory's house that her dad had purchased for her was in Dallas. She hoped she was going to be living alone "Please, Lord, let it be so!" she had prayed over and over. At last, she had succumbed to sleep, too.

Chapter 27

DECEPTION

"Oh what a tangled web we weave.
When first we practice to deceive."

ERIK AND SUZANNE drove as far as Little Rock, before checking into the Hilton Hotel. They had been having a wonderful time together. Erik regretted that they hadn't met years before. Then, he had realized that God had redeemed him and had brought them into each others' lives in His perfect timing.

They were finishing a room service breakfast, and Suzanne had pulled out her steno notebook with her shorthand notes from the previous day's meetings. "I wonder how soon they needed these notes typed up," she had wondered aloud.

Erik had been thinking he should go revisit his two detainees. He had hated to mention it. When she had brought up the corporate minutes, Erik had begun to laugh. "I've heard of 'working vacations'; we might be starting something new with a 'working honeymoon'."

His new wife's laughter had rippled through the room. "That would really make us seem like a couple of over-responsible old people, wouldn't it?" Her giggles were so cute. "So, what's on your devious mind?" she had questioned.

He had told her what he was thinking, and she had sighed, sadly. "I always thought the sheriff was a pretty nice guy; shows what I know. Do you really think he was party to those awful murders?"

She had clapped her hand over her mouth, suddenly. "Oh, I'm sorry; I probably shouldn't ask you about your cases." she had apologized.

He had pulled her back into his arms. His gaze had met hers. "Mrs. Bransom, you may ask me anything you want about my cases. I may, occasionally have to tell you when I'm not at liberty to say; I hope that won't ever be a problem. Sometimes I may tell you things I don't want you to pass along." He had chuckled joyfully. "You're perfect! Actually, you have just already been a tremendous help to me." He gave her a little extra squeeze before releasing her.

"Let's get ready to go; we'll go shop for a laptop for you, and get it up and running. Then, we'll go to the office. You can start in on your work, while I talk to my two guys. He shaved while she did her make-up. They were ready to walk out of the room at the same time.

Suzanne had already given some mental clarity to her new groom. He looked sideways at her, catching her staring at him. He winked at her and reached over for her hand. The new ring from DiaMo Corp. pretty much eclipsed the wedding set he had been able to acquire on his pay grade. She hadn't had a chance to find him a wedding band, at all. He grinned. Things had clipped along pretty fast. His own ring from the corporate meeting was setting off some pretty good shine. He checked his pocket again for the Mont Blanc.

"Tell me some more about Oscar Melville," he had prompted her.

She had shrugged and sighed. "I don't know; that's what I just told you. He was always nice to me. He even offered several times to buy the house from me, just the way it was. It was in pretty bad shape, you know. I wanted to sell it the first time he offered; you can't begin to guess how much that disturbed Mallory. I tried to explain how much we needed the money more than that house. Like I said, I don't know anything"

He laughed. "You just presented me with a goldmine of information. Maybe I should say a diamond mine. How much was he offering you on the house? Did he ever get that far?"

M-m-m, nine thou at first; then, he had gotten it up to ten. I tried to make Mallory understand how strapped we were for cash. She didn't get it."

Bransom was trying to stifle his laughter. Obviously, Mallory had "gotten it", Suzanne was the naïve one. He squeezed her hand and brought it up to his lips.

"So, old Oscar was after the diamonds," he had mused aloud. "What else can you think of to tell me about him?"

Patrick used to spend time with him; I thought they were good friends. Then I heard Patrick telling Mallory not to trust him. I think Pat used the sheriff's office a lot to keep his ear to the ground about everything that was going on in Boston. He was pretty paranoid about his brother. He used to hang out some at the police station, too; same reason. I hope you don't mind hearing me talk about Patrick.

They found an electronics store and purchased a really nice laptop and printer. They purchased discs and printer paper. Then they left the computer in the hands of the geeks while they went for lunch

At lunch, Erik was more fascinated with his new bride than ever. She was wearing a really cute pink dress; she looked feminine and appealing. He could hardly believe she had consented to marry him. "Why did we decide to work during our honeymoon?" he had laughed.

Her blue eyes were dancing mischievously; she shrugged, flashing the diamond ring.

"I honestly don't remember," she had responded.

He had continued to coax more information from Suzanne. Seemed like Oscar had hated being called 'Oscar'. Bransom could see why, but that was interesting. He only ever wanted to be called 'Sheriff'. O'Shaughnessy had dug at him about that, asking him what his name would be if he lost the next election. Actually, no one in town could figure out how the man had continued to be reelected.

They had picked up the electronics purchase and continued into the city's downtown area. Bransom had pulled the big car into a space that was reserved for him in a parking garage. Carrying the laptop, he had taken her elbow, and was guiding her toward the elevator. It was Saturday, so, although there weren't going to be as many people around as usual; he knew they were really going to take some razzing.

Before they had entered the FBI office suite, Bransom had been able to hear Martin Thomas carrying on. He couldn't imagine how the guy could still have any voice at all. He had ordered the two suspects brought here under heavy security; they were in separate interrogation rooms.

Everyone was too freaked out from having to listen to the insane threats to do much more than nod at Suzanne.

When Bransom had entered the room where Martin was sitting in heavy chains, the kid had still tried to lunge at him. "Kid, I'll shoot you on the spot, and be happy to do it! Shut up!"

"Gag him!" he had ordered the agents who were keeping him secure.

"He can't talk if he's gagged," the agent was trying to explain.

"I'm not interested in hearing him talk! He's said a week's worth of too much already. I'm here to visit with the sheriff; he tells me what I want to know!" Bransom had pulled out a handkerchief and jammed it into the suspect's mouth. He jerked the chains tighter; the guy couldn't move; he could barely breathe.

He entered the room where Melville also sat in chains. "Hello, Os-s-car," he had begun, drawing out the name mockingly. He punched a buzzer, and one of the agents had popped his head in.

"Yes, sir?" he had questioned.

"I need you to look into information from Pike County, Arkansas elections for the sheriff's office. See if you dig up anything rotten on good ole Oscar here. Bring me all his financial information I had you pull together. Then bring in the transcription of Thomas's testimony. Turn the heat up in here. I really want to see Oscar sweat.

Seeing the thermostat adjusted, he left Melville to his thoughts, and rejoined Suzanne.

Her fingers were flying on the keyboard, the diamonds sending rainbows dancing around her. He fixed them each a cup of coffee. She started to move from his desk chair, but he motioned for her to keep her seat. She was so enchanting, he had decided not to waste much more time with the two clowns in the shackles. After all, this was his honeymoon.

He had paced around for a few more minutes. Suzanne had said she needed about another hour. Erik raised the temperature for Thomas's room, too. The agent had reappeared with the file on Melville's money; they were working on the election data.

Even if the sheriff had been reelected legally for each term, he certainly seemed to have a little power-hunger. Only call him sheriff? Bransom had seen the financial records earlier in the investigation. Nothing there! Literally, nothing there! No large amounts of cash; no suspicious purchases. The guy simply had nothing. He drove the "Sheriff's car, provided by the county; he lived in a tiny apartment; he earned a small salary. He was accumulating a small 401K and he had some weak health benefits. All that would be lost, if he ever were to lose an election. He had no records of what other types of employment the man had ever held, or his educational background. "Find me everything there is to know about this guy!" he stormed as he slammed the file folder down on the agent's desk. "We've had these guys for days; I don't even know where they were born! Find me stuff about them they don't even know! Stop jackin' with me!"

He had released the deputy who had failed to investigate the Haynes' home crime scene. He had really just been that inexperienced. Learning police work from Melville wouldn't have been the most enlightening education in the world, Bransom was certain.

He lowered the thermostat and re-entered the room where Melville was. "You better tell me your story; you better tell me quick; and you better give it to me straight!" He was in the guy's face.

"Not without my attorney-"

"I'm done! Get em back where they belong!" he turned and strode out.

He looked in on Thomas and barked the same order. "Kill him if you want to," he had added.

Suzanne was finishing up; they returned to the hotel where they e-mailed her files to Daniel Faulkner.

They had decided that was enough work for a honeymoon. They enjoyed a seafood meal and shopped together. Suzanne found a wedding band for Erik right away and slid it onto his ring finger. He kept glancing at it proudly. They both found some more clothes, appearance mattered to all of their new friends. They didn't resent it; they loved the whole thing.

They had decided to drive to Hot Springs for church on Easter Sunday. They felt like traitors to the Andersons, but they still wanted to be more alone with one another. They had both listened attentively to the sermon, nodding occasionally, smiling at one another from time to time.

Later, they had driven through the narrow town, not without some difficulty. There were plenty of tourists. They parked and walked around the popular little resort town, lunching in a cute little spot, then finding fudge and other things to snack on, amidst the souvenirs. They returned to church for the evening service; they both wanted to. It seemed like a heavenly way to begin a marriage.

On Monday morning, Erik had accompanied Suzanne to the Sander's Corporation. Suzanne had told her new husband about her previous employment at the company. Roger had really been successful. Bransom had taken it all in with a lawman's eye for detail. Everything looked new and well laid out. Constance had been pressed into service once again. She waved at them and clapped her hands jubilantly.

Roger had just entered the foyer, laughing as they entered to his daughter's warm reception.

"What are you two doing here?" he had demanded as he pumped Bransom's hand energetically.

Suzanne's smile had given way to her confusion.

"Oh, you still want a job? Hallelujah. I tried to take Faulkner out over you, and then this bird steals you away."

He had invited both of them into his office; quite the change from the cubicle of his beginning days. They took a seat and coffee was served from a silver service. There was a silver plate of petit fours. Roger had a packet that was give to all new prospective employees. They visited for a while, then Roger had invited them to follow him back to the country club for lunch. Beth had joined them. Suzanne was instructed to take off another week for her honeymoon, then begin her new job the following Monday. Her new employment package was very good!

The work on the big black truck with the heavily tinted windows was progressing. The more the crimes had been investigated, the more awful the truth had been of what had happened to the four victims.

To the amazement of everyone who was involved in sorting it out, Oscar Melville didn't ever seem to have been involved in the murders, or to have had any knowledge of them. At first, Bransom had suspected the sheriff's involvement when he had seemed so desperate to get Martin freed after the school fight. Bransom thought the two culprits were hiding something together. Then they had found blood, fiber, epidural cells, and hair from all four murder victims on Melville's clothing and in his apartment. Bransom had intended to hang the charges on Melville, then. But, he knew it was a stretch. The actual crime scenes had each indicated a single madman, enraged and working his evil alone!

The evidence was indicating that Melville had been trying to buy the O'Shaughnessy place from Patrick. Evidently aware that his "friend" was sick, he had offered to take the place off his hands for eight thousand dollars. That had slightly alarmed O'Shaughnessy, that perhaps the diamond pipes were known about, or at least subject to conjecture. Eight thousand wasn't much for fifteen acres, even without the diamonds. Of course that was a really laughable offer, in light of the gems. The sheriff didn't even have eight thousand dollars, anyway. He would have had to finance it. Maybe his meager 401K would have provided a down payment.

The sheriff hadn't even known about the diamonds! He had seen the ramshackle, little homestead as possibly being in his range. His way of achieving the "American Dream".

Bransom chuckled to himself, a wry chuckle. The elections seemed okay. No one liked the swaggering man a whole lot, but they seemed to have thought he was doing a fair job. Rather keep him in office than someone they might be even less sure about. Not good; but not so bad either. Bransom sighed for the good old days when there were sheriffs like in the Westerns. He had yawned wearily. Was it Hollywood fiction he believed in, or had America really been better once? Could she be better again?

He still wondered how, even a poor investigator, like Melville, could ride in such a bloody, messed up vehicle, and not notice anything! It was the sheriff who had driven it off, and hidden it out in the county beyond Tom and Joyce Haynes' house. He had been mad at his dumb friend for sustaining the damage to the vehicle. Thomas was only supposed to scare the "girls" enough so they would sell their house and leave town.

It appeared that, Martin's first attempt at frightening Suzanne and Mallory had been in those wee hours of Sunday morning. The sheriff wanted them scared; evidently Martin had been trying more than that. He had succeeded in pushing Mallory's bedroom window up. David

Anderson, who had somehow anticipated something, had been on the property watching. He had slashed at the big kid with a hunting knife! Martin's scream was what had awakened Mallory. Unarmed, because he figured he could overpower Mallory without a weapon, Martin Thomas had pulled himself away from his attacker and retreated. David Anderson had pursued him until the sheriff had picked Thomas up in his patrol car. That was the incident that had caused Anderson to e-mail Bransom's Little Rock office about the sheriff's questionable behavior.

"Wow," Bransom had mused. The sheriff had set his heart upon a homely little house. The FBI agent pictured the tumbledown abode in his mind. The place didn't seem like enough of a glittering prize to break the law over. Of course, the sheriff hadn't meant it to escalate the way it had. People never did think that their devious plans would get out of hand. Bransom knew they did, more often than not.

First, the sheriff had accused Mallory of having somehow induced her father's fatal hear attack. Bransom couldn't quite figure out why Melville had behaved that way. Trying to ruin her reputation? Then, they would just quietly sell out to him, and leave in disgrace? A lot of stuff didn't make sense. But then, greed and deception usually didn't.

Some of his agents had behaved in ways that had left him disappointed. Morton and Delham, the two agents who had had the oversight of the material in Patrick's bedroom had made an agreement together. They had been partners for some time. Their deal was, that if they found anything of value as they worked together, and it was something that wouldn't be caught, they would divide it If they found a ten dollar bill, for example, in a pant's pocket in the laundry, they would split it, rather than turning it over. They had found some items of value and were trying to decide if they could get away with all of it; or if they should turn part of it over, or all of it. They were kind of afraid it might be a "sting". It wasn't, but there would be some from now on, Bransom had determined. Mallory's interrupting them for the cash and diamonds in the closet had unnerved Delham. She had confessed their activities to him. The charges against them would depend on the total amount of their stolen goods that could be verified. Whatever they had gained, they were now losing far more.

He was grateful for the Treasury Department oversight. Maybe the two agencies had been vigilant enough of one another, that no further crimes had been committed.

Then Adam's appearance on the scene, and the Ryland O'Shaughnessy connection had confused the issues for a while. Compounding that confusion in an even greater way, was the fact that Adams had inadvertently found the Thomas truck which a multi-agency task force had been unable to find. That had made the agencies believe that Melville had ties with organized crime in Boston. Nope! He was just a little local nerd trying to scare a widow into doing what he wanted.

Erik Bransom could hardly believe the events that had taken place within a week. He thought happily of his new bride and all of the corporate friends, of his faithful pastor and newfound faith. The light of God's word was illuminating his paths in ways he had never thought possible. But compared to that marvelous light, the darkness was still very, very, very dark!

He turned the lights off, and locked the big glass door to the FBI office suite. Enough work!

Chapter 28

DIVERSION

MALLORY HAD AWAKENED early. She was still tired. She had gone to bed late, then been unable to fall asleep. The RV seemed quiet; the Faulkners must all still all be sleeping. She closed her eyes and wished to be anyplace but here. She opened her eyes reluctantly and gazed dully at the ceiling. She couldn't see a clock. The room was gradually growing brighter as the sun rose. She felt like a prisoner; the small space was suddenly stifling. She felt like an orphan, step-child, misfit. She tried to remind herself of some of the information that had seemed encouraging. She thought there was a light tap on the door. Shrugging into her robe, she had said, "come in" softly. She wasn't positive anyone had tapped.

Diana pushed the door ajar so she could enter. She was already dressed and looking perfect. She didn't look like she was going canoeing. Then Mallory had remembered Daniel's announcement about his wife; she couldn't go.

"Morning," the woman had greeted her softly. "Did you get any rest? I didn't really make any breakfast, since Hal is ready for us at the lodge."

Mallory had scrambled out of the covers and begun making the bed. Diana had retreated to give her space to get ready. Mallory had quickly showered and dressed in the new, teal, casual outfit. She changed her belongings into the canvas tote and slid her feet into the espadrilles. She was amazed. It had seemed like she had been doing some crazy shopping without rhyme or reason. So far, all of the new stuff was fitting into her life like puzzle pieces. Had the Lord really been that tenderly supplying her with just exactly everything she would be needing? She was awed. To think that in the midst of her desperate fear and uncertainty, the Lord had been providing, too, for the seemingly minor issues. She applied the very barest cosmetics and presented herself in time to head out the door for the lodge.

The tired people from the night before had been energized by the rest and the prospect of a fun day in the beautiful surroundings. Not surprisingly, everyone was already ravenously hungry again. The buffet breakfast was disappearing as fast as it was being delivered from the kitchen. Daniel and Diana had been relieved to see Mallory eating without being fussed at about it. They were both still watching over her with quite a bit of concern. Even though she had exhibited a willing spirit with the judge, they had still been nervous that she might decide to try to run away.

The Anderson family was there, albeit, without David. The Haynes had arrived, and the Sanders. Connie had decided to stay home with her feet up. Delia and Shay were both there. Daniel and Diana were both still livid with them about the suit for Patrick's remains.

Erik and Suzanne hadn't materialized; they hadn't really been expected.

Daniel had looked around curiously for Kerry Larson. This kind of dare-devil stuff was usually his stock in trade.

"Have you seen Kerry around this morning?" he had questioned Diana worriedly.

She had a huge stack of pancakes, heading for the table. She had been helping Cass get situated.

"Baby hungry this morning?" Daniel was teasing his wife good-naturedly. Usually Diana ate very wisely and tried to get the rest of them to follow suit. He couldn't resist teasing her. She was cute whenever she was annoyed, or flustered.

I haven't seen Kerry," she had changed the subject deftly. "Maybe he had to get back to Dallas. Probably best," she had finished cryptically.

Daniel was amazed she had said that. "Thought I was the only one that noticed," he had whispered as he sank into a chair beside her.

"I wish you had been; you know I always pick up on stuff like that before you do. Maybe there should be a law against hormones," she had finished gloomily.

He roared with laughter. "That might be an overly drastic plan. The human race would die out then. Any other ideas?"

Mallory had returned to the table with one of the big apples. They halted their conversation so suddenly that they knew she would feel like she had intruded.

"I haven't seen your attorney around this morning," Daniel had tried to change the subject to keep the moment from becoming even more awkward. Immediately, though, he knew that hadn't been a good topic. He caught that Diana had rolled her eyes at him.

"Haven't seen him," she responded without being seated. She wandered back over to the buffet line.

Alexandra was seated by herself, glaring at the world, so Mallory went over to try to talk to her. "Do you mind if I sit here?" she had asked, feeling pretty shy, herself. The other girl didn't respond so Mallie sat down across from her.

"My name's Mallie," she had begun.

"I know who you are" the girl's enraged whisper had carried, and her dad had whirled to give her a withering stare. She had ignored him. "You are the only subject I've heard about in months. I wish I'd never heard of you!"

"Maybe everyone was really nervous about all that stuff yesterday." Mallory had tried to alleviate the girl's concerns. "I couldn't figure out what was going on. I was more scared than I needed to be. I think things are going to settle back down. I don't plan to give your mom and dad any trouble If we can't be friends, let's at least not be enemies, please," she had concluded.

"Why isn't your picture on your mom's sweater with your brother and sister?" she had asked curiously as she was rising from the table.

"Because I didn't want to pose in her dumb picture!" the girl had responded defiantly.

"But now you're mad you're not in it?" Mallie had guessed correctly.

Alexandra was exasperated. "I told you, I didn't want to be in it!"

Mallory had continued to stare at Diana's outfit in wonder. It was so cute! It was a picture of Jeremiah and Cassandra in a lunar vehicle on the moon, with the Earth floating in the expanse of space behind them. It was cute, and totally jaw-dropping, awe-inspiring at the same time.

"Why wouldn't you want to be in it?" Mallory had probed. "Have you guys been to the moon?" she had questioned at last, honestly perplexed.

Alexandra had finally smiled, then laughed. "Been to the moon?" she had questioned. "How would we have done that?"

"That's what I was wondering," Mallory responded.

Alexandra had shaken her head in wonder at the dumb questions. "That's just a phony Kodak Moment place at the Kennedy Space Center in Florida. Did you really think they were on the moon? How dumb!"

Mallory felt totally rebuked. She couldn't help it that she had never seen any phony Kodak Moment places so she could reference what the wealthy little girl was saying.

She had begun to rise with a dejected sigh.

"I'm sorry, Mallory." Alexandra had begun to cry. "Please stay and talk to me some more."

Now totally confused, Mallory had settled back again onto the chair. "So, do you like Tommy Haynes?" she had resumed the conversation curiously.

"I'm too young to like anybody," came the response.

Mallory took a nibble of her apple, surveying Alexandra. "So, was that a quote from your parents?" she queried between bites. "Sounds like a parental quotation to me. That's good, because I'm compiling a book."

She was suddenly aware her grandmother had been watching her from another table. She grabbed another linen napkin, pretending to write down the quotation on the napkin so she wouldn't forget it.

By this point, Alexandra had begun to smile and then giggle. Delia hadn't been the only one watching; Daniel and Diana had been noticing their oldest child's deteriorating attitude for a week. They had been extremely displeased about her bad manners with Mallory; now it seemed like Mallory might be winning her over.

"She has until the end of the day to be acting a whole lot better, or I'm wearing her out when we get back to the RV this afternoon," he had told Diana. Her face filled with concern, she had nodded agreement.

Mallory had continued to talk about Tommy Haynes. She didn't feel like she knew anything to talk about without looking really stupid again. She was trying to make small talk.

"Why was he hoping his dad would get fired?" Alexandra had decided to hold up her end of the conversation.

"Well, a lot of reasons, I guess," Mallory had begun. "He gets a lot of pressure being the principal's kid. The kids razz him and even get mean to him, if Mr. Haynes announces any new rules or anything they don't like. He makes good grades, so the do-do birds resent that. So, sometimes he's teachers' pets. Maybe it's because he really does try to be a good Christian. A guy named Martin Thomas had really been bullying him lately."

Alexandra's face had blanched and her big gray eyes had widened more. "You mean Tommy knew that killer? That big guy picked on him? How could that happen?"

"It just could; it just does. I used to think maybe it was tougher being a principal's kid than it was being a preacher's kid. Now, I have finally concluded! Drum roll! Here it is- it's just tough being a kid!"

Alexandra was smiling through tears. She couldn't help liking Mallory O'Shaughnessy.

The Andersons had enjoyed more meals out from Wednesday through Saturday than they had in five years. They could still hardly believe all of John's work of studying and gleaning so many spiritual insights was finally going to be rewarded by getting it all published.

Lana kept laughing at his worries. "Just getting it published doesn't mean anyone will buy it," he had confided to her.

"Well, they plan to just distribute some of it, anyway, just to get your name out," she had tried to be consoling and supportive.

"Well, they want the Gospel to be dispersed more; my name really isn't that important. Just printing it and handing it out is no guarantee anything will be read."

Sometimes he was so determined to be humble and self-deprecating there was no use in her trying to talk to him.

"Why does Tammi have on so much make-up?" he demanded suddenly of her. Startled, she had turned to see where he was looking. Tammi had evidently piled it on since they had all left the house together earlier. John and Lana's eyes had met. They were both thinking the same thing.

Now that David's crisis seemed to have eased, were they about to begin a siege with their next child?

"Oh, Lord, no please," Lana had whispered fervently under her breath, once more.

"Hey, Tamara Elaine Anderson!" The pastor's voice had silenced the merry hum in the room.

Embarrassed, Tammi had hurried over. "Daddy, you're always too loud," she whispered.

"Go wash your face," he had lowered his voice, but there was no mistaking the fact that it was an order.

Usually, she tried to explain to him that you couldn't just remove some of it; that you just smeared it and looked like a real freak for the rest of the day. She could tell that he really didn't care.

"Yes, sir," she had whispered.

"Give me your purse!" He was clearing out all of the cosmetic items and dropping them into Lana's bag.

"I told you when you're sixteen, and you begged. So, did I tell you to go easy with the stuff? When you're sixteen you can try it again; until then don't ask."

"Daddy, I paid for that with my baby-sitting money," she was trying not to cry.

"I know that, Tammi. That's why it isn't in the trash- yet! You want privilege, don't abuse it. Go-wash!"

Tammi had begun to confide to Mallory about her dad and the make up.

"Well, you didn't even look good," Mallie had interrupted her . "I was going to tell you that you look a lot prettier without so much-"

"You just don't want me giving you any competition," Tammi had come back at her defiantly.

"What? Competition about what?" Mallie had questioned blankly.

"In the looks department! Don't pretend you don't know!"

"Okay, -I'm not pretending. I think I must just be the village idiot, today; but, what are you talking about?"

"I'm pretty sure we like the same guy!"

"Uh, Tammi, news flash! I like David, your brother! I have for the last-all of my life. This is Mallory O'Shaughnessy you're talking to. Why are you trying to look and act like you just came from Mars? Who do you like that you think I like?" she hesitated, suddenly curious.

"Never mind." Tammi had muttered quietly.

"Oh no! Not 'never mind'! We've been friends; I need to know who you're suddenly so ready to fight me over."

Realization and intuition suddenly hit Mallory. "Oh no, he already has a girlfriend; he told me!"

"No, he doesn't, he told me!" Tammi had come back.

"Well, he will have by the time you grow up enough for him. Did you ask him if he already had a girlfriend? Tammi! What were you thinking about? All that make up didn't make you look "mature" either.

"What's this huddle about?" Roger Sanders had interrupted jovially before he had noticed the expressions on the faces of the two girls.

"Nothing!" Tammi had stormed away.

The day was beautiful, and the reports about the Winding Stair Rapids was that they were exciting. There had been enough snow earlier, then rain.

Mallory had been watching Daniel and Alexandra get outfitted. Diana was worried about it. The guide was good, but it was just risky.

"Honey, okay if I don't wear a helmet?" he had tried to tease her.

"Fine with me; your head's so hard you probably don't need one," she had come back quickly.

Tom and Joyce and Tommy were all going together. Tommy was showing Alexandra how to fix some of the equipment. Delia and Shay were going together. As Roger and Emma were paying and gearing up, Emma had kept paying attention to every move Shay was making. Beth Sanders wasn't going; she and Evan were going to keep company with Diana and Jeremiah and Cassandra. The Andersons had decided to head home from the lodge. They said they might join up again later to just canoe in the float area, after the thrill-seekers had run the rapids.

Mallory was warning the group about the poison ivy and poison oak. Then, she had given them all insect repellent packets. Joyce and Beth knew about the ticks, but Diana hadn't been aware of the problem. She had scrubbed her husband and daughter down vigorously with the towelettes, ignoring their spitting and sputtering.

Then, the moms were applying the repellent to the little children who were just going to be playing in the area of the Little Missouri Falls. It was an area of beautiful scenery. Diana had the most extensive (and Mallory guessed, expensive) array of cameras with her. Photographers did come from all over.

Jeremiah and Cassandra had decided to like Mallory, so they had both hung onto her for the rest of the morning. She had decided not to take the rapids. They had done it before, once as a family; once just Mallory with her dad. One of Mallory's friends had been seriously injured a couple of years before. She had been wearing a helmet, but she had suffered some internal injuries. Mallory had heard Suzanne whisper to one of her friends that the girl wouldn't be able to have babies now.

Even now, as Mallie had watched Diana clambering over rocks to take pictures, she was worrying if she might still lose this baby if she weren't even more careful.

By the end of the day, everyone was sunburned, despite generous dowsings with sunscreen. They all parted company, and Mallie had returned with the Faulkners to the RV. Dinky had been alone all day so Mallory took him out for a walk. The security teams had never been too far away from the group all day. Now, Mallory was still aware of them as she walked her dog. She had wished he could have gone to the river with everyone; she would have had even more fun with him there. She had hated to ask to bring him in the Hummer. When she had returned from the walk, Daniel was sitting in a lawn chair by the steps. Dinky growled at him a little and Mallory told him to hush. She was still pretty nervous around her guardian; maybe Dinky could sense it.

Daniel had unfolded another chair and invited her to sit. Her feet were wanting to run, and she had stood, staring at the chair in a panic.

"I need to be able to talk to you, Mallory." His voice was firm and business-like.

She was trying to be compliant enough that she wouldn't need to be spoken to. She would just do whatever she was supposed to do, and then hopefully, they would leave her alone. She was afraid she was in trouble. Maybe they had heard about her telling Tammi she still liked David.

Her face stark-white, tears welling in her eyes, she had finally sunk gingerly onto the edge of the chair. She sat mutely, staring at him, waiting for whatever he was going to say. He had asked her a question; she hadn't heard it. She couldn't have choked out a sound anyway. She wanted her daddy!

Finally, she had been able to absorb some of what he was saying. They were going to church here tomorrow for Easter. Then, Monday morning, they were going to take her by where her house had been moved out and fences were being erected. She could go by her school and tell everyone good-bye. Then, they would get her established in Dallas. They would be flying home to Tulsa, but they would be keeping an eye on her. If she needed anything she could call either one of them on their cells or at their home, any time.

He sounded relieved; she had just sat like a statue while he spoke. "I'm going to speak to David Anderson." He had begun speaking again, She wanted to clap her hands to her ears; how could he presume to talk to her about this? Her heart was breaking in two; how could she bear any more than she already had? She wanted her mom! The tears had begun to spill down her cheeks.

"Mallory, are you listening to me?" he had asked, his exasperation beginning to show itself.

She had nodded mutely, sobbing.

"I know you aren't going to like this, but I'm going to ask David not to be in contact with you in any way whatsoever for at least six months."

"You can go in now," he stood and folded his chair.

Mallory escaped up the steps, no one in sight. She made it to the little room, and closed the door softly behind her

Chapter 29

DAYBREAK

EASTER MORNING HAD dawned beautifully. There was a chill in the air, and the breeze was cool.

Mallory was surveying herself critically in the full length mirror in the RV bathroom. She thought about how excited she had been when she had been shopping for the clothing on the previous Tuesday evening. At that time, she was still afraid of all of her yard stalkers, but at least, she had been oblivious to the will and guardianship. Five years seemed to stretch endlessly before her.

She hadn't minded not seeing much more of Kerry Larson after Friday, but, she had planned to request the letter from her father be given her. Maybe it had more to it, that he just hadn't read for time's sake. Surely, there was more explanation of what it was all going to mean.

Now, she didn't like the dress and was ashamed she had spent so much on it. There was a tap on the bedroom door, and Mallory had moved quickly to see who it was. It was Diana.

"Oh, Mallory, you look stunning!" she had gasped. "Come out here and turn around!" She had grabbed Mallory by the hand and spun her around. "That is absolutely adorable! That color is delicious!"

"Honey, doesn't Mallory look great?" she was raving to Daniel who was buttering waffles in the small, efficient kitchen.

"Absolutely," he had replied. "Kids, come get a waffle!" He had sat down to enjoy one of his own concoctions. Mallory had figured if he had fixed them, they must be from the toaster. No! They were from scratch and a waffle iron. There were freshly sliced strawberries to go on top, with real whipped cream.

"Sit down, Mallory. Try to eat a little breakfast," Diana was urging. "Would you like a glass of milk or some juice?" Mallory was still too shy to just sit down at the kitchen table with Mr. Faulkner, so she was trying to beg off. Something beautiful was showing on their big plasma TV that had arrested her attention, anyway.

Entranced, she was trying to follow it. "Hey, Mallory," Jeremiah was whispering her name. "Have you seen this before?"

"No, what is it?"

It's a DVD about the Bethlehem Star, but there's a part of it too, about 'the Day of the Cross'. Mom got it out for Easter!"

Realizing how nervous Mallie was around her husband, Diana had skillfully guided Mallory to the sofa. She set up a TV tray, placing a Belgian waffle and a glass of milk in front of her. "Try to eat at least part of it," she had urged again. "I'm going to get dressed."

Diana had dressed quickly in the beautiful silk ensemble with the pink Hydrangeas. Daniel was wearing a gray suit with an ivory French cuff shirt, a gray, ivory, and pink paisley tie, with an ivory silk pocket square. Alexandra was wearing a sunny yellow, linen suit, and Jeremiah had a little gray suit with a yellow tie. Cassandra had on an orchid princess dress with a full, puffy skirt and an orchid floppy hat. Diana was trying to get them all in a picture. Sunrises and sunsets were easier, she had said. They didn't scowl at you and talk back. Mallory offered to take one of the whole family, including Diana. They all smiled better for her.

She missed her dad. He had always insisted on taking pictures of 'his little girl' on Easter Sunday. She felt like she must be an awful imposition. The only thing that was sustaining her at the moment was Daniel's edict that she couldn't be in touch with David for six months. She had figured everyone would try to keep them apart for the entire five years, and then ever after, too.

Mallory had been fascinated by the DVD, but she really hadn't been able to follow it too well. Then they had finally turned it off, because they were about to leave.

"Are you always the church pianist?" Daniel had asked her.

"Oh, no, sir, Mrs. Anderson is. I filled in the other night because she had a headache."

They were early; the children headed to their classes anyway. Security team members didn't actually accompany the children to their classes. They simply set a perimeter and watched for anything that seemed suspicious. The Faulkner children were totally used it.

Mallory had sat by Mrs. Faulkner during the adult Sunday School class. She wasn't sure if she could go with the teens. She didn't know if David was going to be in there, or not. He hadn't been to Sunday School in months, but she didn't want to get in trouble with the Faulkner's. She could still hear David's voice, as he had explained his feelings to the judge. She was sure Kerry Larson and the Faulkners had liked him even less after that.

Her head ached again. She wanted to cry, but she hadn't brought any tissues. She sat there miserably; a ragged sigh had escaped. Diana had glanced over at her quickly. As a nurse, she had been concerned about the grief-stricken girl

After the Sunday School hour, the little auditorium had begun to grow crowded. Lana had begun the prelude.

"You didn't mention they should get a new piano as one of the first things," Diana had whispered to Daniel. He had put his arm around her shoulder and whispered back something Mallory couldn't quite make out.

The congregation had sung "He Lives" and "Up From the Grave He Arose". There was no choir. One of the men had sung "The Old Rugged Cross" as a special. Then John Anderson had preached from: *John 11:25 &26*

> *Jesus said unto her, I am the resurrection and the life: he that believeth in me, though he were dead, yet shall he live.*
> *And whosoever liveth and believeth in me shall never die. Believest thou this?*

The message was powerful and sweet. Some of the congregation that day had never heard the Salvation story. There were more decisions. Lawrence Freeman, one of the attorneys that Delia often employed had come weeping; he had never heard anything like it. Janet Walters had come, although Brad hadn't moved.

To Mallory, the sermon was particularly meaningful because it reaffirmed her faith that her father had never died. He had left his body like a discarded garment, to wing his way to heaven. The pastor had once again explained: "People think they are bodies, and they have souls; the opposite is, in fact, the case! People are souls who have bodies!"

As the crowd was filing out, headed to cars and various Easter dinners, Mallory had noticed that all of the Anderson family had been wearing new things.

"Wow," she had told Tammi, "cute outfit."

Tammi had still acted mad at her about the previous day, and she was mad because her dad hadn't let her even wear mascara with the new outfit. And she was disappointed that Kerry Anderson wasn't around. She had finally asked Mallory where he was.

"Tammi, I don't know anything about him. His mom and dad grow those big apples. I don't know where he is!"

Daniel and Diana had started a rack of lamb earlier in the morning, so they had invited the Andersons to come eat at the RV. The Andersons had accepted the offer, so Mallory and all of the Faulkners had hurried to the campground to get the rest of the meal put together.

Daniel and Jeremiah had pulled some patio furniture from the side of the RV, and had set up some tables outside.

"Do you think it's too chilly out?" Diana had worried.

"Well, we'll really be crowded up, otherwise," he had observed.

They had a delicious salad, with a tangy-sweet dressing they had mixed themselves. Diana had prepared Au Gratin potatoes in the microwave. Daniel had made a sweet potato casserole, and they broiled asparagus. All three children had helped with the setting of the tables.

Diana the magician, had pulled Easter Baskets out for all of the kids. David had driven up, and Diana had a basket for him first; he was the oldest of the kids. It was full of candy, real Easter eggs, and plastic eggs holding money or gift cards. There was an iPod in it, and some speakers. He was amazed.

Then there was one for Mallory. It was composed much like David's, but it held a camera, rather than an iPod.

Then Tammi, and down the line to Cassandra, who was the youngest. By the time everyone had made over the baskets, the meals were beautifully plated, and set in place.

Daniel had instructed the little group to their places and requested Pastor to give thanks for the meal.

Everything was delicious. Mallory had never tasted the delicate, tender lamb with mint jelly before. No one had needed to tell her twice to eat at this meal. Alexandra and Jeremiah had the plates removed and in the dishwasher before anyone had told them to. Alexandra's bad attitude had seemingly evaporated.

Daniel had loaded a tray with cups of coffee and slices of coconut cake and carried them into the living room. He told his three children they could eat a little bit of the candy and play for thirty minutes.

Lana had noticed musical instruments and had asked who played what. "Naturally," Mallory had thought bemusedly, "they all played everything! They were business people, they were fashion designers, they were gourmet chefs, they were scuba divers, they were musicians, and they had practically been to the moon!" They were so accomplished at so much, that Mallory felt like a total country bumpkin! Growing up in rural Arkansas, she had always told herself that she was born in Boston. She felt inept.

John Anderson had asked the Faulkners if they minded singing something or playing the instruments. They didn't mind at all; and were they ever good! The Andersons had insisted that the family take over the music for the evening service; then the pastor had asked Daniel if he ever preached. He had asked Daniel to speak. The pastor said he wished he had known about the family's talents in time to have announced this special event in the morning service.

"Dad, I'll go back to the church and send out e-mails to everyone," David had volunteered. He thanked the host and hostess for the basket and the meal and headed for the church. He composed the message, telling all the membership they didn't want to miss this special treat.

He tipped back in his dad's desk chair after he had turned the computer off. He hadn't said much to Mallory, and she hadn't said much to him, either. He tried not to think about her all the time, but every time he tried to push her image away, her fragrance would tantalize him. When he had left the Faulkner's she had all three of their children playing with a piece of string, showing them how to make a "cat's cradle". He could still picture her in his mind, her laughter rippling, trying to get Jeremiah to pinch the string at the right "X's". He was sure the kids had every toy imaginable, but she had captivated them with a string.

His gaze had shifted out the window. His dad wanted him to finish school, of course, but to help oversee the building of the new camp, as well. Brad Walters was a carpenter, but Roger Sanders had watched Brad work on one of the buildings at his corporate headquarters. He had told all of the guys on the board, that Brad could read blueprints, and he had been telling the contractor how everything should be. Brad was going to be made a contractor to oversee the camp and the ministry headquarters building. His wife had gotten saved this morning, but Brad hadn't.

The O'Shaughnessy house was to have been bulldozed. David and Kerry Larson had quickly had it removed from its place. It was on its way to the site of the camp. David had decided to move it up there so he could live in it until other buildings could be built. It had some termite damage. He had just overheard his dad telling his mom that wanting the pitiful little house was what had caused the sheriff's downfall.

He didn't think his dad should have relinquished his pulpit for the evening service; Brad Walters needed to get save. David had been amazed at the musical talent he had heard. Like Mallory, he wondered if the Faulkner family could really be that good at absolutely everything!

Mallory peeled a couple of her Easter eggs before the evening service, so Jeremiah had followed suit. Diana hadn't been able to keep from smiling. Jeremiah had already developed a huge crush. He had never eaten a hard-boiled egg before in his life! Mallory had also decided to check out her new camera. She knew making the baskets had taken quite a bit of time and money. She thanked Diana again.

Daniel had gone in to work on his sermon for the evening and had come right back out.

He was amazed to find that Suzanne had already transcribed the notes from their meetings and had e-mailed them the previous day.

"Wow, your mom is good!" he had told Mallory excitedly. "No wonder Roger was ready to fight me!"

Mallory had smiled; she was pleased to have recognition given to her mom for her work. It was also a comfort to her that her mom really wasn't far away. It brightened her afternoon.

The blue skies of the day were being chased away by a front appearing from the west. It reminded Mallie of the previous Sunday afternoon. She was suddenly nearly overcome with gratitude. It had been a tumultuous week; understatement of the millennium, she was sure. She still had some major worries, but she could tell the Lord had been with her through everything. She was grateful now, for the Faulkners and the care they had already shown her. They hadn't been forced to assume all of this extra responsibility. They had loved her father and been happy to do this She hoped all the business empire they had been talking about really would work out.

A few raindrops were spattering against the windows.

The concert presented by Daniel and Diana and the children was as amazing as every thing else they did. Diana and the three children made up a string quartet playing "Great Is Jehovah the Lord", accompanied by Daniel at the keyboard. (Daniel had already mentioned to Lana Anderson that she should begin shopping for a beautiful, new piano right away.) Then, Alexandra had played "What a Friend We Have in Jesus" on the violin, accompanied by Diana. Daniel sang "Tell Me the Story of Jesus" as a solo, and Daniel and Diana had sung a duet, "It Takes a Storm Now and Then". Tears had been rolling down Mallory's cheeks throughout; so were they for a lot of people.

The crowd was up, too. David's e-mail had gotten people to respond. Often, people made such a point of being in church for Easter Sunday morning, that the Sunday evening service was poorly attended. Usually rain, or even the threat of rain, could keep people from coming. But, people had turned out, and they were glad they had.

Diana and the kids sat down, and Daniel took the pulpit. He opened his Bible, and spread out his notes. He thanked the pastor for allowing them to participate. He reminded everyone how blessed they were to be part of such a great church and have such a faithful pastor. He told a couple of jokes. He seemed relaxed and natural, and the congregation as a whole, seemed to relax as one entity.

Daniel invited everyone to open their Bibles as he caressingly turned the pages of his. He told how Christians should never be too cool to be seen with a Bible. He read his text:

> *Matthew 10:31 Fear ye not therefore, ye are of more value than many sparrows.*

Tonight I would like to speak to you for the next few minutes about FEAR. I know this isn't anything new to anyone here. I think you can turn to almost any book of the Bible and find the Lord telling us not to be afraid. I think most of you are aware of the fact that some of us have had a pretty scary week. I know you have all heard the acrostic for fear:

False Evidence Appearing Real; F-E-A-R, fear.

He clicked a remote he was holding. The picture shone on the wall of Jeremiah and Cassandra on the moon. He explained where the picture was actually taken, then showed another shot that Diana had taken too wide that revealed the backdrop screen. He told about Mallory asking Alexandra if they had been to the moon. Everyone laughed, and Mallory was glad he had darkened the room. He laughed, too. "You all know that Mallory is smart; she didn't think people were traveling to the moon on a regular basis. But the picture made it look like our children are on the moon. That is false evidence appearing real. We weren't trying to trick Mallory; my wife just thought it was a cute picture. Sometimes, we are deceived when no one is trying to deceive us, because of appearances. That's why we aren't to make snap judgments. Sometimes people are really intending to deceive for purposes of their own. We know Satan is the deceiver. He wants us to think we don't need to receive Jesus' atonement for our sins. Once we are saved, he tries to make us fearful Christians: afraid to witness, afraid to pray, afraid to commit everything we have and are to the Lord.

We serve a great God Who longs to have us come to Him for everything! Here's another picture my wife took; she's the crazy camera lady y'all have seen around this week. At first she was annoyed that, even out here, where it's supposed to be rural, there were wires everywhere. She and Mallory decided that we should have invented wireless first." He paused, and people chuckled.

He showed the picture. Since Diana hadn't been able to avoid high wires, she had decided to zoom in on purpose. She got one of the most delightful shots of the entire trip. The wire was lined up with sparrows, backed by an intensely blue sky. The crowd actually gasped with delight. It was such a vivid illustration of the text verse.

"She was so excited about it, and she was trying to make me see that all 'of their cute little faces are different, and they have different facial expressions; look, this one looks happy'!" He had raised his voice to a falsetto, imitating Diana's voice and inflection.

The congregation laughed again.

We shouldn't fear anything when we serve a God Who is so great that every sparrow is different, every snowflake, every person.

We have all had some really fearful things happen this week. But nothing was out of the Lord's control. He saw us through this past week, and He will carry us through this next one.

He spoke for a few more minutes, and when he began the invitation, Brad Watson had moved forward immediately. So had Delia and Shay. They explained that they had actually received salvation Wednesday night. Now, they didn't want to be fearful of making their decisions known, but they wanted to be bold for the Lord, like Mallory.

Jeremiah had begun to play "Amazing Grace" on the keyboard; it sounded like bagpipes.

After church was actually dismissed, some of the people asked if the Faulkners would mind giving a little more of a mini-concert. They were glad to. They sang some more sacred music, then asked the pastor if he would object to a couple of secular songs. He wasn't sure, but they had begun, anyway.

They sang "Fly Me To the Moon". Then, the last song of the night was for Mallory. All five sang as Daniel accompanied. Their harmony was beautiful: "You're the end of the rainbow; you're Daddy's little girl." Mallory sat, entranced, both smiling and crying Her daddy couldn't sing, but he had always played the song for her. They finished it;

"You're your Daddy's little girl." Jeremiah went up on the ending notes; he had a beautiful falsetto.

The storms had continued, but everyone scurried, beneath umbrellas, to reach their cars. Many of them were headed for the lodge for one more meal together before they were heading separate directions the next morning. The Sanders weren't there; they had responsibilities at their own church. They were also worried about Connie who was having some labor pains too early. Kerry Larson, who had planned to stay in the area through the week-end, had changed his plans and returned to Dallas. Of course, Erik and Suzanne hadn't been seen! But the Andersons, the Faulkners, the Haynes, the Walters, and Shay and Delia with their attorney friend, had all joined up.

They were all delighted about such a wonderful day and the glorious celebration of the Resurrection daybreak, when the stone had been rolled back from the grave to show that Jesus was already risen!

John and Lana were particularly overjoyed. So often, they had continued on without many decisions for Christ, and without much material reward. John had already e-mailed Daniel an article for the financial journal. Daniel had been amazed at the scope and depth of it. Patrick O'Shaughnessy had tried to tell them about the pastor, but Daniel and Diana had both felt that if the man really had that much knowledge and ability, he wouldn't have stayed at this place so long, with so little appreciation and remuneration. Now, God had poured out from the windows of heaven, some marvelous rewards.

Delia was wearing a beautiful, fitted, deep gray linen dress that was embellished with lace. She had on a gorgeous three-strand choker of large Tahitian black pearls, in addition to her other diamond jewelry. She had liked the DiaMo Corporation gift, too. She had sat down next to Mallory, presenting her with a box of linen stationery. "Now, you won't have to write on my napkins any more," she had begun. "Mallory, I apologize for that incident Friday morning. That was my main reason for coming here; I didn't want Patrick's money or whatever, I wanted him! Then, everything here has been so amazing and fun, I forgot. If you can't forgive me, I understand, but please don't be mad at Shay; he tried to talk me out of it from the beginning. He didn't even want to come here."

"Grandmother, I couldn't be angry at you or Shay, either one! I'm glad you and Shay came. I'm so happy you came to church and heard the gospel, and your attorney, too. If you had changed your mind, Mr. Freeman probably wouldn't have been here for today. Grandmother, I have missed my daddy so much!" The tears were flowing again, and she could barely speak. "Nobody has been able to understand, but even though I miss him, I haven't even been to the cemetery. He didn't even look like himself the morning I found him. If having his remains will comfort you and you want to bring flowers, I don't mind."

Delia had given her a hug, and some beautiful monogrammed linen handkerchiefs. This was a test of the new waterproof mascara.

Diana had been watching protectively from a distance. She was glad that the three Boston connection people had received the Lord. "All's well that ends well, I suppose," she had breathed. The woman's tactics had angered her, but Diana couldn't help admiring her. She moved to join them.

"Diana," Delia had greeted her warmly with a peck on the cheek and a little squeeze of her hand. "We have a gift for you!" She caught Shay's attention. He had managed to get the bulky gift carried in, even through the rain. The lovely gift-wrapping was a little rain-spattered, but not too bad.

The large gift had drawn the crowd's attention, and they had gathered around curiously. Diana's eyes were alight with excitement at the totally unexpected gift. Cassandra wanted to help her mother tear the wrappings, but Daniel had swept her up into his arms.

"This is so exciting!" Diana had chortled gleefully. She ripped the paper back, then suddenly cupped both bejeweled hands to her mouth to stifle a yelp of delight. "Oh, Delia! Oh Shay! Oh, you guys!"

"Well, what is it, Honey?" Daniel had finally questioned. He turned Cassandra loose. "Maybe you do need to help your mom," he whispered.

Cassandra had ripped at the paper, but she was disappointed. The gift was a beautiful set of heavy, Damask table linens. Delia and Shay had gone on-line to see if they could find out anything about the Faulkner's home in Tulsa. Delia had suspected that the elegant family's home had been written up for some magazine or other. The search had been successful, and Shay had counted forty chairs at the table in the formal dining room. The linens hadn't required a special looming, which Delia could have accomplished. But it was still a "special order". Sets like this one were not just available at the department store. And- the quality!

Diana was overwhelmed. The tablecloth was gorgeous; no one was ever going to eat on it! Shay had told her there were sixty napkins. Daniel was always glad to see her so excited. He shook Shay's hand and gave him a slap on the back.

Everyone settled into places, ordering food and beverages amidst the banter and conversation. Shay had pulled Mallory into a big, round, corner booth. He got Tommy Haynes, Alexandra Faulkner, and David and Tammie Anderson to join them at a teenagers' table.

Daniel and Diana had exchange startled glances with one another over that arrangement! Even worse than David and Mallory's being in such close proximity, was the fact that Alexandra had joined them, next to Tommy. She was eleven! They both figured they should let it go for now. But, they would be establishing some new ground rules, based on the ever-changing dynamics of raising a family.

Jeremiah and Cassandra were at the kids' table with the three younger Anderson children, Evan Sanders, and the Walters twins.

The teenagers were having fun. Tommy had shyly told Alexandra that he played the trumpet. David had been gloating that the Rangers had won another game. Their conversation had turned to the high school. Mr. Haynes was still going to be principal. Tammi hadn't said much. She was bummed out because Mallory was moving away. Mallory thought it was more because Mr. Larson hadn't showed up all day. They were all excited about the diamonds and the new church ministries. David and Shay had talked quite a bit about plans for the new Bible Camp. Their food arrived. Mallory had ordered a loaded up baked potato. It was huge, and her appetite had disappeared. She pushed it away from her.

"Oh, no you don't!" Shay had noticed. He mixed it up a little and got a forkful. "R-r-r-m-m-m, here you go, open the hangar for the little airplane," he instructed.

Laughing, Mallory had opened her mouth, and the bite flew in. She managed to swallow it, and gulped down some iced tea. "Ow! That was hot!" she had gasped.

They all laughed. Shay was talking about his wool; he could even make that interesting. He and his grandmother were going to Dallas the next day, too. They wanted to help make sure Mallory got all settled in. Then, Shay was flying to Denver, and Delia was going back to Boston. Shay was planning to visit some Alpaca ranches along the front range.

He was trying to put a trip together to visit South America, too, to survey interests in both Alpaca and Vicuna down there. He asked Mallory if she thought she could go on the South American trip with him. He was telling her he could go to Houston with her and walk her through getting an expedited passport.

Mallory was amazed. She had never dreamed of anything like that before. She had taken another little nibble of potato. "What are Alpaca and Vicuna?" she had finally asked; she thought she should know, but she wasn't sure. Shay had explained that they were little cousins to camels, and that their wool was very soft and silky. Luxury fabrics. The vicuna was rarer and more expensive than the Alpaca, but both would fit in nicely with his expanded business model.

David didn't know what to say, so he said nothing. South America didn't seem to him like the safest place in the world for two teenagers to visit alone; even if they did think they were big-shot corporate execs. Maybe they would have all kinds of corporate security; he didn't know. At the moment, it seemed to him like Patrick O'Shaughnessy's devious plan to come between him and Mallory was working. She would be swept into this gorgeous world of wealth and glamour, and travel; she would forget little small-town boy, David. Men like Kerry Larson with their Rolex watches and Porsches would surround her. He almost felt like crying, in front of everybody. He had nearly forgotten one thing. False Evidence Appearing Real!

"Lord, please keep us in love with each other." he had prayed in his heart.

Chapter 30

DEPARTURE

I Corinthians 2:9 But as it is written, EYE HATH NOT SEEN, NOR EAR HEARD, NEITHER HAVE ENTERED INTO THE HEART OF MAN, THE THINGS WHICH GOD HATH PREPARED FOR THEM THAT LOVE HIM.

MALLORY AND THE Faulkner family were up early on Monday morning. The skies were still overcast, and rain continued to spit occasionally. Mallory had all of her textbooks in her backpack to check back in at the high school. Some of her books were still in her locker. She had showered and dressed in the white blouse and the black skirt and high heels. It was dressed up with the beautiful pearl jewelry she had indulged in the previous week. She hadn't been sure about wearing the white blouse again. She had worn it Friday, and she hadn't had a chance to do any laundry.

She couldn't help the anxiety about where she was going. She was really worried about whether she would have any access to a washer and dryer. In her mind, she was picturing a small house, like the one she had lived in all of her life, in a run-down neighborhood in Dallas. It would be unfurnished; she would have to use some of the cigar-box cash to get what she would need. She wondered what had happened to the furnishings and contents of her house. She hoped she could continue to keep the cash. She wasn't really sure about that. Her emotions about the school were mixed. All of the kids had always seemed to like her pretty well, but she wasn't that crazy about any of them, except the little group who were in her youth group at church. She wondered where she would go to church in Dallas.

She had poured a bowl of cereal; it was growing soggy. Daniel had come in, and was telling everyone to load into the Hummer. They were scurrying to do so. His BMW was pulled up behind it.

Diana emptied Mallory's bowl and loaded it into the dishwasher. The RV would be driven to Tulsa to their corporate headquarters where it would be polished down from top to bottom for whoever would use it next. Like Roger Sanders, their corporation owned everything, protecting their wealth from undue taxation and frivolous lawsuits.

Daniel asked Mallory if she would mind driving the Hummer. She couldn't believe she was hearing right. Alexandra was riding with her and Dinky. Jer and Cass with their parents. Diana hadn't felt very well this morning. Mallory was instantly worried about her. They pulled up at the high school at eight, on the dot. The buses were just arriving. Mallory cringed; only a week since her bus ride with Martin trying to maul her.

She had had an eventful week!

Inside, the smells and sounds were familiar and poignant. Everything was so unreal to her that she just checked her books in and received her transcript like a robot. Daniel was at her side, as her legal guardian. She had cleaned out her locker, throwing everything in the trash. If people said anything to her, she didn't remember it later.

By the time they returned to the vehicles, Diana had begun to feel better. The nausea had passed.

Mallory asked them if they could go over to the baseball diamond where the girls' team was practicing. One of the girls had hollered at her, "Hey, Mallory, come pitch a couple before you go, please."

"Go on, Honey," Diana had encouraged her.

Gingerly, Mallory made it to the mound through the mud and damp grass. She wound up and released the ball. Satisfied, she watched the ball sail high, before it dropped quickly and curved in over the plate.

"Yes! Stree-ike one!" she chortled. Clasping her hands jubilantly over her head, she was swaggering back toward the Hummer. "I am the greatest pitcher!" she was singsonging.

David had pulled up to let Tammi out for the practice. Mallory, suddenly self-conscious, weaved in front of him. "I am the greatest pitcher!" she stated again for his benefit.

"I've thrown better pitches than that with my eyes closed!" he bragged back at her.

"Oh! Yeah!" she laughed and did a little dance in front of him. "In your dreams!"

She drew a point on an imaginary scoreboard. "One for Mallory!"

She hopped into the driver's seat of the Hummer, and she was gone!

The rain had ceased, and the sun was peeking tentatively through the pale leaves of the Pecan tree when their vehicles cleared security and entered the DiaMo mine property. Mallory just stared around in wonder. the blocks still marked where the little house had been situated. The shed was still there, and it seemed like that was going to be used as a temporary headquarter for the mine.

Daniel had been leading in the BMW; now Mallory pulled the Hummer up through the mud, to where one of the blocks was located. Her eyes studied the little eroded mounds curiously, one last time. This was where she had spotted the diamond a week ago. She knew that didn't mean it would still be visible. A hundred people had tracked through the little property since that time, tearing the ground up with tires, trampling every inch. The sun scooted out, and to her amazement, the stone blazed in the brightness. Her shoes had already gotten pretty muddy at the baseball field. She alit from the vehicle and retrieved the stone. It was nice!

A large helicopter loomed suddenly above them, then lowered quickly between the vehicles and shed, and the tree line at the back of the yard. Some plyboards had been carried out by the mine foreman and a couple of his guys. Everyone was able to board the chopper without being mired in the mud. Mallory removed her muddy heels before stepping into the luxurious interior of the craft.

She was sure she looked as dazed as she felt. Her feet had never been off the ground! Her spirit thrilled. So much for driving the Hummer, but this wasn't bad! She sat down and buckled in. Daniel grabbed a chocolate from a sideboard and poured himself a cup of coffee. He handed Diana a bottle of water, then tossed one of the chocolates playfully to Mallory. He buckled in beside his wife, and okayed the pilot to take off. Mallory couldn't believe the kids weren't more excited; surely they didn't travel like this often; did they?

In less than thirty minutes they were in Mena. They left the chopper and were hustled by private security onto a private jet. They buckled in once more. The kids had gotten a game out of a storage area. Evidently this was their plane. In a matter of minutes, the jet had been cleared and was tearing down the runway. Mallory was too fascinated to be terrified. This was some of the stuff Daniel had been discussing in the meeting on Friday afternoon; she had failed to grasp the significance of everything.

"What did you pick up back there?" Diana had joined Mallory once they were air-born.

Mallory laughed. "Oh, I already forgot about that." She dug through her handbag, retrieving the diamond. She placed it in Diana's hand. "It looks like a nice one; someone who knows really needs to check it with a loupe."

A flight attendant brought them all a delicious lunch; the hour was early, but the puff-pastry filled with chicken and mushrooms tasted delicious. The five years ahead of her were definitely looking brighter. The tears had rolled down her cheeks again, but they were tears of relief and delight. Never in her wildest dreams had she imagined anything this beautiful and perfect. She gazed at the landscape spreading beneath the sleek craft. The Lord had done this for her; and her daddy had been planning it. Wonders were unfolding!

Chapter 31

DALLAS

Isaiah 55: 8 & 9 For my thoughts are not your thoughts, neither are your ways my ways, saith the LORD.
For as the heavens are higher than the earth, so are my ways higher than your ways, and my thoughts than your thoughts.

THE FLIGHT TO Dallas had been quick. The jet landed at the Addison airport, a private airfield, and they made a dash through an elegant terminal to waiting Suburbans.

There were uniformed drivers at the wheels of both vehicles. Diana, and Mallory, and the two girls were hurried into one, while Daniel and Jeremiah had hastily ducked into the other. Dinky was still being transported in the Hummer. They had thought it best not to have to tranquilize him for air travel. Mallory was grateful to them for their patience about him. The Suburbans entered the North Dallas Tollway heading south and got off at the first exit. There were beautiful office buildings around, and Mallory was fascinated by everything. They pulled into an adjoining parking garage and stopped by a private elevator. Daniel used an odd looking key, and they rose to the penthouse suite of offices. The glass windows of the suite were beautifully lettered Dia Mo Corporation, and below that, GeoHy Corporation. That was the logo Mallory had noticed on the jet and on the flight crew uniforms. She had given her guardian a perplexed look.

"Making a detour here, to show you your father's company offices," he had explained, enjoying the incredulous expression on her face.

GeoHy stands for Geological Hydrology. That's our original corporation. My grandfather was a geologist in Tulsa in the Oklahoma oil heyday. Tulsa has the nickname, 'Oil Capital of the World'. My dad followed in his steps, and they made a fortune. I came along and majored in Geology, and minored in Hydrology. Water is still more valuable in many parts of the world than oil is. I was looking for water for wells in Africa-"

"When he met me!" Diana had interrupted the narrative. "My parents were second generation missionaries. I have nine brothers and sisters who are still at the mission station. I was a nursing student, and I came to the hospital one day; that was the first time I ever saw Daniel. He was nearly dead, but he was still the most handsome man I had ever seen."

"Of course, she fell in love with me at first sight, and tenderly nursed me back to health," he finished the story.

The story was so incredible that Mallory wasn't sure whether to believe it, or not. She guessed it must be true; how could they make anything like that up?

"So, is that what GeoHy still does? she asked.

They had entered the suite, and the receptionists had perked up attentively. Mallory had picked up on the movement. Somehow, she was sure they wouldn't have acted so relaxed and indifferent if her dad had been present. Daniel had spoken a couple of words to them and had introduced Mallory. "Here's our little heiress!" he had concluded. They had both acted pretty indifferent.

Daniel was leading the tour, and he halted when they were around a corner. GeoHy does many different things. Your dad came to us because he wanted us to do a study of water as it relates to the diamond erosion. Where would high water have deposited the diamonds? How would they be situated along the creek and river beds, according to the movement of water currents?. We had never done anything like that, although other companies similar to ours, have. We liked your father very much. Diana was reluctant, at first, because growing up in Africa, she had experienced the Conflict Diamond heartache first-hand."

They had moved forward once again. The space was large and beautifully done. At last, they had come to the inner sanctum. The office was huge with stunning views of the Metroplex to the south and the east. Mallory could sense her father's personality through the furnishings and appointments of the space. She no longer felt amazement at what he had done! The clever space in the shed was all linked here. He could come screaming here in a jet, if necessary. But mostly he could work from the shed; and none of the nosy gossips of Murfreesboro had ever had a clue. Tears of pride filled her eyes, but they didn't escape.

A woman was sitting at Patrick's desk, talking to someone on the phone. Daniel had hesitated courteously, thinking she would end her conversation and explain what she was doing. She swung the chair around to gaze out the window, almost turning her back on them completely.

At last, she hung up. "And you must be little Mallory," she had gushed, not bothering to rise. "The Faulkners must be showing you your father's office."

Mallory had advanced forward, swiftly and purposefully. "No, they are not! They're showing me my office! I believe-you-are-sitting-in-MY-chair!"

The woman had glared defiantly, but Mallory's steady gaze won out. She rose angrily to her feet and headed toward the door.

"Whoever you are, you may have your resignation on my desk by five," Mallory had informed her. "Unless, you would like to try this again."

Diana was stunned at Mallie's acumen. Tom Haynes had told Daniel about Mallory's poised personality at the school office, so he was already forewarned that she could be a force to reckon with, if need be. He was only pleasantly surprised.

Mallory had sat down behind the huge desk. She steepled her fingers upward and practiced her "executive face". Then she had spun around in the big chair a couple of times like a little girl.

"Where to, next?" she questioned.

David had watched the vehicles carrying Mallory and the Faulkners pull out across the highway and head away. Tammi hadn't gotten out of his car.

"You gonna be okay?" she asked him. They weren't without their sibling rivalry and differences of opinions, but they did have a strong bond. Now, she was worried that her brother might be so bummed out, he would quit the efforts he had been making over the past week. She sat there.

"You can get out," he had told her. "I'll be okay. Sit with me at lunch, though, will ya?"

"Sure." she was flattered. With Mallory gone, she wasn't sure who would want to eat with her, anyway. She and her brother would be moral support for each other while they made the adjustment.

David parked in his space and walked slowly into the building. He wanted to go someplace and cry, get under control. But, he couldn't. His missing first semester had been stupid. No wonder Patrick thought he was such a loser. Now, he had raced ahead of his class, and was working on his senior year. Mr. Haynes had helped him; now David knew he needed to stay at it. He didn't have time for the luxury of licking his wounds.

"Please, help me, Lord!" he whispered silently.

He was sitting on the steps reading his Bible when a helicopter raced across the clearing sky above him. He had surveyed it curiously. He had no idea it had whisked Mallie away. He figured she wasn't even to Hope yet.

He plowed his way dismally through his morning classes and joined Tammi at lunch. He unrolled a site plat of the future Bible camp, and he and his sister made a study of it as they ate their hot school meal. They had guiltily thrown away the meager sandwiches their mom had always fixed for them. Using some of their money from the plastic Easter eggs, they had decided upon the luxury. What they had listened to most of the kids complain about for years, was a treat for the pastor's two children. They devoured everything. Sometimes, they could get seconds, if there was anything left. They both eagerly accepted seconds of everything, except for the blue Jell-o. Tammi ate her second coleslaw and left the rest for David. They were having fun talking about the property development.

Coach had called him out into the hallway during his study hall to ask if he had changed his mind about going out for track By far the most athletic of the upperclassmen, David was flattered. And, he loved sports.

He thanked coach again before returning to study hall and hitting his books.

Tammi rode home with him, but he had grown withdrawn again. As they neared the parsonage, David caught sight of the FBI car. He tried to stay calm; it didn't mean anything about Mallory, he had tried to reason with himself. He pulled up beside the house.

The agent seemed to be waiting for him. David was kind of nervous; he didn't really know why.

"Hello, David," Erik had greeted. "Can I buy you a cup of coffee?"

"Oh, sure, why not?" David had decided. He got into the big sedan with Bransom.

They headed toward Hope; the guy hadn't said much. "How's Suzanne?" David had plunged in.

"She's good. She's all squared away to start working for Sanders Corporation next week. We ate lunch at a country club with Roger and Beth. She has a good deal. They gave her a pretty nice clothing allowance, so I left her at the mall to look around. She has some security people keeping tabs on her."

"What's the latest about Thomas?" David had questioned to fill in more of the awkward silence.

"Nothing new," Bransom had responded noncommittally. "Shannon O'Shaughnessy recovered from his injuries enough that he's returned to Boston under Federal custody.

Treasury Department seized his dad's stuff. He was so indebted, though. His stuff won't even bring much at auction. With some people, it may look like crime pays. O'Shaughnessy was a classic case where he never did well enough to even make it look like it pays. He should have gone into the table cloth business with his mom and daddy."

The agent continued, "Melville, I'm convinced, just wanted the O'Shaughnessy property. Suzanne told me he had made her several low offers. He didn't have any money; would have had to finance even that humble little abode. Go figure. He didn't have a clue about the diamonds. He had no idea Martin Thomas had murdered those four girls. He just paid the guy a little bit to help scare Suzanne and Mallory into selling. No terrible crime, just a little something underhanded, so he could get what he wanted. You remember a story about a dog with a steak?"

"I think so," David responded. "The dog was crossing a bridge with the steak in his mouth. The reflection of the steak in the water made the steak appear larger. So, the dog dropped the steak in the water snapping at the reflection. Was that one of the Aesop's Fables?"

"I'm not sure about that; been a while since I was in school. That's exactly what's gonna happen to Melville! I hope he does some jail time. Even though he didn't know Thomas was a killer, he still exposed our ladies to terrible danger when he brought Martin in. Just because he didn't know, doesn't change the facts! Even if he wiggles out, he dropped his little dab, grabbing at what belonged to someone else. He'll have less than nothing!"

David's stared past the man grimly. He thought that was small consolation.

"Suzanne heard from Mallory this afternoon," Bransom had continued. "She was all excited, getting settled in. She had a chopper ride to Mena; then private jet to Dallas; then she visited her dad's office. Suzanne never knew he had an office in Dallas."

David had been glad when the agent had broached the subject of Mallory; but the fact that she was happy and excited buzzing around in choppers and jets while he was missing her, stuck here in Dullsville, didn't exactly delight him.

Bransom had turned the radio on, and the Rangers were playing. Rangers had the bases loaded when the two reached the Target store in Hope. Without waiting for the inning to end, Bransom had turned off the engine and was sprinting toward the store.

There was a Starbucks. Bransom ordered a large coffee, to be told he meant a *Venti*. Not sure what she was talking about, he had irritably responded, "whatever!" David hadn't been to a coffee house like this before either. He had hated to tell the burly agent he wasn't a coffee drinker. He surveyed the menu, which made no sense to him, either. Finally, he had asked for a small "mocha" and was informed that smalls were not called smalls, but talls, which made no sense either, as they were really the shortest! When they got their beverages and sat down, both of them had burst into laughter. Bransom was laughing so hard the tears were rolling.

"Good thing- ha ha- we made a trial run-" he was laughing so hard he couldn't talk. "at this thing! Ha-ha, whoo! before we brought the ladies. So we didn't look - this stupid for them !"

Bransom had tipped his chair back on the back legs. David thought about how his dad and Mr. Haynes wouldn't like that.

"So, agent," David had begun, "what are we doing here sipping Starbucks together?"

Bransom continued to sit, surveying him intently. "I dunno," he had finally responded. "I just keep thinking about what I heard Mallie tell you the other night; what night was it? Friday night? Wow, what a week; my days are kind of jumbled. Oh, yeah, it was just before Suzanne and I went back to the church so your dad could get us married- I better not forget that day. Oh, yeah, Friday the thirteenth, I think it was. Hey, it was my lucky day! Mallory said you were trying to get her to jump the fences her daddy had set up around her. She said she wasn't going to be a fence jumper like you. Remember that?"

David had cringed; then started to rise angrily.

"Sit down!" Bransom barked.

"How could I forget it? She didn't have to give me a lecture in front of everyone. Now Faulkner, Larson, Sanders, you, nobody's gonna give me a break!" The only reason he had obeyed the barked order was that it was a long walk back to Murfreesboro.

"You see, that's where you're wrong. I shouldn't go here, as a federal agent I can get in a lot of trouble with my mouth about this. Feminism and sexual harassment, and all that. I mean, I know some female agents that aren't too bad, I guess. But, here's what I see, and you don't have to agree. Most girls and women aren't fence-jumpers. They want to be pretty safe and protected. The way I see it, guys are supposed to be more the daring fence jumper type. I don't think those guys think less of you; at least, I don't."

David was amazed. He had smarted under her words all week-end.

"But, here's the thing, Cowboy. Even if you're jumping fences, you should look before you leap. I mean, never go in without back-up. Even the Lone Ranger had Tonto, you know?"

"Uh, no, Sir. I think you lost me when you called me 'Cowboy'. Who's the Lone Ranger and Tonto?"

"You've never seen the "Lone Ranger" on TV? "the agent questioned unbelievingly. No wonder the country's in a mess. I thought it was because the Bible got ripped out of schools. Now I see there's more to it than that. They took the "Lone Ranger" off TV too!"

David laughed; he couldn't help really liking the guy. Well, you better fill me in, otherwise your illustration is totally lost on me."

Bransom told him about the old, popular TV western. The Lone Ranger was the main agent, and Tonto was the Native American who was his backup. Every week, Tonto got pistol whipped and was unconscious throughout most of the program. At the close of each episode, when good had still somehow prevailed, Tonto would sit up and say, 'head clear now, Kemosabe!' You know, the theme song was the William Tell Overture?" he had ended, certain that would jog David's memory.

"Never saw it, but what's your point?" David had continued laughing through Bransom's recounting of the classic show. He was sure it was losing something in the interpretation.

"Always watch your backside. Don't try to be a lone ranger; even the lone ranger had a partner. You should have confided to your dad what you thought about the sheriff and what you knew about Martin's coming on her property. You shouldn't have been over there alone."

"I tried to tell him." David had interrupted.

"But you didn't tell him you were going over there by yourself, with your little knife and beanie, sitting in her tree?"

"You make it sound stupider than it was."

"No, it was a poor plan. That night she got her phone; you punched in your number and told her not to call the sheriff, but to call you if she got scared! What were you planning to do? Run in there and hold her tight? You have to think through your plan, and you have to bounce it off people who don't believe you. Your dad would have told you not to go over there like that. If you had leveled and told them her mom was gone; she was alone with no power and phone, couldn't they have helped come up with some better ideas? How's your stuff taste?" he had changed the subject.

"Kinda bad," he admitted. "It's kind of a cross between hot chocolate and coffee."

Bransom sipped it gingerly. "Gyah! You're right! They should pick one or the other!"

⥈ ⥈

From the DiaMo offices, the Suburbans had sped along the NDT to the George Bush Turnpike to a north Dallas suburb. The homes were mansions. Mallory had seen a few such places on TV, but she didn't know there could really be so many. And they were the real thing, not just movie or TV sets. The lead vehicle had pulled in where there was a gate with Mallory's monogram worked into it. A button was pressed, and the gates swung away. The Suburbans hummed up a long, concrete driveway. The iron fencing and lush landscaping everywhere were beautiful. They were approaching from the front, and the home had loomed into view. Mallory wasn't familiar with architectural styles, but, the sight was impressive; she thought she counted eight chimneys. It reminded her of a European influence she had seen in books There was a sparkling pool, barely glimpseable, as they had sped along the drive. The Suburbans rolled to a stop on the circular drive before massive double doors. Delia's car was already there, and Shay had been watching for them.

An antique grandfather clock in the soaring foyer was chiming two o'clock as Mallory entered her front door for the first time. Diana had stepped forward to lead her from room to room and area to area. Mallory was pretty sure she could recognize Diana's style in much of the décor. There were beautiful sunrise or sunset pictures in a couple of rooms; then the delicate tints were repeated throughout the spaces. Amazed, she realized that Diana's designs expanded into interior design, as well as clothing. There were some beautiful Christian decorative items. They looked elegant. No "Country Art" flea market things here! At the completion of the tour an hour later, Mallory was dazed and still not sure she had seen a washer and dryer, or an iron and ironing board. Somehow, it seemed less important now.

Daniel had called Mallory into the beautiful library. He had sat down behind an ornate desk.

"We are going to be heading home in just a few minutes. There are a few things I want to go over with you first. The security cameras are positioned mainly on the perimeters. Your private areas are to be private. Security will sweep daily to check for anything out of the ordinary. If you want to swim, you can do so in privacy, although, it's not a good idea to swim alone, either. Here are keys to the house, remotes for the gate and garage doors. Here are car keys; credit cards, be sure to save receipts with a brief notation about the expense. That will come with practice. Don't try to outrun your security; let them stay with you. You're pretty much free to come and go as you wish. You don't have to explain yourself to the help. If you need anything, call any of us. We're all in touch. Just call your mom (she's had enough time to honeymoon), your grandmother, Shay, Diana, me. Don't have things you just worry and wonder about when you can find out. We'll keep in touch by e-mail. Here's a refund check from the IRS. Endorse it tomorrow, and Kerry will have the CPA advise him where to put it. He opened the safe. You should place the rest of your cash in here. Here's your jewelry, including your diamond ring from your dad. Leave it in here when you're not wearing it. He pulled the diamond from his pocket that Mallie had found earlier and had given to Diana. This is some kind of diamond! Makes me nervous carrying it. Save the cash and use the corporate credit cards. Makes record keeping easier for the CPA. You have lots of money so get what you want and need. Here are the keys to the offices."

She obediently retrieved the cash and placed it in the safe, and he twirled the dial. He had hollered for Diana and the kids, who had responded immediately. Diana had given her a hug, telling her to be sure to remember to eat. They had all told her good-bye before loading up and disappearing down the driveway.

It was about time for Shay to depart for Denver. Mallory had slid into the elegant car with them. They navigated quite a bit of traffic, but managed to drop Shay off at his departure gate in plenty of time. He kissed Delia and Mallie on the cheek, telling them both he would e-mail them as soon as he knew anything. A security car had been following; two nicely attired men got out, following Shay into the terminal. They would be traveling first-class a couple of rows behind him.

The sleek Rolls exited the DFW airport at the north exit. The security car followed. There were still two team members guarding them. Delia had invited Mallory to have dinner with her. They decided on Ruth's Chris Steak House.

Delia ordered first, then Mallory. They had a team of servers.

Delia had begun to cry softly. She had reached for Mallory's hand across the table. Mallory clasped it and blessed the food. Delia was smiling. Having been saved for less than a week, the blessing was something she wasn't in a habit of doing. Even as a devout Catholic, she had never realized she should be grateful for everything.

"Mallory, I thought about spending the night here. I will if you would like me to. I think you are a lot like Patrick was; about not minding being alone. I think he thrived on it. I'm glad the Faulkner's were so nice to you, but I felt sorry for you cramped up in that little trailer."

Mallory had laughed at that. The luxurious coach owned by GeoHy could hardly be considered a cramped, little trailer- by anyone other than Delia!

"Come on, you know you were suffocating!" Delia's tears had dried and the mischievous twinkle was back in her eyes. "You'll be fine! I'm going home tonight! I'm never gone this long. Guess I'll be gone longer, though, when we go to Turkey! You are an amazing girl, Mallory!"

She had paused, turning serious. "Shay and I went to the cemetery before we left this morning. We took flowers. I won't be moving my son. I'm truly sorry about everything!

Do you mind terribly if I keep his Bible?"

Tears had sprung into Mallory's eyes.

"We prayed every day for you to get saved. I'm so happy. I want you to have Daddy's Bible. He does, too, I'm sure of it!"

Salads finished, their steaks had arrived. "Tell me about David." Delia winked conspiratorially.

An hour later, Mallie's grandmother knew David' life history, but the girl had barely nibbled at the steak.

"You aren't taking that home to that dog!" Delia had finally interjected.

The captain had presented the check, and Mallory had placed a corporate credit card with it and returned it to him.

"He can have an occasional steak!" she had defended.

Chuckling, Delia pulled out her cell. Shay had e-mailed his safe arrival. Delia briefly explained the nature of his trip.

"Write on the receipt that this was about the Alpaca deal!"

Mallory had signed for the meal, including a reasonably generous tip. She left a gospel tract.

On the receipt she scrawled: "Alpaca deal and the Service of the King!"

Delia had summoned her car and one of the Suburbans Mallory had ridden in earlier in the day. Delia gave her a squeeze and a quick peck on the cheek, slid in where her driver had opened the car door for her.

"I'll e-mail you when I'm in, Dear!"

Chapter 32

DREAMS

DIANA HAD PHONED Mallie that they had arrived home safely; then had asked her briefly about her evening. Mallory had recapped it, telling her that she was nearly home.

Diana was worried that Delia hadn't stayed.

"She knew I was going to be fine," Mallory had assured. "Thank y'all for everything. Now, I'm going to go wander around my lovely new home and try to decide which TV to watch the news on. Then, I may enjoy the hot tub before I go to bed."

Diana had broken the connection, still worrying. "I thought Delia was going to stay." she had repeated again. They had sent their three little ones to get ready for bed. Diana didn't want them worrying about Mallie.

"You know, Honey, Mallory told the judge she would adhere to her father's wishes." Daniel had pulled her into his embrace. "She knew she didn't have to. She's like Patrick was. When he gave his word, you didn't have to keep checking on if he planned to carry through. Delia was right. Mallory needs some space now, just to catch her breath and think. She's not going to 'jump the fences', as she so aptly described it. Let's pray and go to bed."

"Hey, kids, y'all ready to come in here for a prayer?" he had questioned into the intercom. They all came tearing into their parent's master suite.

They thanked the Lord for safety for everyone and asked the Lord to bless them with a good night's sleep.

He did!

Dinky had arrived and Mallory wasn't sure what she should do with him. She wasn't sure the housekeeping staff would be too crazy about him. Then, she had smiled, remembering she was the mistress of the house! Not an intimidated little guest! She gave him his steak in the kitchen; then she checked the refrigerator. She had assumed it would be empty. It was full; so were the pantry and cupboards. She had found the large utility room: the washer and dryer were brand new, matching, top-of-the-line. The garage had four different cars in it: she didn't know where her little car had ended up. Like the contents of the little Arkansas house: it didn't matter!

She gazed back into the refrigerator. She was trying to decide between a diet soda and a bottle of water. She grabbed one of each. Reaching back into the pantry, she pulled out a can of Cashews. With Dinky at her heels, she had returned to her own bedroom suite. It was a tribute to Delia, a dream confection of snowy-white, fine linen. The ruffles billowed everywhere. Pillows covered the bed. Everything was monogrammed in white on white. The floors were carpeted in white which flowed into white marble tile. The fireplace was white marble. Her father's original letter that she had intended to ask Kerry Larson about, was matted with white nubby linen and had been framed in a Swarovski crystal frame It stood on a bedside table beside a picture of her father.

She had picked up the remote before settling into a chaise lounge. The plasma came to life. She nibbled at the cashews and opened the beverage; she was fast asleep.

Light was filtering softly through the linen semi-sheers that covered the French doors which opened out onto a terrace. Mallie rose from the chaise, looking around, still half asleep. The enchanted castle hadn't dissolved into nothingness while she slept. It still spread around her, real stone, and glass, and concrete. Tears had come! It was so beautiful, so perfect. She had asked the Lord to show her what Heaven looked like.

"It's still even more beautiful than this, isn't it?" she had whispered in awe.

She found the camera that had been in her Easter basket and her Bible. Silently, she had moved out onto the terrace. The air was chilly and still. The fragrance of shrubs and flowers, mingled with the faint hint of Chlorine from the pool, hung in the morning air. There was a slight mist, causing the atmosphere of the rising sun to shimmer.

The dewy mist had dampened the table and chairs. While she was wondering where there might be some old towels, a woman in a maid's uniform had emerged to wipe away the moisture. Mallory thanked her, sitting gracefully. A cart arrived with coffee and cream and sugar, and fresh raspberries.

Mallory fixed her coffee the way she liked it. Then, while she sipped it, she began photographing the indescribably beautiful sunrise. She poured the rest of the cream and sugar onto the berries, then ate them slowly, delighting in the taste sensation.

She opened the Bible:

> *Psalm 34:8 O taste and see that the LORD is good: blessed is the man that trusteth in him.*

The beauty of the morning in the palatial surroundings engulfed her. She thought about the previous Tuesday morning when she had run from study hall and shopped in Hope. In the beautiful warm sunshine, the events of the past few days had begun to fade. God had worked everything together for her good. She was wise enough to know she needed Him.

Material goods could slip away. Looking around her rapturously, she was praying they wouldn't.

A plate of steaming Eggs Benedict had appeared. She devoured it hungrily, drinking an entire carafe of milk with it.

She turned to the book of Ephesians, once more staring at the pictures of the beautiful site located on the Aegean Sea. She was going there! She was grateful for the wonderful new friends who would also be going. Even her dreams of world travel were coming true. As she sat there, the corporate pilgrimage to Turkey was being arranged! What a beautiful and exotic destination!

God had brought her through the long, dark tunnel of grief to bring her again into the DAZZLING light of His Presence!

She thought of the six months ahead, at least, before she could possibly see David again.

She reread her father's letter.

She went into the white marble master suite, starting a bubble bath in the Jacuzzi. She was singing!

Her path was shining brightly toward the perfect day!